THE REPLAY

THE REPLAY

Michael Curtin

GEORGE BRAZILLER
New York

Published in the United States in 1982 by George Braziller, Inc.
Originally published in Great Britain in 1981 by Andre Deutsch Limited
105 Great Russell Street, London WC1

For information contact the publisher:
George Braziller, Inc.
One Park Avenue
New York, NY 10016

Library of Congress Cataloging in Publication Data:

Curtin, Michael, 1942-
    The replay.
    I. Title.
PR6053.U77R4   1982   823'.914   81-15536
ISBN 0-8076-1027-5   AACR2

Printed in the United States of America
First Edition

For Kieran

1

The Challenge

The early suburb of Southview Gardens was constructed by a man who thought flatteringly of himself as a jerry builder. The march of time so left him in the shade that fifteen years later the estate was considered a jewel of architectural planning. It comprised five cul-de-sacs of four-bedroomed semi-detached houses; the front lawns were capacious enough to accommodate two-a-side football and the back gardens stretched a hundred yards until they ran into the protective boundary wall of a convent. The development was small enough for the exercise of control by the inhabitants and sufficiently populous to justify a residents association. Southview Gardens won the National Tidy Estate Competition six years in a row – every year since the award was initiated, and was so very much instrumental in the setting up of CRAM – the Combined Residents Association of Mellick – that their very own Stanley Callaghan was its President for the third year running – every year since its foundation in fact. Stanley Callaghan was president of SGRA and CRAM. Stanley Callaghan was a primary school teacher. Yet he was the only original settler who did not have a knot in his stomach in the face of the mortgage fifteen years earlier. He was anything but wealthy then and the mortgage was steep – three thousand one hundred and fifty pounds, the weekly repayment two pounds four shillings and seven pence. He did not have a knot in his stomach then because he had not yet begun to systematically shed his first self and he was in love.

Now, the Southview Gardens houses were worth on average twenty-six thousand pounds and the Callaghan abode had been valued at thirty-two thousand five hundred. Stanley enlisted the school handyman to see to maintenance through the years, chutes and such, exterior business involving ladder climbing and roof attention. Inside, his wife Kate was deft at papering and painting and curtaining. The school handyman put Stanley in the way of knowing a man who was a postman by trade and a cabinet maker by nature and there was hardly a nook or a cranny that Stanley had not seen fit to improve. Capital expenditure, the school handyman, the postman and a few helpers converted the attic into his very own bedroom and study for Conor, who was now thirteen. It was Stanley Callaghan's own idea to take down the number 29 and replace it with Katstanco.

Within Katstanco on Friday night Stanley and Kate Callaghan sat at their respective desks, correcting; in his attic bedroom/ study Conor was reading the third book on the home curriculum set by his father. The first two had been *Treasure Island* and *The Vicar of Wakefield*. Stanley went methodically through his batch of headliner copies, gloating over the lower case marching along between the faint blue lines and the upper sprouting to caress (no more, no less) the red lines. A gorgeously scripted 'f' he shared with his wife.

'Kate . . . Kate . . . '

'Yes, sweet?' The response was automatic; she did not raise her eyes from her own work.

'Kate, look at this. Look at Finbar Crowe's f's. Note Crowe's f's.'

Kate accepted the copybook and murmured: 'Very good. Very, very good.'

'Last September Crowe thought a pen was a sprinkling can. It just shows what can be done.'

'It shows who can get it done, Stanley.'

'One can do no more than put one's finger in the dyke. How are you getting on yourself?'

'Another ten, fifteen minutes.'

'Up to standard?'

Kate shook her head: 'W-e-n-s-d-a-y. N-e-s-s-a-c-e-r-y.'

Kate's was a Leaving Cert class. Stanley shook *his* head.

At thirty-eight his hair was already grey and parted at the left. On one side it was unruly from the constant professorial running of his fingers through it. His moustache was still ninety per cent brown, a combination of nature and nicotine. He wore leather patches on the elbows of his beige working cardigan. His sockless feet were in slippers. It was a regret of his that he was unable to master a pipe.

'You'll be finished early then, Kate?'

'Yes. I must be going easy on them.'

'You're not to worry about them. I've told you. The damage was done long before they reached your hands. Would you like to go out?'

Kate nodded happily.

'Right then. I'll go up and change and see how Conor's faring while you finish.'

Kate nodded again. They hadn't missed a Friday night drink in years and yet Stanley always suggested the outing as though it were a treat. Kate quickly stuffed the essays into her case. She would finish them on Sunday morning while Stanley and Conor would be out for their walk. Stanley Callaghan had a horror of putting things off. On Friday night father, mother and son put their chores behind them.

'Kate . . . Kate, put the kettle on. We'll have a cup before we go.'

This was ritual but again Stanley invested the suggestion with novelty.

It was a balmy night for March, the very weather to gull the precipitate into foolish exposure and the inevitable chill, Stanley thought, as he doffed the cardigan and raised his hands into a heavy duty Aran pullover. He tucked his vest and shirt into his underpants and adjusted the braces attached to his baggy brown corduroy trousers so that a quarter inch of fawn wool sock grew visibly out of his brown brogues. He climbed the steps to Conor's study and knocked.

'It's open, Dad.'

He sniffed the complete absence of cigarette smoke; *that* had not yet started. Everything was very far from panic stations which didn't surprise him given the attention that had gone into ensuring that Conor should turn out recognisably human as distinct from the cut of his contemporaries. But his satisfaction was academic and didn't travel from his head to his heart.

'Finished?'

'Yeah. We didn't get much.'

'Not "yeah". Yes. They probably don't want to have to correct much. How are you getting on with *Glenanaar*?' Canon Sheahan's novel was the third book on the home curriculum.

'What does Hagar and Ishmael mean, Dad?'
'Pardon?'
'Hagar and Ishmael. It's a chapter title.'
Stanley took the proferred novel and leafed through the chapter.
'Yes. Sheahan was in many ways an underestimated talent. There are people who would knock Sheahan today. Take Dara Holden . . . '
'Dad, can I go down and watch telly now?'
'Television, Conor. Not telly. It's almost nine. You want to watch the news?'
'Charlie's Angels is on after it and a sports special.'
'American rubbish.'
'Mammy is American.'
'There's America and America. What's the sport?'
'Highlights of Liverpool's European Cup match.'
'Soccer!'
'You played soccer yourself, Dad.'
'Yes. *I* played *soccer*. What it is that Liverpool play has yet to be classified. In my day if the goalkeeper chewed gum and rolled the ball on the ground the crowd would roar for their money back. Stanley Matthews played in Mellick once, he came over with Stoke City . . . '
'Can I go down now, Dad?'
' . . . past his prime, still, had all the magic. What? Oh, I suppose so, your mother and I are going out for a short while . . . '
'Bring back Kentucky Chicken, Dad.'
Stanley had one slice of bread and butter with the tea to line his stomach; every little helped with the breathalyser in action he told Kate who had once listened to Dara Holden accuse her husband: 'You don't drink any more as supposedly befits a representative of this country. You're gone prim Anglo in your old age, Stanley.'
The kitchen sported a wall to wall carpet. 'One need not go in for squalor because there's a child in the house, Kate, and tiles are common.' When Kate came down after applying a trace of powder and lipstick she found Stanley with the vacuum cleaner in action where crumbs from his one slice of bread might possibly have fallen.
'Stanley! After a cup of tea.'

'Now, Kate. A little at a time and often. Besides ... the president of CRAM must show the flag.'

Kate purposefully unplugged the cleaner and replaced it in its corner. Stanley had a last look around, patted the keys in his trousers pocket: 'Ready then?'

Dara Holden had attacked the 'then'. 'I can take the leather patches on the cardigan, Stanley, but this "then" business ... are you trying to sound like an English gentleman?'

They both kissed Conor good-night, Stanley performing stiltedly. Kate strode out the gravel path and waited the twenty seconds for her husband to catch her up. The short, frenetic stride of one in danger of not reaching the bookies before the off was now a slow motion lope. He handed the keys to Kate.

'I'll drive back. You can let yourself go tonight.'

Kate was only dimly puzzled by the pretence that the breathalyser curtailed his drinking. Apart from the belated wedding of Jake O'Dea two years before Stanley had not exceeded the three pint mark. But gearing himself for the challenge was out of the same stable as the warm woollies on the night of an east wind. As Kate slipped into gear Stanley placed his hand on her leg beneath her skirt and winked. It was Friday night.

'Stanley!'

'It's Friday night, Kate.'

Retaliating, Kate clutched her husband between the legs. They smiled briefly at each other and then released their grips. Kate started the car. It was not true for Dara Holden: Stanley was not a dryballs. He was a man of probity, honour, standards. He was already a legend in his own school, the *Irish Times* had mentioned him in an editorial as an example of the type of spirit lacking in the country. Dara didn't understand. 'Kate, leave him, come with me, I don't know what you see in this changeling.' Dara's comic whine only thinly hid his longing. A foundling herself, Kate was attracted by Dara's description of Stanley. Dara was a humanist, had the concomitant jaundiced outlook, and was a man Kate and Stanley both held dear. Stanley and Dara accused each other of not having grown up. It did not matter to her which was the adult: Bush Vine had figuratively laid hands on Stanley. Bush Vine at sixty-eight years of age had come across Kate, a sixteen year old foundling, when he was researching *Without a Past* at the convent with the blessing of Sister Aquinas. That had been all of twenty-seven years ago. Bush was her past and had signposted her future.

'Your instructions, darling?'

'Let's try that new place – Tramps – and then settle in Brigid's.'

He would have one pint in Tramps and two more in Brigid's over a two hour period. On his last visit home Dara had said: 'Kate, I love you, lovely company, but I'm off to the Nook. I remember when he'd throw back five whiskeys and six pints before settling down to serious drinking.' Dara resurrected that anecdote in Brigid's and after he had left Kate tried to draw Stanley out. All he offered was: 'Kate, there is no point in growing old without growing wise.'

They parked the car outside Tramps on the main street. Stanley addressed her across the bonnet as she locked the door: 'Kate, who in God's name are Hagar and Ishmael?'

'You're kidding me, Stanley.'

'It was the title of a chapter in *Glenanaar*. Conor asked me.'

'Don't the Irish ever read their bibles?'

Stanley offered his arm to link her into Tramps.

'No need. We have the faith, our theologians know the bible on our behalf. When the Witnesses and the chaps with the short back and sides come to the door we refer them to our theologians – a gentleman has his seconds. Biblical people, were they?'

Despite the facility of speech Kate was mildly irritated at the Celtic camouflage of ignorance.

'Stanley, you're a thick.'

Inside Tramps, over a pint of beer and a Winter's Tale that yielded no change out of a pound, Kate patiently related the story of Abraham and Sarah. From the lesson Stanley was able to decipher Canon Sheahan's justification for the chapter title and then he let himself go praising *Glenanaar*, the book shoved down his throat by Bob Tracey, the teacher on whom he modelled his own magisterial ethos. And while instructing Kate on the merits of Sheahan's oeuvre, of which he had read nothing but *Glenanaar*, Stanley condescended to notice and comment on his surroundings. Tramps was chandeliered, sumptuously carpeted and upholstered in purple velvet.

'New Yorkish. Ersatz New Yorkish.'

Here was her Celt again. She didn't bother pointing out that he had never been to New York.

'Conor won't have any trouble with chapter headings in *Lady Chatterley's Lover.*'

'Kate . . . ?'

'Yes. The book falls open at one spot. He has it covered with brown paper with "Algebra" written on it.'

'How did you find it?'

'Stanley, I'm his mother.'

'I'm his father. I didn't come across it. I see I have my work cut out.'

'Leave the boy alone, Stanley.'

Kate had offered to teach Conor the facts of life on his eleventh birthday but Stanley pointed out that it was his place to give such instruction if such instruction should be given and he didn't think it should. Conor knew the facts of life, Stanley maintained, and if he didn't it would be better if he learned off his own bat. Then he had contributed one of his weird observations: 'One should preserve what remains of one's nationality.'

His equanimity in no way disturbed by the news or by his awareness that nothing was more ersatz than his comment on New York, Stanley ploughed on: 'Judging by the size of the menu card the maitre is flashing this place caters for expense account merchants, bookmakers, notables of that sort.'

In his capacity as standard bearer for old Bob Tracey, he detested the notion of people earning more than himself. No matter how much a teacher of his calibre received it was less than he earned.

'Just think, Kate. The long haul before you secured a post?' His wife nodded. She had heard it before many times. It was as much part of the evening as being in Tramps or any other pub before going on to Brigid's on Friday night. 'When I think of you without a smithereen of Irish having to swot for the Ceard Teastas. The curtains pulled on the windows all the time while we saved for furniture. I doubt if there's a human being saving today. All hire purchase.'

The maitre proferred the menu. Stanley waved him away.

'Uncivilised, letting food interfere with drink. Look at them. They all have homes to go to, presumably. But no. Now that they have a few bob they must be seen paying through the nose for bad drink and worse food. A pound for two drinks.'

'Stanley . . . Stanley, cheer up. Remember Bush left all his money to the lawyers. He said all money brought him was three alimonied bitches and two worthless daughters.'

Stanley smiled, thinly. 'It was a neat stroke to die intestate, the bitches and the daughters battling it out in court for five years. He showed great confidence in you, Kate, not leaving you anything.'

'You were his bequest to me. He said that.'

'Yes. Wonderful man.' Stanley drained his beer and contemplated the glass. 'No change out of a pound,' he laughed, 'all I can say is fair play to Mr Tramps, there's no excuse for being poor in this country – if you're rich in neck.'

He pulled back Kate's seat to help her get up. Tramps was the red herring of the night; it might be Tramps again sometime – although more likely not, no change out of a pound – or it might be the Royal George Hotel where they had their drinks in the lobby and Stanley observed all round him with scorn. They always went someplace before Brigid's because it was not on to 'set out' for Brigid's; that smacked of dependence on a local. Stanley Callaghan knew all about shaking off dependence on a local, having exorcised the pull of the Nook where he had not visited for fifteen years.

He held open the door of Brigid's to allow Kate precede him. Over her shoulder he saw Henry Corr.

'Kate, you order while I wash my hands.'

Tony O'Neill lowered his mouth into his hands and whispered: 'That's him.'

'Yeah,' Henry Corr grunted, 'I remember. Who's the piece?'

Drunk but worried, Tony O'Neill began to sweat. He did not like what they were doing or rather what Henry Corr intended doing.

'His wife.' Again Tony O'Neill whispered. At half past seven Henry Corr had collected him and insisted on going drinking. 'We gotta be in there before he comes,' he explained.

'Maiden's Piss,' he had christened O'Neill's hopeful request for beer and ordered them both Scotch; now, two hours later O'Neill could hardly keep his eyes open and had toppled over in the lavatory, mercifully without witnesses.

'Jesus Christ, his wife? Where'd that motherfucker pull a bird like that?'

Tony O'Neill lowered his head. He had seen Mrs Callaghan often in town. Hazily, he remembered thinking it unusual that a school teacher should be married to the most beautiful woman he had ever seen on or off the screen.

'Tony . . . look at those tits! The legs, the arse. Where'd the cunt get her?'

'I don't know,' Tony O'Neill mumbled into his hand. He was no prude; often he told his own brothers to shag or feck off in an argument; sometimes he said jeez instead of gee.

'Okay. Now I'll make the intro and you know what to say, but wait till I nod. Don't come in too early. We mightn't need it at all, the shithead might be dumber than we think.'

With Scotch courage Tony O'Neill whined his defiance: 'I can't do it, Henry. I can't do it.'

'What chickenshit's this?' Corr looked down his nose. 'All right. Shit, I'll do everything. Always have. Fifteen years I dreamed of this. Had a set of goals and achieved every one of them. Except this. This is the big one, this is goin'a be the sweetest. I swore I'd get that cocksucker,' Tony O'Neill dived for his glass. 'I said that shower of pricks wouldn't get away with it . . .'

Stanley Callaghan tried to smooth his hair in the lavatory mirror and wondered why he did this after spending his academic life tossing it. And he wondered what had suddenly taken hold of him that drove him into the lavatory at the sight of Henry Corr and Tony O'Neill. He gathered together what he remembered of his old self and decided he had not recognised them. He fixed his eyes on Kate as he passed them by. She sat with her back to the wall on which hung the large mirror advertising Gold Flake at 6d for ten. Kate's Winter's Tale and his pint of beer were already on the counter. Brigid was preparing a cup of tea and a sandwich for the huddled figure of Mrs Trehy toasting her talons at the fire. Two old men – silver watches grew out of their waistcoats – sat drinking bottles beneath the window.

'Good-night, Brigid.'

Brigid indicated Mrs Trehy: 'I'll be with ye shortly.'

Kate made as though to rise so that her husband could sit with his back to the wall but Stanley held up his hand.

'I'm fine here, Kate.'

'I thought you liked the commanding view.'

'I have a commanding view of the most beautiful woman in the world. Isn't that enough for me.' But he was not looking at his wife. In the mirror he saw Henry Corr and Tony O'Neill glancing in his direction.

'Stanley, don't turn round. There are two people near the door . . . '

'I see them, Kate. Yes. They *are* discussing us. But we don't know them. Remember that. We don't know them.'

'Stanley . . . *do* we know them?'

He nodded, smiled at Kate and patted her knee then turned to look at Mrs Trehy. Mrs Trehy was a regular client of Brigid's in Brigid's capacity as field operative for Al Anon. Brigid, an ex-school teacher herself, had taken to running the pub ten years earlier after her husband had died a gallant failure in the attempt to drink his own pub dry. Since then it was common-place to have a comparative stranger of either sex stagger into Brigid's desperate with the longing but terrified of the con-sequences. Brigid sat her patients by the fire, furnished tea and sandwiches and philosophy and risked losing some of her more squeamish customers.

Stanley knew from his old Nook days that Mrs Trehy was a fraud. She was a prostitute by trade but now at fifty-nine years of age she preferred drink to work and in fact worked to drink. She spent her time between the docks and the drying out department of St Joseph's Mental Hospital. When hungry and skint she called at Brigid's, ostensibly in the throes of the struggle. After tea and sandwiches she accepted fifty pence and sometimes a pound from Brigid to buy a bit of breakfast for the morning and used the money as entrace fee to the Nook where she opened her coat and crossed her bare, mini-skirted knees. The Nook was a regular port of call of the dock disgorgement and it was not unusual to hear four or five different languages all enquiring of the fuck.

In the mirror Henry Corr began to make his approach.

'Hiya, fella. Stanley Callaghan, right?'

The teacher's cliché had been carefully chosen and cocked a full minute: 'You appear to have the advantage of me.'

'The Institute. The Nook. Fifteen years ago, remember? Ye claimed ye beat us but we all know better, don't we?'

Stanley Callaghan frowned and turned to Tony O'Neill.

'I know this man's face. You'd be one of the O'Neills?'

'Of course you know him. He was playing.'

Henry Corr was prominent in the chin and held his head as though he were tracing the flight of an aeroplane with the sun in his eyes. It was a belligerent stance and in spite of a pastel pink shirt and floral tie that of a fit man, a live wire. Stanley Callaghan felt ten years his senior.

'I'm sorry. You'll have to forgive me. It was so long ago. You're mister . . . ?'

'Look fella, don't mister me. Corr. Henry Corr. I remember that match like it was yesterday. You remember, Tony? The Nook? Goalkeeper escaped from a circus or something. He had a nickname. Four foot ten. He couldn't have been more than four foot ten.'

'Bazook was five feet three and a half inches.'

'Yeah. And Mickey Rooney's King Kong. Anyway, what's past is past. If there had'a been crossbars we'd have stuffed ye, but so what? What else is new? Your good wife?'

'Sorry. Kate . . . Kate, Henry Corr. Tony O'Neill.'

'Pleased to meet you.'

'And you, ma'am. And you. What are you drinking?'

'Thank you all the same. We like to stay on our own.'

'Horse manure, Stanley. Hey! What's her name? Missus, Missus, give my friends here another shot of their poison. And two large Scotches.'

'Henry, a half pint will . . . '

'You're okay, Tony. You're fine. I been fifteen years in the States. Great country.' Henry Corr's voice softened. 'Great country but home's home. What are you at yourself, Stanley?'

'I'm a teacher.'

'Uhuh. A teacher. I'm with Datalog myself, you know, manufacture integrated circuits, you probably heard of us, world-wide, we're just setting up here in the industrial estate, hey, where's a good spot to live? I'm out of touch, we're renting at the moment, can't decide where to build. Where you live yourself?'

Stanley raised his pint in acknowledgement: 'Good luck.' He was grateful for the diversion. Such half-wits did not fall into one's lap every day. He did not blame the O'Neill chap for trembling with discomfiture.

'Southview Gardens,' he admitted, hating to part with the right time to such a person.

'No kidding?' Henry Corr looked at Tony O'Neill. But Tony O'Neill stared at the floor. 'I know Southview. That's real nice. And costs a few bob. But you got things lined up in the summer?'

'Pardon?'

'You know. You in caravans? Taxis? No. I don't see you in taxis. Development. Development's a good line. But you don't look like a developer, Stanley. I'll put two bucks on caravans. You're into caravans, right? Right, Stanley?'

Kate didn't take her eyes from Henry Corr.

'I'm sorry. I don't know what you're talking about,' Stanley bluffed.

'Look, Stanley kid, don't get uptight. I'm not knocking it. Gee, it's no secret teachers are badly paid. Even in the States. There's no sin in pulling a stroke during vacation. All I wondered was how you make the few bucks during the holidays.'

Stanley looked to Kate for help. She offered simply: 'During the holidays we holiday.'

'You mean . . . he's not into *anything*?'

'Stanley has neither the time nor the inclination to be *into* anything. We rent a chalet in West Cork for a month. That's as long as we can afford and anyway Stanley has to come home to prepare for the new term.' Her answer was frosty and definitive.

'Hey! You're American?'

'After fifteen years I think of myself as Irish.'

Kate lied. Although she had dual nationality she still thought of herself as American in honour of Bush Vine and she lied out of respect for her husband.

'If it's all right I ask, how'd you two meet up?'

Henry Corr looked from one to the other. The implication of the question decided Stanley that he'd had enough. He and Kate remained silent for a few moments, then Kate stepped in.

'I was taken to a soccer match fifteen years ago. The Nook and the Institute. I was introduced to Stanley. It happened from there. Although why I'm . . . '

'Hey, are we into coincidences. Now honey, don't let that result put you off. If there were record books they'd show the Nook won, but we know better, eh, Stanley? We know the difference between those two teams. Right Tony? Right?'

Crimson, despite the Scotch, Tony O'Neill croaked in agreement: 'We were surprised all right.' He grinned at Stanley and Kate by way of not giving offence. All he could remember of the game was having had to go to the Nook afterwards on behalf of the Institute. Henry had been offside in refusing to shake hands.

'Surprised? Yeah, you could call it that. They had a dwarf in goal, intimidated the referee ... '

Stanley was still listening to 'how'd you two meet up'. Mechanically he let slip but with venom: 'The referee was an Institute appointee celebrated for his impartiality. And Bazook is five feet three and a half inches. We measured him.'

'Bazook! Bazook! Yeah, ye all had nicknames. Where'd he get a name like that?'

Stanley gestured with his hands and wrinkled his forehead. Assaulted once in the heat of a poker school by a blow-in who accused him of dealing from the bottom Paschal Halvey later claimed his attacker had gone bazook. The name stuck. Stanley was fond of retailing the anecdote on the right occasion. This was not one of them. He hated disciples of the Institute. Hockey, tennis, cricket and bowls, castle Catholics, snobs, sons of merchant princes. How Corr had ever become a member puzzled Stanley and yet pleased him: if that was their class then it would be easy talk to them now.

Henry Corr shook his head like a comedian. 'Jesus, what a bunch!'

'Excuse me. You may consider me old fashioned, but I won't have people swear in front of my wife.'

The quiet authority drew the attention of Brigid, Mrs Trehy and the two old men. Tony O'Neill thanked God that Henry had offended with merely the tip of his repertoire. Henry Corr looked all round him for support. Kate Callaghan was shocked – by her husband. It was true Stanley didn't swear but she had never heard him object to another's colourful language. He would have had to cut her ears off to protect her from the strings of fucks and jaysuses that were part of the vocabulary of social Ireland.

'Fella, I'm sorry.' Henry Corr's voice was soft again. 'Look, I really am sorry. I keep forgetting you're a teacher. Ma'am, my apologies. Look, I got an idea. Tony, you listen to this too. I got a sudden idea. Stanley, I think I have a brainwave. What do you think of this? We're going to replay that match . . . are you on?'

Although it was fifteen years since he had visited the Nook Stanley was, after all, Nook trained. He took his time about answering and clung to a neutrality of tone that was fast deserting him.

'I don't see how we could.'

'Why not? Where's the problem?'

Tony O'Neill relaxed. It seemed that Henry wasn't going to go as far as he had threatened.

'I don't use the Nook nowadays. As far as I know they don't have a soccer team. A pool team more likely.'

'No, no. You're not with me. I mean we replay the match with the *same* two teams. Somebody – I think it was Robert Flanagan's brother – photographed both teams before the game. I got one of the Institute. And one of your bunch must have one someplace. We just round up both teams fifteen years later. What do you say?'

Mellick is a sporting city. The two old men and Mrs Trehy – who should have long since taken up her stand in the Nook – and Brigid all stared nakedly at the teacher who tried desperately to shake off the accumulated rust of fifteen years' absence from the Nook. Jake O'Dea or Cocoa Brown or Dara Holden himself would have weighed the proposition to a gram's milli. Stanley observed that Corr and O'Neill were in splendid shape for men of their ages and he recalled having spotted in the local that Tony O'Neill was runner-up in last year's South of Ireland – no matter that tennis was to Ireland as rugby to an Eskimo. Fleetingly, what had filtered through to him of the afterlife of that Nook team, claimed his attention. He banished the demoralising thought, forced a smile and shook his head: 'Sounds romantic but I'm afraid we're long in the tooth now, Henry.' He managed not to choke on his first use of the christian name.

'Life begins at forty. Come on fella. Thirty-eight? I'll vouch for our crowd. And just for – just for the crack – we play for something – say, a thousand pounds a man.'

Brigid laughed, a short cackle of derision. The two old men smiled wistfully. Tony O'Neill coughed up a dribble of whiskey. There had been no mention of money during the rehearsal. When he recovered he smiled sheepishly at Stanley, though he addressed Henry Corr.

'Henry, go easy. Speak for yourself, a thousand pounds! Phew!'

Stanley decided to buy drink to buy time. He was alarmed at the state of his reflexes. There was a stink to the proposition that he could not identify. He was only sustained and oddly charmed by the memory that no one he had known in the Nook would have so undermined the authority of a Nook spokesman as Tony O'Neill had done.

'Brigid, the same again, please.'

'No, no, fella. I'll get this.'

'Nonsense. It's my round.'

'Look, no offence, but – how do I say it without getting your back up? But look, I more or less got it made. Let me treat you, okay?'

Kate watched the blood drain from her husband's face. She had only seen the white anger twice before, during the strike when he was assaulted passing the picket and the night in the snug of the Nook with Dara Holden and Bush Vine. She grabbed her bag from the counter.

'Stanley will not buy this round. Neither will Mr Corr. I'll buy. Brigid, I'll take care of this.'

Henry Corr shook his head while Kate poked in her purse. 'No need for this. None of this lib sh ... none of this new freedom, I thought I got away from that coming home. The hell with it. Let Stanley buy it.'

'I earn more than Stanley.' Aghast at what she'd said Kate bit her lip and clung to her temper.

'No kiddin'? In that case ... what's your bag anyway?'

'I'm a teacher.'

'Aha! I see! Two salaries. That's it. I made a deal with Norrie, Norrie's my wife. We had it tough but I said Norrie, you're the mother, I'm the breadwinner. 'Course it's different two teachers. Fair play ... '

'Brigid, same again, please.'

' . . . Yeah. But listen. Stanley, what about it? A thousand quid a man.'

'It's not a realistic proposal.'

'Why not?'

'Eleven thousand reasons, Henry,' Tony O'Neill cut in.

'Tony, you don't need to worry. I'll handle it, leave our side to me. Now, I remember you Nook lot used to boast you were never beaten and never avoided a challenge. Am I right?'

'Yes. We were never beaten.'

'But I say ye were.'

Brigid placed the Scotches, the beer and the Winter's Tale on the counter. Kate paid. Though ready to leave – she had swallowed half the tea and managed a sandwich – Mrs Trehy was rooted to her crouch by the fire. She remembered the teacher from his days in the Nook. He was one of a very few who had not fucked her for a half a crown. In those days he had never acknowledged her presence but in Brigid's he treated her with respect. 'Good evening Mrs Trehy,' he often said. In the Nook people whom she didn't even know brazenly called her Birdie.

Stanley was aware of all eyes being on him now, including Kate's. The eyes that should have been on him were those of Bazook, Cocoa Brown, Jake O'Dea, Dara, Stevie Mack. The Corr article was trying to goad him into commitment.

'I don't see why you persist in saying we were defeated when we never were.'

'I say we beat ye that night. The Institute beat ye and there's one easy way to prove it. Good for the goose as the gander. We're all fifteen years older. I'm sure our crowd can raise the dough but I won't let them. I want to put up the eleven grand myself. And there must be someone in the Nook amounted to something . . . hey, Dara Holden, I didn't think of him, he was playing, he could chuck in eleven grand out of his hip pocket. So whaddya say, Stanley, buddy? Deal?'

Though the proposition came from your typically returned fool from America, Stanley could not deny its fairness. But he was puzzled by Tony O'Neill. All night he had been uneasy, sweating, licking his lips, not knowing whether to laugh or cry.

'I'm sorry. I must have grown up faster than some of you. I haven't the appetite for a replay.'

'Horse manure.' Corr downed his Scotch. 'Listen, Stanley. Why don't you think about it? You don't have to decide right now. I think on my feet myself. Had to. No rainchecks on decisions in America. The money is immaterial – you have Dara Holden for that. You know I wasn't talking about yourself personally, two salaries or not. How does it go? Those who can, do. Those who can't, teach.'

Stanley's hand tightened round the glass. He nerved himself not to drink from it and in an effort to remain calm he tried to recollect the source of the quotation. It was probably Henry Ford.

'Is that your own?'

Henry Corr looked briefly around him and at his clothes. 'What? Is what my own?'

'Those who can, do. Those who can't, teach.'

'Oh. Yeah. It's good but not mine, I'm afraid. Wasn't it Oscar Wilde?'

Accustomed to Stanley's mute pleading in such circumstances Kate nodded.

'Of course. I should have recognised the remark of a pervert.'

'I thought there was live and let live nowadays. No offence meant, fella. But look, we gotta go. Why don't you think about it? Round up your cronies. Here's my card, you ring any time, give your name, I'll take the call straightaway, you won't be kept hanging. Okay?'

Stanley ignored the card. Henry Corr placed it on the counter.

'Tony, let's go. Slash first. Nice meeting you both, ma'am.'

Kate ignored him and continued to look at her husband.

'Come on, Tony, just shake hands with the devil and then we're off.'

The pub fell quiet and the muffled voices of Corr and O'Neill could be heard from the toilet. Stanley couldn't look at his wife or Mrs Trehy or Brigid or the two old men who, he knew must all be staring at him. There was laughter in the toilet, Henry Corr's unmistakable transatlantic guffaw and: 'You bet that guy Wilde was right.' A glass partition separated the bar from the toilet, six feet of it up to the ceiling. Mrs Trehy rammed the rim of her cup into her mouth and the two old men heaved from their watch chains up with fright as Stanley's pint sailed through the air and crashed through the glass.

It was Tony O'Neill and not Henry Corr who shouted: Jesus. They came running out of the toilet to be greeted by Stanley Callaghan on his feet, his face bloodless:

'The Nook will play the Institute for eleven thousand pounds that I will personally put up . . . '

'Fella, you've got a deal, now we gotta firm this up . . . '

'ENOUGH! ENOUGH OF YOUR TUPPENCE HA'PENNY-JARGON. I said it's on and let that be enough for you. O'Neill is a witness.'

'Okay, okay. We'll just shake on it then.'

The teacher sat down. He did not shout now. He hissed at the outstretched hand: 'Get out. Get out of my local. I'll appoint my second who will deal with your representative.'

'Fella . . . '

'Get out. Get out. Get out.'

'Okay, you want it that way, buster, I'll give it to you. Same teams, same venue, no substitutes.'

'Same result.'

'We'll see about that.'

Stanley cradled his forehead in the palm of his hand and continued in the direction of the spillings on the counter, 'Never, the Nook, the street, never, never beaten.' He did not observe Corr and O'Neill gingerly withdraw or hear Mrs Trehy's hoarse 'good-night' to Brigid. Kate tugged at his cardigan sleeve and gradually he became aware of the two old men studying him. He glared at Mrs Trehy who immediately gathered herself and left.

'Kate . . . '

'Yes, love?'

'Kate . . . I'm sorry but . . . '

'Don't be sorry. You're lovely angry. It was like that very first night, you were lovely then, really lovely then.'

'Kate, you're not to worry. The eleven thousand – pure rhetoric, I lost my head but tomorrow I'll ring the imbecile and undo . . . '

'Stanley!' Kate tapped her chest. '*I* was a witness. I know we haven't eight hundred between us but put me down for five and a half thousand, however we raise it.'

He took her hand and held it gently. 'My Kate. He made me lose control. Caravans. Caravans!' Stanley fingered the business card. 'Embossed.' He threw it in the fire.

'Brigid, forgive me. I'll be in touch with a glazier's first thing in the morning. I'll have that put right.'

'No apologies in this house please. And aren't you the gay dog? Go down on that and have a drink on me. If Charles were alive he would have run that fellow.' Beaming at the two old men Brigid added: 'And a drink for everyone and why not.'

The two old men touched their caps at Stanley acknowledging him as the true instrument of Brigid's bounty. Stanley raised the index finger of his left hand by way of returning the salute.

'Brigid, on top of your round, five large brandies on me.' He put a ten pound note on the counter. He put two of the brandies in front of the old men. Then gulping down the brandy, sipped a chaser of beer and tried to think.

It was plain to him now that the Institute pair had deliberately goaded him. They knew what they were doing. That was why O'Neill was on edge. The O'Neills were a harmless family. Henry Corr was an animal. He would make an entry in his notebook about Henry Corr and use it as ammunition to hurl at Dara Holden the next time the actor was home. He remembered once reading in James Stephens' *Crock of Gold* that it was amazing on what slender compulsion people go to America. What was astonishing about Henry Corr was that he bothered to come back. Brigid and Kate were sitting quietly over their drinks so that his wonderful brain could function but his wonderful brain would not function without Dara. The two old men couldn't help. He had never spoken to either of them other than to bid good-night and not contradict their weather forecasting. Brigid was a good sort but had never been out to the house or anything. In the teachers' room he did not get on with any of his colleagues; not after the Locky strike when he scabbed. It was true that they ran caravans, taxis, what have you – but he did not object to that *per se,* he couldn't very well, he of the double income family. But he would have welcomed their even pretending that teaching was a vocation and not a fitful interregnum between the launching of mobile homes.

As president of CRAM he was naturally in touch with all manner of persons – within the limitation that members of CRAM could be distinctive – but there was no fellow traveller in the Association. His neighbours kept themselves to themselves which was in its modern way an ideal method of not falling out with each other. He had to face the fact now that the buttyless isolation he had sculpted over fifteen years was chilly company. He went back to the counter.

'Dara, Kate. Dara.'

'He wasn't exactly fit as a fiddle last time we saw him.'

'I hadn't thought of Dara as a *problem*. But, relax Kate, we're not being as quixotic as you might think. We can't lose.'

'How can you be sure?'

Now he no longer needed Dara. 'I never believed in it, Kate. Losing. It's as simple as that. Did you ever hear me mention Tolly Holliday?'

'He was at Jake O'Dea's wedding. The big man.'

'Big is a nice way of putting it. He was sixteen stone then. Who else. Bazook. Jake. Thank God for Jake O'Dea. I have that photograph at home someplace. I must look it up later.'

'Stanley, not tonight. Not Friday night.'

'Jake is sound.' He continued, not having grasped Friday night. 'Jake, myself, Dara, Tolly. Johnny Green was playing. We didn't know whether to put Johnny or Bazook in goal. Having no crossbars decided that. Stevie Mack. In England. He's the one I bleed for. Curious the way he confides in Dara now. How many is that? Seven. And Cocoa Brown. Eight. And some strangers. We had to pick up a couple of strangers because of the short notice. I remember that. It wasn't even our best team. But we won.'

'Stanley.'

'Yes?'

'Tell me. What were you like before I met you?'

By way of inviting Brigid into the conversation Stanley answered in her direction: 'Empty.'

'Brigid, Dara Holden – Stanley's best friend – Dara claims Stanley sowed wild oats as though seven years of famine were predicted.'

'Boys will be boys, Kate.'

'Dara refuses to grow up.'

'That's what he says about you.'

'I've proved him right tonight. Where is he again?'

'New York.'

'I thought he forecast New York about to become an out place?'

'It's in again.'

'Now that he's there. He must have wangled his way into the latest fashionable disco club. Dara's their type of client I should imagine.'

'How can you talk like that about your best friend?'

'Because he's my best friend.' Stanley looked at his watch and raised his eyebrows. Brigid nodded. She came out from behind the counter and announced to the two old men: 'Young fellas, home to bed. Come on. Throw it back.' Meekly they tipped their caps at Stanley and Kate and allowed Brigid to see them to the door. Brigid put out the lights and silently accepted Stanley's brandy glass. Stanley took the drink from the counter and by the light of the dying fire, his face heated with drink and the memories of the life without restrictions that he had known before Kate made her appearance, he tried to see the photograph.

Kate fed Brigid news of Conor which Brigid lapped up, not having had children of her own. It was difficult for children today, Brigid proposed, and while they discussed that subject they became gradually aware that Stanley was not joining in with his authoritative commentary on how best to deal with children nowadays. He was prodded by Kate.

'Stanley, Brigid is talking to you.'

'Pardon? Sorry. Sorry, Brigid.'

'A grand book for a child. Kate was telling me. *Glenanaar*. A lovely writer, the Canon, no dirt and no need for dirt. No filth and sex and muck and dirt with the Canon.'

'Yes. Old Bob Tracey introduced us to the Sheahan work. Wonderful teacher, Bob Tracey. You know, about six months before he died, I saw him strolling in the park talking to himself. His beard was white and he was bent a little, a bit slow on the feet. I saw him talking to himself and it struck me that's how I'd like to go out. Talking to myself in the park, life's labour behind one.'

'Thanks.'

'Dear Kate. . . I like to think I take after him in so far as I can – given today's conditions. Set a steady course. Stick to it.'

'Not have the noiseless tenor of your way rocked.'

'Ah, Brigid. Goldsmith never lets us down.'

'Stanley! Not Goldsmith. Gray.'

'Of course. Silly of me. One for the road?'

Kate shook her head: 'You've had enough.'

'Calligraphy and manners, Brigid, equals education. Correct?'

'Ah yes, Stanley. The three 'R's.'

'I think at times it's doing for me, Brigid. The three 'R's. One has lost one's grasp of one's *Golden Treasury*. We'll have one for the road, Kate?'

'You have one. I'm the pilot.'

'Rubbish. I'm quite capable of driving.'

They brought home Kentucky chicken for all, Stanley driving slowly and badly. Before sitting down to what he referred to as the object of false appetitite he went upstairs to the attic over

Conor's study and rooted out the old photograph. He was immediately preoccupied with the youthful and, at the same time, aged faces in the photograph. It was the short back and sides that accounted for the oddity. By comparison with Cocoa Brown Stanley had wintered well. Cocoa's quiff hung over his forehead in the snap but he was as bald now as he ever would be. Tolly Holliday grinned, arms folded, eleven stone. A hawser would scarcely hold up his trousers now. The muscular six foot Dara Holden – he *was* a fine cut of a fellow then, Stanley had to admit – these days Dara sported the film star's inevitable gut, camouflaged by held breath in the Dara Holden File on television.

Kate shouted up that his chicken was getting cold. As he was about to leave the study he spotted Conor's Algebra book. He flicked through the pages. *Lady Chatterley's Lover* did not stand the test of time. Clutching the photograph he rejoined his wife and son. He picked absentmindedly at the chicken before bequeathing the box to Conor with the observation: 'Conor, I'm afraid you have the makings of a family bucket man. America is dying from junk food.'

It was his custom after such a remark to grin from ear to ear but now he concentrated grimly on the photograph. When the time came he mechanically kissed his son good-night. It was twenty minutes later that Kate announced: 'Stanley . . . I will arise and go now . . . '

'Ah yes. Yes. Coleridge.'

'Not Coleridge. Yeats. And have you forgotten that it's Friday?'

'No. I won't be one minute, Kate. One minute and I'll be up.'

They made love regularly, either last thing at night or on awakening, encounters that indeed sprang from love. But every Friday night and Sunday afternoon – when Conor was despatched elsewhere – they indulged in sex. Stanley rummaged for a last cigarette as he thought about the twins who had been press-ganged into action. He couldn't even remember their names. His cigarette packet was empty. There were some in his coat in the bedroom.

Kate was standing on the bed dressed in a short nightie under which he could see the black bra and panties he had asked her to buy. As he entered the room Kate lifted the nightie, made a pelvic thrust at him and groaned theatrically.

'Just getting a cigarette, Kate. Be back in one minute.'

He smoked two cigarettes trying to christen the twins. There was also the young fellow in the back row between Johnny Green and Jake O'Dea. In an effort to identify him Stanley marshalled every individual he had ever come across in the Nook but with no success. He fell asleep, his cigarette smouldering between his fingers. When he woke an hour later there was a hole in his corduroys and ash all over the carpet. He threw water on his face in the bathroom and then went to Kate. She appeared asleep. Stanley lay awake beside her and continued to grapple with the stranger.

'You don't love me, Stanley.'

'I thought you were asleep. Do I love you. "Let me count the ways", and I know who that is Kate so don't ask.' He took her platonically in his arms. 'I'm not myself tonight. After I see Cocoa Brown and Jake O'Dea I'll be over it.'

Kate snuggled sleepily into him. They had an encounter that sprang from love. Stanley did not even take off his pyjamas. After the usual interval Stanley said: 'Good-night, my sweet.'

'Good-night . . . . . . Stanley?'

'Yes?'

'Who in fact was it?'

'Was what?'

'Stop bluffing. You know what I mean.'

It was obviously one of those chaps who wrote their poetry to women all the time.

'It was Browning, wasn't it?'

'No. His wife.'

He was close and he thought this a very good omen.

2

The Nook

'How could you possibly be skint on Saturday night?'

The question was liturgical. No one understood better than Cocoa Brown how easily Jake O'Dea managed to be penniless on Friday evening let alone Saturday night. But Cocoa Brown also understood how understanding led to sympathy and weakness and fatality of the purse. Jake O'Dea gently sloshed life into his ebbing pint.

'If you were married yourself, Cocoa, you'd know all about it. Out of what she gives me I pay Tom. What's left isn't worth a wank so it goes on the horses. If I click, grand. If I don't, I'm as well off with shagall as too little.'

'You did that when you were single. People are supposed to grow up when they get married. You could at least keep the price of the liquor. Save me having to buy it.'

'You were always a mean bollix.'

'What did you want to get married for anyway?'

What remained in the glass – the second pint bought for him by Cocoa – was not worth nursing any longer. Jake finished it off and replied: 'I was deserted.'

Even though, after an absence of fifteen years, Stanley Callaghan was due at any moment to enter the Nook, Jake O'Dea could not rise above the depression of being broke in Cocoa's company. Listening to people sometimes Jake had the idea they thought he liked being a bum; it wasn't true. He had come from a good family – much too good a family – and had reacted accordingly. His mother had been a teacher, his father a superintendent in the gardai before on retirement becoming manager of a building society. One of Jake's brothers was a priest, the other an engineer and his sister a nurse. Jake left

school after succeeding in failing his intermediate certificate
and then carried a ruler and a set square to the technical school
for a year where he learned to stop adults in the street and ask:
Excuse me sir, would you have a light, please. The O'Dea family
assembled often and wondered what would become of him.
Their mercantile influence was negligible and they managed no
better than to get Jake into Stephen S. Kelly's, the timber
importer's where wages were not great. But Jake was delighted.

'A dog with a mallet in his arse could do the work and I have
enough for fags and drink and the bet.'

Tall, six one, and with the strength that stems from all bone,
Jake O'Dea was a gifted athlete but without any interest in the
formal pursuit of sport, without any interest other than
smoking and drinking and gambling. He was particularly
uninterested in women. In the Nook women were not
mentioned but at intervals someone's attendance fell short of
the seven nights a week and it was mournfully accepted that
that someone had an interest outside. A stag night was
announced; money was borrowed to buy the departing a
present and the proprietor, Tom Splendid, tapped for a few
bob on the morning of the wedding. That kind of gradual
evolution was stoically understood. What had remained a
mystery to Jake O'Dea was Stanley Callaghan, nowhere near his
peak, *disappearing*. One moment he was there, streaking. The
next he was married and gone for ever.

It was many years later, alone in the bar chatting to Tom
Splendid, Jake O'Dea announced: 'This place is gone to the
dogs. I hardly know anyone except Cocoa and he wouldn't give
you the steam. I'd be better off married. Know anyone would
marry me, Tom?'

'Splendid job. Splendid.' Tom Gilligan had been called Tom
Splendid as long as anyone could remember.

Molly Leonard worked in the county council with Cocoa
Brown and pestered him discreetly. She let it be known to her
pals that she wanted Cocoa to take her to the annual dinner; she
sat by his side on staff bus outings. Molly was not crazy about
Cocoa Brown but she had a low opinion of herself and she had
no money. She was a country girl and ready to set her sights as
low as Cocoa Brown. Tom Splendid confided in Cocoa: 'Jake
says we're to look out for a woman for him, he wants to get
married.'

'He should marry Molly Leonard so and get her off my back. She'd be dumb enough.'

'Ah, now, Molly is your girl.'

'Was he serious was he? I could kill two birds with one stone. Get Molly off my back and if he was married the fucker wouldn't be tapping me all my life.'

'Splendid job.'

Molly Leonard was informed that *a certain person* was interested in her. She assumed it was Cocoa and said as much.

'Jesus, no. It's not me. It's Jake. Jake O'Dea. He asked me to put the word in.'

It was sad but true that Molly Leonard, approaching her middle thirties, would have married anyone. She knew Jake O'Dea from the Nook. She was not thought of in the Nook as a woman because she drank, smoked, swore, played poker and could calculate a yankee, accomplishment she could not fail to develop working beside Cocoa Brown. The proposition was put to Jake O'Dea by Tom Splendid.

'I'll marry her,' Jake said as though accepting a bet. After a degree of dilatory horseplay a date was arranged. Jake O'Dea set the tone.

'Molly, I haven't one clue about going with women or sex or anything, all that will have to be up to you. Do you know all about that?'

'Yes, Jake.'

'Good. That's out of the way anyway. As Tom would say, splendid job. Listen, will we go for a jar, have you anything?'

Molly turned out a gem. She was adorable for all the little ways she had that Jake thought exclusively the properties of the male – she understood he liked a drink every night and found the house confined. And when they got to know each other – after the first sex made them temporarily strangers – Molly shared Jake's opinion of Cocoa.

'He's a mean cunt that fucker,' Jake said and Molly agreed.

'What's that supposed to mean – you were deserted?'

'Everyone went off and got married or went away.'

'I didn't get married.'

'Who the fuck would marry you. Come on, buy a drink.'

'I bought two already. Get them on the book.'

'I can't. The No 2 account is too high. I have to get it down a bit.'

'Wouldn't you draw in your horns and settle down. You're married now.'

'Will you get the drink, will you? You invited me here.'

'Stanley Callaghan invited you and you're here every night anyway.'

'He invited me through you, so you buy or else I'll fuck off and when I see him explain I had to go away because I was skint.'

'It never changes. Tom, two pints.'

Tom Splendid closed Jake O'Dea's No 1 account at one hundred pounds and twelve pence. The No 2 account stood at forty-six pounds seventy-four pence. The No 1 account would be cleared when Jake's ship came in. That was how Jake himself put it and Tom Splendid had no difficulty believing him because he knew it certainly would not be cleared sooner.

'Give us one of your fags.'

'I'm supposed to be at the dogs. Stanley said he'd see us here tonight. It's half nine, what time does he think the night begins? You've no fags either. Jesus.'

Stanley Callaghan returned to the Nook. He closed the door behind him as students are taught to at drama school. There were no more than a dozen customers propped in their privacy at the long counter. The pub had not changed an iota. Jake and Cocoa sat at the table under the television. Stanley stretched his hand across the counter to the proprietor.

'Ah, Mr Callaghan himself. Splendid job.'

'How are you Tom. I see you have the television.'

'Fourteen years now, Stanley.' The teacher grinned in acknowledgement. He nodded at the customers with none of whom was he familiar and walked towards Cocoa and Jake.

'I missed the dogs over you.'

'Sorry, Cocoa. What time did I say?'

'You said tonight. It's half nine.'

'How are you, Jake?'

'Terrible, Stanley. Terrible. I can't do a thing right.'

'Tom, give us three pints. We'll have them upstairs.'

'Listen to him. Upstairs is closed ten years,' Cocoa Brown began but he was cut short by Tom Splendid. 'That's all right, Cocoa. Look after the pints. I'll see Peggy.'

Tom Splendid's wife, Peggy, was happy to vacate her upstairs kitchen to oblige Stanley Callaghan. It was a poky kitchen comprising sink, gas cooker, one cupboard, a table and two chairs. The Splendids also had a living room, a bedroom and access to a toilet which was also shared by the hairdresser's, the car rental company and the Sarah O'Malley Staff Bureau. Tom and Peggy were childless, comparatively poor as publicans go, not that they leave anything behind, Tom was grimly fond of saying, they are taken away from it. The building itself was over one hundred and fifty years old. The bar was filthy. Tom once hired a temporary barman when Peggy broke her leg falling down the cellar and when Tom spotted the young chap zealously dusting bottles he remarked: 'No need for that, the drink is on the inside.' Customers sat on barrels or stood at the counter or by the card table beside the fire. There was a snug immediately off the street. And there was a downstairs toilet for men. It consisted of a wall for urinating against and a bowl secreted by a half door on which there was no lock. The bowl did not have a seat. Patrons supplied their own strip of newspaper.

Upstairs in the kitchen Stanley indicated that Jake and Cocoa occupy the chairs. He sat on the table, sipped his pint and began: 'Fifteen years ago we played the Institute a soccer match. They want a replay.'

His audience continued to look at him expectantly.

'Well, what do you think?'

'Did I miss the dogs for this?'

'What I want to know first: are we all agreed in principle?'

'What the fuck are you talking about? You said it was *important*.'

'It is important, Cocoa. It is. Henry Corr – you remember him, Jake?'

'Yeah. He went to America. He was a bit of a bollix.'

'Correct. He's home now, Jake. I bumped into him last night. He claims we played a midget in goal, that they scored a few goals we managed to get disallowed because they went over Bazook's head. There wasn't a crossbar.'

'I remember that,' Cocoa Brown hesitated, 'that was the night, Dara was with the film star, you . . . '

'Yes, Cocoa. That was the night. Now listen, Jake. Two items. Henry Corr wants a replay. The same two teams. The exact two teams. I have our photograph here in the envelope. Tough luck if we can't round them all up. If we can only find nine we can only play nine. No subs. And item: He wants to play for a bet.'

'What do you mean "a bet"?'

'Cocoa, a bet is a bet.'

'How much?'

'Not an insignificant amount.'

'How much?'

'A thousand pounds . . . '

'A thou . . . '

' . . . a man.'

Cocoa went down on his pint. He stood up and with his hand on the kitchen door announced: 'To think that there are young children in your care. And that I missed the dogs. Fuck you and goodbye.'

An indication from Stanley was correctly interpreted by Jake O'Dea as a licence to haul Cocoa back by his jacket collar, plank him back on his seat and stand guard by the door.

'All right. I'll listen to you. Because I'm not strong I get bullied. You always bullied me. Took my money off me because I was better at minding it than the rest of you. I'll listen but I'm buying no more drink. This fucker has nothing, who's surprised. I'm not parting with a penny let alone a thousand. Right?'

Stanley handed Jake a fiver. 'Get three more pints.'

In Jake's absence Stanley withdrew the photograph from the manilla envelope. 'Cocoa, you look different from the snap. But you haven't changed. Here.'

Cocoa progressed from a serious perusal to a sudden fit of laughter. He took off his glasses and dabbed his eyes with the cuff of his shirt.

'Oh Jesus. Gabriel! Gabriel!'

'Who's Gabriel?'

'Come again?'

'Who's Gabriel?'

'Are you telling me you don't know?' Cocoa's mouth remained open and his eyes grew wide as he stared out over his glasses.

'The third from the left in the back row? I couldn't place him. Well, who is he?'

'Stanley, tell me something. You didn't put any money – down?'

'Not yet.'

'How did you propose to finance the bet? Dara?'

'I thought every man would find his own thousand.'

'Did you? Well, you're looking at a man who's not going to find a thousand. I have a thousand but I'm not finding it. And Jake – let's leave the sick jokes out of it.'

Jake nudged the kitchen door open with his elbow and placed the tray of drinks on the table. Cocoa handed him the photograph. 'Third from left back row. Stanley doesn't know him.'

Jake O'Dea didn't laugh. He looked straight at Stanley. 'You don't know Gabriel?'

'All right. Give it to me. Who's this Gabriel. He's not dead, is he?'

They told him.

Stanley lit a cigarette and considered. 'Right. We'll cross that bridge when we come to it. Cocoa, you and Jake and Bazook, none of you, as a matter of fact nobody, will have to put up any money . . . '

'I knew it had to be Dara.'

'It's not Dara,' the teacher shouted and then added, 'I'll put up the lot. Anyway who puts up what is incidental. We'll win. Jake, what do you think?'

'Cocoa had hair on him here. Tolly Holliday. My God. If I were you I'd get out of it Stanley.' He put the photograph on the table.

'Jake, the bet is a thousand pounds a man. If we lose you lose nothing. But if we win everyone gets a thousand.'

'Gimme that photograph.'

Jake re-studied the bygone faces. 'Stanley, you're on the level? I get a thousand pounds? Straight up?'

'If we win.'

'Bazook. Tolly. I hope he doesn't count as two players with the size of him now. The twins. Gabriel. Skip him. Keep the hard ones till last. Dara Holden, pluck him out of the television slot. Cocoa . . . hey, that cunt isn't going to get a thousand, is he?'

'Shut up.'

'He's loaded.'

'The labourer is worthy of his hire.'

'Myself. Yourself. Johnny Green. Stevie Mack. Last time he was home he was gone back just as I was beginning to understand his accent. We've one good thing going for us. None of us is dead. And that's all we do have.'

'Cocoa?'

'I'm trying to think of something. Apart from Bazook and the crossbar we were outsiders that night. They had that tribe of the O'Neills, all younger than us and fitter from tennis and hockey. They had other fellas, Jake, they had someone . . . oh Jesus, I remember . . . Jake, remember who they had?'

Jake O'Dea still held the photograph in front of him but he did not see it. He was trying to see a thousand pounds. He saw the No 1 account cleared and the No 2 manageable. He saw clothes, the baby things Molly said would be necessary in four months. It had taken them a long time to get it right, the sex. Molly had mentioned the price of prams, an amount that had sent Jake straight out to top up the No 2 account.

'Jake wake up.'

'I am awake. Too awake. Don't you remember their team, Stanley?'

'No. I remember Corr and the O'Neills. Who's Cocoa talking about?'

'I'm talking about Timmie Stockil and Ralph O'Shea, that's who I'm talking about.'

'Jake, he's joking. They weren't playing?'

Jake nodded solemnly. Stanley calculated that Ralph O'Shea could have been no more than sixteen at the time seeing as he was now still holding his place at centre on the Irish rugby team. Timmie Stockil was probably seventeen – he held a midfield position with Birmingham having already played for Manchester City, West Bromwich Albion and, of course, Ireland. Jake broke the silence: 'I have to hand it to you, Stanley. Were you drunk?'

Omitting the Wilde reference Stanley told them of his meeting with Henry Corr and finished: 'You're right, Jake. Can't win without confidence. I'll have to back out of it somehow.'

Cocoa Brown knew enough to remain silent. Jake O'Dea *was* the team.

'All right, Stanley. If you say we'll win, we'll win. Your money is safe.'

'Thank you, Jake. It's not the money. It's the principle.'

'Of course.'

'Cocoa, you and Jake set it up. Contact Stevie Mack. I'll take care of Dara, Johnny Green, Tolly. Forget all about Gabriel. The less he knows the better. I want nothing whatever to do with Corr. Anything crops up, ring me, arrange a meeting. Now, Cocoa, the bet itself is important. You make sure it's a cash deal, tell them bluntly we don't trust their cheque not to bounce.'

'Yessir.' Cocoa answered smartly, relaxed for the first time that night in Stanley's company.

'Good. Now, how about a small game?'

'The two of us?'

'I'll back Jake.'

'Small ones out.'

'Up to the four.'

'Up to the six.'

'All right. Down ahead with you Cocoa and order the drink. Jake, I have a further instruction for you concerning this replay. Join me in a slash.'

In Tom Splendid's toilet Stanley instructed: 'If I'm carrying I'll make some comment about the drink: the pint is bad in Brigid's these days, Tom's drink is as good as ever. If you have them talk about the match, how Timmie Stockil is playing with Birmingham or Ralph O'Shea with Ireland. Follow?'

'Right.'

They played poker until two in the morning. Jake O'Dea lost the eighteen pounds lent him by Stanley; Stanley lost a total of sixty pounds, the proceeds of two cheques negotiated with Tom Splendid. They adjourned to Patsy Naughton's grill in Parnell Street where Cocoa paid for sausage and chips and tea and bread and butter for three.

Kate had not yet gone to bed.

'How did you get on?'

'A juvenile evening.'

'You managed not to tear yourself away from it.'

'Yes. I'm sorry. That was part of it. Time has stood still for them. I was with Jake and Cocoa. I actually had to sit down and play poker to keep them happy, took a few quid off them. They're practically gaga over this contest, the whole thing is so childish . . . Kate, Kate, come here . . . '

Seventy-eight pounds out of pocket, the teacher did not know how to adjust to the elation he felt. In a few hours he had shed the cocoon of prudence methodically spun over fifteen years. Kate was on his lap.

'Remember the time I thought I'd lost,' Stanley coughed, ' . . the . . you know?'

'Yes, Stanley.'

'Let's try the cure.'

'Yum yum.'

Kate stripped slowly and provocatively, throwing each garment snappily over her head. She stood by the door, beckoning with her index finger and affected not to notice the graceless and hasty way he undressed. She went to the third step of the stairs and waited until he knelt in the hall and stretched his hand until it reached her ankle. Kate wore nothing beneath her slip that she held in a fistful about her curly hair and one of the straps was off her shoulder. She climbed a step, stopped and waited as his hand reached up. By the time they reached the landing it was Friday night again.

3

Stevie Mack

From Wood Green, where he was on his third day back on the buildings, Stevie Mack travelled seventeen stations on the Piccadilly Line as far as Earls Court where he changed to the District Line that brought him two further stops to Fulham Broadway. He tossed a tenpenny piece at the black London Transport official.

'Here mate!' The darkie shouted after him. Stevie Mack walked on. In his capacity as an Englishman, which he had become, he hated wogs, geezers, layabouts, sods and foreigners. The black man ran after him and placed an authoritative hand on his shoulder.

'How I know where you come from, mate? Three days in a row you chuck me ten pence.'

'Take your hand off me.'

'Ten pence. Ten blimey pence. Where's your ticket?'

The black man extended his palm revealing the evidence of the ten pence. Patiently Stevie Mack took back the money. 'You don't want it? Right then. Fuck you.'

He took the Fulham Broadway steps three at a time and ran the eight minutes home. Three days on the dry, three days back on the buildings, he felt the good of it already. A light sweat trickled the scars on his face. He had eight. He loved his strength and his drunkenness in the Saturday night Paddy pubs and when the questions flew on the Monday morning he loved to deliver the laconic: 'Got into a rumble, didn' I?'

Old Bill was on his way to the pub as Stevie Mack turned into the street. "Allo, Stephen,' Old Bill called. Stevie ignored him. He pushed open the hall door and shouted: 'Eed, you got the bath on?'

Eed answered from the kitchen. 'Christ. That bleedin' time. Clean forgot it, Steve. Sorry.'

Stevie was already half way up the stairs to his room. He stopped and gripped the banisters. Slowly he walked down the hall to the kitchen. Eed was standing, with a long-ashed Embassy dangling from her mouth, over the frying pan in which white sausages had not yet begun to perform. They were smothered in grease although,he had told her a hundred times how to cook them.

'Sorry? Sorry? What the fuck you mean sorry. I told you free times this mornin' I was 'avin a bath tonight.'

Eed brushed past him to the table where potatoes were haphazardly chopped. 'Keep yer shirt on. I'll chuck on the chips and then fix yer bath. Okay, darlin'?'

She saw the danger signal on his red face. It was bad when his lips moved and no words came. At length he muttered: 'What . . . what I say first thing this mornin'? Did I say, Eed, I want a bath tonight minute I come 'ome, so's I can sit down an' watch Dara Holden. Did I say that? Did I fuckin' say that, Eed?'

Coquettishly, though an emaciated fifty-eight-year-old who had had one breast removed, Eed sidled towards him. 'Steve, come on Steve, let's don't be nasty, eh?'

Eed put her hand between his legs and fondled him. Savagely he pushed her away and though she was not altogether taken by surprise she could do nothing to stop her forehead crashing into the shelf. Stevie Mack planted his boot in her arse and she lay in a heap with its print on her slacks. 'You Irish fuckpig,' she hissed.

'And dump that grease out of that frying pan and don't let them sausages get burned either or I'll yank your other tit off an' all, fuckin' cow.'

At the door a thought struck him. ''Ere. Old Bill. Fought he was skint. I just see 'im goin' down the pub.'

'Tapped me.'

'Yeah. Tell us another, Eed.'

'All I 'ad was sixty pence. Can't do much with sixty pence, can I? Thought 'e may as well 'ave it. Honest.'

'Yeah.'

Stevie understood that he was about to be tapped himself. Eed knew when to pounce, nearly always on Wednesday night, Dara Holden night. He went and sat on the bed in his room, time to kill now that he was not having a bath – the immersion took three hours to heat. Eed never had enough money, the poor sod, he didn't blame her, she got up in the morning at five and went to the betting shop on the corner and scrubbed the place on her hands and knees for an hour; then herself and a mate cleaned two pubs.

It was her income together with his rent. She went to bingo on the Broadway three times a day and she liked her tipple. She might have got one book for the sixty pence she gave Old Bill, Stevie wasn't sure, but she liked her bus ride and her fag and her tipple. It was true; she couldn't do bloody much with sixty pence. Stevie had two choices. He could lend her a fiver that she would pay back next time she clicked or he could give her the rent two days earlier the following week. He had only those two choices because otherwise Eed would stay in and make Old Bill and himself miserable on Dara Holden night. She got stubborn on skint nights, claiming it was her house and her TV and that she preferred Coronation Street to Dara Holden. He would give her the bloody fiver although he remembered distinctly telling her about the bath.

Stephen McNamara had a marvellous head of red hair and a blocky frame when he arrived in London. He had been seven years a member of the Thomond Weight-Lifting and Body Building Club in Mellick and yet he was timid and shy except when crossed. He gratefully accepted the Marian Employment Agency's recommendation of a safe Catholic house and a job in a nut and bolt factory. He stayed three months in the safe house unappreciative of the breakfast fry or the four course dinner at night; it was what he had been used to in Mellick. He went to mass and communion every Sunday and to confession three times in the three months. He was susceptible to influence and fell so much in love with the English language as spoken in his new surroundings that he complained to his landlady of having been overcharged fruppence in the corner shop and added: 'I fought people were honest here.'

Over tea-up in the factory Stevie compared notes with Halpin who was three years younger but who had been in London since he was eighteen. Halpin said: ''Ow much you payin' then, Pat?'

'Five knicker.'

'What you get for that then?'

'Breakfast. Dinner at night.'

'Got your own meter?'

'Naw. Electricity's free.'

'Not bad, not bad. Same as me nearly. Four quid. 'Cept I get the 'ole an all, don't I?'

Stevie Mack nodded, rinsed his cup and returned to work. Halpin was puzzled. Everyone to whom he told his story was impressed and envious of the fact that he slept with his landlady, a widow. The next day Halpin began: 'Ivy – that's me landlady – Ivy's got this sister, you know? She's lookin' for a lodger. Four quid she charges, same as Ivy. Breakfast and dinner.'

Stevie Mack rolled a cigarette. He had not yet managed to do so with one hand but he did call the packet of Rizzla's Rizzlers. 'Four quid. That's a quid less than I'm payin'.'

'Yeah. And there's the . . . '. Halpin gripped his right elbow with his left hand and jabbed shortly with his fist. Stevie Mack blushed a little or a lot, it was difficult for Halpin to tell, Stevie was so red headed and red faced. 'I seen 'er a couple of times. This Eed. That's her name. She's a bit of all right too. I could swing it for you.'

Stevie Mack sucked on his Golden Virginia.

'Well, what you say then?'

'I dunno.'

'You still go to mass?'

'Me? Nah. Gave up all that.'

'Well then, you want I should fix it or not?'

'Yeah. You do that mate. And ta.'

Stevie told the people in the safe Catholic house that he was going home and they congratulated him on his wisdom. He took the tube from Kilburn to Fulham Broadway – paying the correct fare – and walked to the address. But approaching the house his nerve failed him and he turned into the pub. He ordered light and bitter. It was half five and the bar had less than ten clients. It was a strange part of London to him. At least in the Kilburn bars the faces were Irish even if he didn't know them. To flash his accent and establish himself with the barman he pretended not to know the number of the house.

'Scuse me, guvnor. You dunno where a Missis Rogers live

round here by any chance?'

'Rogers? That must be Eed. Old Bill'll soon put you right. Bill, say Bill, chap here lookin' for Missis Rogers.'

Old Bill was short and very fat with an open shirt to allow his thick neck to breathe; he wore a fairisle pullover inside his short coat. He waddled to the counter bearing a Teacher's and light ale, both of which he downed before speaking. 'You must be Stephen McNamara. Eed's expecting you. How are you, boy?'

They shook hands.

'Yeah, all day we been expecting you. Let me get you a drink, then I'll take you over. Albert, same again Albert, and what's yours, Stephen?'

'Light and bitter, thanks.'

'And a light and bitter. Yeah, Eed was only sayin' afore I come out, expect the chap Ivy's sendin' any minute.' Old Bill searched his coat and trousers pockets. 'Hold on. Come out without me bleedin' wallet. Sod.'

'That's okay. I'll get it.'

'Thanks boy. Cheers.'

'Cheers.'

During the next half hour Old Bill had three Teachers and two light ales to Stevie's two light and bitters. Stevie thought they were two nice blokes, Old Bill and Albert, asking him where he came from and how he was getting on, Old Bill adding: 'Always liked the Irish I 'ave. Like blokes what can drink.' The glasses were empty and Stephen McNamara showed no sign of buying again. 'Yes, we'd better get along then, Stephen. See you later, Albert.'

Old Bill had a key to the house. He opened the door and immediately shouted: 'Eed, Eed, new lodger for you.'

Stevie Mack's first sight of her was as she opened the kitchen door and walked out the hall wiping her palms on her slacks. ''Allo Stephen. Welcome. Just gettin' your tea. You like scrambled eggs, Stephen?'

He muttered assent and followed the woman into the kitchen. She was thin and walked quickly in her slippers. She wore a high-necked black jumper inside a black cardigan that was clasped with a cameo brooch. Her thin, wide mouth camouflaged the fragility of her body. Halpin had said she was just gone forty like Ivy but she looked nearer fifty to Stevie

Mack. He was given a seat near a pallid fire that consisted of a single briquette thrown into the grate a second earlier by Old Bill. The table was laid, homely crockery and hybrid cutlery. The mantelpiece was painted green and various shades of wallpaper fought for expression. The linoleum was worn and patched.

'Where'd you two meet then? Sayin' your prayers in church I bet?'

'Now, Eed, Stephen just dropped in the pub for directions and we had a couple. Couldn't just run outa there, could we?'

'He catch you for much son?'

'Pardon?'

'Bill. How much he take you for? 'Ow many Teachers?'

Stevie didn't know where to look or what to say. He blushed. Old Bill had taken his shoes off and was toasting a toe that stuck out from his sock.

'Don't mind Eed, Stephen.'

It was no help to Stevie that he was not a lover of scrambled eggs at the best of times. These were dehydrated and cratered and resembled foam rubber upholstery.

'Where you from then, Stephen?' Eed asked.

'Mellick.'

'That's in the South? Never been to Ireland, often thought I'd like to go there.'

'You wasn't much places Eed, was you?'

Eed thought about that for a moment and then admitted: 'Yeah, truth is, Stevie boy, I been fucking no place an' that's a fact.'

'I've never been to Ireland neither,' Old Bill paused from chomping gummily on his scrambled eggs. ''Eard of it 'course, Killarney an' that. Like to 'ave seen Killarney.'

'Hear 'im. Never been no fucking place neither. Missed the war an' all 'e did. Fucking dodger.'

'That's not fair, Eed. Turned me down they did. You know that. Me bleedin' back.'

'Yeah, you codded 'em. Not eatin' boy?'

'I'm not very hungry, Mrs Rogers.'

'Mrs Rogers! Sod that. Eed, everybody calls me Eed. Have another cuppa an' then I'll show you to yer room.'

Stevie had two cups of tea and six slices of bread and margarine. He was used to the margarine in the safe Catholic house. Anything to be away from Eed and Bill and to sort himself out he said: 'Can I see the room now then?'

'Sure. You clean the things up Bill an' do it proper or I'll belt your ear 'ole.'

Eed skipped up the stairs in front of him and pushed open the door of the bedroom. It contained a double bed, the sheets had that very day been put through the wringer at the launderette. The blankets were faded beige and later Stevie was to discover that they were full of holes where his legs rested. A single wardrobe, a chest of drawers, a table and a chair completed the inventory. Here again the wallpaper was of the mongrel breed. Eed was talking.

'... four quid the lot. I likes to be a month in advance, I don't know did Ivy explain that to 'Alpin, an' I does yer washin' an all. If you find it cold just ask for a bottle, don't believe in those bleedin' fires, we's all family here, you treat the 'ouse like you was at home, Stephen, come an' go as you please. All right boy?'

'Grand, Mrs Rogers.'

Eed shook her head. She had both breasts then. She scratched them absentmindedly, her hand sliding from one to the other inside her cameo-clasped black cardigan. 'Eed, Eed, Stephen son. Now wot else. You think you'll be 'appy here, fit in all right?'

'Yeah. I think so.'

'Sure you will.' Stevie continued to stand, holding his suitcase. 'Anythin' on your mind, best you come out with it now, Stephen, you tell old Eed, you'll find I'm understandin'.' She smiled and winked.

Stevie's face took fire as he recognised the growth in his trousers.

'You like we get to know each other now, ease things a bit?'

The enquiry was gentle, considerate as Eed insinuated herself to within a foot of him. His mouth opened: 'I – I – I ... '

'Go on love. Speak your mind.'

'I – ah, I ... am, you see, I 'aven't ... '

'Youwhah, Stephen?'

'I've ... never done it before.'

'Oh! Oh, you poor sod. Silly buggers. I didn't know, son. Ivy didn't say. That 'Alpin bloke, 'e musn't a said anything. Well, I suppose, you like me to show you then?'

'I – I dunno.'

'Close this door. Don't want him creepin' around, I'll just put the chair agin it. A bleedin' virgin! Tell you what, Stevie boy, Eed's gonna enjoy herself an' all. Right then, trousers off. Come on, come on, get 'em off you.'

Eed took his suitcase and pushed him on to the bed. She coaxed his trousers off and then stepped out of her own slippers. Stevie did not then see the dirt of her feet because she was wearing a pair of men's socks. Eed undid her brooch, opened her cardigan and lifted her pullover high enough to expose her breasts. 'Go on, son, they won't bite you.' Stevie did not notice the dirt of her skin as she directed his hands to her breasts. And through the entire initiation he was not once conscious of her lack of cleanliness. Eed spoke continuously.

'What we got 'ere then. Out you come. 'E's a big un. Cooo. Look at 'im.'

Stevie Mack only spoke once when Eed was attempting to guide him in. 'Oh Jesus. Oh, oh, oh. Jesus, lovely. Give us a kiss.'

He put his arm around Eed and roughly pulled her towards him and kissed her all over her face. Suddenly Eed eased herself off him.

'That done it,' she said examining herself. 'Waste o' bleedin' spunk. Better luck next time, Stephen.' Stevie lay on the bed exposed from the stomach down while Eed had taken off nothing except her slippers. Before zipping up her slacks she used the cuff of her cardigan to wipe his sticky mess off her leg.

'All right, Stephen?'

'Yeah.'

'I gotta go to me bingo now. You can 'ave another go tonight, okay?'

'Yeah.'

'Right then me old son. Can I 'ave that rent now love, you got it, you 'ave?'

'It's in my pocket. I'll . . . '

'Stay's you are. I'll get it. 'Ere we are. Five, ten, fifteen, no nickers 'ere. I'll just take the twenty an' owe you four. Okay, love? Now you watch that Old Bill. Don't leave things 'angin' about. 'E's got itchy fingers, 'e 'as.'

'Is he your brother?'

'Youwhah?'

'Your brother? He's not your dad?'

'Me dad? Coo, you are a one. Bill's me fucking 'usband, 'in he. Didn't you know that then? Guess not. Yeah, Bill's me better 'alf. Little fucker. Wouldn't blame you if you took him for me grandad an' all. You 'ave yourself a rest now. I'll nip off to me bingo. Watch telly, make yerself at 'ome till you go drinkin'. Bet you like yer gobble, eh? See you boy.'

It was a very confused Stevie Mack she left behind. Screeching for his attention was his sudden loss of virginity, as he thought of it, and the fact that Old Bill was her husband. He was no more than five minutes lying contemplatively on the bed when Old Bill startled him by shouting up: 'Stephen. Stephen?'
    'Yeah?'
    'Nippin' over the road. Won't be long, all right?'
    'Yeah.'
    Out of her haul Eed had given Old Bill a quid and the proviso: 'Don't you go tappin' 'im first night or I'll belt you one.'
    'I wouldn't.'
    'An' you leave 'im be. Keep yer filthy habits to yerself.'
    'Now what you want bringin' all that up again for? And look who's talkin'. You just fucked him, didn't you?'
    'Mind yer own bleedin' business.'

Stevie went down to the kitchen and sat by the dead fire. He found briquettes in the scullery and chucked on a half dozen. He couldn't understand her, chancing it like that with her husband downstairs. He had been taught at school about pagan England but somehow he had always thought it had something to do with the fact that they didn't do the nine Fridays in England and didn't say their three Hail Marys for purity or pray for happy deaths. Even though he was able to take care of himself it was still comforting that Old Bill was not a bruiser. And then the cool way Eed reverted to landlady and looked for the rent. The rent! He sat upright in the chair with the shock. A month's rent in advance and, worse, she took twenty and owed him four. He couldn't believe that he had been so dumb. He remembered that apart from being pagans they were also fiddlers and knackers and didn't know the meaning of honesty. He heard the front door open.
    ''Allo Stephen. Nippy out. What's on telly then?'
    'Dunno.'

'Gettin' a fire goin'. Eed doesn't feel the cold you know. Always runnin' about. The Avengers. I like The Avengers.'

Old Bill made himself comfortable. He took off his jacket and shoes and cocked the bare toe at the fire. He had to crane his neck. Stevie said: 'Am I sittin' in your place, Bill?'

'Whasthat? Oh? Nah. You're all right boy. I sits there but you 'ave it. No fear of Old Bill. Expect you'll be hittin' the pub soon, eh?'

'Yeah. Might do.'

'May as well enjoy yourself while you can, lad. Me, I'll just sit 'ere an' watch telly. Never know, Eed might click an' treat me later. Very decent, Eed, when she wins a few bob.'

Stevie smiled at Old Bill with frank admiration.

'I may as well go and 'ave a couple. You comin'?'

Old Bill reacted with rare talent. He opened the palms of his hands; he might have been mildly irritated at having to disturb his viewing to answer such a daft question. 'Can't, can I? Ain't got nothing.'

'You skint?'

'Yeah. Comes o' this bleedin' back. Can't work or nothing. What I get down labour don't last long.'

'That's all right. I'll treat you.'

'Nah. Wouldn't be fair. You treated me earlier.'

Stanley Callaghan would not have reminded Old Bill that he had earlier laid claim to the possession of a forgotten wallet; neither now did Stevie Mack.

'Come on. Let me treat you. You treat me when you 'ave a few bob. Okay, mate?'

'That's decent of you, Stephen. You'll find me okay when I 'ave it. Ask anybody.'

In the pub Old Bill answered: 'Teachers, Stephen, please. An' Stephen, would you mind, could I 'ave a drop of ale with it, whisky's bad for me stomach neat.'

In the safe Catholic house Stevie had struggled to write a letter home to the Nook that he tore up without posting. There was nothing in the letter worth telling. Anyway there was nobody to write to in the Nook any more. Stanley Callaghan was gone and without Stanley Callaghan there was nobody. The pub had died overnight. It would have survived the loss of Dara Holden or Stevie himself but not Stanley. Dara was really making a name for himself. Stevie had gone in to Leicester

Square to see the picture; he had roared his head off at Dara up on the screen thumping Charlton Heston. It was a pity. He would like to have shared Old Bill with the Nook. On his fifth light and bitter Stevie drew praise from Old Bill.

'You can drink an' all, Stephen, can't you?'

Stevie did not bother to return the compliment. Instead he shared a little of the Nook with Old Bill. 'I got two mates back home can drink. Well, one's not back home any more, 'e's a film star. Dara Holden. Ever hear of 'im, Bill?'

'Dara 'Olden? Yeah, I 'eard of him. Don't go to the pictures myself, but I 'eard of 'im. Isn't 'e the bloke in that picture with whatsisname, chap who plays all the Bible blokes, Moses an' that lot . . . '

'Charlton Heston.'

'That's 'im. Now I recall Holden is Irish. You really know 'im, Stephen?'

'Lived in the same street. Dara can drink. But that's nothin'. There's another mate, Stanley Callaghan, 'e's a teacher. Should see him drink. Greatest bloke in the world he was. Got married to an American.'

''Ere, Albert. Albert, you know that film star bloke, Dara 'Olden? 'E's from Stephen's home town. Neighbours, grew up together.'

'Sthat so? Go on.'

'Yeah. 'E's been tellin' me.'

Because of his friendship with Dara Holden Stevie was now introduced to Taffy and Jock. They shook hands and called him Pat. They were all nice blokes, old Bill, Taffy, Jock, Albert behind the counter. This was really England. That bloody place Kilburn wasn't England at all.

Taffy and Jock were delighted to meet a pal of Dara Holden. Stevie offered them a drink and they consented to join the round. Old Bill could hardly believe the never-ending flow of Teachers let alone the chasers of ale. A rarity for him, Old Bill began to feel drunk. He slapped Stevie on the back and he put his arms around Taffy and Jock and urged them to sing. Taffy sang although he was far from being merry. He sang at the slightest encouragement. Jock sang something but nobody understood the words. Drunk and maudlin, Stevie sang Galway Bay. Old Bill took over and rendered a trilogy: Underneath the Arches, Hometown, Any Umbrellas. A few dart players were at first peeved but when told that the Irish bloke – the chap with the red hair – was a mate of Dara Holden's, they downed weapons and applauded and joined in the chorus.

'Ere, what's this then? Havin' a party? An' look who's singin'.'

Eed had her arms folded, her bag dangling from the crook of one, an Embassy limp and long ashed in the corner of her mouth.

' . . . any umbrellas, any umbrellas – to mend . . . today!'

'Bleedin' Gigli. Any large Haigs goin' 'sall I want to know, not a bleedin' black, am I?'

'A drink for Missis Rogers, Albert, please.' The formality was a conscious effort to dispel the notion that he could possibly have been almost raped by her a couple of hours earlier.

'Mrs Bleedin' Rogers. 'Ear 'im. You enjoyin' yourself then, Stephen, with this lot?'

'Yeah. Yeah, I am.'

Taffy was singing again: Ken Dodd's Tears for Souvenirs. Old Bill, about his business, asked: 'Any luck, Eed?'

'Nah.'

Three middle-aged ladies entered and hailed Eed.

'Congratulations, Eed. How about that then.'

'Lucky bleeder, mine's a brandy.'

'Well done, Eed.'

Alert, Old Bill asked: 'What you goin' on about, Lisa?'

'Hear 'im. An' you havin' a party. Don't forget Lisa, when Lisa wins the 'undred she'll have a party an' all.'

Old Bill stared at his wife. Stevie, Taffy and Jock made pathetic attempts not to appear to be looking at her.

'What you all gapin' at? I was keepin' it as a surprise, I was. Think I wasn't goin' to treat ye, silly buggers. Albert give the bleeders a drink, an' yourself.'

'The 'undred, Eed?' Old Bill almost pleaded.

'Deserve it, don't I? Look at all I been losin'.'

Stevie had not taken his eyes from her. She confronted him now and he noticed her change colour a little. Then she winked.

Back in the house Stevie had a cup of tea with Eed and Old Bill. He had drunk fourteen light and bitters and felt high-spirited but not drunk. Eed recited a catalogue of near misses at bingo and reckoned the hundred pounds didn't cover what she felt bingo owed her. But Stevie Mack had been schooled in the

Nook. He nodded politely at the tale and then yawned.

'I think I'm for kip. I'd like me four quid change, Eed, if that's awright. Spent more than I fought in the pub.'

'Sure, I'll just get it for you, son.'

'Night, Bill.'

'Eh? Oh. G'night, Stephen. 'Ave a good sleep.'

Old Bill was dribbling into sleep beside the white ashes. Confident, Stevie went to his room and waited. Eed came and counted out four pounds.

'And the rest, Eed. Kidded me, didn't you? A month's rent. Never heard of no one givin' no month's rent in advance. So gimme sixteen an' keep the four for one week.'

'You've a bloody cheek. I always charges a month in advance.'

'Not with me you don't. Aren't you goin' to stand me outa yer winnin's?'

Eed laughed. 'Listen to 'im. Cool, you are.'

'I'm buying drink for Bill all night. You think I was a millionaire?'

'Bill? Fuck Old Bill. Not payin's his debts I'm not. Ivy said you was supposed to be a quiet kid. That 'Alpin. 'E said it.'

'Am too. Just don't like to be done.' Stevie was groping now. 'Earlier, 'member what you said, you know ... '

'Yeah?'

'Well, could we – you know, you could keep eight, if we did it again.'

'Horny then, Stephen?' Eed leered at him till he blushed. She put the four pounds on the table by the bed and continued gravely, 'Stephen, you ever been sucked off?'

'Don't know what you mean.'

'Course you don't. You don't know nothin', do you? Lie down.'

Later, as Stevie lay back on the bed, sweating from pleasure, Eed climbed down and whispered: 'Good-night, Stephen.' Stevie leaped from the bed and blocked the door. He was naked, his penis glistening like an urchin's nose.

'My money. Sixteen quid.'

'You said I could keep eight. I fucked you didn't I?'

'That's part of the rent. That's what Halpin said.' He managed to smile. 'Didn't Ivy tell you.'

'I'd a known that I wouldn't a sucked you, would I? How long's it goin' take you get it up again? You dunno, do you?

Holy Mick you was couple hours ago. Now listen to you. Errol bleedin' Flynn. You know somethin', Stephen? You wanna know somethin'?'

'What?'

'I like's you boy. Eed likes you. You an' me's goin' hit it off.'

'I still want my money.'

'Oh, fuck you then. I'll get it. Let me by.'

Stevie was slow about letting her pass. Eed grabbed his penis and yanked him from the door.

'Ow.'

'Got you there, mate. Christ, left me purse on the table an' Dick Turpin below. 'Scuse me.'

Stevie was in his pyjamas when she returned.

'In we lovely. 'Ere you are Shylock. 'An e're's me cunt to you an all. Come on.'

Stevie lay on top of her reaching her through the opened zip of her slacks and clutching her breasts in mouthfuls, coming up for air to mutter: 'Oh God, oh God'. An hour later as he waited to rise for the third time Eed slipped out of bed. 'Got to get some sleep love. 'Ave to rise early. See you in the mornin'.'

'Hang on. Tell us, how come you're not afraid he'll catch you.'

'Silly. He knows.'

'He – knows?'

'Sure. He knows. 'E'd watch if he was let.'

'Doesn't he mind?'

'Give us one of yer fags. Rolls your own? Oh, bloody shit. Can't stand them. Roll us one then. Yeah, he knows an' he don't mind.'

Stevie had not thought her capable of sadness but suddenly she didn't look happy.

'Can't mind, can he? Not after I caught him. Chap workin' over the pub time Albert done six months on a GBH. Young kid, no more than seventeen. Bill bring 'im over for a night cap. Caught 'im, didn' I? Buggered the fuck outa the kid, 'e did. Fucking queer. Never was no good with me, then I knew why. 'Cept he's no fucking queer, is he. Poor bastard. Just couldn't get it up no more an' turned to kids. I don't 'old with it. I told 'im. Bashed his head in with the poker. Eight stitches 'e got. I said let's have no more of that then. Lazy fucker, 'im an 'is back. So now you know that much. Keep it to yourself, all right.'

'I will.'

'Good-night, boy.'
'Good-night.'

Eed did not like to talk about Old Bill. During the two months up to Christmas Stevie had to drag piecemeal from her that she had married when she was nineteen and he was thirty-four, at the beginning of the war. 'I just fell for 'im, with 'is moustache an' all, had a moustache then.' Old Bill did have a bad back and would not have been accepted by his country but the disability was overlooked by employers. ''E used to work at this an' that okay but that's cos he liked to dress neat.' Eed spoke wistfully. ''E was a ladies' man. Had to keep my eye on 'im but 'e managed to do the dirt on me just the same. But with 'is size 'e got fat, didn' 'e. His hair began to go. Moustache on its own fuck all good to 'im then. We 'ad some right rows about 'is women we did but I never minded that much did I, I mean it was honest, they was women. Then 'e couldn't get off with them no more 'cept for old bags, chucked work an' all, become a tapper, haunted the bettin' shop an' I's on me hands an' knees scrubbin' floors. Funny, end up he can't get it up for me no more.'

'Did you have men yourself?' Stevie's acquired accent slipped when he was being personal.

'Yesterday's yesterday son. Ask me no questions an' I'll tell you no lies.'

Stevie began to treat Old Bill as the cypher he was. He made him yield the better chair by the fire; at half five in the morning, once he had taken to the buildings, he was woken up by Old Bill with a cuppa and when he rose Old Bill had Readybrek steaming on the table and two boiled eggs in the saucepan. Stevie always wanted to talk about Old Bill after sex, thinking it was a safe subject between them but Eed did not respond. Once Stevie asked her a question that genuinely puzzled him. 'How come you didn't divorce him then?'

He was astonished by her reply.

''e's me 'usband. We're not film stars that 'as divorce, nor want it.'

After that Stevie softened towards Old Bill and was happier because he liked him. He noticed in the pub that Old Bill and Eed were not everybody's favourites but Albert liked them and Taffy and Jock and Lisa and her bingo pals. The guvnor when he was on duty wore a cardigan and sported gold cuff links on his white shirt; the guvnor did not like Old Bill. He called Old Bill Mr Rogers.

Christmas came. Stevie went home leaving a suit behind him with a fiver in the jacket inside pocket and a tenner in the trousers back pocket so he would not be skint when he returned. It was a prudent move because on holiday at home he spent like a Paddy on holiday at home.

It was eight o'clock when he reached the house. He had missed Eed and Old Bill and Taffy and Jock and Albert while he was at home. The Nook had fallen apart. Jake O'Dea was the only company. Dara was in America; Stanley Callaghan had not been seen since the night Bush Vine and the woman had taken over the snug. Johnny Green was off with the band. Cocoa was there but Cocoa was as mean as ever. The house was empty. Eed was at bingo as he expected and Old Bill over the road. Stevie went to the wardrobe to get his fifteen quid but the pockets were empty. All he had left after the holiday was seven pounds. He went to the pub where Old Bill greeted him like a long lost son and emphatically put his empty glass on the counter. Stevie bought.

'Bill, I left fifteen nicker behind an' I goin' away. It's not there now. Someone nicked fifteen nicker belongin' to me.'

''Ere! You're not lookin' at me, Stephen. I 'ope you're not lookin' at me?'

'Who am I goin' to look at then? The 'ouse wasn't broken into, was it?'

'Course it wasn't. Are you sure you left it?'

'Yeah, I'm sure. I'm not a fucking eejit, am I? What you know about it?'

'Stephen, cross my heart. I didn't touch your money.'

'Where'd it go then?'

'I don't know, Stephen. You ask Eed. Maybe she knows. Straight up, son, I don't know nuffin' about it.'

Eed came in from bingo at ten o'clock. Stevie had ignored Old Bill's empty glass for so long that Old Bill bought a round.

''Allo, Stephen. Welcome back. Thought you was gone for good. Who's buyin' then?'

'Not me, Eed. Blew me lot.'

'What lot. Ain't you goin' to treat me, Stephen?'

'I left fifteen quid in the wardrobe when I was goin'. It's not there now.'

'What you mean?'

'Someone nicked it.'

Eed looked at old Bill.

'Now don't you look at me like that. I already told him I know nuffin' about it.'

'Well don't look at me neither, Stephen. I never touched your money.'

'Did you 'ave people in over Christmas?'

'Nah. 'Cept Ivy called. 'Er an 'Alpin. That's it! I bet that bleeder 'Alpin took it. I wouldn't put it past him.'

Stevie glowered into his light and bitter. He drained his glass and ordered again, ignoring Eed and Old Bill.

'All on our tod then, are we? I didn't touch yer money boy an' if you feel that way about it you get yer things an' clear off. I didn't go near yer bleedin' suit.'

Stevie restrained himself from booting her there and then. The guvnor was on duty. Stevie imagined Old Bill having to step in for Eed; he saw the three of them barred from the pub.

'All right, Eed. I'm sorry. I just got angry, that's all. Shoulda known you wouldn't touch it. Probably Halpin. Come on, let's drink.'

During the hour until closing time Stevie recognised Old Bill as being Old Bill whereas Eed was on her guard – too polite in enquiring about his holiday, not shouting across the pub at Lisa when a thought struck her. The atmosphere was worse in the kitchen as Old Bill dropped off and Eed made tea. When she came in from the scullery carrying a cup in each hand Stevie stretched his legs and tripped her. She fell helplessly, the tea spilled and the cups broke.

'The fuck . . . '

'My money. I want my money, Eed.'

'I haven't got yer bleedin' money.'

He lifted her a few inches from the ground by the hair of her head and began to choke her with his free hand. 'I didn't say nothing about the money bein' in my suit. I never said where it was.' He allowed her feet to touch the ground and then elbowed her in the face. Eed started to cry. Old Bill rubbed his eyes. ''Ere, what's goin' on?'

'You shut your trap. I'm givin' her a beltin' cos she stole my fifteen nicker. Didn' you? Admit it. Didn' you?' He grabbed the poker and beat her on the back with it. She slumped sobbing to the floor.

'All right. All right, you fucker, I took it. Only a loan it was, I was skint ... '

Stevie went to the scullery thinking he was going to be sick but nothing came. He realised the sickness was in his mind and yet he did not know what it was that disgusted him.

'Serves you right, Eed. What you want to rob the boy's money for?'

It was Old Bill that sickened him. He helped Eed up from the floor and shouted at Old Bill.

'You. You, you fat fucker you. You knew an' all, didn't you? Bet you knew. Stand up, Eed. Let's show 'im. Come on, get your duds off, let's show 'im how it's done.'

'Not now. I'm in fucking agony I am. Nearly killed me.'

'I might do that if you don't get those clothes off. Or you want me to tear 'em off.'

He had to use every ounce of muscle developed in the Thomond Weight-Lifting and Body Building Club of Mellick to get the better of her. With every item of clothing he tore from her it dawned on him, as more flesh was revealed, that up to now he was the one who was always naked and Eed always dressed. She was grimy. Her ankles were black and so were her knees. She did not have pubic whiteness. Eed, stripped, was a filmy grey all over.

'Jesus, don't you ever wash yourself.' Stevie looked at Old Bill who said simply: 'Bath don't bleedin' work, do it?'

There was a colour in Old Bill's cheeks that owed nothing to whisky or the fire and the fatalism of his observation made Stevie think of the fifteen pounds as inconsequential. He was ashamed of himself and so crazy with anger that he should feel shame that he carried on: 'Up with you outa that chair.' He threw Eed on the chair and straddled her, shrieking as he sawed: 'Ridem cowboy! Wanna grab a tit, Bill? Come on. 'Elp yourself.'

Old Bill did not move. He leaned against the table, watching. Eed spoiled the whole business by crying. She cried softly as though it was unmanly to cry, as though she was not Eed at all but a woman. Stevie rose when he'd finished and tried to resurrect his anger. 'Now. I just don't care for bein' robbed, that's all.'

Eed went naked to her room. She returned, naked, and put fifteen pounds on the table. 'There's yer money.'

'Right. I'll clear out in the morning.'

In the morning, with his money repaid, Stevie could not even summon the recollection of anger. He had slept badly, waking at intervals. He got up at seven o'clock and packed his case. Eed knocked first and then came into the room.

'You goin' then?'

'Yeah.' Stevie had his back to her and could not turn round.

'You really want to? You don't 'ave to. Less you want to.'

'You nicked my money.'

'Got it back didn't you? An' yer bit of fun.'

He closed the suitcase and leaned on it with his knuckles. He looked sideways at Eed and then away from her. A few moments earlier he'd been miserable at having to leave. He didn't know what to say now.

'All's I sayin' you want to stay, stay. You want to go, go.'

He turned to face her. 'If I stay, I'm goin' to buy a lock for that door.'

'Suit yerself.'

'Don't want to be robbed, do I?'

'Oh, can't you forget it. You loved it, thumpin' me, didn' you? A sadist is what they calls people like you. Go on, tell the truth, you got a kick outa thumpin' me.'

'Yeah, I'll admit it, it got me dick up.'

'Well, you want to thump me go ahead. I knows the world, boy. Anytime you like. But not with 'im around. It's not proper. So long as you don't hurt me too much, I may's well tell you, I don't mind. You think you could fix that bath, I'd clean meself right. We do some real fucking.'

The Nook was behind Stevie now, a shadowy place; they would never believe him; he could not imagine himself telling them anyway. He smiled at Eed.

'I think I prefer you dirty.'

'Bleedin' sod. An' I late for work. Costing me money talkin' to you. Is everything okay then?'

'Yeah. Yeah, I guess so.'

Stevie gave Eed a fiver and packed her off to bingo. She had changed little in thirteen years. Her hair was greyer but he didn't mind that. He liked it grey especially after she had been to the hairdresser's – after a click – and he didn't mind that her breast had been removed. But he could not bear to have her in the house while Dara Holden was on. She had no reverence for Dara Holden or any of the famous people Mellick had produced. 'Don't tell me you're goin' on about those bleedin' sods again?' At least Old Bill showed respect. Whether he meant it or not Stevie wasn't sure but he didn't mind so long as Old Bill showed respect. Sometimes it was as though Stevie himself was on television and Old Bill the entire audience. Looking back on it Mellick was a place to be proud of. It had produced Dara, Ralph O'Shea, the Irish rugby centre, Timmie Stockil, midfield now with Birmingham after service with Manchester City and West Brom; and to cap it all a woman Stevie had never heard about until her death in some part of Kent, Kate O'Brien, it turned out she had written books and also came from Mellick. Stevie never tired of reminding Old Bill:

'Yeah, there's Dara Holden. Ralph O'Shea, you seen 'im with your own eyes on the telly scorin' the try at Twickenham. Timmie Stockil, no need to tell you who he is, is there? And then there's her nibs what wrote the books. All from Mellick. I played a soccer match against O'Shea and Stockil, me and Dara Holden, we played for this pub, see?'

'You told me 'bout that, Stephen.'

'The Nook, great pub, we played against this Institute, shower of snobs they was, O'Shea an' Stockil played for them. There was me an' Dara an' Stanley Callaghan, told you about 'im, greatest bloke on earth he was. Cocoa Brown, he's another bloke but he wouldn't give you sweet Fanny Adams, an' Jake O'Dea, now he was the best footballer I ever seen in my life but he 'ad no interest, you know? You listenin' Bill?'

'Oh, course I'm listenin'. Timmie Stockil an' all that. Yeah.'

'An' Johnny Green. We all come from the same street you see, Johnny was younger than us but the greatest bloke of all time was Stanley Callaghan. He gave us two commandments. Commandments 'e called 'em. He said any man who would see another man's glass empty was a bastard.'

'Sounds a good bloke, Stephen.'

'An' the other thing he made us all swear that if anyone of us ever struck it rich none of the rest of us would take a penny from him. Only for that I could put my hand out to Dara Holden an' 'e'd fill it up with how much I wanted.'

'Would 'e do that, Stephen?'

'Course 'e would. But I wouldn't ask, would I? Unless me

glass was empty. That's different. Stanley said that's different. Cocoa Brown, ever told you what 'e done to me one night. This night, see, I owed 'im a quid, owed it to 'im for near a month an' I had to fix a date to pay 'im back otherwise he'd never lend me nothin' no more, that's the way 'e was. I 'ad twenty-five bob the night I 'ad to pay 'im back the quid so I paid 'im an' 'e asked me if I was goin' for a jar. I told 'im all I 'ad left was five bob hopin' he'd say hang on to the quid but 'e didn't. Five bob was enough for two and a half pints then an' I explained to him that two an' a half pints was worse than nothin', couldn't sleep after two an' a half pints. Know what he did, Bill? He pulled out this little bottle an' he give me two pills. Sleepin' tablets they was.'

'What he do that for then?'

'You don't listen do you, fucking akip all the time you are.'

It ws ten minutes to Dara Holden time and there was no sign of Old Bill. Sixty pence Eed said she gave him and he couldn't last long with that unless Taffy and Jock were standing to him. If Old Bill didn't turn up to watch Dara Holden Stevie decided he wouldn't give him a quid as he had done the past two nights. On his third night on the dry he was not in good humour. Every time he went back on the buildings after the winter in a factory he stayed off drink until he was used to the work. He also went on the dry in preparation for a holiday at home. His abstinence now was a combination of both although Eed hated him going home. It was a chasm between them. He tried everything to sort her out. He beat her and buggered her but no matter what he did to her the one thing she would not admit to was interfering with his post, not even when he rifled her handbag and waved his mother's letter in her face. It was not as though his mother ever sent any money. The letters were as one paced as the horses Eed backed, slobbering references to pagan England and news of mushroom apparitions of factories at home. Eed steamed open all his letters and released some, not realising that those she released testified that others had been suppressed.

Old Bill sometimes turned quisling when he was in desperate need of a hansel. 'Stephen she'd kill me if she ever found out I told you but a letter come for you today. You get it, Stephen?'

Stevie was always grateful for the information. It was a golden excuse to beat her. And so it went on and on until instead of dying as expected – Old Bill was pale for weeks in terror of being left alone – Eed had a breast removed. Like father and son Stevie and Old Bill visited her in the hospital every night and in the pub afterwards Stevie let Old Bill have his head in the mourning stakes. 'I worry about 'er you know,' Old Bill said to Jock and Taffy and Albert and once the guvnor asked: 'How's Mrs Rogers?' It was while they were all worrying about her for three weeks – Lisa and her pals went to see her one Sunday afternoon – that Stevie discovered something in himself that surprised him; so much so that when Eed did come home Stevie left her to herself. After four days during which Eed was very down, which wasn't like her, she said late at night while Old Bill snored by the fire: 'Don't want me no more, do you boy? No good to you without the two tits, eh?'

'What you talkin' about?'

''Ear 'im. You know an' all mate. Gettin' it in the Paddy pubs again?'

During his six years in the house – up to the time Eed had the breast removed – Stevie had negotiated intercourse out of the Paddy pubs no more than five times. And what Eed never understood was that he did not go to the Paddy pubs in search of it. Fits of shame drove him to the Paddy pubs, fits that could not be anticipated, as likely to be induced by the depression after an episode of the Dara Holden File as by the memory of Stanley Callaghan knocking on the door on Saturday morning when they were ten year olds with the proclamation: 'Mrs Mack, will you tell Stevie get up, we're at war with Ballysimon Road.' Driven thus outside himself and forced to look at the shabbiness of his existence Stevie imagined the nightmare of Stanley Callaghan and the Nook knowing what he did with his landlady. He had related in confidence a glamorous version of his affair to Dara Holden because Dara was an abroad man himself and Dara had his own stories to tell. But the thought of anyone else knowing brought sweat, shame and anger. Anger that could not be worked off on Eed. Angry, Stevie put on his leather jacket, shaved, blotched himself with deodorant and took the tube to Harlesden or Hammersmith, Kilburn or Acton – paying no fare at all. He took up a position at the counter of a Paddy pub and listened with disgust to the ceili group on the stage. Here he flexed a strength that came from not caring any more whether he lived or died; here were the people he most despised – ringers of himself. There were often as many as three generations of them in the Paddy pub on Saturday night, sullenly stamping their feet to the mangled inheritance of fiddle and accordion; illiterate nomads unacceptable back at home, barely tolerated in England.

Stevie sat and stared until obligingly approached by a kinsman.

'That's my bird you're starin' at, mate.'

'I wasn't starin' at no bird.'

'Well, see that you don't.'

'Nothin' to you where I look.'

'When you're lookin' at my bird it is.'

'Look, you lookin' for a rumble, Pat?'

'Who you callin' Pat?'

'Cos if y'are, just you an' me outside. You don't go back to your crowd, we go straight out. I'm on me tod, 's you can see.'

Outside the boot was put in, forehead and nose clashed; sometimes there were knives, cuts, blood. And sometimes too there might be a redheaded nineteen year old not long removed from the influence of the Legion of Mary who obliged the winner up against the back wall of the Paddy pub. The ritual cleansed Stevie Mack but it was a side of him that he shared with no one except, silently, with those he fought. Certainly he would not tolerate Eed raising the subject but because she was only out of hospital a few days he answered her patiently.

'I haven't been near a Paddy pub in twelve months. You know that, Eed.'

'Savin' up to be a monk then? Or's wankin' keepin' you goin'?'

'Look, I just thought you'd want to be left to yourself after your operation.'

'I'd a died back in the 'ospital, what was you goin' to do? Stay here with 'im? Not bleedin' likely. You was hot foot back home to your mother you was.'

'No I wasn't. And you wasn't goin' to die. We knew that. Doctor said it, didn' 'e?'

'Better off if I did an' all. Gettin' old anyway. Fifty-three I am. You realise that, Stevie boy? Fifty-fucking three. I'm not tight for you no more. Already you been makin' me turn an' use all me tricks, 'aven't you? An' now me tit's gone.'

Stevie's mouth opened and closed but not now as a prelude to

violence. He glanced dumbly at snoring Bill for support. He did
not know what to say to console her. He had never before seen
her depressed.

'I don't know what you're goin' on about, Eed. Really, I just
don't.'

'Yeah. Me tit's gone, fanny's wide as a barn door, next thing
you'll be gone an' all, won't you.'

'No, I won't be gone. Never said I would, did I? Did I ever say I
was goin'? Ever? Did I? Well, did I?'

'You wouldn't say, would you? Not goin' to turn around and
tell me, 'ere, Eed, you're too old for me now, I'm on me way.
Are you?'

'Okay. I'll never leave you. Okay?'

''Ear im.' The misery in her snort angered him. Reddening,
he blurted out: 'I loves you, don' I?'

It sounded ridiculous to Eed, funny, unaccompanied as the
remark was by his penis lunging inside her. She got angry
herself now.

'What you want sayin' a silly thing like that for? Makin' fun of
me.' She was surprised by her sudden tears. 'Christ I can take
anything but don't make fun of me. I can take your thumps, but
don't make fun of me now. Not now with me tit gone.'

They were seated at the table, cups of cold tea between them.
Stevie stood up and told hold of her shoulders and lifted her
chin so that she had to look at him between her tears. 'You
fucking git, I love you. Don't you understand? I'm never goin'
home for good to me mum. I don't want no Paddy birds neither.
You I want. I love you, don't care if you had no tits and no cunt
or fuckall arsecheek, okay? I fucking love you, Eed.' He put his
arms around her and squeezed her to him while she sobbed on
his chest. He repeated, as though it also surprised him: 'I do
love you, you know.' Eed did not go so far as to tell him she
loved him but she did say when he let her go and she was wiping
her eyes: 'I get's frightened. I gotta look after 'im, you know
that, but I get's frightened times lookin' after meself. Don't
know where I'd be you hadn't happen to come along. On me
knees scrubbin' it gets to you. I want a bit of 'appiness, that's all.
And you don't 'ave to go pretendin' you love me. Just that I'd
miss you.'

Stevie was madly proud of her struggles now and of how she
had never let anything get her down. For her sake and his own

he repeated: 'Eed, honest, I'm only goin' to say it once more, I don't care any more if you think I'm bein' silly buggers, I love you, Eed. I love you. I'll take care of you – and 'im. Always. Okay?'

'I'll make another cuppa. Dry me eyes. Sit down, son.'

The Dara Holden File began. The habitual pre-credit opening showed the black secretary opening the office and raising the blinds. The office was a mess. The telephone rang. Lorna answered: 'No, sir. Mr Holden hasn't come in yet.'

A moan from underneath the couch contradicted her. Unkempt and hungover, Dara Holden assembled himself and went to the phone. Lorna smiled a big white smile and shook her black head. Across the screen as Dara Holden silently nodded into the receiver and then held the telephone under his jaw while he took notes, flashed the legend

THE DARA HOLDEN FILE

It was twenty-five to nine when Old Bill came in.

'Blimey. Started already. I miss much, Stephen?'

'Course it's started. Twenty-five to nine now. Fought you was supposed to 'ave only sixty pence?'

'Met a bloke who owed me a couple of quid.'

'How'd anyone owe you money? You never 'ad fuckall to give to no one.'

'Now, Stephen. That's not fair. Good tonight, is it?'

'Always good. You missed the best part. Two black blokes 'ad 'im. You know the way 'e talks, Bill. "Gentlemen, I must adjust my tie. If a man has to go he should go tidy." You see they was two black blokes what went in for bein' all dolled up to the knocker themselves. Always cleanin' their finger nails, you know. Dara spots this, see, knows the form. While they're lookin' at 'im tying his tie, wham, out shoots the boot, get's of 'em in the knackers and then the other guy with the elbow . . . '

'Missed it then. An' I had a feelin' it would be good tonight, I said it to you, Stephen, 'member I said, I bet your pal will be good tonight.'

At nine o'clock Stevie made tea and offered a cup to Old Bill who refused: 'Early for tea.'

Stevie took the tea and a spam sandwich to eat by the fire and pretended to read the *Evening News*. Old Bill got up once and drank a cup of water. 'Bleedin' thirsty.' Old Bill did not deserve money for drink, Stevie thought. All he had to do was watch one hour with him. But because Stanley Callaghan had once proclaimed: 'A man who would see your glass empty is a bastard,' Stevie melted after half an hour. Till then he had peered at Old Bill over the rim of the paper while the insult to Dara Holden was being avenged.

Old Bill cracked just before Stevie. 'Stephen, Eed give you anything 'fore she went out tonight?'

'Me give 'er you mean.'

'Didn't she give you no telegram then?'

Telegrams had only one meaning. If his mother was dead and Eed had tried to keep it from him he would kill her when she came in from bingo. Kill her stone dead. And Old Bill with her. And Ivy and Halpin if Halpin had been still around.

Whitefaced, Stevie whispered: 'D'you say a telegram?'

'Yeah. You want I should tell you where it is?'

'Tell me.'

'In the scullery. Saw her put it in the sugar caddy for safe keepin'. Expect she forgot it. Probably goin' to show it you later.'

The telegram did not contain the formula: Mum dead. Come immediately. It read: NEED YOU URGENTLY STOP RING COCOA STOP STANLEY CALLAGHAN.

'Bad news, Stephen?' The Irish went bonkers when their mothers died. Bought all round them. Stevie sat down by the fire and read the few words a dozen times. He ran his fingers through his hair. 'Nothin' wrong is there?'

'Naw. Don't think so. It's from Stanley Callaghan. Greatest bloke on earth he was. He needs me. I dunno what for but he needs me. Gotta phone another bloke tomorrow to find out.'

'You happy about it all then?'

'Happy? Yeah, I'm happy. Why?'

'If you wasn't on the dry, bet you'd be celebratin'.'

The remark took a few moments to penetrate Stevie's high good humour. He beamed at Old Bill and grabbed him playfully by the crotch.

'Come on then. Let's hit the pub, you an' me, get you pissed as arseholes I will. An' Jock an' Taffy an Eed. See if I don't.'

4

Mikimoto

Eight ones are eight
Eight twos are sixteen
Eight threes are twenty-four . . .

It was the same classroom in which Bob Tracey had taught him twenty-eight years earlier. And it was the same chant. Stanley did teach the new maths as per the curriculum but he taught the old maths also.

'Crowe.'

'Yes, sir.'

'Twelve thirteens.'

'One hundred and fifty-six, sir.'

Stanley nodded and turned his back. The class finished the eight times tables and chanted the nine times tables. Stanley knew the lay teachers laughed at him but he did not mind just as he scorned their hostility. Theoretically, bygones were bygones, and as though to prove it Mr Locky of all people waved the *Echo* at him that morning coming in the yard and asked: 'Is it true, Stanley?'

'The bones of truth is there someplace.' Mr Locky had no dignity. If he had he wouldn't have spoken to Stanley after what Stanley had done to him.

'Seriously though, are these facts?'

'I'm not at liberty to elaborate. You understand it is a team game; one has obligations. If I may put it, the matter is sub judice.'

Thus, mysteriously, did he avoid being pestered for the time being. It was a development he had not anticipated, that *Echo* chap, O'Grady of the O'Grady Says column, having the gall to ring him at the school. He had told O'Grady frostily that he had a class to teach and put down the phone. And yet it was all there in the *Echo*: 'A chance meeting in a hostelry of two friendly football rivals has led to a romantic challenge. Mr Henry Corr, Managing Director . . .'

The credulity of the common herd was no longer to be wondered at if the gospel according to O'Grady was acceptable to them. In this pastiche Henry Corr emerged as a gentleman, bearded in his local and vulgarly challenged to a football duel by a humourless teacher. O'Grady went on to reveal that there would be no shortage of funds on the Nook eleven as the original team boasted Dara Holden as a member. O'Grady paraded the Institute luminaries . . . Timmie Stockil, currently in the twilight of an illustrious career with Birmingham, having served Manchester City, West Bromwich Albion and Ireland. (Incidentally, Timmie Stockil had turned down a quarter million move to the New York Cosmos. This may or may not have been true, Stanley Callaghan was in no position to verify. What he did know was that half the soccer players in England were contemplating or turning down moves to the New York Cosmos; the other half were under thirty.)

Stanley checked his watch and brought the guillotine down on the sing-song. He turned the blackboard around to reveal NOW IS THE TIME FOR ALL GOOD MEN TO COME TO THE AID OF THE PARTY and silently indicated with his pointer that this apposite legend was the day's headliner. Crowe went around the desks with the litre bottle of diluted ink and topped up the wells; he distributed the straight pens. A request for a new nib was not in his bailiwick to grant. Stanley himself made that decision. He patrolled the aisles carrying a ruler. Now and then he paused and measured the distance between a scholar's nose bridge and copybook. Bob Tracey had always held that the correct distance was nine inches. Bob Tracey had learned this in a *Reader's Digest* of the time, an issue that also carried a simple cure for nicotine addiction.

In the silence, punctuated by the scraping of thirty-nine nibs, Stanley took stock. Himself, Cocoa, Jake, the twins, Bazook, were sound. And Tolly Holliday. Kate had written to Dara. He himself had telegraphed Stevie Mack. Johnny Green was due home from his tour of Birmingham and Stanley was to call on him that night. That left Gabriel.

He also had to call to the Nook to sort out the sponsorship business. That very day lunch at Katstanco was interrupted by

Cocoa's telephone call. It dawned on Stanley that he was now a busy man. He had to attend the monthly meeting of CRAM – he was now struck by the acronym – he had to visit the Nook, he had to see Johnny Green. And he had to watch the Dara Holden File. A busy man and in the news. Conor reported that the O'Grady revelation in the *Echo* was the talk of secondary, so many of the pupils there had gone through Stanley's hands. Conor was a hero.

On his way back to school after lunch Stanley was greeted by Brother Gibson's: 'We're making a comeback, I believe?'

'Newspapers, Brother. Their silly season.'

Brother Gibson shook his head. 'Not in March, Stanley, not in March. Pity, if only it had been hurling or Gaelic football.'

It was almost time for the litany and home. Ten minutes. Stanley leaned on the window-sill, his head in his cupped hands. It was raining inspiration. He foresaw how one could take a stand. The game was actually taking root in America, affording counterpoint if indeed counterpoint were needed. He had read someplace where an American soccer player had scored twice and provided two 'assists'. He supposed an 'assist' meant a pass. They had a facility in America for making sows' ears out of silk purses that wrung from him his reluctant admiration. The boys began to cough. Stanley crossed himself: '*In anam an Athair . . .*'

The boys stood and joined him in prayer. Stanley consulted his *Treasure of the Sanctuary*. It was printed in Ireland, bound in Belgium, edited by the Sisters of Charity, bore the *Nihil Obstat*: MATTHAEUS CANONICUS MacMAHON, Censor Theol. Deput. and the *Imprimi Potest*: EDUARDUS, Archiep. Dublinen, Hiberniae Primas.

'Sancta Maria,' Stanley invoked and the class intoned: *Ora pro nobis*.

The Latin litany had been his Churchillian gesture to the other teachers. It had been a Bob Tracey practice. In search of where he might lay his hands on the Latin, Stanley had called to the Jesuits and the courteous young cleric produced in answer to his summons listened and shook his head. 'I haven't heard a word of Latin since I left the seminary. Will it not do you in English?'

'No.'

'No? I think you should see Father Moore. He's having his afternoon nap at the moment, he's getting on. Call back later.'

Father Moore was ninety-six. With the aid of two sticks he

shuffled along the hall to the waiting room. He too listened, then he produced the *Treasure of the Sanctuary* from his pocket.

'You'll find it under the *Benediction of the Blessed Sacrament*.'

Stanley thanked the old man who in turn asked Stanley to pray for him. He saw Stanley out with a civil 'good day now'. The request and its gratification might have been to Father Moore as everyday an occurrence as a beggar looking for a few coppers only that a beggar of the day in question would have opened the bidding at twenty pence.

'Mater admirabilis . . . Ora pro nobis.'

At the beginning of term the class were in thrall to the novelty of their own contribution. But gradually the whole business became a tedium to be suffered before being allowed home.

'Sedes sapientiae . . . Ora pro nobis.'

For a moment the class was on the alert. Stanley obliged them.

'Causa nostrae laeTITiae . . . Ora pro nobis.' They giggled.

It had been so under Bob Tracey, was now and would be saecula saeculorum. The litany dragged on. But there were no more dirty bits.

Conor did not need to be chivvied into doing his homework on Wednesday nights. It was accomplished a good half hour before the Dara Holden File started. Conor was a celebrity at school because of his friendship with Dara Holden who brought him presents from America. Dara brought presents to Kate and Conor but he never brought anything to Stanley. It all went back to the night in the Nook when Stanley, Dara, Jake O'Dea, Cocoa Brown, Stevie Mack, Bazook, Johnny Green and Tolly Holliday were nursing half pints. A stranger had come in and cleaned out the school. It was Tom Splendid's night off and his wife, Peggy, who was on duty was an intolerant woman who thought a slate kept the rain out. The stranger returned a week later and Stanley and Jake, instead of playing against him, studied his form. The stranger won the first ace pot of the night but as he was taking in the pool Jake O'Dea leaned across the table and gripped his wrist. Then Stevie Mack took the stranger up the post office lane.

But on the night they were cleaned out and Peggy was on duty, Stanley Callaghan issued his commandments. There was nobody at the table who thought then that any of them would ever amount to anything so they all agreed never to accept money from any one of themselves. Except porter money.

The introduction to the Dara Holden File launched Stanley.

'You see, Conor, we are being led to believe that Dara is a hard man given to incessant bottle orgies. He rises from beneath the couch, hungover, unkempt, his apartment a mess. But. What are we missing here, Conor?'

'I don't know, Dad.'

'You can't see what is conspicuous by its absence? My generation were brought up in the flea pits, Conor. Fourpenny forms we sat on and watched cinematic magic – Franchot Tone, Deanna Durbin . . . '

'Stanley, let him enjoy it in his own way. And Deanna Durbin was before your time.'

'We caught her on Sunday nights, Kate. The forms are gone now. All luxury now.'

'It's starting, Dad.'

'Roy Rogers, Gabby Hayes. I could go on. But your private eye then, Conor, was a hero. Yes, he rose from beneath the couch in those days and the empties strewed his office – BUT – here's the missing link, Conor. ASHTRAYS! *Overflowing.* If a picture starred ashtrays and coffee cups then it was a private eye or a newspaper picture . . . '

The Dara Holden File was on. Stanley, the third member of the household to do so, lost interest in his own thesis. He went to the kitchen and got his notebook. He wrote: What's an 'assist', Dara? The entry before that read: ACUPUNCTURE?

Back in the sitting room Stanley watched Dara slap a cigarette out of the black man's mouth.

'Filthy habit, black man. Pollutin' your insides, huh? Okay, wise guy, who sent you?'

'Nobody sent me, whitey.'

Dara stared hard at the black man. Dara should have been smoking; he should have drawn slowly upon his cigarette, inhaled deeply and blown the smoke in the black man's face. But all Dara did was to edge nose to nose to the black man and hiss: 'You fulla shit.'

Stanley wrote in his notebook: Dara, best white actor in world at saying you fulla shit.

Sex jokes and bad language were ignored in Katstanco. Kate
had triumphed in debate. Early in their marriage Stanley
belonged to the school that wanted the television thrown into
the docks. As Conor grew this attitude was moderated to
censorship. But Kate's liberal stance finally won through the
night in Brigid's when Stanley, unknown to himself, dealt her
the winning hand.

'In our day,' Stanley said, 'we entertained ourselves.'

'Faith we did,' agreed Brigid.

'Pleasure was simple and healthy and free. You could always
duck into a circus or carnival. You'd never see a circus now, or a
carnival. I'll never forget the Great Blondini. He used to set
himself on fire and dive two hundred feet into a vat of water.
Before the Janesboro Housing Estate was built, they used to
hold the carnivals there.'

Brigid and Stanley swopping tales of jumping ditches for
entertainment did not always hold Kate's attention but she
found herself enthralled listening to Stanley talk of the Great
Blondini and how Stanley saved Stevie Mack's life in the canal.
They were around twelve years of age, Stanley was relating,
when the Great Blondini was soaking himself in petrol and
diving his ball of fire into the water two hundred feet below.
Stanley could not remember exactly whose idea it was but
Stanley, Dara, Jake, Cocoa and Tolly Holliday were all there.
Stevie Mack had left school and helped his father who was an
upholsterer. They filched an old mattress out of Mr McNamara's
shed. It was a Sunday afternoon. The Guinness crane used in
those days to lift the barrels from the barges in the canal lay
idle. They tied the mattress around Stevie Mack and climbed to
the top of the crane. They had soaked the mattress in paraffin
oil. It was lucky that Stanley had remained by the canal edge,
the better to watch the splash. The experiment was a success
because it proved that anyone could emulate the Great Blondini.
Stevie Mack leapt from the crane and landed in the canal where
the mattress quenched. But the weight of the mattress made it
impossible to swim and also drove Stevie to hit bottom – the
water was five feet deep – and he was concussed. Stanley dived
in and managed to save him. He had to be taken to Barrington's
Hospital where he was detained overnight for observation. Mr
McNamara had to be informed. Mr McNamara visited the
parents of his son's friends. 'I'll never forget the hiding my

father gave me,' Stanley concluded.

Brigid slapped the counter with glee but Kate didn't as much as smile. And when next Conor wanted to watch the Late, Late Show – a professor and her husband were promoting their book of sex instruction entitled *The Oral Examination* – Kate insisted that Conor watch: 'It can't be much worse than watching the Great Blondini.'

Stanley closed his notebook on 'fulla shit' and left to attend the monthly meeting of CRAM. At the meeting Stanley proposed that CRAM take it upon itself – in the continued absence of action from the city council – to wage war on litterbugs by organising a massive sweep-in. This proposal was passed unanimously.

Next he poked his head in the door of the Nook. His glance took in Jake, Cocoa, Bazook, Tolly Holliday and the twins, Tom and Joe Lewis. He didn't greet them. He extended three fingers to Tom Splendid and beckoned Jake and Cocoa to follow him upstairs.

'Why didn't you come in? They've been waiting for you all night.'

'Cocoa. Bring me up to date. I have to see Johnny Green later. Did you sign my name to the wire?'

'Yeah. He rang me this afternoon. He can come any time.'

'Good. Kate's written to Dara.' Jake joined them with the three pints. 'Thanks, Jake. You pay for them?'

'On Wednesday?'

'I'll fix it later. All right, Cocoa, what's all this sponsorship business?'

'It was Jake he contacted.'

'Who?'

'I'll tell it. It happened through Tolly. Peter Dempsey needed a taxi home from some function and he rang Tolly. I know Dempsey was pissed but what do we care. I tell you Stanley there's a God there after all. Dempsey saw it in O'Grady Says in the *Echo* and Tolly told him he was on the team. That's when Dempsey came out with his proposition. You know how mad Dempsey is for publicity. A thousand a man Stanley and all we have to do is wear jerseys with Mikimoto written across the chest. That's if we win of course. Dempsey wasn't that drunk.'

'He has the agency for that Japanese boxcar?'

'Eleven grand, Stanley. Buckshee. If we win.'

'A clever man, Dempsey.'

'He thinks we haven't a chance, Stanley. Imagine him sitting beside Tolly in the taxi. What am I saying, he couldn't fit beside Tolly, he must have been in the back. I'm surprised he didn't make it fifty thousand. And he knows Stockil and O'Shea are playing for them.'

'And all we have to do is wear jerseys with Mikimoto on them?'

'That's all. And win. We have to win.'

Stanley noticed the cuffs of Jake's coat as he raised the pint to his mouth. A neat strip of leatherette was ironed onto them. Molly was an economical woman. She would have to be.

'A pity, Jake. A pity,' Stanley said and brought Cocoa to life.

'What d'you mean "a pity"?'

'I wouldn't mind relieving Dempsey of a few bob, Cocoa. But it has the game ruined. All games ruined. At the same time we'll have to thank him for his offer. Cocoa, you draft a letter at work, sign it on behalf of the Nook with my name. Be polite, but firm.'

'What the fuck are you talking about? Jake, what's he saying?'

Jake fished a nobber out of his top pocket and did not reply.

'Don't you see,' Stanley continued after a swallow of porter, 'this is our chance to make a stand? Get on to O'Grady Says. Let him know what we're on about. My wager with Henry Corr – that has nothing to do with money. At least not on our side. There is a glorious principle involved here. Gentlemen at play. It's even a pity we had to resort to vulgar coinage at all. A quirk of genetics and it might have been my trusty hunter against Henry Corr's gun. Or my chef.' Stanley drank again from his pint. Cocoa looked at Jake who stared at the floor. 'They may play soccer in America today, England may be represented by pop stars chewing gum on the pitch, but the lights are not yet out all over Europe. A flicker is visible in the modest hamlet of Mellick. Look at the publicity we're getting already. O'Grady and the two Dublin evening newspapers. The Nook must stand tall and clean in this, we may be a mere catacomb in the influential sphere but ours will be the widow's mite of good example – in short, for no amount of money will we wear Mikimoto across our chests. Agreed?'

Cocoa Brown rose and leaned his hands on the back of the chair.

'A – lunatic. A – fucking – lunatic. What did I always tell you, Jake? He's a fucking header.'

'Shut up, Cocoa. Stanley's right. I agree with him. Almost. Stanley, I'm not thinking of myself. You know that. All right, we'll pretend you know that. But Stanley, think of Bazook. Peter Dempsey could put Mikimoto on his chest with a branding iron and he'd be thrilled with a fiver let alone a thousand. We've all got jobs but Bazook hasn't. He hasn't a tosser. At thirty years of age he became a redundant docker with a widowed mother to keep. We – he drank it in six months. Stanley, just think of Bazook.'

Stanley Callaghan thought of Jake O'Dea. 'All right, Jake. All right. But I'm not wearing Mikimoto. I'll get my own jersey. Tell Dempsey he has a deal. For ten thousand. The rest of you will wear his jersey and he coughs up if we win. But on one condition.'

'What condition?'

'I'm serious about this, Jake. You and Cocoa can paint me any way you like to Dempsey but the money must be in cash and down before the game, the same as the Institute's money. I won't allow even Bazook to look ridiculous if there's even the remotest danger of a welsh or a bounced cheque.'

Jake O'Dea nodded. He drained his glass and said to Cocoa: 'I'm just after making you a thousand if we win. Go down and buy a drink.'

While Cocoa was downstairs getting three pints and a brandy – Jake insisted on celebrating – Jake said: 'Stanley, why do you have to give me heartburn?'

'Jake, Johnny Green. I have to see him later. How's he doing?'

'Johnny's doing fine. Rakin' it in.'

'How's he doing – domestically?'

Jake shrugged: 'I don't know. I suppose it's the same.'

'Still petticoat government?'

Jake nodded. They shared the pain.

After the pubs closed Jake persuaded Cocoa on the strength of the good news to treat him in Patsy Naughton's grill. Over sausage and chips Jake said:

'Stop calling him a lunatic. It's beginning to dawn on me how much money a thousand pounds really is. Stanley walked out of the Nook fifteen years ago and never came back. You have to learn to treat him like nitroglycerine.'

'But he is a lunatic.'

'You don't understand these things, Cocoa.'

'I'll tell you what I understand. When we were twelve that lunatic persuaded us that we could outdo the Great Blondini, remember. And 'twas me he wanted to tie up in that fucking mattress until Stevie, the nut, volunteered. Stanley didn't even climb up on the fucking crane. He directed operations from the ground.'

'Treat him like nitroglycerine. I'd eat another chip, they're lovely.'

5

Johnny Green

Stanley Callaghan had met Teresa Green twice. The first occasion was the very night that the Nook were celebrating the victory over the Institute and that was just six weeks after Teresa and Johnny Green celebrated their shotgun wedding at six in the morning in Cratloe Church with no representative from the Nook present. Johnny was with the Colorado Showband then and about to set off for a gig in Co. Dublin when Stanley contacted him and demanded his presence. Teresa was six weeks married and two months pregnant and, at seventeen years of age, always accompanied her seventeen years old husband to dance-halls up the country. But this time Johnny had managed to persuade her to stay at home after swearing a solemn promise not to go near a groupie. Shanghaid by Stanley, Johnny did not bother to tell Teresa he was not going with the Colorado after all.

They met in the first place in the Oyster Ballroom, Dromkeen. Johnny was on drums. He had jet black medium length hair then that could be adapted to any trend; and he was always smiling. He had smiled through childhood and brief adolescence; and it was this smile which was as constant as another's dimple that cut short Teresa's career as a groupie and ended his adolescence. She jived all night in front of the bandstand and returned his winks. Outside the Oyster Ballroom while the lads were loading the instruments, Johnny Green had her up against a tree. But she did not become pregnant that time. She began travelling with the Colorado, herself and two pals, and it was some night in the wagon that it happened.

By the time Stanley met her they had a flat in the same street as the Nook so it wasn't surprising that Teresa spotted Johnny going into the pub when he was supposed to be in Co. Dublin with the Colorado. In high spirits Johnny called his drink and grabbed Mrs Trehy; he was giving the old dear a swing when Teresa poked her head in. Stanley Callaghan was in the snug with Dara, Bush Vine and the celebrated actor's ward, the then Kate Flynn. He stood up and peered over the partition at the commotion. He saw Teresa pour the pint of Guinness over Johnny's head and try to stick the broken glass in his throat; he saw Johnny cower defensively while Teresa spat at him, pulled his hair and scratched at his face. He was thoroughly embarrassed.

Stanley did not see Teresa Green again for thirteen years. The occasion was Jake O'Dea's wedding where Johnny – now with the Blunotes – was combining business and pleasure.

There was nothing Johnny Green could do about his smile and it was no more than good and second nature that prompted him to smile at Jake's bride, Molly, as the couple led the dancing, such as it was, given that most of the guests were from the Nook. Molly blew Johnny a grateful kiss and then for the second time in his life Stanley was ashamed in Kate's company. Teresa, who was sitting alone near the bandstand, picked up her chair and threw it at her husband, shouted 'bitch' at Molly and ran out of the hall. Johnny Green smiled through the rest of the evening.

Stanley had rung Teresa Green and been informed that Johnny was due home from Newcastlewest where he was playing with the Blunotes at about seven minutes to one. Stanley was not surprised at the exactitude. At fifteen minutes to one he drove his car to the entrance of Caherdavin Park and waited, thinking bitterly of what had become of little Johnny Green who was six years younger than the rest of them and who had been once the pride of the Fairgreen.

Johnny Green tried to reach a count of a hundred. During the fortnight's tour of Birmingham and the Midlands he counted eleven; from last year's tour of London he counted fourteen, not counting the one in the Paddy pub where Stevie Mack had taken him.

'What time is it?'

The driver, Paschal Simpson, rhythm guitarist and founder of the Blunotes, answered: 'Johnny you asked me ten minutes ago. For fuck sake, relax. We're on time.'

Teresa knew they were doing a cabaret spot in a pub before their gig as relief to the Royal Showband in the Olympic in Newcastlewest. She knew how long it took to travel from Newcastlewest home to Mellick. She worked it out on paper before Johnny left the house and calculated that he should be home by seven minutes to one at the latest. Johnny was twenty minutes behind schedule now and he had done no more than sit smoking in the wagon watching Paschal and Butch Madden, the organist, on the job. Paschal was gone fifty and never got over how easy it was. The girl tonight was younger than Paschal's youngest daughter.

Butch offered Johnny one of his cigarettes. Butch was nineteen. Johnny Green shook his head. 'No thanks. And you watch it, Butch. Next thing you'll want the hard stuff.'

'Not me, Johnny. I've too much sense. Thirty-five quid for two short gigs the one night only an hour from home. Boy!'

'Big money to you, Butch?'

'Isn't it to you?'

'I'm not complaining.'

'Why didn't you ride the one tonight, Johnny?'

Butch was part of the trio six months. Paschal owned the group. He was married to a sister of John the Man Collins, the biggest impresario in the south. John the Man booked them seven nights a week. They had two days off at Christmas, one week in the summer and the annual fortnight in Birmingham or London was so that John the Man could bill them 'back from their successful tour of England'. The almost governmental security of the job robbed Johnny Green of even the daydream of ambition. Johnny Green had seen all the changes since first the Clipper Carlton and then the Royal Showband opened the floodgates. When Johnny was with the Colorado there were six hundred and fifty-eight showbands in Ireland, all doing good business, twelve of which (not including the Colorado) would have filled the largest hall anyplace on any night in any weather. The Jack Dillon Orchestra was on the road then – four violins, sax, trombone, two clarinets, three guitars, drums, electric organ and piano and three backing singers. Now there were fifty showbands including the Blunotes, none of which had talent except for the Royal which had lasted but the Royal spent six months of the year in Las Vegas. Johnny Green had survived. The clarinet was gone, the horn, the bass, but they still needed a drummer. The Blunotes needed a drummer and they needed Paschal Simpson not so much for his rhythm guitar as for his brother-in-law, John the Man Collins. And they needed a thick, fornicating, iconoclastic representative of youth to remind them of what they should rehearse. Butch Madden was the latest recruit in that line. Only six months with the Blunotes, Butch Madden had not yet heard the Johnny Green Story.

'Why didn't I ride the one tonight? I was tired, Butch.'

'You weren't tired in Birmingham.'

'No. I wasn't racing against the clock. I'll tell you something, Butch. I didn't enjoy it. All right, okay, eleven times but I still didn't enjoy it. At least I can't remember enjoying it. Jesus . . . Butch?'

'Yeah?'

'Never get married.'

Johnny Green was over thirty. They all said the same thing. Butch did not like the thought of ending up like them. But he didn't tell that to their faces. He humoured them with the old formula.

'It's good to have a bit at home when you're stuck, isn't it?'

'Sex isn't everything.' Johnny's smile tightened. He did not have to love Butch Madden to warn him of the dangers. 'Butch, whatever you do, don't put a bird up the pole.'

'Her tough luck if it happens. She can fuck off over and have an abortion.'

Johnny considered that escape route retrospectively but it didn't appeal to him. He had five children whom he loved. He focused for a moment on what class of parents produced the Butch Maddens.

'There was none of that then, not when I was your age. Paschal, what time is it?'

'It's only half twelve. Relax.'

'We won't make it till ten past one. Fuck. There'll be murder.' Then, going back to his story. 'Butch, let me tell you something, I was only seventeen years of age; I was still waiting for my voice to come back. Then, wham! An old man overnight. And now look at me. A drummer. A ventriloquist. Butch, I sang solo from the high altar in the Redemptorists on Christmas night. Three years in a row. I was only fourteen years of age the last time. Did you know that, Butch?'

'No.'

'But you've seen the Redemptorists Christmas night with all the candles.'

'I haven't. I live the other side of town. Anyway, I don't believe in all that shit.'

'Shit or not, it's some scene.' Johnny Green closed his eyes. All that shit. To call it shit. He ploughed on: 'There's a thousand candles on the altar, Butch. Exactly one thousand. You can see the altar boys lighting them . . . There's no getting in there Christmas night. You'd want to be there half an hour before devotions start. I'll tell you the routine. The choir sings for half an hour. You know, Silent Night, the Adeste, all that. Then there's a sermon. Then benediction. And then at the end they switch off all the lights and the place is in darkness except for the thousand candles on the altar. And then . . . and then the soloist steps out in front of the choir on the high altar and sings. I was the youngest ever to sing it. Eleven years of age. The boy soprano sings Holy Night.'

Johnny Green turned away to look out the window. It was wasted on a Butch Madden, so wasted that Johnny couldn't help pursuing it further.

'And you were never there Christmas night?'

'No. I'm not knocking it, Johnny. It's just, I just don't believe in all that crap.'

'Maybe you're right, Butch. Maybe you're right. I didn't know then how beautiful it was. Because it is beautiful. My parents, the neighbours, they all came and told me 'twas lovely. And Father O'Riordan. But all I knew was that I could sing. I knew that from scout concerts and charity shows since I was nine. I was in the same concert one night as Josef Locke and they clapped me as much as him. Hey Paschal, Paschal, remember me and Josef Locke?'

'Yeah, Johnny. I remember.'

'You see Paschal remembers. Yeah, I knew I was good then but I didn't know anything else. Until last Christmas, Butch. I was stuck in all day. Stuck in a wagon all year round and stuck in front of a television on your day off. I had to get out of the house, had to get air. I took the kids with me. I walked into town and then I saw the crowds all heading towards the Redemptorists. I followed them. Outside of christenings and first communions I wasn't inside a church since the day I was married. I let the kids run around and I just leaned against the railings in the yard smoking and listening to the choir inside. I could see in the main door. When the choir stopped I knew the sermon was on although I couldn't hear it. Then the benediction, I saw the lights go out. So I went in and stood at the back . . . I . . . I . . . a soprano sang it all right, a girl, but I thought, it sounds stupid, I thought I was up there, I thought Holy Night was coming out of me, and I was up there . . . '

Butch Madden did not know if Johnny Green had finished his story. There had been no punchline. It seemed for a moment to Butch as though Johnny was going to cry. But Johnny must have finished his yarn because Paschal muttered: 'You were one hell of a boy soprano, Johnny.'

'Yeah.'

There was no point in finishing his story now. Butch Madden would only think him daft. And Paschal – Paschal was John the Man Collins' brother-in-law. He had walked home from the Redemptorists in a trance carrying a weight inside him that he could not fathom until he had re-crossed Sarsfield Bridge and left the crowds behind him. He had leaned over the parapet and stared down the river and at the spire of the Redemptorists. And he had clutched the stone and cried. Butch Madden would not understand tears.

'Well, you got your voice back.'

Startled, yet mollified, Johnny Green looked at him: 'Butch, you think I can sing, *now*?'

'What were you doing tonight? Every other night? Of course you can.'

Johnny Green chuckled. He examined Butch to see if Butch was having him on.

'Hear that, Paschal?'

'I know, Johnny.'

'Listen to me, Butch. Listen. When I was twelve, when I was twelve, Butch, Josef Locke was in his prime. They wouldn't let me go off the stage. 'Twas in the Savoy, fifteen hundred seats. I sang Ave Maria, Happy Moments, 'I Dreamt I Dwelt in Marble Halls'. You know what Josef Locke said? He had to keep calling me back on stage and let me take a bow and he whispers through his teeth; Sonny, that's enough now, scoot. He was *jealous* of me. *Josef Locke*! Ask Paschal. Hey, Paschal, you ever hear of me stealing the show from Josef Locke?'

'I was there, Johnny. I was there.'

'Tonight I was playing drums and doing my ventriloquist act and croaking out ballads. Fucking ballads! Some world. Some world, Butch. Let me give you two pieces of advice. Butch, never put a bird up the pole. And never strike a woman either. What time is it?'

At a quarter past one the wagon reached Caherdavin Park. Stanley Callaghan got out of his car and hailed it before it reached Johnny Green's house.

'Stanley! Stanley Callaghan! How are you kid?'

'Johnny, sit in the car a minute, I want to talk to you.'

'Okay. I'll just tell Teresa I'm back. Hold on.'

Stanley watched him run down the road. He was wearing knee length black cowboy boots into which were tucked red corduroy trousers. His shirt was yellow and his waistcoat black as his now shoulder-length hair. He wore a tweed peak cap. It was fifteen minutes before he returned.

'Sorry, Stanley. What's the problem?'

'Sit in. Tell me, does Paschal Simpson dress like that?'

'No. He wears a bainin pullover and a red beret.'

'You were always a great kidder, Johnny.'

'I wish I was kidding now. Butch, that's our organist, he has a sort of Napoleon outfit ... '

'Forget it. Teresa told me you only got back from Birmingham today and you had to go straight to a function. Did she tell you about the match?'

'She said something funny, we had a small bit of a row, nothing serious and just as I was going out the door she shouted something like, that's right, go and play your stupid match. I didn't know what she was talking about.'

Stanley handed him the photograph. 'Look at this.'

'We were crazy in those days.'

'We still are. Here. Read that. That's O'Grady Says in the *Echo* last week.'

Johnny read snatches aloud: ' ... another well known member of that Nook team was Johnny Green, one time Colorado Showband star and currently with Paschal Simpson's Blunotes ... '

'Hey, how about that. Is this for real, Stanley? Eleven thousand?'

'Yes.'

'Look at our haircuts. God. My old fella. My old fella's a barber, he . . . '

'I know, Johnny. He cut my hair up to three years ago.'

' . . . imagine then, looking at that photo, who'd think . . . he said to me once when I was a kid, when I wanted to chuck school, he said on one condition, that I apprentice myself in the shop. People will always want their hair cut, he said. The poor bastard. I told him what was happening. Myself, I couldn't even go to him, I had to go to Unisex. He said it was all a fad. He's in security now. A fucking night watchman.'

'Johnny, how are you for this match?'

'How am I? What do you mean how am I?'

'I can depend on you?'

'Of course you can depend on me. What a thing to say.'

'Good. How's Teresa? How're the kids?'

'Great. Great. All fine. How's your own wife and son? Brian, is it?'

'Conor.'

'Conor. That's what I meant.'

'They're both fine. I'll let you go. It's late. Keep in touch.'

'Hold on Stanley. Hang on a minute. Just stay talking for ten minutes. There's a bit of a, you know, hang on till I see the light on upstairs. D'you mind? Just till she's gone to bed.'

'Not at all. Have a good tour?'

'I envy you, Stanley. A woman like Kate. No trouble, I bet she doesn't shout, no rows?'

'We have our moments, Johnny. Marriage is marriage.'

'I only met your wife once. What she must think of people like me. Teresa going bazook. Some world . . . '

'Are you settling down, Johnny?'

'Jesus, that's a laugh. Settling down. I'm nailed down. You know why I kept you waiting a few minutes ago? I was explaining to Teresa that we had to change a wheel. She didn't believe me. She never does. She threw a plate. A willow pattern. If I hadn't ducked it would have cut my throat. You'd think a woman never heard of having to change a wheel.'

Stanley gave him a cigarette and noted the shake in Johnny's hands.

'Did you change a wheel?'

'No. We didn't change a wheel. You want to know had I a bird

in the wagon. That's what you're thinking. Right?'
'Wrong.'
'Well, we had a bird in the wagon. Two of them. Paschal
fucked one and Butch fucked the other. I sat there smoking.
That's how we were late. I couldn't very well walk home.'
'Why didn't you explain that to Teresa?'
'What's the point? I do fuck about. She knows the scene. But
the funny thing is any time I do it I always arrange to be back
home in time. And I don't hear a word about it. She gets at me
all the time for things I don't do.'
Stanley had always thought of Johnny Green's as a ludicrous
problem. Now it was the ludicrous problem of a member of the
Nook eleven once more. Wearily he said: 'She needles you?'
'Hi, that's good. That's it exactly. I'm ballsed up, Stanley.
Everyone knows it. That time at Jake's wedding, I couldn't look
Jake in the face that night. And everyone there. Dara, yourself,
Cocoa, Stevie Mack, Tolly. I suppose everyone laughs at me.'
'I don't. And neither does anyone else. Johnny?'
'Yeah?'
'Does it really happen like I read about, the Rolling Stones
and those people, does it happen all the way down – or should
that be up – the line, girls throwing themselves at musicians?'
Johnny nodded, with Stanley thought, a faint pride.
'So. What's the problem?'
'I don't follow you, Stanley.'
'You work in a flour mill you come home with a white face.
You're a printer, you have ink under your nails. You're in a
band, you fuck about. Why can't she understand that?'
Johnny Green chuckled at this novelty. 'Would you like to
explain it to her for me, Stanley?' He was surprised when
Stanley turned in the driving seat and said bluntly. 'Listen to
me. I'm serious. You're fifteen years working. You've never
drawn the dole. Your house is in a fashionable area. You keep
your wife and kids well shod and fed. And you no more than
anybody else can make an omelette without breaking eggs.
You're a star, you fuck. Now you go and put it to her, Johnny,
and make sure she sees it. Or I'll drop you from the Nook team
and play with ten men.'
'It's easy to say, Stanley, but she's a woman.'
'Then you be a man. Belt her. Kick her arse in. What kind of a
nancy boy are you, Johnny? Do you think I don't give Kate a

puck in the gob? You think Jake doesn't have to give Molly a dunt now and then?'

Tentatively, Johnny Green, unable to decide whether or not Stanley was serious, said: 'I never thought I'd see the day that Stanley Callaghan would recommend beating a woman.'

'I'm not talking about women,' the teacher shot back, 'I'm talking about wives. The next time she nags you chuck the drums at her, tell her go off with Paschal Simpson and earn the few bob.'

'They have women's aid shelters now . . . '

Johnny's smile would have disappeared if it could as Stanley hissed at him: 'Beat her. Follow her to the women's aid shelter. Drag her home. If she gets the guards, attack the guards. In the name of Jesus, make a stand.' Stanley leaned across him and opened the passenger door. 'Go on. Get out. Hit her hard. And don't hold back.'

6

Gabriel

St Patrick's Day fell on Saturday that year and so the pupils were entitled to a free day on the Friday. On top of that the teachers' association had negotiated a day off on Thursday so that they might have a long, long-weekend 'to see to their caravans', Stanley conjectured to Kate. Stanley never knew what to do with himself on a day off and from his point of view, it was catastrophic that on the Monday the central heating failed and the Superior had no option but to close the school. For the first three days of St Patrick's week only one class attended: Stanley Callaghan's. He brought in his own gas heater and cylinder. But on Thursday morning he had to observe the long weekend. He rose early and rang Cocoa Brown for a progress report. The fact that the county council were working that Thursday highlighted the wantonness of teachers in laying down tools.

'What do you want?' Cocoa answered.

'What news from the Rialto?'

'Did Jake ring you about the boots?'

'Boots?'

'He mustn't have finalised it yet. He knows someone in one of the Leary shoe shops. The manager there is willing to supply us with Three Star boots. And fifty pounds a man – if we win. Same idea as the Mikimoto. It won't cost Leary anyway. Three Star will foot the bill.'

'Cocoa, you're even insensitive to your own wit. Now listen to me. I'm not having this. We have an image to protect.'

'You have, Stanley. You have. Is it really true you brought your gas heater into school? Jesus. Jake told the Leary manager that we had a lunatic on our side who might not be willing to accept his sponsorship. The manager understood. So it's ten pairs – and ten fifty quids if we win. You can stay pure, Stanley.'

'All right. You get it in cash though. Same as Dempsey. Now let's get on to something constructive. We've agreed the match has to take place at night same as the original. We've agreed ref and venue ... '

'They're not sure yet about the venue. The Institute trustees have to sanction that. It's their pitch.'

'All right. But wherever it takes place no crossbar. You make sure of that. And listen. We didn't fix an exact date. Make it the first Saturday in May – the fifth. Not the last Saturday in April. The first Saturday in May. Do you think you can organise that?'

'Why not the last Saturday in April?'

'You'll find out soon enough. You should know without my telling you. Good day to you.'

It occurred to Stanley that the fifth of May was a more suitable date for the replay than the last Saturday in April after reading in his morning paper that Mike Gibson, the British and Irish Lion, had retired.

Stanley had no difficulty enlisting Conor for a stroll. The boy had suffered occasionally when an eccentricity of his father's was brought to his attention and all he had ever been given in justification was Stanley's: 'Conor, pay no attention to what you hear. Someday you will understand that I am the finest man you know.' The replay changed all that. Everyone in class wanted news of the match and Conor aped his father by declaring he was not at liberty to divulge information. They took a turn by the docks – 'a change is as good as a rest, Conor' – where, sitting on a bollard, Stanley observed people his own age knocking at public houses for a cure.

'Isn't that the Nook up there, Dad?'

'Yes, that's it.'

'What kind of a place is it, Dad?'

Stanley looked from his son's hungry eyes to the pub. Every night, he knew, they were all in the Nook savouring the replay.

'Conor, how would you like a Seven Up?'

'Rapid.'

'Conor, please.'

'Sorry. I mean, great.'

'Come on then.'

There was only one other customer – a stranger – and the proprietor.

'Good morning, Tom.'

'Ah, Stanley. How are you? Splendid job. Splendid.'

'Two Seven Ups please, Tom.'

'Seven Ups coming up. In training, Stanley?'

'And ten Players Medium, with the government health warning. Quiet this morning?'

'At twenty to eleven, yes. The days of the early risers are going. God be with the days,' Tom Splendid glanced at Conor, 'God be with the days when I used to be knocked up at eight o'clock.'

As Stanley lit a cigarette he became aware of the stranger who suddenly began to mime. The long counter, shaped like a horizontal walking stick, curled into the wall near the fireplace where the stranger was closeted. He brought two fingers to his mouth and sucked an imaginary cigarette and raised his eyebrows at Stanley. Stanley raised his eyebrows in turn, looked down at his packet and back at the stranger. The stranger nodded. Stanley gave him a cigarette. The stranger mimed a light. Stanley gave him a match. The stranger spoke: 'Thank you.'

The two deep syllables were enough for Stanley to realise he was in the presence of an educated man. He thought it sad that an educated man should have no cigarettes. The stranger coughed and gingerly pointed with his little finger at his empty half-pint glass. The longing in the nutant gesture was harrowing to witness.

'Drink?' Stanley interpreted.

'Please.'

A rich voice.

'Tom, a drink for the gentleman.'

'Splendid.' Tom grinned, it seemed to Stanley, conspiratorially. The beneficiary was middle-aged, looked nearly fifty. His grey hair was closely cropped and balding at the crown. He was a few days without shaving. He gulped half his drink and suddenly announced: 'I've two uncles dead.'

Stanley genuinely disliked sadness but he was always stoic in the face of sadness for which there was no cure. Johnny Green's troubles were ludicrous. But Stanley could not bring people back from the dead.

'I'm sorry,' he condoled.

'One of them died ten years ago.'

Tom Splendid smiled over the newspaper he was pretending to read. Stanley understood now that the stranger probably had a problem. But he had no sense of humour where the deranged were concerned and he detested those who had. He was disappointed in Tom Splendid. He enquired politely, 'When did your other uncle die?'

'Twenty years ago.'

The combination of properly enunciated words and their lack of sense prompted Stanley to reflect that it was mostly the educated who became winos or went off their heads. It was a commentary on the state of society. There was total silence in the pub for a few moments.

'One of them was no good at hurling.' The stranger looked straight ahead. Stanley coughed. This information begged a question.

'Was the other uncle good?'

'He was useless.'

The stranger drained his glass and without another word left the pub.

'Poor chap,' Stanley observed to the proprietor.

'Yes. It is sad and no doubt about it. You have your work cut out, Stanley.'

'Pardon?'

'I say, you have your work cut out there.'

'I don't seem to follow you, Tom.'

'Our friend.' Tom Splendid nodded at the corner where the stranger had stood.

'What about him?'

Tom Splendid studied the teacher. 'Stanley, you *do* know who he is?'

'No. Should I?'

'Well, isn't it customary for the captain of a team to know his outside right.'

Stanley couldn't quite believe him though it did tie in with Gabriel's history as related by Cocoa and Jake. 'Tom, he looks fifty. I only saw Gabriel once. The day of the match. He was only a kid then.'

'I forgot we don't see you these days. That's Gabriel, Stanley. I wish it wasn't for your sake. But it is. It is.'

*   *   *

On his way to the Institute grounds on the night of the match, Jake O'Dea took a short cut through Caledonian Park, a municipal hotch potch of soccer pitches and grazing for tinkers' horses. Stanley had told him to bring a player with him as the Nook were likely to be short. Jake delayed ten minutes watching an inter-firm game. He had not yet picked up his player. Beside him a youngster with a faraway look in his eyes leaned against a goal post.

'Youngfella, you play soccer?'

The boy nodded but didn't look at Jake.

'Have you boots?'

The boy shook his head.

'Come on. You can play in your tackies.'

The boy fell into a trot beside Jake. 'I'm better with tackies anyway.'

'Whether it's hobnailed boots or tackies you better be good. We have to win this match. Where d'you play?'

'On the wing.'

'Good. That's where I would have put you anyway.'

After the game, as Jake began to undress, he noticed the boy walk off. 'Hey, hey, youngfella, whatsyername, Gabriel, hey, where are you going?'

The boy walked on. Jake ran after him and had to stand directly in front of him to impede his progress. He had the same vacant look on his face that he had had while leaning against the goal post in Caledonian Park.

'What's wrong with you? You were brilliant.'

The boy had his hands in his pockets and stared at the ground. He tried to move around Jake.

'Listen. You could play for us again. We're always short.'

The boy wouldn't answer. Slowly Jake stepped out of his way. He stood looking after the boy until he was out of sight.

Nobody understood what happened to Gabriel Storan.

He grew up in Mount Pleasant Avenue, the only child of parents who had married in their late thirties. The avenue was a cul-de-sac of twenty-three houses. It was two hundred and ten yards long and sixteen yards wide. Every day the children played soccer on the road. Three electric light poles grew at intervals out of the footpaths. In the cramped surroundings it was a natural ploy to kick the ball around a pole while running straight ahead and then collect the rebound off a garden wall. A touch was never conceded when the ball went into a garden passage. Opponents chased in after it and fought for the ball in the passage, an area of four by two yards. The ball itself was no bigger than a tennis ball. The children did not use the through pass or the forceful break. Because it was a cul-de-sac it was not permitted to shoot hard at the goal leading to the main street and it was common for a player to beat the same opponent three times in an effort to walk the ball into that goal. All the players were agile, knacky and possessed of remarkable ball control. And of all the children, in the matter of agility, knackiness and ball control, Gabriel Storan was the best.

Gabriel's only interest outside football was study. He was eligible because of his father's low income, to sit the secondary scholarship exam. Neither of his parents nor any of their relations had ever gone beyond primary but they dreamed of a better future for their son. Every day after school Gabriel played football till tea time and then did three hours study, going to bed after listening to Perry Mason. Gabriel got his scholarship easily. It amounted to one hundred and twenty-five pounds payable over five years secondary at twenty-five pounds a year which was in turn payable at Christmas, Easter and Summer in instalments of eight, eight and nine pounds. The money was intended to pay for books, fees and clothes. And it did. The scholarship was also subject to the maintenance by the pupil of a certain academic standard.

At the same time that Gabriel won the scholarship, Caledonian A.F.C. signed him for the under thirteen side. At first Gabriel had difficulty adjusting to football boots and grass but then so had the other players who were in their first year off the streets. At under thirteen, fourteen and fifteen Gabriel shone at outside right for Cals. No cliché was spared to praise him: he could run rings around people, he could turn on a sixpence, he could talk to the ball. But he did not have a strong shot or a strong kick. His method of crossing the ball was to beat defender after defender until he was close enough to goal to loft the ball in the air for the centre forward.

Timmie Stockil played outside left on the same Caledonian team. He lived near the Institute and had played all his football on grass. He was orthodox, direct and had a powerful shot. The contrast between the two wingers was not lost on the Caledonian manager, Jack Lipper, and whenever rival full backs were taking the measure of either of them or both, Jack Lipper switched wingers. Caledonians won the under thirteen league and cup, the under fourteen league and cup the following year and the under fifteen league and cup the year after that.

It was definitely true that the selectors of the Irish International Schoolboys soccer team had a notorious bias against the provinces. They held a lip service trial every year between one half of the Rest of Ireland and the other half of the Rest of Ireland, excluding Dublin players from either side. Gabriel Storan and Timmie Stockil were picked to play for one half of the Rest of Ireland in the trial during which they switched wings to confuse the other half of the Rest of Ireland. Both played so well that they were picked to go forward to the Final Trial – usually one half of Dublin versus the other half of Dublin. It was pointed out though to Jack Lipper that the Mellick lads would only get half a match each.

It was unprecedented for one let alone two boys from the backwater of Mellick to go so far. The excitement in Mount Pleasant Avenue was such that the neighbours ceased complaining that their windows were in danger; they nodded benevolently at Gabrial Storan dribbling his ball to the corner shop for his father's MacSmile blade.

On the train to Dublin with his two protégés Jack Lipper went over every facet of Gabriel's play and added: 'Timmie, all this applies to you too.'

Gabriel played the first half of the trial and performed better than he had ever done for Caledonians. But he was outshone, not by the full back, but by the left winger on his own team and both opposition wingers, all three of whom were reared in alleyways that would have fitted comfortably in Mount Pleasant Avenue. In the areas of agility, knackiness and ball control what Gabriel Storan had to offer the sourdough metropolitan selectors was old hat. They were impressed though by the well fed, solid, direct approach of Timmie Stockil.

All the way home in the train Jack Lipper did his best. He and Timmie Stockil agreed and both told Gabriel that he too should have been selected. Gabriel did not want to cry but he could not help himself. Jack Lipper leaned across the carriage and held his arm gently. 'Don't let it get you down, Gabriel. You'll come into your own.' Jack Lipper recalled brilliant players of the past who had not even made the metropolitan trial. Jack Lipper was a good man, married with young children of his own and unique in schoolboy football management in that there was not even the suspicion of the paedophile about him. He said, 'Mark my words, Gabriel, you'll come into your own and those selectors will be ashamed for life.'

Jack Lipper was in error.

Too old for schoolboy soccer Gabriel graduated to the minor ranks, but he was not a success. Never garrulous, content with football, study, the radio and *Charlie Buchan's Football Monthly*, Gabriel became further withdrawn as he grew older. He arrived for a game, located a dry stone, stripped and played without talking to anyone. And he discouraged all attempts to be friendly. In particular did he avoid Timmie Stockil. Timmie improved in the minor division. His strength and direct approach served him better than the light touches profited Gabriel. And Timmie's confidence had soared from having represented Ireland against England, Scotland and Wales – all three of which games Ireland lost heavily. In contrast Gabriel developed rather than arrested all his own worst faults. He would not part with the ball. He performed tricks. After Gabriel's two years at minor level Jack Lipper was unable to recommend to the committee that Gabriel be allowed play junior.

It was at this time that Jake O'Dea found him leaning sullenly against the goal post. The Nook thought Gabriel a wonderful player. They did not notice his lack of shot – the Lewis twins could not walk in football boots let alone shoot – and the heavy drinkers and smokers on the Nook team – all ten of them – were quite happy to watch Gabriel playing with himself out on the wing for as long as he liked while they recovered their breath.

Gabriel Storan was an excellent scholar. He was intelligent. He reasoned that the envy that consumed him was not an acceptable emotion in the eyes of the world and he contained it as best he could. He knew that Timmie Stockil was not responsible for his not having made the schoolboy international team, still less Cals junior side, and so he kept his hatred of Timmie Stockil to himself. He studied, he listened to the radio and he read his *Charlie Buchan Football Monthlies*. And he took

refuge in daydreams. A metropolitan selector on his deathbed
would own that they picked the wrong boy; he would be
spotted in the local park by a scout who would take him to
England where the canny dribbler was appreciated. He read and
re-read Len Shackleton's *Clown Prince of Soccer*.

Timmie Stockil was snapped up by Mellick United, the local
League of Ireland team. Gabriel began to stay away from the
home games, praying that Mellick would lose and that Timmie
Stockil would be the architect of defeat. Timmie Stockil and
Mellick United prospered, winning the League. And when
Gabriel was only three months off sitting for his Leaving
Certificate (Honours), Manchester City signed Timmie Stockil.

On the day Timmie Stockil left Mellick to join Manchester
City the Boherbouy Brass and Reed band assembled near the
Institute. Timmie Stockil and Jack Lipper and officials of
Mellick United stood on the back of a lorry. Neighbours,
friends and wellwishers collected behind the lorry. The band
struck up Marching Through Georgia and the throng set off.
The emigrating footballer was played all the way to the station,
down O'Connell Avenue, right into Wolfe Tone Street, the
street that had Mount Pleasant Avenue as a tributary. Mr and
Mrs Storan themselves walked down to the end of the avenue to
watch the cavalcade. Gabriel looked out the skylight of his
bedroom. The lorry was decked with the black and amber
colours of Caledonians and the claret and pale blue of Mellick
United. Timmie Stockil waved shyly at the cheering crowds
lining the street. Gabriel Storan climbed slowly down from the
chair. He sat on the bed, lifted Len Shackleton's *Clown Prince of
Soccer* from the table and clutched it to his chest. He rolled over
and lay face down and bit hard on a mouthful of pillow. His
sobbing was quiet but it was fierce. Not alone was the boy's
heart broken, his soul was being torn apart.

The point of life escaped him gradually. He reasoned that it
was not necessary to get honours – or pass – to play for
Manchester City. He knew this was specious logic but he could
not resist the flirtation. He found it easy to find it difficult to
focus on his examinations. He managed two honours that he
could hardly have avoided, English and Latin, and he passed
History, Geography and Irish. He failed Mathematics and
Physics. With such a poor Leaving Certificate he had to take a
job in a factory in the Shannon Industrial Estate where he was

inducted to the lathe. He lasted two years until Timmie Stockil got his first full Irish International cap.

In the world of the three-cycle shift Gabriel Storan discovered belatedly why he had not been picked for the Irish Schoolboy International team. It was a labyrinthine revelation that began when he noticed the shift in emphasis in the newspapers from Irish to English soccer. He could not be sure when the change occurred or if it happened overnight; but as far as he could recollect coverage of English soccer in the Irish dailies had always appeared on the bottom left column in the leanest sports page under the heading: CROSS CHANNEL. Now – he was six months on the lathe – he realised that the bottom left column of the leanest sports page was devoted to: ON THE HOME FRONT, pride of place having been allotted to cross-channel, to another country. How had this happened? The answer was all around him in the factory.

Gabriel was in a position to reason at first hand that the multi-national pathfinders in Ireland were set on pre-empting the dumbest Celt's discovery that the three-cycle shift went against the national, indolent grain. The piped music in the factory fulfilled its function of deadening the thought processes but it was still necessary to provide food for the lobotomised appetites. It was here that certain interests had combined, Gabriel deduced. With the abolition of the maximum wage in English football soccer had become a business. Football club directors – businessmen – newspaper moguls – businessmen – and multinational troubleshooters – businessmen – had come together and hatched a plot to plug the individuality gap in football reporting as the first step towards plugging the individual. *They* established a central agency which fed *identical* coverage to any newspaper in the British Isles desirous of receiving same. At first the *Irish Times* heading: Law to Level Liverpool, the *Irish Press* heading: Brom to Blitz Brum, and the *Irish Independent* heading: Man. Utd. Mangle Leeds were all headings over one and the same article on English soccer published in the three Irish newspapers. The headings differed, the articles were word for word identical. Gabriel researched further and discovered that occasionally a conscience-stricken editor juggled paragraphs in an attempt to come up with a format that might have been more identifiable with that newspaper's patois of presentation. But that was a hopeless task. The journalese employed by the central agency was couched to find a snug home in every newspaper from the *Mirror* to the *Telegraph*. The principle of establishing the lowest common denominator all but sufficed. Like currants dropped on to assembly line buns the *Daily Mirror* style was peppered with purple clout to satisfy the man in the pin stripe and bowler on his way to the City.

Heading, in *all* newspapers over *identical* article: Bolton Brio Clobbers Chelsea.

Closer to the bone, in the three cycle shift belt, Gabriel could not help but notice that management and workers, regardless of their taste in dailies, were becoming equally informed of every detail affecting the lives of cross-channel footballers who, because of their new wealth, superseded the pop stars as harbingers of fashion and thought. On the hungover bus on its way to the Shannon Industrial Estate at seven in the morning a nose might extract itself from the *Daily Star* (the basic *Mirror* ingredient had to be diluted by the central agency) and declare: 'I see Spurs were beaten by Chelsea last night.'

Gabriel noted that strikes on the industrial estate were of a frequency higher than in most European countries but he also spotted that they were far short of multi-national predictions of what should have been par for your sensitive and/or lazy Celt. And he saw how this was achieved. Piped music; the central agency's unvarying diet; and the entry from each factory of at least three teams into the inter-firm league. For the sane, Gabriel observed, idle moments were not spent contemplating differentials; they were used in putting replicas of the central agency's notion of footballers on the field. And for the unhinged, he concluded honestly and bitterly, idle moments were consumed with the dream that someday, somehow a wrong would be put right.

Aware of the conspiracy and having traced it from more or less its inception, Gabriel yet allowed himself be sucked into the miasma of common interests. Modestly he played for his factory's 'A' team in the inter-firm league.

In 1966 England won the World Cup without using wingers; Timmie Stockil was capped for the Republic of Ireland – at midfield. Ninety per cent of the work force in the Shannon Industrial Estate hailed from depressed rural areas and their introduction to soccer was through the newly established Irish television station. The television could do no more than show what was going on and what was going on was now the product of the central agency's really putting its shoulder to the wheel. Having converted footballers into pop stars with uniform long hair, every single one of whom uniformly chewed gum, the club directors – businessmen, the newspaper moguls – businessmen, and the multi-national troubleshooters – businessmen, would all be *fucked*, Gabriel realised, if they were going to allow some flashy winger to flaunt himself on television, thereby jarring the carefully orchestrated diet of the three-cycle shift. All it needed was one *prima donna* of a Len Shackleton entertaining himself out on the wing to inspire one *prima donna* of a three-cycle shifter to decide he wanted the piped music turned down, up or off. But all went smoothly. Wingers were redeployed to midfield. England won the World Cup. True, Danny Blanchflower raised a dissentient voice. In his *Sunday Express* column the morning after the final victory Blanchflower suggested that if that was soccer then God help England. No one expected any better from such a blimp and Blanchflower was left to cry in the wilderness without the consolation of knowing that Gabriel Storan, clock number nine hundred and fifty-two, agreed with him.

The manager of the factory's 'A' inter-firm team, Austin Durack, a native of Tulla, Co. Clare, was by nature suspicious of knacky little hoors who came from little streets in cities and so, armed with the authority of his television viewing, his *Star*, *Mirror* and *News of the World* reading, and his never having heard of Len Shackleton, thought Gabriel Storan, where the fortunes of the 'A' inter-firm team were concerned, *the* clown prince of soccer; and dropped him.

At the time Gabriel gained admittance, St Joseph's was no longer an establishment that catered for the half-section prospective heir tormented by greedy relatives who had the connivance of the parish priest. True, it did house a quota of unwanted old and some dangerous lunatics but mostly the inmates were voluntary admissions who complained of pressure; the ability not to throw up a Roche 5 vouchsafed their credibility. Before he summoned the despair to enter Gabriel clutched the wall of St Joseph's for an hour crying silently with rage. He was certain that there was no trace of the lunatic about himself but he could no longer rationalise what he could have done to deserve being passed over for the schoolboy international team. It had been an agony he had done his best to live with. He had suffered the progress that might have been his – Timmie Stockil's – bravely. His reward came in the shape of being dropped from a factory team by a culshe from Tulla. His club directors/newspaper moguls/multi-national troubleshooters thesis no longer sustained him. He began to suspect – despite all the evidence – that his thesis was unsound. Greater brains than his would have exposed the conspiracy. He had heard of pressure but he had no idea what that meant. Did he suffer from pressure, he wondered. Did they have tablets that would take away his unhappiness the way Mrs Cullen's Powders eased toothache? He opened the gate of St Joseph's knowing he was sane and knowing he was sad. He signed a form, was sedated and put to bed.

The following day Gabriel had four meals of a quality far superior to the food served in the industrial estate canteen. He had slept in a comfortable bed. The grounds of the mental hospital contained a pitch and putt course, a football field, a croquet lawn, and pathways and shrubbery to while away a walk. Because of the sedation Gabriel was not fully appreciative of his surroundings and it was not until late in the afternoon, as he wielded a mallet on the croquet lawn, that the pleasant aspects were brought home to him by his companion, an alcoholic named Dineen.

'Better than the Royal George this place. It's breaking my heart to leave. I said to myself this morning, Dineen, you'll be back. MacArthur won't be in it. Go on a batter. Do damage. Your shot. What's wrong with you anyway?'

'I have pressure. Look, I don't know how to play this game.'

'Neither do I. Far from it we were reared. Just give it a poke and try and put it through that thing. That's it. Now you've the hang of it. Short, though. Didn't eat your boiled egg. Pressure? You want to do better than that. They can cure that. Fuck you out into the cold, cold snow. Two rashers and a sausage I had for breakfast. Four cups of tea and loads of brown bread and butter. *Brown*. And a roast for dinner. Horsemeat they give the hardchaws. Someone making a packet somewhere. Take my advice youngfella and stay fucking mad if you can. That was my mistake, the drink. I can't fool them. They know it's the drink

with Dineen. The whole of fucking Mellick knows it's the drink
with Dineen. You take a leaf out of old Martin's book. Over
twenty years he's here. What an act! "I've two uncles dead."
Sorry to hear that Martin. "One of them died ten years ago."
When did the other die, Martin? "He died twenty years ago." I
see. "One of them was no good at hurling." Oh. Was the other
uncle good? "He was useless." A topper, Martin. Maybe he is
daft. Who knows? Your go, son. No, I'll concede that. Next tee
or whatever they call the fucking thing. What's your name
again?'

'Gabriel.'

'Gabriel. That's a good name. Silence, I think. I'd recommend
silence in your case. Back into a corner and squirm. Classic
symptoms.' Dineen lit a cigarette. From the moment he had
first spoken Gabriel discerned immediately that Dineen was a
man of good humour. But now Dineen, briefly, looked down-
hearted. 'Two rashers and a sausage. Roast for dinner. Choice
of a fry or salad for tea. A bed. Television. Croquet. Fuck them
anyway, throwing me out, the cunts. But I'll be back says
MacArthur.'

Gabriel had signed himself in for the minimum fourteen days
committal. Most of the voluntary patients wanted to depart
after twenty-four hours. After leaving Dineen, Gabriel toured
the grounds and contemplated his position. He was not mad.
Yet listening to an alcoholic like Dineen was more soothing
than puncturing the assembly line day in the factory surrounded
by culshies who'd never heard of Len Shackleton. He paused
near the deserted football pitch. It was ironic. Football had
brought him here. And here was his answer. Here was inspiration. He would stick to the truth. If they asked him who made
the world he would tell them of his conspiracy theory. If they
asked him to open wide and say 'Ah' he would tell them again.

The day before Dineen was due to be discharged – they were
playing pitch and putt – he tapped in at the sixth for a seven.

'Yes. Tomorrow the long walk. You know, I got a brilliant
idea last night. Watching Quicksilver. The way the contestants
just sit there having questions shouted at them. You can get
away with that sort of thing on telly, it's respectable, the chap
who asks the questions is a fucking celebrity, but do you think
you'd get away with it on the street? Or in a pub? I doubt it.
Good putt. What's that, a five? Your honour. FORE! But you

know what I mean. Imagine if I had a handful of little pieces of card, say three inches by two and I stopped someone in the street and flashed a card and barked at them, who painted the Laughing Cavalier? I'd be locked up, wouldn't I? I haven't the courage though. I'm going to be too busy drinking. I'm a fucking alcoholic. Sorry. I didn't realise you were about to drive. Take it again, we won't count that.'

The night after Dineen was discharged Gabriel was lonely. He was allowed out at night on condition that he return before eleven but so far he had not taken advantage of this furlough. It dawned on him that he could do with a drink. Gambling that it did not necessarily franc his sanity he asked for and was granted permission to go as far as Dessie Quaid's pub a couple of hundred yards away. He bought a half pint and joined silently with the throng watching television. After the news the Irish team to play Turkey was announced. It was a four-four-two formation with the captain, Timmie Stockil, playing midfield. Gabriel understood then that Dineen was correct: there was happiness behind the high walls. He climbed up on the counter and waved his fist at the television.

'BRING BACK WINGERS.'

Three men were holding him and trying to calm him down.

'I HAVE TWO UNCLES DEAD.'

They were strong men, labourers with rough hands but they were so gentle that they might have been wrapping him in swaddling clothes. In a committee they stood over him with Dessie Quaid himself as the chairman. 'Are you all right now?' Quaid asked with solicitude. Quietly Gabriel answered: 'In what town in Ireland do they have the most chamber pots?' The committee giggled but Dessie Quaid indicated that this was not the right way to treat him. 'It must be Dublin, Dublin has the highest population,' Dessie Quaid answered. 'Correct,' said Gabriel. They were not going to drag him back to the hospital. They were happy that he was calm. He was served another half pint and told it was on the house and then, at Dessie Quaid's instigation, everyone made a point of ignoring him. Gabriel pondered the discovery that extrovert behaviour was tolerable, if not expected, from the deranged. He had raised his voice in anger and release and had been rewarded with a free drink. He felt a contentment that he had never known. He muttered: 'They call it soccer and no wingers.'

Dessie Quaid glanced at Gabriel and then back to his customers. 'It's true for him,' the proprietor said.

While Stanley Callaghan contemplated his soft drink as he listened to Tom Splendid's pocket history of Gabriel Storan as it was known to Tom Splendid, Gabriel went to Brigid's. Tom Splendid had stood him a drink; the gentleman who had come in with his little boy had given him a cigarette and a half pint. And he had started out with two half pints in Dessie Quaid's. And here was Brigid.

'Yourself, Gabriel. And how are you love?'

'Morning.' Gabriel picked up a beer mat, scrutinised it and asked: 'In what town in Ireland was Elizabeth Taylor born?'

'Gabriel, don't be daft now. Here, drink that.'

'In what town in Ireland was Elizabeth Taylor born?'

'Oh, to please you, Listowel.'

'Wrong. Abbeyfeale. In what town in Ireland do the biggest whores come from?' Gabriel read from a second beer mat.

'Be nice now, Gabriel. When I was a lassie they used to say Waterford.'

'Wrong. Adare. In what town . . . '

'That's enough now Gabriel. I've to do the shelves.'

Gabriel took a half-smoked cigarette from his top pocket and lit up. He sipped his half pint. That morning had been his first visit to the Nook since he read about the replay in the *Echo*. He had discovered the Nook five years earlier and had been startled when recognised by Jake O'Dea. Jake O'Dea had mentioned the original match and Gabriel had replied: 'What town in Ireland has the most milliners?'

From time to time Jake O'Dea insisted that Gabriel had played for the Nook but Gabriel either read a question from a beer mat or else repeated: 'Don't remember. Don't remember.'

Gabriel had long ago given up religion and God in return for God having abandoned him but during the past week he had begun to pray again. This was the vindication he had yearned for all those years. To play in a soccer match *against* Timmie Stockil. And for the one team in the world who appreciated wingers.

'He started to come in here four or five years ago. To me he was just one of the unfortunates, I gave him an odd drink, but then Jake was here one day and recognised him as having played for us that time. Jake – when he has the money – often buys him a drink on the strength of it but the funny thing is Gabriel can't remember. He just goes into his act. Reading from beer mats – what town in Ireland has the most chamber pots or else talking about his dead uncles.'

'Does he know anything about the match?'

'I don't know. This is his first time in since the replay came up. I was just about to sound him when you came in.'

'The next time he's here hold on to him and get word to me. I want to talk to him.'

'He'll be here this evening around six. The warders pick him up here. But he'll be very drunk. He's gone off crawling the town.'

'That's good of them, isn't it?'

'It suits them. They put him in the boot of a car and say he's escaped. He's entitled to go out but he's up there so long that they pretend he causes a disturbance in town. Which I suppose he does.'

'Did you say the *boot* of a car?'

'Yes. They drive him out past the gate office. Release him in town and spend the day looking for him.'

Stanley Callaghan looked at his son but could not help saying: 'Jesus.'

In the afternoon Stanley went to the bank. Both sides had agreed without debate that the eleven thousand pounds would have to be paid in before the match. Stanley knew very little of banking practice. His deposit account was modest and the current account received the lodgement of his and Kate's monthly cheques. Money was withdrawn piecemeal throughout the month to pay ESB. Oil and mortgage was charged as a direct debit. He had once toyed with the habit of overdrawing because he thought being a few pounds in the red fitted his professional image. A curt note from the bank disabused him of this.

Stanley had some idea that he would have to make an appointment or at least be made to wait a half hour or so. But he was shown directly into the manager's office. The manager was standing with his hands in his pockets staring out the window. He nodded at a chair. 'Sit down. Make yourself comfortable.'

'Thank you.'

'I detest being idle,' the manager continued and remained standing. 'Our business – mine, the assistant managers and one or two others – our business is merely to oversee lending. Anyone,' the manager threw back his head in the direction of, Stanley interpreted, the general staff, 'anyone can take in money. We oversee lending. And I can tell you, sir, and this is not a confidence, we will not have any work to do for another ten months because, believe it or not, money *is* tight. The central bank is merciless.'

Stanley was oddly flattered. He said: 'I see.'

The manager's last remark to the window was: 'Ah well.' He sat down, produced a packet of tipped.

'Smoke?'

'No thanks.'

'You don't indulge?'

'I prefer the non-tipped.'

'What can I do for you, sir?'

'I wanted to negotiate a loan. But if there's a squeeze on . . . '

'Every case on its merits. Mister . . . ?'

'Callaghan. Stanley Callaghan.'

'Mr Callaghan. Frawley. John Frawley.' The manager extended his hand. 'So. A loan. In the amount?'

'Eleven thousand.'

'That's a sizeable figure.'

'It's only a temporary loan.'

'Have you securities?'

'I'm told – you see my house was valued last year – I'm told it's worth at least thirty-two thousand five hundred. And the original mortgage was around the three thousand. I thought I'd be covered there for eleven thousand in a second mortgage.'

'Well covered. But you said it was a *temporary* loan. What do you mean exactly? There's no such thing as a permanent loan. But *how* temporary?'

'Anything from a day to a week. A week at the outside.'

The manager had a round face and half a dozen sandy strands of hair partitioned his otherwise bald head. Though he did not smile it was plain that he was a jovial individual. He pushed his horn-rimmed spectacles down his nose and peered at Stanley.

'A day? A day? And the purpose?'

'I beg your pardon?' Stanley's interrogative ran together and was not icy. It conveyed surprise.

'We have to ask. I'm not prying I hope you understand. For one thing it might be possible to facilitate you without the rigmarole of a second mortgage. I say "might". Money is tight at the moment.'

'Oh. I see. Well, it's all rather juvenile, I'm afraid. And it's a long story. How will I put it? It's a bet actually. I have a bet with a chap and I only need the money in case I lose. Mind you, I won't lose. In fact I expect to be in to lodge my winnings.'

'A *bet*? Ahah! I know. Callaghan, that's it. That's the name. You're the teacher? That pub and the Institute. It's the soccer match, am I right?'

Stanley nodded.

'I didn't know you were with us. I've followed your progress before, you know. That strike. The Locky incident. This is wonderful. Wonderful.'

'Is money – loosening?'

The manager chuckled. He stood up and went to the window. He thrust his hands thoughtfully into his jacket pockets, the thumbs sticking out in military fashion. After a couple of minutes he sat down. He nibbled at his biro. He said 'hmm'. Finally he clasped his hands in front of him on the desk.

'Mr Callaghan, do you mind if I speak as John Frawley – man to man – rather than John Frawley, banker?'

'Not at all.'

'We must tread warily. I was fond of the turf myself as a young man. You'd be forty? Forty-two?'

'Thirty-eight.'

'Exactly. Now how am I to put this to you without offence? I'll speak delicately – if you'll indulge me. Now. I don't think mortgage is our answer. Far from it. Anyway, it's not banking policy to chuck people on to the side of the road. Not done. Unless as a last resort. Now don't get me wrong. As I said, I was fond of a flutter. I read the O'Grady chap's column and I think I can read between the lines. But I must tell you about John Frawley the banker. He looks for – for *stability*. John Frawley the banker looks for stability.' The manager leaned across the desk and almost whispered: 'He's *not* a sportsman. *Not*. Quite definitely.' The manager winked. Stanley nodded in return.

'What are we talking about after all? We're talking about money here. Money to your banker now, money is like a little puppy to your spinster – we think of good homes, if you follow, where one can anticipate respect . . . I don't know if you're with me?'

'I'm not,' Stanley said mildly.

'No matter. Only testifies that I'm on the right, the *delicate*, track. You're married? Children?'

'One boy.'

'Hmm. Just the one?'

'Yes. It was something to do with pituitary glands.' John Frawley, man or banker, Stanley was not sure to whom he was now listening, coughed delicately.

'Yes, of course. I understand. Insurance?'

'If I died in this seat my wife would come into forty thousand.'

'Good. Your good wife has a position?'

'She's a secondary teacher.'

'Excellent. Excellent. Now, to sum: House valued thirty-two thousand five hundred, insurance forty thousand, two solid professional incomes, modest demands on resources. You would agree with John Frawley – man to man – good collateral.'

'That's what I hoped.'

'Of course you did. And what are we talking about? Eleven thousand. Eleven thousand pounds for the right purpose. *The right purpose.* Are we coming closer – may I call you Stanley – do I detect a meeting of minds?

'You're turning me down.'

'Please, Stanley. We're being precipitate. John Frawley, banker, is talking about money. Mon-*eey*. He has to report to his Regional Manager. About money. The Regional Manager . . . take the computer. *Very* delicate stomach. Imagine feeding it a wager as distinct, say, from that compact back garden swimming pool?'

Stanley nodded. 'I understand.' A suffusion of gratitude enabled John Frawley – man to man – to sink back in his chair. He rounded off: 'Stability. You understand. We were all sportsmen once. It's Cheltenham week, isn't it? God, there was a time. Gone from it now. Swimming pools. Car ports. A modest boat. A pair of mobile homes. There's a thought, Stanley. What dish shall we serve the computer.'

Despite the manager's geniality and the fact that there were so few about now who made the effort to be cordial, Stanley shook his head. 'I want eleven thousand pounds to wager that my old pub will beat the Institute.'

'Mr Callaghan,' John Frawley – man to man still – injected a quiet astonishment into his timbre, 'I'm doing my best. I thought you understood.'

'I do. I don't want a swimming pool in my back garden. *Or* a modest boat. I want money for a bet. Can you facilitate me?'

'You reward me with implacability. Why? I don't understand.'

'I'm honest.'

'Honest?' The manager symbolically washed his hands. 'So be it then.' A red spot appeared on the upper left side of his forehead. 'John Frawley – man to man – has failed. And honourably, I take the liberty of believing. Now here's a word from your banker: In cold blood you confront me with a lack of stability. Have you any idea of the consequences were I not to remain obdurate? Do you seriously expect me to stand by and watch the financial wheels grind to a halt, undermined by the inoperable rust of flippancy?'

'You will not facilitate me?'

'Facilitate you? I'm *trying* to facilitate you. You won't let me.'

'Would you lend me the money on a guarantee?'

John Frawley could not avoid smirking. He managed a paragraph of scepticism in one word. 'Whose?'

'Have you ever heard of Dara Holden?'

'Of course. I watched him last night.'

'Does he deal with your crowd on this side of the Atlantic or your – your blood brothers in the States?'

John Frawley, both man and banker, was frankly appalled in the face of such innocence.

'I'm sure you can take it that he deposits – ubiquitously?'

'I understand. Who knows, maybe there might be a possibility of my persuading him to deposit with a little more – narrow-mindedness? Anyway, Dara Holden will act as guarantor. If that's acceptable.'

'Yes, yes. Of course it is. But – do you mind, I don't want to interfere, I'm only thinking of saving you the trouble of unnecessary paper work, but wouldn't, couldn't Dara Holden simply put up the money?'

'No.'

'No?'

'No. Suppose I call in again in a month or so with Dara Holden, will the paper work and that take long?'

'Two minutes.'

'Thank you. It's been a pleasure talking to you.'

'The pleasure is all mine – Stanley.'

Kate halted the fork en route to her mouth. 'You were with whom?'

'Dr Jekyll and Mr Hyde.'

Stanley recounted his interview with the bank manager and drew from Kate: 'He implied you were off your head?'

'One of him did. Damn it, I have to get Dara to sign a guarantee. He'll love that. Bankers. Implying I'm crazy. I had visions of riding around in the boot of a car, like Gabriel.'

'Pardon?'

'I heard that this morning. That's what they do to Gabriel. The warders. When they want a day off they put him in the boot of a car and smuggle him out and then pretend he's escaped. *They* should be in the boot of the car, and this Frawley fellow. Kate I have to rush out again. I have to see Gabriel. I'll try not to be late.'

It was just after half five when Stanley reached the Nook. Jake O'Dea and Cocoa Brown were there for their regular pre-tea drink. But the first person Stanley saw was Bazook. The goalkeeper looked even smaller than Stanley remembered him. He had the predictable porter belly. He had sideburns and a moustache and had let what he had of his hair grow. His teeth were as prominent as ever. Small, fat, balding, buck-toothed – Bazook ran the gamut of establishment ugliness. The three of them – Jake, Cocoa and Bazook – stood leaning against the counter a few yards away from each other. They might have been strangers. A handful of people unknown to Stanley sat by the fireplace watching what was supposed to be a children's programme on the television. Bazook bared his gums in recognition: 'Hello, Stanley. Long time no see.'

'How are you, Bazook. You're looking fit.'

Bazook tapped his stomach. 'I don't feel fit. I feel fucked. Is it really true we're playing this crowd again? No one is having me on?'

'We're playing them, Bazook. And we're going to beat them

with the help of your cat like saves. Seven Up,, Tom, please.'

'Splendid job.'

'I couldn't dive to save my mother.'

Stanley turned to Cocoa. 'Tolly?' Cocoa shook his head. 'No problem. He just wants to know who's going to lift him on to the pitch and who'll tie his boots.'

'He has a sense of humour then?'

'If that's what you'd call it. Anyone who can laugh at twenty-stone must be sick.'

Stanley looked at Jake O'Dea. Neither of them spoke. Stanley turned back to the proprietor. 'Where's Gabriel?'

'He's been in and out half a dozen times since this morning. He's well cut. I told him you wanted to see him but he has no idea who you are. Speak of the devil . . . '

'What town in Ireland has the cleanest streets?'

Gabriel stood smiling innocently in the doorway. He was drunk. Gabriel was not in his fifties, Stanley could now see that but he certainly looked older than thirty-two. The ill-fitting Martin Henry suit might indeed have been inherited from a dead uncle so posthumously avuncular was it cut. His teeth were yellowing. A hair grew out of his nose.

'What town in Ireland has the cleanest streets?' Gabriel repeated, this time impatiently. He directed the question at Stanley.

'Adare.'

'Wrong. Mellick.'

Nobody laughed when Stanley did not laugh. Jake O'Dea cut in: 'Gabriel, everyone knows Mellick has the dirtiest streets in Ireland.'

Gabriel ploughed on. 'What town in Ireland has the most whores?'

'Listowel,' Jake replied.

'Wrong. Killarney.'

'The last time you were here it was Listowel.'

'They were thrown out of Listowel.' He was rewarded with laughter now even though Stanley still did not laugh. 'In what town . . . ' Stanley grabbed his arm and held it firmly.

'Listen. My name is Stanley Callaghan. You played for the Nook fifteen years ago. We have to play again. We need you. What do you say, will you play for us?'

Gabriel shook himself free and went to the end of the bar

where he had been stationed that morning.

'Pint, Tom.'

'A half pint, Gabriel.'

'Pint.'

'They'll be here for you in a minute.'

'Pint.'

'Now, Gabriel ... '

'Tom, give him the pint.'

'If you say so, Stanley. Splendid job.'

The Nook was suddenly very quiet. Bazook, Cocoa and Jake nursed their drinks as they watched Stanley Callaghan watching Gabriel. The customers watching Tom and Jerry had not taken their eyes from the set when Gabriel made his entrance. Gabriel stared straight ahead of him until his pint was placed before him. He took a sip and then, quietly, to no one in particular, said simply: 'I'll play.'

Jake O'Dea pounced upon him, patted him on the back and hugged him. Cocoa and Bazook cheered. Gabriel brushed Jake away shyly. Tom said: 'Splendid job.' And suddenly there was silence again. Stanley was content to sip his Seven Up and smoke a cigarette. Gabriel took a mighty sup from his pint and declared: 'I've no gear.'

'You don't need any gear, Gabriel,' Jake O'Dea told him. He was beginning to realise that Gabriel, far from being a liability, was probably their star turn. 'I'll look after all that. We're getting a present of jerseys, socks, tights, boots ... '

'No boots. I won't wear boots.' Gabriel spoke reasonably.

'What are you going to kick the ball with?'

'No boots. I hate boots.' Again he was firm but not hysterical.

'Gabriel ... '

'FUCK OFF.' Now he was hysterical.

He took his drink from the counter and sat on the floor with his back to the corner, muttering to himself. Stanley Callaghan walked over to him.

'You don't have to wear boots. You can play in your bare feet if it suits you.'

'Can I wear tackies?' Gabriel smiled up at Stanley. It was an innocent smile.

'Of course you can. Jake will get you a brand new pair of tackies. That right, Jake?'

'Fresh from the factory.'

'Not new. An old pair. I don't want to have to break them in . . . '

Seated on the floor, Gabriel's head began to go from side to side as though he were following the play at a match. 'In under his legs, nip around him, bang, top corner of the net . . . '

And then he began to cry. He remained sitting on the floor, his eyes bloodshot, sipping his pint and whimpering. Tom and Jerry ended and the Angelus pealed. Everyone rose for its duration. At the door of the Nook one of the male nurses said to his mate: 'He's here.' Gabriel was immediately on his feet. He jumped on to the window ledge on which rested the television. He clung to the set and cried: 'Don't beat me, sir. Please don't beat me.'

'Now don't start that, Gabriel. Tom, three pints. I'm getting you a pint, Gabriel, and then we're off. So don't start.'

Gabriel remained on the window ledge. Stanley looked from him to the male nurses. They were continuing a conversation apparently broken by their arrival in the Nook. It was about a horse that would have made up a treble if it had won instead of finishing third. Nothing that Stanley knew of Mellick was more redolent of normality than a horse failing to make up a treble; if they were Gabriel beaters they were cool about it. The drink was put on the counter by Tom Splendid. One of the male nurses shouted: 'Come on, Gabriel. Come down and drink it.'

Gabriel didn't move. Stanley took the pint from the counter and brought it over to him. He held out the glass and motioned Gabriel down. Slowly Gabriel descended. He beamed at the nurses: 'You can beat me now, sir.'

Stanley went back to where he had been standing beside the male nurses. 'Tough job?' he enquired politely.

'Ah, you wouldn't want to pay too much attention to Gabriel. The way he carries on anyone would think he's off his head.'

'Isn't he?'

The male nurse laughed: 'Yes, of course he is, officially, but you know what I mean. Who's sound? Who's unsound? Who knows? I'm ten years at this lark and I can tell you the line is blurred.'

'Tell me this. Have you heard about this match that's coming up?'

'Heard of it? We're hearing nothing else for this past fortnight. He's in training. Running around the grounds above with a towel around his neck.'

'Will he be let out to play?'

'Of course. Leave it to us. We'll see to it.'

Gabriel was seated on the floor again. He couldn't hear the conversation as it hadn't risen above a whisper. But Stanley spoke a little louder now and Gabriel could hear: 'Don't bring him out in the boot of the car. He must sit in the back seat with the windows down, in full view.'

Both the nurses coloured and one of them snapped: 'What exactly do you mean by that?'

Stanley drained his glass of Seven Up. He looked around him and saw Bazook, Cocoa and Jake O'Dea. Jake O'Dea took his free hand out of his pocket. Stanley would have preferred to see Stevie Mack. But he carried on.

'You know what I mean. Bring him out in style.'

The nurses looked at each other. The bigger of the two had been sitting on a stool. He stood up.

'Just who the hell do you think you are? We don't have to take that kind of talk from you.'

'You do have to take that kind of talk from me, sir. Now take Gabriel back and be nice to him. And bring him out in style the day of the match. Good evening to you.' Stanley paused at the door. 'Otherwise we'll go in and bring him out ourselves.' The big male nurse opened his mouth but Stanley was gone. He shrugged at his partner and then said: 'All right, Gabriel. Let's go.'

Without glancing back, they left. Gabriel followed them. Cocoa Brown and Bazook and Jake O'Dea avoided each other's eyes. Jake O'Dea blushed with embarrassment. He finished his drink and went home to his tea.

7

Breakfast

There was a full muster at the Institute breakfast in the Royal George Hotel. Tony O'Neill, the eldest of the O'Neills, delivered his four brothers. Bertie and Stafford Foy were present. And Robert Flanagan. Henry Corr presided. Excusably absent were Timmie Stockil and Ralph O'Shea. Bertie Foy was the first to order. He asked for bacon, egg and sausage. His brother Stafford, Robert Flanagan and the five O'Neills indicated they would have the same. Henry Corr was dressed in a blue pin-striped executive suit. He had taken a shower at six and shaved. He glared over his menu at his sleepy companions.

'What kinda stomachs you guys got?' He turned to the poised waitress. 'Orange juice, four slices of toast lightly done, not burned please, honey, a few plain scones with margarine, not butter, coffee with cream, no sugar.' The waitress departed on his last word having scribbled with the speed of a shorthand typist. 'Okay, we work while we eat. We'll start with you, Staff. What's it with you?'

'How d'you mean, Henry?'

'What's your ambition?' Henry Corr patiently made himself clear.

'I'm a bit old for ambition now, Henry.'

'Horse manure. That's the trouble around here. People retired at thirty. Staff, you and Bertie got your old man's printing works and you know what your problem is? You run it like it was your old man's time. What'd I ask you on the colour brochures? You said you don't do colour, what kind of dumb answer's that? My goddamn business cards, you don't do embossed. You know what I said to myself the very first day in the office? I said Staff and Bertie will be along any minute chasing the account. Jesus, Staff, printing is our *raw material*. Do

I hear from you? No. *I* ring *you*. And all I hear is we don't do this, we don't do that. You know, your two kissers weren't in this photograph you could go and fuck yourselves. But I'm not like that. I wouldn't do that. Just because I had to fight my way to the top where its tough at the top *and* the middle *and* the bottom, I'm not an animal . . . '

The waitress began to serve the fries. Henry Corr did an obvious double take and then said: 'I'm not really hungry, sweetheart. Don't worry too much about me.'

'I'll be with you in a moment, sir. I've only two hands,' the waitress snapped and departed.

'See what I mean? Everyone has an excuse. I know the bitch has only two hands. You think this hotel, getting eight people for breakfast on a regular basis is going to find another bitch with another two hands? No fucking way. That'd be thinking. Okay, Timmie and Ralph, they're in action regular, we have only us here to whip into shape and I'm not just talking about bodies . . . ' The waitress brought the remainder of the fries. There was no sign yet of the orange juice, toast, scones or coffee. Henry Corr stared angrily at her. She out-stared him back. Everyone else began to gobble their breakfasts.

'How does it take so long to serve orange juice, toast, scones and coffee here? Because nothing has changed in this damn country. There must be an assembly line of that greasy shit in there. Don't any of you guys have ulcers? If you worked in the rat race you'd have ulcers.'

The waitress brought Henry Corr's breakfast and laid it before him. He said, uncharacteristically it seemed to his team members, 'Thank you honey, thank you.' He threw back his orange juice and grimaced. He tasted the coffee. 'Christ! Okay, let's stay with it. Staff, I ring you some morning I want yankee-doodle-dandy printed embossed in full colour on an enamel bucket, you say "right on" and go figure how it's done. I don't wanna know your fucking problems, Staff. Gettin' there's a state of mind. Fifteen years I been waitin' to get those Nook cowboys. Here, Tony, what am I lookin' at here? Five O'Neills all in brokerage, how many O'Neills kicked down my door to put in pensions, how many? Fuck all, that's how many. I had to put the words into your mouth. Okay, okay, this is Ireland, not New York. I know. I know by this fucking bog of toast in front of me. The minute I put my foot in Shannon Airport, no need to tell me this is Ireland, everyone goin' around in their goddamn sleep. Now I want to level with you on this, America might not be heaven but it has its good points and I brought 'em back with me. So what have we got? Huh?'

Henry Corr first looked at Staff and Bertie Foy, both of whom managed to return his look without saying anything, having nothing to say. The O'Neills did not take their eyes from their plates save for the eldest, Tony, who got them into this situation and whom they expected to get them out of it fast – each person was *paying* for his own breakfast. This was the first formal gathering. A few days earlier Henry had telephoned Tony O'Neill and instructed him to haul his ass over to meet him. He had given the elder O'Neill a dozen OTIS cards for distribution – Original Thinking Induces Success. The youngest O'Neill – Eric – who had been only fourteen when the Institute played the Nook commented to his brothers irreverently: OTIS means Going Dutch. And he had also ribbed Tony by asking: 'Have you to bring your ass with you to the breakfast?'

'Fellas, am I talking to myself? Tony, what do you think? Straight up, will we beat the Nook?'

'We should beat them on paper.'

'Yeah?'

'Their goalie's small . . . '

'Fucking midget you mean. Fucking cock . . . '

' . . . and another player is in the mental home. The twins, the Lewis's, were hopeless and I never heard of any of them playing again.'

'What do they do?'

'I don't know.'

'You should know. Find out. All right. Go on.'

'Another chap's in England. Stevie Mack, he's a real tough character . . . '

'I remember. Cunt put the boot in.'

'Tolly Holliday, he's a taxi driver now. He's so fat he could be in a circus. Dara Holden could hardly be fit. Though he was a sound player. Stanley Callaghan isn't great, it's all in his head. Johnny Green is okay but he won't be fit either. Cocoa Brown, well, you saw him. He's like an old man.'

'Who else? This Jake O'Dea.'

'He beat us on his own last time.'

'Now, Tony, get that out of your head. He didn't beat us, they didn't beat us, we beat the motherfuckers by five clear goals, an honest referee . . . '

'Henry, he was our referee. Ronnie West is a member of the Institute.'

'Bloody Englishman. A fair play merchant. Leaned over backwards to show he wasn't biased. None of that this time. You get through to him, Tony.'

Motherfuckers and cocksuckers did not shock Tony O'Neill as much as the suggestion that Ronnie West might be approachable in that light.

'Henry, if Ronnie was a Catholic he'd be at mass and communion every day. As it is he's a practising campanologist.'

'Don't hand me hundred dollar words. What is he, a scout-master?'

'He's a bellringer. He's the only non-Catholic ringer in the Redemptorists. He's even more respected than Stanley Callaghan.'

'Callaghan. That motherfucker respected. Okay, go on. Jake O'Dea.'

'He's the best soccer player I've ever seen in my life.' Tony O'Neill spoke boldly and looked around the table and was rewarded by nodded corroboration, even from Robert Flanagan who did not like to draw attention to himself. Robert Flanagan had not yet married. He wore spotted dickey-bows and a coloured handkerchief in his breast pocket. It was common knowledge that he drank in a literary pub with odd bods. It was generally known that Robert Flanagan was a – but nobody liked to dwell on that.

'Okay. They've one man. We got Timmie Stockil for that.'

'He's better than Timmie Stockil.'

'Christ, Tony, Timmie Stockil plays first division in England.'

'I don't care where he plays. Jake O'Dea is better.'

'All right. Still one man. What's this about on paper? Why only on paper?'

'I'm not saying only on paper. We should hammer them. We've Timmie, Ralph. We're all fit from tennis and hockey. Staff and Bertie play squash and . . . and . . . '

'I'm in shape. Don't worry about me. When the going gets tough I get going. Had to, to be where I am today. So none of this paper shit. We're better and we'll beat them. Think positive. Now what about them? Are we in touch?'

Eric O'Neill responded to his brother's glance.

'I met Jake O'Dea coming from work yesterday. He says they're down to a hundred cigarettes a day . . . he says they'll stuff us.' Eric O'Neill had all the rashness of his youthful twenty-nine years of age. He smiled at his report.

'Yeah, they're the type of bunch would think that funny. Cheap wit. One thing I can't stand is cheap wit. I have a good sense of humour, you have to to get on in the world, but if that's funny count me out. Still, I don't trust them. O'Dea, Callaghan, none of them. Low class fuckers. A teacher, okay, how'd he get to be a teacher? Good at fuck all else. The rest of them glorified messenger boys. Pop singers. Taxi drivers. That Bazook freak, Christ, he was a docker. And that half-assed actor. Right. We're clear. Let's affirm this in our minds: We're the better side, we're going to win. But we're going to make sure. You, Eric, how fast can you run twelve miles?'

The youngest O'Neill forced himself not to laugh. He tended the clerical side of the brokerage, not having had much interest in insurance in the first place, not grave enough to confront people with the benefits that would accrue to them on their demise. He answered simply: 'I don't know.'

'How come?'

'I never ran twelve miles.'

'How far did you jog?'

'I never jogged.'

'Jesus. They're jogging in America at eight fucking years of age.' Eric O'Neill took out his cigarettes; he did not any more have the strength to face Henry Corr and he did not have the courage to laugh. 'Don't jog and cigarettes for breakfast. Bacon and shit fried in grease. Jesus. Think clean! All right, all right, all right.' Henry Corr relented, closing his eyes to induce the serenity to continue softly: 'Eight of us, tomorrow morning at half five, track suits and running shoes. Twelve miles. We're going to establish each other's pain threshold and we're going to crash it . . . '

Although all of his brothers and the Foys and Robert Flanagan stared at their plates Tony O'Neill knew they were spiritually looking at him.

'Henry, we're only playing a soccer match, not the Olympics.'

'We're not *playing* anything, Tony. We have a – clear – goal. And we achieve that like any other goal in life by method and

application and the elimination of anything that interferes –
cigarettes are out, the fucking frying pan is out, you guys can
fuck up your stomachs *after* we beat the Nook.'

Stafford and Bertie Foy were at their printing works at quarter
past eight, three quarters of an hour before any of the staff of
seven ever turned up. The brothers did not as much as take the
covers off the machines; they did not know how to operate
them. The business fell into their laps when their father died.
They added 'and Sons' to the Charles Foy masthead and left the
work to the workers. It was now the last letterpress-only shop in
the country and as such, the last craftsman's house.

'It's not my fault,' Bertie Foy exonerated himself.

'And it's certainly not mine. Tony O'Neill dragged us into
this. Anyway, you think I'm running twelve miles at half five in
the morning? You could be arrested for that. End up like that
Gabriel, in the loony bin.'

'Hold on, Staff. Think. You heard what Henry said. Printing
is their *raw material*.'

'Yeah. That's when I switched off. They're not as thick in the
States as Henry'd lead you to believe. They'll fly over a half
dozen A.B. Dick's when they see what printing in Ireland costs
them.'

'Maybe. But it'll take at least a year until they look at the
audited accounts. Might even go fifteen to seventeen months.
Staff, we could *milk* them for a year.'

'If we live that long running twelve miles in the middle of the
night. Embossed cards! Full colour! Bertie, we have five
printers, the youngest is forty-eight. You see what Monday is
like with sick heads? They have a job centering a black and
white letterhead in the middle of an A4. They haven't even
accepted A4, what am I talking about, they still say quarto and
foolscap. After being pisseyed drunk Sunday, can you imagine
them *registering* four colours? They'd go on strike. Close us
down.'

'Staff, take it handy. Let me deal with it. I'm younger than
you are.'

'Yeah. Well it won't be me. I can't handle people like Henry.
It's America. I mean look at what he calls the simple letterhead.
He doesn't want anything fancy for DATALOG, just computer

lettering and gold ink, *gold* for Manufacturers of Integrated Circuits. Keep it simple, he says, eight point italics will do. Then the directors. I mean, Bertie, this is a simple letterhead. American directors: J. Martinez, E. Kumm, R. Eckert, E.Z. Jones, fine, no trouble, they can be in eight point italic as well, just when you're doing H. Corr, the Irish director, print the name in silver in keeping with company policy abroad. Bertie, when Chucky Lysaght comes in this morning belching and farting, would *you* like to hand him that simple little job . . . '

8

The Referee

Ronnie West's tongue protruded like a safety net to catch the
single tear that had taken so long to navigate his cheek. His
fawn clad foot rested on an antique coffee table as he lay back
on the settee in his luxury flat and clasped his fingers together
behind his bald fifty-nine-year-old head. The fruits of temperance, they had called the flat and furniture, though he was a half
dozen sherry man in company but of course they measured
drink by the score of pints and bottles of whiskey. He did not let
loose the tear at the memory of his first nine years in the public
house in St Ives of which he thought his parents were the
owners; he did not sigh at the revelation that his mother Bridie
West (née Dunne) had been the barmaid and his father Henry
the governor's right hand man; the uprooting in response to an
advertisement in the Mellick *Leader* to the gate lodge in the
Institute no longer caused him pain. His father had explained:
'Your mother did cough a lot. Never expected TB though. We
were hardly settled in when she went.' The Institute committee
went into four hour conclave, emerging with the proposal that
Henry West be allowed to stay on if he thought that, with the
help of young Ronnie, he could look after what was always
thought of up to then as the distaff side of things. The double
salary was no longer on though. Salary and a half was the best
they thought they could manage. The boy was only ten.

Before school every morning Ronnie West helped his father
at the distaff side of things – cleaning and waxing the pavilion
on his knees. At four Ronnie was proud to be traipsing around
after his father cutting the grass, putting out the stumps, lining
the hockey pitch or tennis court or helping stock up the bar for
the night which Henry would tend while Ronnie ploughed on

with his school work. These were happy memories; helping his father.

And, though he didn't understand how now, he had been content playing tennis against himself with an abandoned racquet on wet November evenings. He lobbed the ball high over the net and ran to return his own serve. And he distinctly remembered being happy to insinuate himself into an out of bounds fielding position at cricket and standing behind the hockey goals as a retriever. 'Young fellow,' Major Ring called him. 'Young fellow, do this. Young fellow do that.' The plate in Major Ring's head dated from the first world war. Those were happy days. As was the occasion when another young fellow – who went on to become the father of the O'Neills – challenged him to one set, a duel witnessed by Major Ring from his Oldest Member eyrie by the bay window of the pavilion. Both young fellows were admonished that night, O'Neill by Major Ring and young Ronnie by his father. *That* memory could not draw a tear now either. But it must have been the end of the happy days because there was a gap in his recollections of Institute incidents during which he studied assiduously and allowed his father to perform on his own.

Ronnie West came tenth in Ireland in the junior executive civil service examinations and was posted to the Cork tax office. He joined Three Rock Rovers as a non-playing member and took to refereeing the hockey matches. Transferred, on promotion, to Dublin he became a social member of Lansdowne R.F.C. where after three years he was appointed assistant fixtures secretary and also refereed with an implacable impartiality that was rewarded with his being given the Leinster Schools Junior Cup Final. His eventual return to Mellick as Tax Inspector occurred one week before the death of his father. He had by now also refereed League of Ireland soccer matches, not that there was any upward mobility attached to that carry on. But it served to round him off as the complete referee. In any match in any code Ronnie West only saw two different sets of jerseys to be punished or rewarded on merit and if some team was seventy years since winning a trophy and that team was trailing fifty-eight points to nil with a second to full time and committed an infringement, then that team was penalised. And if the Pope's favourite cousin captained the same team and used an expletive then the Pope's cousin had an early shower.

In short, his fame had gone abroad and he was heartily welcomed home to the Institute and so much had the times changed that he was invited to take out membership. That was a happy week for him. He remembered having to stay at the lodge while he searched for a suitable flat; and he remembered modestly admitting to being in the tax office. He was three days a member of the Institute when his father died of a stroke. There was a big turnout at the funeral and his hand was well shaken in the pavilion. He moved his things immediately to temporary accommodation in an hotel not wanting to in any way inhibit the appointment of his father's replacement which item was naturally foremost on the agenda of the weekly committee meeting.

On the night of the meeting Ronnie West happened to be in the pavilion and was surprised to be summoned to assist the committee in its deliberations. At this stage of the century there was no one on the committee with a plate in his head from any war but all the same there was a sufficient presence of the past for it to ensue that he be offered his late father's position. Cleaning ladies would be brought in to see to the distaff side of things and with the membership as it stood the bar would need strong management what with stock control and the proliferation of late night functions. Cognisance would be taken both of the perk of the lodge and the need for a salary assessment commensurate with what he was receiving in the tax office. At any rate the particulars could be ironed out as they presented themselves; the main point was that it was the consensus that they should not go for a new man; after a thirty year tenure it was felt the West incumbency should be perpetuated.

Ronnie West drew on the even temper of the referee within him to subdue his horror. He might have been a Pierrepoint. He choked back his bile under the guise of throat-clearing preparatory to speech. While he was conscious of the honour, he told the committee, he thought he should point out that, strictly in the interests of sound husbandry, he did not think any treasurer or auditor worth his salt would sanction a caretaker's salary equal to that of a tax inspector. With one gasp the committee agreed with him. No one had realised he was the *Inspector*. They adjourned the meeting and hauled him out to the pavilion and stood him drinks and as he mellowed vengeance swelled up inside him. Had they not insulted him he would have used his position for their good. But now they would pay for their sins. Within a year they would all be so in hock to his knowledge of their affairs that he would *be* the Institute.

That had been all of twenty years ago and he was now as much the Institute as ever he would be thanks to his age and the death of the old guard. And the Institute was all new money now, a shower of hustlers in comparison with the old days. As for that Corr individual. He did remember the original match. The lack of crossbars had been a godsend. That had been his finest hour converting a rout in favour of the Institute into a victory for those public house messenger boys. But that awful moment when young Corr refused to shake hands after the match! It was as well that nobody possessed of a plate in his head was around to witness that. He had had to send one of the O'Neills to the public house to apologise on behalf of the Institute. Mercifully Corr shoved off to the only Irish colony there was – America. Only to apparently escape and turn up among them again after fifteen years, stir crazy, and dissipate what remained of the tone. Ronnie West had been in the bar politely explaining to the Foys that they could not claim a refund of five years value added tax on a leased printing machine on which they had paid one month's rent when Corr had burst in shouting 'Hi' and announcing 'drinks for the house', a vulgarity Ronnie West had never before witnessed in the club. And later when he heard 'cocksucker' unmistakably for the second time he had been obliged to point out to Corr that he was no longer in America. Corr had replied, apparently contritely: 'Sorry fella. Dickens still rules OK? That's okay by me.'

Eleven thousand pounds the fellow stood to lose. It was probably true that America was a great country for money. They had all thought him a great fellow to have purchased a luxury flat for twenty thousand – the mere cost of a house at the time. The 'fruits of temperance'. They saw little wrong with any of themselves owning a house and being able to guzzle spirits. They saw no contradiction in this. When they looked at him they saw no tax inspector. They still saw the caretaker's son, worse, the man who would be caretaker had he known his place. He could still cry at that. The same teams, the same old rules, the same referee. He trusted the Nook would help him this time. No crossbar – surely they must understand the blatancy of propping a midget between the posts would not succeed a second time. All he wanted was anything remotely like a close game and he would do his bit.

9

Training

Cocoa Brown, Bazook, Jake O'Dea, Tom and Joe Lewis, the twins, Tolly Holliday and Johnny Green all now haunted the Nook again to savour developments so far. But they were often a gloomy group. They felt they should be doing something or that something should be done. It was unnatural to carry on as they were especially since Johnny Green, returning from a late gig, claimed to have seen nine of the Institute team running in the dark at half five in the morning. At first Jake O'Dea tried to persuade himself that he did not believe this news, that Johnny was on drugs or something. But then news came from an unexpected source. A sister of Tom and Joe Lewis worked as a receptionist in the Royal George and she heard from a waitress that the Institute arrived every morning for a shower and breakfast at seven. The twins' sister also learned from the waitress that they used foul language talking about the Nook. It was dragged out of their sister by the twins that they called the Nook cowboys and cocksuckers. Cocoa Brown reported to Stanley Callaghan who commented: 'Good work. See that they keep it up and see that I'm informed.'

'Informed? What has fucking informed got to do with it? What are *we* going to do, Stanley? We're all in the Nook every night. Why aren't you? Do you intend meeting us the morning of the match?'

'Relax, Cocoa. We'll meet when Dara and Stevie show up. Time enough to talk.'

'Who's talking about talk? What about training?'

'Please, Cocoa. We're amateurs. Gentlemen. Training indeed.'

'Come on, Stanley. What do I tell the lads?'

'Tell them not to panic. We lost a lot of men at Dunkirk through panic.'

Cocoa and Jake O'Dea discussed Stanley's response in the snug where all decisions relating to the match were plotted. The two of them represented Stanley Callaghan.

'Cocoa, I think you're right. Get me a pint there while I figure this out.' Cocoa ordered through the hatch. 'A thousand quid a man there for the taking. My God. Maybe Stanley thinks the Institute will burn themselves out.'

'Listen, we'll burn ourselves out bending down to tie our boots. He's a lunatic, Jake. It's as simple as that.'

'I know, Cocoa. I know. Give us one of your fags there a minute. I agree with you, Coke.' The crafty use of the diminutive almost stuck in Jake's throat. 'Here's what we'll do. All day tomorrow both of us will try and think of some plan. I'm not good at thinking. That was always your department, Coke. I'm depending on you. We'll meet here tomorrow night and put our heads together . . . shit!'

'What's wrong?'

'Molly.' Jake O'Dea slapped the heel of his hand against his forehead.

'What's wrong with her?'

'Nothing's wrong. It's the bloody sausage and chips. You know how pregnant women are.'

'What would I know about pregnant women? Speak English.'

'Some of them go mad for ice cream. Or buns or cakes. Molly has to have sausage and chips. She'll kill me.'

'What have you to do with it?'

'I spent the money.'

'Your wife's sausage and chip money?'

'Yeah. Christ, a dog's life all for the sake of a pound.'

'A quid for sausage and chips? Does she get them by the hundredweight?'

'I'm supposed to bring her back fags too. Listen, this is serious, Cocoa. Pregnant women – just take my word for it. Look, I've only taken one sip out of the pint. Will you buy it off me for forty pence?'

'Jake, I'm just after buying you the pint.'

'Let me sell it back to you. You've no idea, Cocoa, when a woman is in that condition . . . '

'Jesus. Drink your pint. I'll give you the quid on one condition.'

'What?'

'That you pay me back the quid and everything you owe me if we win the match and you get your thousand.'

'What do I owe you?'

'Nineteen fifty including the pound now.'

'Are you serious? I don't owe you nineteen fifty.'

'You owe me five since the day Tolly drove us to Navan races . . . '

'That was before I was married, that's over three years ago.'

'So?'

'I just . . . I dunno, I dunno what I thought . . . '

'There was a fiver that day. Then there was the night . . . '

'Cocoa, I'll take your word for it. I'll tell you what I'll do. 'Tis worse than I told you. I took a loan of a few quid belonging to my mother, she keeps under her sewing machine. I'll make a deal with you. Gimme a fiver now instead of a pound and I'll pay you back the full twenty-three fifty after we win.'

Jake O'Dea bought a double sausage and chips and ate them on his way home. Neither his mother nor Molly liked sausages or chips. Now that he was officially into Cocoa Brown for twenty-three fifty he saw no reason why he could not go to forty or fifty pounds. A prospective thousand in his case had the same collateral as a million pound note. He could play the same card with Tom Splendid and add to the No 2 account. He could tap the whole of them. He saw himself rapping on the window of Tolly Holliday's taxi: 'A life saver, ten quid to keep the wife happy, first thing after the match you'll get it.'

But next day at work, with four pounds burning a comfortable hole in his pocket and knowing he could abandon television and go to the Nook earlier that night, he was still not happy. He began to take a sober look at the prospects of winning. What was Stanley up to? He had absolute faith in the teacher. And when Stevie and Dara arrived there would be more confidence to play around with. But he, Jake O'Dea, had been the team. Was still the team. A thousand pounds. Having four in his pocket was like dripping diamonds. He could not figure out what Stanley was up to but he decided that afternoon at work that whatever else happened no one would blame Jake O'Dea for letting a thousand slip.

Immediately after tea Jake rummaged under the stairs and found the mildewed beach shoes that he had worn two years before when his mother and Molly had managed to save enough to rent a caravan for a week at the seaside. He put on two heavy pullovers to induce sweat and set off alone into the crisp March night. Jake lived in a terraced house in the Fairgreen. He passed Stevie Mack's house, Dara Holden's, Johnny Green's mother's house, Tolly Holliday's and the house that had once been the Callaghans' but had reverted to the landlord when Stanley's parents died. Jake never understood why Stanley had not moved back to the old street to hang on to the council house. Even Dara Holden's parents had refused to go to a house in the country that Dara wanted to build for them. Jake trotted a mile until he had access to the river bank. He was in no condition to trot but he had the will power that once enabled him carry the Nook on his back.

When he reached the river Jake tried to break himself in by running sprints, walking, trotting half a mile, sprinting, walking again. Then he had to stop to be sick. He sat on the grass and lit half a cigarette. He had two draws and flicked it into the river. He did a few push ups and he tried to touch his toes. His eyes were full of sweat now but Jake did not kid himself that it was anything other than the beer breaking out in him. A mile away from the stile that gave on to the river bank was a cluster of trees. He ran the mile and back again and then collapsed. He was so knackered that he hadn't the energy to walk home and yet he knew that this was the very condition to run the mile to the cluster of trees and back again. He could barely see through the sweat now. Twice he slipped down the bank, once landing his feet in the water. He squelched on in his beach shoes. He thought, staggering the return mile, that a thousand pounds equalled pain. He was so steamed up that he took off his clothes and plunged into the March river. The cold was worse than the sweat. He swam to the far bank and back. He was practically out on his feet when he emerged shivering from the river; he trotted to the cluster of trees and back to dry and warm himself. Dressed, he sat down and smoked a full cigarette. In the darkness, barely able to distinguish the river and the trees, he contemplated the odds against his being able to go off drink.

Bazook, Cocoa and Tom and Joe Lewis were in the Nook two hours before Jake arrived at half ten. He had sat exhausted at home watching television until the longing came over him.

'We thought you must be dead,' Bazook greeted him.

'I feel like it. A beer shandy, Tom. And ten – just a beer shandy.'

'Splendid job.'

'What's this with beer shandies and no cigarettes?'

'I was training, Cocoa. Fags would kill you.' Jake sat on a chair and put his feet on another.

'How did it go?'

'Terrible. The body is wrecked.'

'We should all be doing something. Tom and Joe, the two of you'll have to get into shape. And you Bazook. I'm going to start myself tomorrow.'

'I don't need to be fit, do I, Jake? I'm the goalkeeper.'

Jake O'Dea laughed wistfully. The twins in any condition were not going to be much help. Neither was Cocoa. Neither was Stanley. Stevie Mack was all right and Dara had authority–a way of hovering over the ball that convinced the opposition that he was better than he was. And the actor's voice calling for the ball rang with command. The tragedy about Tolly Holliday was that Tolly was good. But exercise would probably kill him.

'It's all up to yourselves, Bazook. The only reason I'm training is to be fit when Stanley decides to get moving. If Henry Corr can have his gang running like phantoms in the middle of the night, can you imagine what Stanley might come up with? And goalies still have to be able to see the ball, Bazook. Look at you. You're bollixed from drink. Drink and fags.'

'It's not my fault. I thought I was retired. Do you see this,' Bazook patted his stomach, 'do you think that'd be there if I knew there was a match coming up for a penny? Let alone a thousand.'

'You know now, Bazook.'

'You see this,' Bazook held out his pint, 'and this?' he pulled the cigarette out of his mouth. 'After I go home tonight I won't touch a drink or a fag till after the match and I'll get out the fucking bike too. Wait'll you see.'

'Good man, Bazook. Now we're moving. And I'm going to do my bit. Jake, I'll run with you tomorrow night.'

'Please, Cocoa.' Jake was already beginning to stiffen. Laughing hurt him. He held his arms tight across his stomach while tears ran down his face. 'Cocoa, please. It's hard enough. Do your own training.'

Jake had only sipped his beer shandy. He struggled to his feet, waved goodnight and left.

Stanley Callaghan and son Conor cooked the breakfast on Sunday mornings and treated the woman in their lives to a meal in bed. But this Sunday morning Conor had to fend for all of them. His father was reading the article in the *Sunday Express* for the tenth time. It was the Sean Senior column. The first paragraph dealt succinctly with a Pakistani who owned eighteen houses that he rack-rented and was fined fifty pounds for drawing unemployment benefit. On the Pakistani's behalf it had been pleaded that he was occasionally not in full possession of his faculties. 'I'll tell you this,' concluded Sean Senior, 'somebody hasn't all his marbles, but it's not Paki.' The next item on the agenda began:

> Now hear this. Paddy the Bomber, we know. Paddy the Lush, he's always with us. Paddy the dosser, look out of your window any afternoon in the direction of the bookies. Paddy the idealist. Paddy the Idealist? Yes, we are in full possession of the old faculties this morning (not having eighteen houses we don't have much choice, do we?) Paddy the Idealist is indeed alive and well and living in the city of Mellick in Southern Ireland. He is one Stanley Callaghan. So meet Mr Callaghan. He is a teacher. Not for our Stanley the new maths. His ten year old pupils sing out their old table books. Not for our Stanley the new literacy. His class make do with *straight pens*. Remember them? And in case you might think our Stanley is not up to date his pupils too are artists. *After* they have mastered their reading, writing and 'rithmetic, then they are allowed free time to indulge the Picasso we are told is lurking in all of us these days. There was a strike once in Stanley's school. Guess who passed the picket? But it is Stanley Callaghan the footballer who concerns us this morning. Apparently in his halcyon days Stanley played Sunday football for his local pub, quaintly named the Nook. Fifteen years ago the Nook defeated a local upper class club known as the Institute. It appears both sides are willing to replay that game with the exact same personnel as fifteen years ago. But here the plot thickens. A local car dealer has

decided to sponsor our Stanley's team to the tune of a thousand pounds a man if they win. *If* they win. Your local car dealer – be it in Mellick or Auchtermuchty – is, I can vouch, in full possession of the old faculties at all times. You see, the Nook can't win. Not on paper. For who played on the Snobs XI all of fifteen years ago? None other than Timmie Stockil. Yes, *the* Timmie Stockil. And one Ralph O'Shea, centre on the current Irish rugby team. The Nook must of course wear jerseys supplied by our friendly car dealer with Mikimoto emblazoned across the chest. Who do these people think they are, I hear you ask, England? Not quite. For here's the rub. Our Stanley Callaghan refuses to wear the jersey. Our Stanley doesn't approve of commercialism. What a fuddy duddy, you cry. Wrong again. Our Stanley does have the gaming instinct. There is also a wager of a thousand pounds a man between the two sides, with Stanley putting up the entire eleven thousand for his side despite the fact that Dara Holden (*the* Dara Holden) plays for the Nook. No, last night's grappa has not gone to our heads. We state no more than facts. Furthermore, a local stockist of same has offered the Nook fifty pounds a man to wear Three Star boots. Stanley? No sir. I tell you this: the England team may have sold the backs off their shirts, poor Paki Rachman might be down to his last eighteen mansions, but thank God and St Patrick there is one among us who holds fast. Altogether now this morning: Hello, Mr Chips.

The following Wednesday night Stanley Callaghan was restless. Dara Holden, wandering across the television screen, slapping cigarettes out of gangsters' mouths, appeared to Stanley derelict in his obligation to the Nook. Kate had written to Dara in good time and they should have heard from him by now. The one aspect of the match that worried Stanley from the beginning was not that Timmie Stockil and Ralph O'Shea were playing but that they were fit. And the news that the rest of the Institute team were training like paratroopers was hard to swallow. The Nook was too far gone to approach the game from the fitness angle. They had beaten the Institute fifteen years before without it. So everyone was fifteen years older, he consoled himself, so what? He needed the understanding Dara, Dara the humanist. 'Humanist? Humanist?' Stanley had roared with delight. 'You can't reconcile the religion of your forefathers with your inability to resist whores of actresses so all of a sudden you're a humanist?'

'Kate ... '

'Yes, Mr Chips?'

'Please, Kate. I'm getting enough of that at school. How about a drink?'

'Love it.'

'I want. to go to the Nook.'

'The Nook, Stanley? You mean it?'

'I've dragged myself back to that level, Kate. I may as well operate at that level until I've seen this through. I need you to keep me sane, Kate. You don't mind?'

'I'm always begging you to take me there.'

'We won't take the car. It's not possible to practise continence in the Nook.'

They clocked in at half past nine. Stanley expected and was modestly prepared for a shout of acclamation to greet his arrival. But the pub was empty save for Mrs Trehy.

'Ah, Stanley. And Mrs Callaghan. Splendid.'

The proprietor shook hands with Kate across the counter.

'A pint of Guinness and a gin and tonic, Tom, please.' Stanley Callaghan was puzzled. It was still Lent but that hardly accounted for the presence of only Mrs Trehy. She sat on a stool at the corner of the bar and had a clear view of all who entered, affording them, in return, the prospect of her tightless legs up to four inches above the knee. Her overcoat was unbuttoned and through a feat of legerdemain unintelligible to Stanley she seemed now to be possessed of a cleavage. She wore the flop hat with the feather in it. She had a raw mouthful of lipstick.

'It's quiet, Tom? People on the dry for Lent?'

'I doubt if my clientele would forswear drink from motives of piety.'

'True. True.'

The Callaghans were seated on the stools at the bar counter. Stanley had never before spoken to Mrs Trehy in the Nook but having developed the habit of saluting her in Brigid's he now nodded in her direction. Mrs Trehy nodded back. It was her experience that she never knew where the next customer would come from. Ten pints was a powerful aphrodisiac. She would have nodded at the Pope.

'Dull, Kate?'

Kate indicated the sign: ONLY SAD SONGS ON SAD OCCASIONS ONLY.

'Oh. Tom, I see you've put up your sign again.'

Tom Splendid grinned: 'I haven't needed it for years. Probably don't need it now. But you never know.'

Stanley chuckled.

There was a shuffling outside the door and the pub was suddenly full. None of the newcomers looked more than seventeen. They were all muscular and clean-shaven – if indeed they had reached the shaving age. They had short back and sides and held their caps under their arms – ten naval cadets from the *Bismarck*, docked earlier in the day. Lager was their common language although a few of them made guttural requests for Guinness. One of them had a better command of English than his fellows and he ordered for the entire party. He was standing next to Mrs Trehy who affected not to notice him.

'I should have known.'

'What?'

'Mrs Trehy in full regalia. The flop hat with the feather, that's reserved for when the fleet's in. She has a cousin a stevedore, he processes the whole business. It's enough to make one bury one's head – we're a city in name only. Charter going back to King John and we have no concert hall and no brothel. There is still great credit to the Germans – it isn't every navy would take on Mrs Trehy.'

Kate narrowed her eyes and peered at her husband. 'Stanley, you're not serious. She won't . . . ' Solemnly, Stanley nodded twice.

'Where will she take them?'

Stanley raised his eyes to the ceiling. 'She rents standing room in Tom's kitchen. There is only standing room. I witnessed the procedure years ago when she wasn't so repulsive – I mean, I assume she wasn't so repulsive then . . . They line up on the stairs and go in one at a time. Like a dispensary except that they come out buttoning flies instead of clutching labelled bottles. I believe it still goes on. We shall watch developments.'

The navy sat under the television – which was not on – and giggled over their drinks. They put their heads together, they broke away laughing, they glanced at Mrs Trehy. The cadet who had ordered the drinks went to the counter again and asked for cigarettes. He stood a whisper away from Mrs Trehy. His mates began to sing. Tom Splendid was immediately out from behind the bar. 'No singing.' He pointed to the notice. 'No ... sprechenzee ... ' Tom mimed singing and then clapped a hand over his mouth. At the counter the ambassador showed Mrs Trehy her own business card which read: 'Madam Trehy, Entertainer.' Mrs Trehy nodded. She gathered herself together and descended from her stool and exited by the hall door which led to the stairs up to the kitchen. Kate giggled: 'She should have a receptionist with a white coat and painted fingernails who would disinfectantly announce: "Next." I can see her collating cardex paraphernalia between turns.'

Six of the ten cadets were ushered in Mrs Trehy's wake by the commander of English. The remaining three concentrated ferociously on drinking. They were probably Catholics, homosexuals or might have been initiated elsewhere. Stanley's thoughts began to drift from Mrs Trehy and her clients.

'What time are you, Kate?'

'Ten to ten.'

'Ten to ten and nobody in the Nook except ourselves and a few sailors. Tom, where is everyone?'

'Everyone? I have no idea. No idea, Stanley.' Tom Splendid looked him straight in the eyes. Stanley said no more. Only liars looked one straight in the eye. The just man fell ten times a day and had the grace to be permanently guilty. Fresh shuffling outside the door announced Bazook, Cocoa, the twins and Jake O'Dea. Stanley thought he caught the word 'shandies'.

'Gentlemen.'

'Hello, Stanley. Hello, Kate.'

'Hi, Jake.'

'Jake, what are you having?'

'A shandy please, Stanley.'

'Bazook?'

'I'll have a shandy too.'

'Cocoa?'

'Shandy.'

'Tom, Joe?'

'Shandies, please.'

'Tom, five pints of Guinness and five whiskeys. At your leisure.'

'Splendid job.'

Jake O'Dea sat on a barrel with his back to the wall. He was at home, in the Nook with Stanley Callaghan. He had done another eight miles – including rivers – and he felt able for porter and whiskey. Cocoa Brown had gone to Cals Park with Bazook and the twins and managed a few laps and push ups.

'Stanley, clean the wax out of your ears. Five shandies we ordered.'

Stanley put his packet of cigarettes on the counter: 'Smoke, Cocoa?'

'No thanks.'

Stanley extracted a cigarette and threw it at Jake O'Dea. He placed one on the counter in front of Cocoa. He offered the packet to Bazook and Joe Lewis, both of whom accepted. Tom Lewis declined. 'No thanks, Stanley. I never touched them.'

'You're not too young to learn. Here.'

'Honest. I don't smoke.'

Stanley lit the cigarette himself and then extended it to Tom. 'Now smoke that or otherwise you won't be on the team. We were short that night or you wouldn't have been on it in the first place. All right?'

'Stanley, don't be acting the maggot . . . '

'Shut up, Cocoa. Now you – smoke!' Tom Lewis accepted the cigarette and drew mildly. He coughed the smoke directly into Stanley Callaghan's eyes. 'That's it. Keep it up. You'll get the hang of it. You see, Cocoa,' Stanley continued as the whiskey and porter was served, 'this is more than a soccer match. This is a battle against chewing gum, unisex hair shops, transfer markets, yobbos, dirty chants, midfielders and the fact that you can't charge the goalkeeper any more. Jake . . . ten o'clock, Jake?'

Stanley handed him the pint and the whiskey. Jake downed the spirit neat in one gulp and sipped his pint.

'I was training, Stanley.'

'Aha! Well?'

'Eight miles and one river. The body is wrecked.'

'Drink up then, drink up. Restore lost energy. Tom, the same again all round. Your twist this time, Cocoa.'

'I give up. Your husband is a lunatic, Mrs Callaghan. With all due respect to you, your husband is a lunatic.'

The side door was opened from the hall and two of the cadets shuffled in. They joined their mates and ordered drinks. At intervals they were joined by later initiates until they were again a full muster and Mrs Trehy's clinic was closed. The six debutantes blended in without comment – it was a golden though unwritten rule of the house that no one ever sniggered or noticed another satisfied customer re-enter the bar after being treated by Mrs Trehy. Mrs Trehy herself proceeded out the hall into the street and then turned back into the snug where fifteen minutes later she was huddled knackered and contented in a corner, brandy dribbling from her lips.

The talk in the bar had drifted to Dara Holden and how soon he was likely to return when the cadets began to sing again. They performed in their native tongue but the song was familiar to all:

> I love to go a-wandering,
> Along the mountain track;
> And as I go I love to sing,
> My knapsack on my back.

'That's enough now.' Tom Splendid pointed to his sign again.

Jake O'Dea interposed, glancing back towards Mrs Trehy in the snug: 'Maybe this *is* a sad occasion for them. It might be a sad song too.'

But Tom Splendid was immovable. The sign had gone up many years before Stanley Callaghan and company were old enough to enter the Nook and they had inherited the restriction. Only once had Tom waived the rule. That was the night ... Stanley would never forget that night. On the occasions when the occasion was sad and the songs sung sad it was possible to appreciate why Tom Splendid preferred only sad songs on sad occasions only. His favourite, cheery offering was Pal of My Cradle Days. He was in a rage now at the cadets' blithe ignoring of his demands for silence.

'Enough now, that's enough. If ye don't shut up I'll clear the house.'

Jake O'Dea, having tasted the blood of two small ones and two pints, rose from his barrel and whispered: 'Stanley, he'll do it, you know. He'll clear the house. Throw us all out.'

His hour come, Stanley Callaghan alighted from his stool and walked towards the choir. For all Tom Splendid's rage and determination he could not get his own way in his own pub. The

Nook bathed in quiet pride at Stanley Callaghan in action. Stanley smiled at the cadet who had negotiated with Mrs Trehy: 'Lads, I'm sorry to interrupt but there is no singing allowed here.'

The cadet took a huge swallow from his pint of Guinness; his eyes closed from the strength of the draught and his nose fizzed. He raised his hand to conduct and led his comrades once again.

I love to go a-wandering . . .

He was the cadet who had spoken the English. There was no possibility of his not having understood. He had flagrantly disregarded Stanley's instruction. Stanley began to take their glasses, one by one, and put them on the counter. But the cadet, while continuing to bellow, took issue with Stanley by clutching his glass simultaneously with Stanley. There was a brief tug of war; the drink spilled; the international imprecation 'fuck you' was followed by the German lad's fist in Stanley's throat. Stanley fell backwards knocking Bazook off his stool who in turn fell on to Kate's stool, knocking her to the floor where she landed with her legs in the air.

Jake O'Dea shouted 'right lads' in the general direction of Cocoa and the twins and jumped on to the table in front of the navy and from the table on to the lap of the cadet who had thumped Stanley. All ten of the cadets managed to land a blow at Jake. Terrified of being branded a coward, Cocoa Brown charged in, his eyes closed. The twins and Bazook and a bemusedly recovered Stanley followed on.

It was no contest. When the two military policemen arrived fifteen minutes later each of the cadets was kneeling on the floor with a Mellick body beneath him and giggling drunkenly at the unscheduled entertainment. Kate was pulling the hair of the cadet astride Stanley and the cadet, laughing, tried to spare a hand to feel Kate's leg. The military police lined their charges up against the counter while the Nook, including Tom Splendid, struggled to its feet. One of the policemen apologised to the proprietor and promised that those under his command would be thrown in the brig. The policeman barked an order that brought the cadets to attention and quick marched them out of the pub. Bazook saved a little face for the Nook by slipping behind the counter, taking down a bottle of Jameson 10 and breaking it over the last cadet's head as a result of which blow the cadet received twenty-three stitches in Barrington's Hospital. Tom Splendid, who rarely swore, exclaimed: 'Bazook, you dumb bollix, wouldn't you use a shovel?'

Stanley and Kate left almost immediately. Back in the Nook Jake O'Dea and company drank on into after hours, Tom Splendid having recovered from the loss of his Jameson 10. The conversation returned over and over to the lament: If only Stevie Mack was here. Tribute was paid to Bazook for his deed but it was hollow and enforced. They all knew that the incident, stripped of drink and legend, amounted to the fact that Stanley Callaghan had let them down. He had charged boldly in to take command and it hadn't worked.

'We hadn't a chance,' Bazook developed the point. 'Ten year ago maybe. Them fellas, they're all fit and trained same as the army. Even if we'd known 'twas likely to happen, if Stanley warned us, or if Stevie was here ... '

In Brigid's Kate tried to console her husband but there was no need for he'd found somebody else to blame.

'It's Dara's fault, Kate. He should have been here. He'd have stopped me. Of all the daft things to do. When we were kids I wouldn't hit a crippled child unless Stevie Mack was behind me.'

'Stanley, that's not a nice thing to say.'

'I'm merely being hyperbolic,' Stanley lied.

10

Dara Holden

Dara Holden was not listening to his agent. He was after all an actor and could have played the agent's part without effort. The agent, Hank Harold, with his hands clasped behind his back, paced the floor of his dingily appointed Madison Avenue office. He was seventy-nine years old. He wore glasses and had a full moustache and a stoop. He reminded Dara of Groucho Marx. He paused, drew a hand from behind his back and plucked the cigarette out of his mouth to facilitate delivery. He brandished the cigarette at Dara Holden while he bared his amiable teeth to Rena Ryan, the sorter, stenographer and mother to them all.

'Ingrate! Rena, tell him. Tell the Mick what I done for him.'

Rena Ryan opened and shut her mouth like a stamp dispenser and without further acknowledgement carried on sorting. The pigeon holes were labelled Australia, Britain, Canada ... Ireland ... and so on. Hank Harold resumed his patrol.

'Two things I know. Don't fight City Hall and don't fuck up CBS! That I know. I'm a dummy? So what? Three weeks I'm stalling. You heard me, Dara. Yeah, sit there and grin. If I was Swifty you wouldn't grin. You'd hop. Whipped you from under his nose. Boy, was he sore. All over town I keep hearing it. Is he sore. Now you listen good, Dara. Just half an hour ago you heard me. That Simon Legree pusher, Cardone! Hey, he shouts. Down the phone at me, hey Harold, you know who this is Harold, this is Cardone, CBS, you got that, Harold? Cardone, CBS, not Cardone your goddamn tailor for Chrissake. Okay, I tell him. Okay, Tony, relax I read you. Tony, everything's okay, I tell him. Relax my ass, Harold, he shouts. Shouts! At me! Hank Harold! Can't be. But yeah. And why? Cos it's that time of year, Dara Holden's on his integrity jag again. In spring his fancy turns to integrity. Yeah, I can quote, so what? I'm a dummy? Okay kid, I tell him, howsabout I buy you and Dara lunch, kick it around. That got him. Some guys you think they never had a meal. Do I get thanks? Huh? I get shit for thanks. Dara, I'm *talking* to you.'

Dara Holden sat with his hands under his thighs on the agent's desk. It was a naked table but Hank Harold called it a desk. There was linoleum on the floor. The chairs were tubular. There was no shade over the bulb. His clients found it difficult to knock him down a percentage in those surroundings.

'Hank, you know I don't eat. I drink.'

'You're telling me? I put that story out. One of my best.'

'After you discovered it was true. Eight years ago. The only true story you ever put out about me.'

Dara Holden stood up, tucked in his gut and notched his three inch deep leather belt. It was an incongruous yet necessary buttress to his blue pinstriped suit but not half as much out of communion with it as was his red beard. He was in mufti with the suit and the beard – hoping and generally succeeding in being unrecognisable from the clean-shaven, bejeaned and sweatered protagonist of the Dara Holden File.

A sub-division of the Ireland pigeon hole was titled 'Mellick'. The actor answered all the Mellick correspondence himself. He had a mother back there and did not want her stopped in the street and accused of having a big-headed son. Dara began picking letters at random from Rena Ryan's geographical piles.

' . . . you think Swifty Lazar could stall Tony Cardone? You think you could tell Swifty you don't eat, you drink? . . . Jesus, you buck CBS!'

The letters CBS meant only one thing to Dara Holden – Christian Brothers School. Christian Brothers School now meant only one thing to Dara Holden – that was where he shared a desk for ten years with Stanley Callaghan, including the year in old Bob Tracey's class, and Stanley was now a bigger prickpot than Bob Tracey ever had been. On his last trip home Dara discovered that Stanley had his class writing with straight pens, wherever he got the pens from let alone the nibs. It would not have surprised him to hear that Stanley sent the kids out to rob post offices. The bastard had said to him last trip home: Dara, we're getting further and further away from O'Neill.

Hank Harold had not wiped Lazar's eye. Dara inherited the agent from Bush Vine. Swifty Lazar would have got him

O'Neill. He was sure. He said: 'Swifty would have got me O'Neill.'

The agent stopped, shocked, began pacing and gesticulating again. 'O'Neill? Don't mention O'Neill in this town. Robards was jocked off for that titled Limey and you want O'Neill, with our image? Willie Fucking Shoemaker is ahead of you in the O'Neill queue for Chrissake.'

Dara had long ago acknowledged to himself that the agent spoke the truth but it was difficult to accept. There was a long day's journey into night aching inside him for expression, but with his image! The very thought of his image drove him to reach for his cigarettes. He had some Gold Flake left since his last trip to Mellick. Bringing Gold Flake to the States was a combination of homesickness and arrogance. Stanley Callaghan claimed that it was on a par with the English soccer team bringing their sausages with them to dago France.

Dara's image, as in the Dara Holden File, was Hank Harold's invention. Hank was a three packet a day man; Dara had been smoking since his first surreptitious pulls at twelve years of age; to Rena Ryan cigarettes were an antidote to not being beautiful herself amidst all the glamour she dealt with. It was ironic in the smoke filled dinginess of Hank's lair that the idea should have come to him nine years earlier.

'Dara, I've got it! Whoever heard of a shamus who didn't smoke?'

'Yeah. Whoever did.'

'Schmuck! Whoever heard of no butt advertising on TV? That's what's in the air, Dara. They're goin' to phase it out. I got this contact in Washington. The health of the country is fucked up. Curing sick people we got fuckall left to beat the Russians in space. They're bringin' in preventitive medicine – don't get sick, we can't afford to cure you. I see it, Dara. I see the deodorant people on top. The toothpaste merchants, they're gonna have the clout. And you have one helluva mouthful, that's it Dara, flash 'em at me, kid. Yessir, since I got that job done on you. I bet it's the diet in Ireland. All the praties and stirabout . . . '

'And fuck you too, Hank.'

'Okay. Listen, Dara. You got this shamus. Knocks people over with a smile. Doesn't touch the weed. I see him goin' into a pool room. My name is Dara Holden, I'm lookin' for a fella,

name of Mr Big, and take that cigarette out of your mouth
while I'm talking, punk, pollutin' your body. Get it Dara? You
see it?'

'I want to do *The Iceman* on Broadway.'

'Yeah, yeah. You walk in this town before you run. Just
think, the toothpaste interest, the health food freaks, I see big
money bein' put up . . . '

Hank Harold took the idea to Tony Cardone in CBS. He
managed to persuade Cardone that it was worth a pilot shot.
Cardone wanted to put a couple of writers on it but Hank said
no. He would deliver the script himself. He lifted a plot out of
Rockford that had previously been lifted from Hawaii Five-O
and before that had been lifted from Ironside and years before
that had been a sub plot in a Gene Autry western. The result
was sensational. In a fit of inspiration Hank threw into the end
of the story the idea that Dara Holden, the non-smoking Dick
Tracey, should round up the three hijackers in a warehouse –
say two blacks and one white – and Dara would let Whitey
escape because he was the only one of the three a non-smoker.
Hank saw Whitey with asthma. But Cardone had antennae
more sensitive than Hank Harold's. He said: Not with this civil
rights thing blowin' up all over the country. They changed the
personnel to two white and one black man – a non-smoker with
asthma.

And now after nine years Dara said he didn't want to do the
File any more. He said the same thing every year but Hank had
always managed to sort him out. But now Dara had more
money than sense and there was that cowboy back in Mellick,
that cowboy Callaghan that Dara was always going on about.
That Callaghan character really seemed to be working on Dara
this time. And to think he was married to Kate Flynn! Three
weeks now, Hank was stalling Cardone.

'I know. That prickpal of yours back in Mellick, he's workin'
on you again, right?'

'Stanley Callaghan is the only human being whose opinion I
respect. Stanley and Kate.'

'Yeah, Kate. Kate Flynn. Bush could sure pick 'em. But let's
stick with it. Leave respect out of it. We're talkin' about six
million dollars! Six million dollars, and you know something. I
didn't say this to Cardone, if Cardone knew I was thinking this,
Dara, this could be the last six million. You know?'

'What do I know, Hank?'

'Old Hank's got a wrinkle. My man on the Hill tells me John Doe in the street has had it up to here. Joggin's helpin', Dara. If you jogged now with a whole packet of Lucky's in your kisser that GASP crowd would have to cheer you. I smell a backlash. What you want today is a shamus goes in to see Mr Big, Mr Big's all scent and perfumery, the queer type, he's just wiped out a whole family, includin' a pipe smokin' grandpa and he says: Mr Holden, *if* you please, I don't allow that filthy habit in my office. Dara Holden sucks his butt, blows the smoke in Mr Big's eyes: Mr Big, I don't allow whole families bein' wiped out – anyplace. Dara, this could be our last fling, Dara.'

'I'd love to believe you, Hank. You made me into a monster who can't do O'Neill because of his image. You're a goddamn Mary Shelley, Hank.'

'Hey! I don't like that talk. Call me anything but don't call me a puff. Okay kid. We meet Cardone right?'

'Okay. McNamara's Bar.'

'Dara! You can't bring Cardone to no Mick bar! Besides, he wouldn't go.'

'Then fuck Tony Cardone, Hank. And fuck the Dara Holden File. Who needs it? I can do it back home. The Abbey asked me once. I got a raincheck on it. Next *Long Day's Journey* I guest star as Tyrone. Yep. Nip over to Dublin . . . '

'Don't you mention Dublin in this office. The Black Hole of Calcutta, yeah. Dublin, no. Not after what they done to The Champ. The Champ and Young Mulcahy from the Bronx. They said I couldn't do it. No way, everyone said. Word got back to me Swifty nearly bust a gut. He said old Hank's gaga at last. But I did it. The Champ v Young Mulcahy in Dublin: In the middle of that fucking field. Whatcha callem? The GAA crowd. They gimme their hurling field. Red tape? More red tape than fucking Russia. I had to agree the proceeds were for charity. Charity for Chrissakes! They put me on your Irish television talking to a nun. Me! This biddy peepin' out at me from her starch. "Of course we couldn't anticipate such largesse without the wonderful work of dear Mr Harold." Largesse! What happened? Those dumb dagos of Irish cousins of yours, they didn't show. That Croke Park field looked like the Sahara . . . '

'Hank, Young Mulcahy from the Bronx – he spent the first sixteen years of his life at home in Naples.'

'Fuck Young Mulcahy. What about the Champ? The nun still writes me. Twenty grand's all I cleared and she wants some of it for her charities. You know what the Champ said in the dressing room after the fight? Everyone's afraid to look at him cos of the bad turnout. He took it as a personal insult – from me. He spoke a poem about me:

> If 'n I ever see Hank Harold again,
> It's bye bye to you all then.'

'You really raided Ireland that night, Hank. I really love you, you know? I think I'll do the Abbey. The Abbey Theatre presents . . . Dara Holden by kind permission of Hank Harold, the man who brought you Young Mulcahy . . . '

Without a word Rena Ryan handed Dara the letter. There were already three letters in the Mellick pigeon hole – two fan letters and one from his mother – but Rena Ryan did not put *this* letter in with them. She recognised the handwriting; the childish script had not changed since the days Kate Flynn used to write to Bush Vine c/o his agent. Dara was excited when he saw there were seven pages to the letter. The usual letter did not go beyond two pages: 'Stanley was saying. . . . Stanley thinks . . . ' Stanley's thoughts, even when spread thin, did not amount to much. And that was all that a Kate letter contained. He was too lazy to write himself. This letter was all about Stanley but with the difference that it was Kate telling the tale as she saw it herself. Dara chuckled over the Wilde epigram. Hank Harold began to pace again.

' . . . six million dollars. For once we'll all be serious around here. Rena has to eat, I gotta eat, okay you gotta drink, Dara . . . '

The actor held up his hand as he raced through the pages.

'Huh? Oh, from her. Okay, read your letter and then we all wake up around here.'

' . . . Stanley needs you badly. Not just to play the match but to share the load. He doesn't say so directly but I know there's no one he can turn to, the Nook are all delightful of course, but Dara, I think you know what I mean . . . '

'That a letter or an encyclical?'

The first dreadful inkling Hank received that his attempt at facetiousness was close to the bone came the moment Dara finished reading.

'Rena. Get me the first flight out of Kennedy to Shannon.'

'I'm hearing right? Rena, put down that phone.'

'Do it, Rena.'

'Rena, drop it. What have we got here? What kinda mutiny is this?'

Dara handed Hank the letter. 'Read it yourself, Hank.'

For once in his life Hank Harold did not understand. He was capable of understanding and disagreeing but never had he failed to understand.

'Dara,' he groped. 'Dara, I don't understand.'

'It's all there, Hank. Stanley Callaghan's in trouble. He needs me.'

'But – it says here he wants you to play a soccer match for a bar. Jesus, Dara, we're not even insured against that kinda thing, you could break your ankle, if he's so hard up for some bucks why don't you send him eleven grand, why don't I send him eleven grand, for Chrissake.'

'Rena, Kennedy.'

'Now hold on a minute, Dara. Something I didn't tell you. The backlash. You know where I got wind of that? Not my Washington contacts, Dara, those guys on the Hill wouldn't pick up yesterday. It was Cardone. We *are* on our last hurrah with the File, Dara, an it's a fact. It's a six million buck fact. So let's pitch some vittles into Cardone and tie it in and then you fuck to the moon if you want and play polo with the Duke of Edinburgh. So long's the deal's signed. Okay?'

'I can't talk to Cardone today, Hank, even if it was McNamara's. I can't talk to that creep unless I fuck someone first and get to feel down, you know that, I gotta be slummin' before I even look at the shit. And I'm full of high thoughts now, my old buddies need me and I can't even think of Cardone now and I've had Cardone and I've had the File and stuff the six million. Gimme that phone, Rena.'

'All right. Rena will do it. Rena will make the call. All I'm askin' is this afternoon – you need a woman, Rena will oblige – then we'll see Cardone. Rena, you'll do it?'

To soften Hank's crudity Dara kissed Rena on the forehead. He had successfully avoided marriage by reading the alimony news in the trade magazines. He knew that only religion and drudgery held marriages together unless somebody was married to Kate Flynn; anyway he wouldn't ever marry anybody while he loved Kate Flynn. There was always the hope that Stanley would get a falling blackboard in the neck. Dara's name was linked with many women principally because his body was linked with theirs the night before and Hank leaked the tit bits in the same way that he put out that stroke about Dara undergoing acupuncture to get him off cigarettes and slow down his sex drive.

'I'll talk to Tony Cardone. After the match.'

'Dara, Cardone won't be there. I didn't tell you. I didn't want to upset you. Cardone said three o'clock today, *we'd talk*, we're going to have to talk *him* into another year. We don't show today, we're out on our ass!'

'Hank, you beat him to it. I can see the headlines, Hank: Holden turns down $6,000,000 to play football! You get on to it, Hank, salvage something from the wreck. Say I want to do O'Neill. Now, Rena, Kennedy, I mean now Kennedy, or else gimme the damn phone.'

There was no better man than Hank Harold for salvaging from wrecks. He had escaped out of Dublin with twenty grand from the Young Mulcahy put up, nuns hounding him. When the Kennedy flight had been confirmed and Dara Holden had kissed him and Rena goodbye, Hank immediately started shooting instructions.

'Rena, get them all, one by one. First the newspapers. I want this on the streets early morning. Then the mag bitches, you tell all the face-lifted crones Hank's got inside stuff won't make the papers . . . I see this one as a put over on Swifty, you think Swifty got a client with integrity, throw up six million bucks to save a buddy? No way. And what am I sayin', soccer's shot up now I think of it, get on to that kraut whatsisname, Beckenbauer, I wanna shot with my arm around him, Rena, good could come outa this. Dara won't get O'Neill after this blows over but I'll milk this, I'll keep this going he'll be such news that fuck O'Neill, the Polaroid people will come to *us* . . . '

11

Prologue

Dara Holden wrote to many actors and film stars. All he asked of them was advice. He wrote to Richard Widmark: ' ... I thought you were absolutely fantastic as Tommy Udo in *Kiss of Death* ... '

He attached to the letter his credits to date:

1960 Played Pats Bocock in the Mellick College Players production of John B. Keane's *'Sive'*.

Understudied Eamonn Martin who played the Covey in the Mellick College Players production of Sean O'Casey's *The Plough and the Stars*.

1961 Played Curley in the Mellick College Players production of John Murphy's *The Country Boy*.

Understudied Eamonn Martin who played Dinzee Conlea in the Mellick College Players production of John B. Keane's *Sharon's Grave*.

1962 Spent a year's sabbatical in London absorbing the theatrical milieu.

Besides Richard Widmark, Dara Holden sent this information to Charlton Heston, Jason Robards Junior, Kirk Douglas, George Hamilton, Eddie Fisher, Charles Laughton, Bush Vine, John Wayne, Sidney Poitier, Chief Dan George, Geraldine Page, John Frankenheimer, Frank Sinatra, Thelma Ritter, Slim Pickens and Burt Lancaster.

Stanley Callaghan summed up: 'Dara, this is a begging letter. You want someone to claim you out to the States and get you a part in some picture.'

'Exactly.'

'Why did you pick this lot? You left out Peter Ustinov and Mickey Rooney for instance.'

'The addresses of their agents were in a movie magazine I picked up at the barber's. The way I look at it, fate put that magazine there.'

'Yeah, like fate put the clippers in the barber's hand.'

Dara received fan fodder in reply from all the agents except those of Chief Dan George and Bush Vine. Chief Dan George's agent had no time even to send fodder – he was attended daily, at his own residence, by a psychiatrist who was trying to help him persuade Chief Dan George that it would be lunacy to sink twenty million dollars into an epic starring Chief Dan George as a cavalry officer.

Bush Vine, whose fan mail was nothing like as voluminous as Chief Dan George's, folded the begging letter and put it in his pocket.

In 1952 Sister Aquinas interviewed Bush Vine. The famous star had written that he was about to make *Without a Past*. His part was to be that of the grand, crotchety, old backwoodsman whose daughter has defied him for the big city lights. She becomes pregnant by a touring base guitarist, lives in terror for eight and a half months, abandons the child at birth, returns home and years later confides in her boy-next-door husband who, the secret too big for him, confides in his father-in-law. It is all of twenty years later that the news is broken to Gramps and because his daughter and boy-next-door husband have no children of their own, Gramps sets out on an odyssey to the big smoke to try and trace the abandoned offspring. There was marvellous scope in the part for an old man's hayseed philosophy in his encounters with big city cynicism.

Gramps has little money and a lot of innocence. He wrings casual employment for himself from the most unlikely sources – star names queued up for these cameo slots. At any rate goodness breaks out all over the place and the child – a young man – is eventually tracked down (with the aid of the Mafia). But the youth had been adopted and is now himself the happily married father of a baby daughter. Almost within physical touch of his grandson the old man finds the courage not to make himself known. At the end as Bush Vine is put on a

Greyhound bus by a farewell party of all those who have discovered their finer feelings through his agency, Bush fights back a tear and tells his new friends huskily: 'There's good in folks. Always knowed it.'

Bush Vine won the Academy Award for his performance but months before the shooting even started Sister Aquinas failed to be won over during their initial interview.

'Mr Vine, we live a sheltered life here, the community *and* the children. And may God forgive uncharitable thoughts – but – a certain notoriety has attached itself to your life style. You have been divorced three times, your name linked with scarlet women . . . '

Bush Vine was seated in Sister Aquinas' reception room, a tray of tea between them. From the nun's clamped lips and virginal vocabulary he could see that she lived a sheltered life indeed – his reputation having scaled the convent walls notwithstanding. Dara Holden was to inform him twelve years later that the director of the Mellick Confraternity mentioned Bush Vine by name from the pulpit as an example of the gifted turning his back on God. Bush now had his knees irreverently crossed despite the frigidity of his reception. He brought the tips of his fingers together under his chin.

'Sister, I have to agree your image of me is not inaccurate. Be that as it may, it is a very small scene in which the old man visits the orphanage. The Mother Superior is going through her records trying to help him. A young girl enters on some errand. The old man has one line of dialogue with the girl. He merely observes in her presence: "Purty little thing." That's all. Don't you think – ogre no doubt that I must appear to you, that it would help me get the feel of that one line correctly if I could speak to one of your charges. Just for one moment? I can't say that line to a camera. I can't say it to an actress.' Bush Vine spread his hands and concluded: 'The words must be wrung from me.'

'You go to such trouble over one line. More tea?'

'Thank you. Sister, that's my job.'

'I must parade deprivation before you to lend verisimilitude to your three little words. Is that really what life is to you, Mr Vine? Sensibility – others – sacrificed for – what shall we call it – Art?' Sister Aquinas inclined her chin to accompany her victorious debating point. Quietly, Bush Vine landed on it.

'Yes, Sister. That is precisely what life is to me.'

Bush Vine was left alone with his thoughts for a few moments as Sister Aquinas stood up, folded her hands under the sleeves of her habit and paced the room. Bush was reminded absurdly of Hank Harold. Hank was a pacer. But Hank did not stop to gaze at a picture of Our Lady of Perpetual Succour as did Sister Aquinas. It was true that he had come in search of three little words. He was that professional. But he was aware that he had been acting from the moment he introduced himself to Sister Aquinas. He had always acted when he wanted his way with women. He acted his way into three marriages and three divorces and hundreds of affairs. He felt disappointed now that he should have to seduce a woman of the cloth.

Before she entered the novitiate Sister Aquinas had seen all of Bush Vine's early films. He was then a clean cut cowboy, swashbuckler, light romantic. She had thought a lot about him from the moment she opened his letter. The matinée idol of her adolescence had seemed then incapable of divorce or fornication. She had not seen a film for over thirty years. How had he changed from all that was manly and good into – into – into the distinguished looking gentleman who now graced her leather armchair, she was forced to concede.

'Mr Vine, I am going to accede to your wish, improbable though it appears to me.'

'Sister, I am most grateful to you.

Sister Aquinas became suddenly matriarchal. She lifted the bell from her bureau and pealed it imperiously. The response was so immediate that Bush Vine imagined a pair of nuns on guard, arms folded, outside the door.

'Yes, Sister?'

'Sister Agatha, would you be so good as to send for Kate Flynn.'

'Yes, Sister.'

'And Sister Agatha.'

'Yes, Sister?'

'May I introduce Mr Bush Vine the celebrated actor.'

Bush Vine had already risen at the nun's entrance. Sister Agatha curtsied but the actor took her hand warmly: 'Pleased to meet you, Sister. Charmed.'

Sister Aquinas directed a wry look at Sister Agatha's receding figure and also at Bush Vine. The actor did not flinch.

'The girl you are about – the girl I am about to display to you, Kate Flynn, was abandoned in St Patrick's as a baby sixteen years ago. She is a sweet girl. A good girl. Will you do me the honour of displaying your better nature?'

'I'll try, Sister. St Patrick's? That's where the child is found in *Without a Past*. What a coincidence.'

'Hardly that,' Sister Aquinas said primly. 'The cathedral is the official dumping ground. Some have the cheek to put a little note with their deposits – 'the baby is Methodist'. Where we are concerned here, finders keepers. You don't – worship – by any chance?'

Bush Vine smiled, gestured helplessly. Sister Aquinas sniffed. Kate Flynn was announced by Sister Agatha. Bush Vine remained standing. His silver hair was full and of theatrical length. His nose was crooked and long. His eyebrows bushy and white. His jacket and slacks – contrasting shades of light grey, had come from Harrods. The denim button-down-collar shirt, grey socks and black shoes might have and did in fact come from any old shop he happened to be passing. His mauve tie was a present from Rena Ryan. He looked fifty at the outside and did not feel within a mile of his sixty-eight years. He confided once to Hank Harold that the only exercise he got was in the sack. Hank rushed the quote to the columnists. Bush Vine made love and drank regularly. He ate often but very little at a time. He was six feet two inches in his stocking feet. He weighed a trim one hundred and eighty two pounds.

The autumn sun cajoled its way through the stained glass windows and bathed the actor in their biblical light. Sister Aquinas took her hand from her sleeve and extended the palm in the direction of the actor.

'Kate, we have a distinguished visitor to the school. The famous actor, Mr Bush Vine.'

The girl stared at him for so long that Sister Aquinas and Bush Vine exchanged a brief glance.

'All right, Kate. Thank you, that will be all.'

Sister Aquinas was obeyed without any leavetaking on the girl's part. 'Have you got your "three little words", Mr Vine?' she asked drily.

'I would have liked to get to know the girl.'

'I'm sure you would.'

'I could help her.'

'She is sixteen years of age. A young woman. Kindly be more explicit.'

'How can I defrost you, Sister? All I'm saying is that I have more than I know what to do with. I want to help – somebody.'

'Please sit down. You came here to research three little words. Your attitude has changed. Why?'

'I don't know why. I'm an old man. Maybe the surroundings are getting to me. If I could do a small bit of good I might sneak into heaven.' He beamed the celebrated Bush smile but it landed on stony ground.

'Sixty-eight years of age. Your last three year old marriage ended in divorce six months ago. What am I to understand is the nature of your patronage?'

'I thought – with your permission – I might befriend the girl, get her to trust me. Then I could take advantage of her, ravish her and sell her into white slavery. Do I read you correctly, Sister?'

Sister Aquinas coloured. 'Mr Vine, if you are affronted, so be it. I have your acquaintance less than half an hour. Your reputation has preceded you and your reputation is unsavoury. You may interpret my thoughts as the cap fits.'

Bush raised his hand in a gesture of helplessness. 'All right. Point taken. Let me establish myself in the only way us vulgarians know how. Cheque book charity. Will the Community accept my cheque for one hundred thousand dollars? If the name is unacceptable I can have it delivered anonymously in cash.'

Sister Aquinas softened. 'I – don't understand.'

'I admire you and your sisters in charity. I would like to make a donation to your cause. I ask nothing in return. You could use money for that girl's further education I imagine?'

Bush drew out his cheque book and waved it questioningly. Sister Aquinas bowed her head indecisively. Bush held his pen poised in mute petition. He interpreted the continued silence as consent. He put the cheque on the tea tray and rose. Sister Aquinas took a handkerchief from her sleeve and put it to her nose. 'I am a sinful woman,' she moaned softly.

At the door Bush Vine paused. 'No you're not, Sister. In fact you're a purty little thing. I'll see myself out.'

*   *   *

It was Sister Aquinas' ambition that Kate Flynn should teach, and Bush Vine insisted that he should pay for the girl's education –and that the hundred thousand dollars was for the community in general. He begged Sister Aquinas to accept him as a Daddy Long Legs to Kate. The nun was embarrassed at her earlier misjudgement of the actor. He visited the orphanage every Saturday, had tea and scones and chatted briefly with the girl. And during her years in college he haunted the campus when he was not on location. He was now, for the first time in his life, he admitted to Sister Aquinas, a good father. He continued to make love indiscriminately and often, as he had always done, but when he was with Kate Flynn or thinking of her he was a different person. It took the actor six months before he could persuade the nun or the girl to call him Bush. He detested Mr Vine, he persuaded them. From then on their confidence in him was complete. He told Sister Aquinas truthfully:

'Sister, I've been surrounded by what are supposed to be the most beautiful women in the world, but I've never seen anyone like Kate. I've never met anyone like yourself if it comes to that. But it is expected of the religious. But, Sister, is she as beautiful inside?'

'Yes, Bush. She is.'

'I'm plagued with the nightmare of some witless, crew-cutted quarterback deflowering her.'

'There's no fear of Kate.'

'I know. I know. But I still worry.'

'Don't worry, Bush. We understand temptation.'

Unsatisfied, on his next visit to the college, and desperate for information as to how Kate might be faring, Bush offered to teach her the facts of life and he made the suggestion with a quite Victorian delicacy. Kate blushed and cut him short: Sister Aquinas had taken care of all that when Kate was thirteen. Helplessly, Bush let it pass. Whether it was thanks to whatever Sister Aquinas knew about the facts of life or no, Kate majored without the loss of her virginity.

Bush treated her to a celebration dinner at the Algonquin. She had become a great reader. Over coffee the father in Bush gave expression.

'Kate, we've got to have a heart to heart, now's as good as any time. Kate, I don't think you should teach.'

Kate was revelling in the heads turned in their direction.

'Kate, pay attention. Do you *really* want to teach? It's a vocation, you know, especially these days with the type of pupil you're likely to get.'

'Sister Aquinas always said I'd make a good teacher.'

'Of course you would, Kate. Do you think I doubt that? But all your life you've been in schools. There's a world out there, I want you to meet it, not bury yourself in a classroom. You should have a career.'

'Bush, I never thought of myself as an actress.'

'Don't, Kate, ever. That wasn't what I meant.' During the shooting of *Without a Past*, fretting over Kate in her first year in college, Bush diverted himself by sleeping with the leading actress – his daughter in the film – and both her hairdressers. 'Over my dead body do you go to Hollywood. Listen, you have a good head, you're beautiful, people pay attention to you. That's enough for any career. I've money in this and that, mostly with Hank, he's *more* than my agent, we have a real estate concern. Kate, we want you to work for us, would you like that? I see you a real hot shot negotiator.'

'But Bush, I don't know the first thing about real estate.'

'Now that's an answer. You didn't say "Bush, I can't do anything but teach, my heart weeps for little ones . . . " So you don't *have* to teach, Kate. As for real estate, Hank will get someone – the best – to show you the ropes. I trust Hank, the only goddamn guy I do trust. What do you say, Kate? If you don't like it, then go teach. Well? Going to work for old Bush, make Bush a packet?'

'It sounds wonderful. But Sister Aquinas . . . '

'You leave the old buzzard to me.'

A packet was exactly what Kate did make for the real estate concern. She began at her own insistence humbly drumming up trade by knocking at doors. It was not until she had proved even to her own satisfaction that she was too good to knock at doors that she agreed to an inside seat at the wining and dining of big property. Bush himself always took her to the parties. Through his introduction and patronage, Kate's rare looks and character, and the Hank Harold fed gossip columnists it soon became not done – where a Malibu excrescence was concerned – to deal other than through Kate Flynn.

What Bush all the time feared might happen did not happen.

Two years of hard work and hard party going still saw Kate Flynn a virgin. She had her own apartment on riverside on the same block as Bush himself and Hank Harold. Bush reported as much to Sister Aquinas.

'The power of prayer, Bush.'

'Yes, Sister.'

For Kate's twenty-second birthday Bush threw a party. He was standing by her side when Merv Murray introduced himself. Merv was as decent a guy as there was in New York otherwise Bush would not have invited him in the first place. He was in his late thirties, just old enough to have some idea of what charm and manners once used to be.

'Bush, when are you going to mingle with your guests? I want to have a word with this young lady.'

'Sure, Merv. Kate, you be nice to Merv. He's got talent.'

Bush mingled – with Hank. 'Hank, you just stand there talking, I want to see over your shoulder. Merv Murray's taken a shine to Kate, or I'll eat my eyeballs. It's lookin' good, Hank. She's laughing. *He's* laughing . . . he's getting her a drink, that's not so good . . . although her glass *is* empty . . . '

'Bush, don't you trust Merv?'

'Of course I trust him, Hank. You know that.'

But even though Bush did stop spying, Merv Murray was unsuccessful.

After the party Bush escorted Kate down the block to her apartment. 'Enjoy it, Kate?'

'It was a lovely party.'

'That's because there wasn't an actor or actress among them. Hey, you and Merv Murray, you seemed to get along?'

'He's nice.'

'Sure he's nice. He ask you to dinner, Kate?'

'Yes.'

'And you said?'

'No.'

'Why, Kate?'

'Why not, Bush?'

'Come on, Kate. That's no answer.'

'It was no question.'

'Kate, you should have a boy friend. Merv's a fine man.'

'I don't want to go out with Merv, Bush. I just don't.'

Bush went to see Sister Aquinas and shared his new fear. He

was astonished by her attitude.

'Bush, are you out of your mind? She's only twenty-two and you're worried because she hasn't a boy friend? My mother was thirty-eight when she married my father. He was forty-three. They came over here when I was a year old.'

'Sister, this is America – America *now*!'

'So?'

Bush gave up on Sister Aquinas. That night he called to Kate's apartment. He broke out her liquor. 'We're gonna talk this out, Kate. You tell me what make of Sir Galahad you have in mind, I'll find him. I'll put Hank on to it. You name it, Hank delivers. Right kid?'

'Please, Bush. I don't want to talk about it.'

'You know, I've been thinking. Maybe we're going to the wrong parties. Look, I know some people in the Kennedy set, can't stand the Micks myself but you have to admire neck, but maybe, yes, I can see you there, Kate, you'd like them.'

Kate listened solemnly then stood up, turned her back to him and contemplated her glass.

'I can't go on any more, Bush.'

Bush walked over to her and put his hand on her shoulder and when she turned there were tears in her eyes. 'Kate, what in hell's the matter?' Kate moved away from him, threw her glass at the wall and clenched her fists.

'All this time. Six years. Bush, don't you know anything? I don't want Kennedy people or Merv Murrays. You should know what I want, Bush.'

The actor spread his hands. It sounded as though she were accusing him. 'What, Kate? What?'

'You. I want you, Bush. I love you. There. It's out, it's taken me six years. I loved you the first minute I saw you under the stained glass window. You know what you were to me? The transfiguration.'

'Kate . . .'

'I said it. I love you and no one else and I don't care what you say.'

'All right. Let's sit down, Kate. Have a drink. And we'll talk about it. Let's – talk – about – this. You're twenty-two. I'm seventy-four. Let's talk about that.'

'You only look seventy-three.'

'That's my girl. I thought you were never going to smile

again. Now let's stop beating about the bush – hey, I like that –
let's talk straight, Kate. Now listen, I know women – but this
part of it, I guess it happens any age, is it that you feel ready
for – for – do I spell it out?'

'Yes, yes. I am ready for it. Six years I'm ready for it.' Kate
went and put her arms round him as he sat stiffly on the sofa.

Deliberately, Bush removed her hands from around him,
stood up and held her at arm's length. 'Kate, maybe you're
upset. And even though I am seventy-four, I'm still ticking
over. Suppose you turn in and I'll drop round and we'll talk
about this in the morning. In daylight?'

Kate showed him she was a woman. 'You'd prefer me to sleep
with Merv Murray? All right. I've always taken your advice. I
will.'

'Kate, please . . . '

'Yes I will. I *need* it.'

She turned away from him again and began to chew her
handkerchief. Bush went to her and held her gently by the
shoulders.

'I'll call round for breakfast in the morning. See how we feel
then.'

Kate didn't move. She didn't respond to his 'goodnight'.
Bush walked slowly back to his apartment. He did not sleep
easily.

Kate was in her dressing gown when Bush joined her for
breakfast. He kissed her tenderly on the forehead and breezed:
'Good night's sleep cure you?'

'Even at breakfast you slay me, Bush.'

'Not as great a compliment as it sounds. I toilet elaborately
before I descend the stairs. Now kid, let's forget all about last
night. Deal?'

'I meant every word last night, Bush. If you don't fancy me, I
understand.'

'Kate, I have to know. Which is it? Me – or sex?'

'It's the same. I believe it's called love.'

'Kate, I'm not moonstruck any more. You must understand
that. You want to move in the adult world? That's what it would
mean with me.'

'Bush, you know what I want. Pour yourself some coffee.'

'All right. I didn't sleep much. I thought it out. It is going to
happen to you some day. I had to battle with my conscience, a

thing I didn't know I had. So. You may as well be initiated by the best there is. Gloria Hazelbeck – wife No 2 – I ran into her a few years after the bust up, the parting had been nasty. I was dining, funnily enough, with a friend in the Algonquin. Gloria paused at our table on the way out. I remember she just stood there shaking her head. I thought she was about to make a scene. She says: Bush, you were some bastard, but boy did you go in like Flynn. She was a coarse bitch, Gloria. But her testimonial was valid nonetheless. So my dear sweet Kate, if you insist, you're in for a treat. Are you ready?'

Kate blushed and stammered: 'Now?'

The actor chuckled: 'Not exactly. We'll do it in style. You get dressed and pack a few things. I wanna go and ring Hank. I'll call for you in one hour.'

Bush Vine lay on his sofa with his feet up as he dialled his agent.

'Hank, listen Hank, I want you to phone ahead and get the lodge ship-shape, okay? I'll be there early this evening. No television, Hank, but the rest as heretofore, the logs, the calico and especially the music, Liszt, Chopin, you know, Hank, the music is very important . . . not sixty-nine, Hank, seventy-four, you're falling for your own handouts. No, Hank, I can't tell you her name. Maybe when I come back. If it works out I'll need a lotta help. And Hank, this is not like any other time. No, Hank. I don't want you to guess the name. I don't care, Hank, I don't care how sure you think you are. Take care then, Hank. See you buddy.'

In Hanrahan's Hotel in Mellick, Bush Vine at eighty years of age lay on the bed after a long bath. He was not afraid of killing himself climbing in and out of the bath; he was as agile of mind and body as he had ever been. But internally he was dying and had been for two years. He was too old to be foolish enough to consult a doctor – he did not want to be opened up simply to provide fuel for a prognosis. He lay on the bed with a hotel towel draped across his midriff and coughed through one of those Gold Flake that had been recommended to him as a tolerable non-tipped. The contraction in his chest had grown progressively worse over the last few months. He tired easily. There was no great pain yet but he knew he was on the way out and he did not mind. Kate aside, what was there to live for any more? And since she was now twenty-eight it was high time he was on his way. Even with reading glasses he could no longer pare his toenails and his helplessness appalled him.

'Kate . . . '

'Hmm?'

. 'Can't wield the goddamned scissors again.'

'Coming. Nearly finished.'

She was having a shower next door – in Hanrahan's as in every hotel they stayed in they had separate though adjoining rooms. Bush could afford it and it was his way of paying her due respect. Not for a second had he ever thought of Kate as his mistress and he had always wanted to think of their sexual relationship as evanescent. He contemplated his toenails and chuckled as he always did at the thought of Sister Aquinas. The coincidence of Dara Holden's begging letter and Sister Aquinas' constant urging that they should take a trip to the old country – a country Sister Aquinas herself had never seen – what would the good sister think if she could see them now?

Kate had rather overdone the pilgrimage on behalf of Sister Aquinas.

'I know I'm home, Bush. I can feel it already.' She had gushed in Dublin airport.

'Kate, it's a goddamned airport.'

The guy who drove them to the Gresham remarked after pocketing his tip: 'I hope it keeps up for you now.' Bush glowered at him. But later, having heard more of the same, he conceded that the driver had probably been referring to the good weather – it was only drizzling at the time. They crossed over to Connemara where Kate bought two of those big white pullovers from a state sponsored peasant outside a thatched cottage. Worse, she insisted on their wearing them. She also amassed a crateful of Waterford glass and on the stone floor of a falling down pub in West Clare gave vent to the few steps of a jig taught a few minutes earlier to her by a wizened fiddler.

Kate emerged from the shower. It was a more impressive barometer of Bush Vine's experience than any encomium of Gloria Hazelbeck that he was not immediately aroused. Kate released her hair from the plastic cap and shook her head to release whatever auburn strands might have become matted; her breasts bobbed. Even at twenty-eight she was not yet at her peak, Bush was sure, and if so, he was not destined to take her in the height of her glory. Whoever, if anyone, inherited her would be a lucky man.

'The royal chiropodist at your service, sire.'

She knelt beside the bed and flexed the scissors. Tenderly she fingered the small toe of his left foot.

'Bush, they don't really need doing.'

'I know,' he said.

Dara Holden sipped a lager downstairs in the bar. He did not want Bush Vine to think him a lush. He wanted to exude the chemistry of the pro who would be there at six in the morning, lines word perfect, popular with the crew. Hank Harold had written that the actor would be passing through Mellick on his way to Shannon airport on his way back to the States. Dara was to present himself at seven o'clock. It was now five minutes past.

Upstairs, finished, Kate Flynn sat on Bush Vine's stomach and smiled down at him.

'Kate, I think we better dress. The young hopeful is probably downstairs already.'

'What exactly does he want from you, Bush?'

'I suppose he wants me to take just one look at him and then announce that he looks just right to be a star. Now let's keep the conversation clean tonight, huh? None of that Joyce and stuff tonight. Or Beckett. I'm too old for it.'

'Bush, I'm ashamed of you. I'll never forget the look that bus driver gave you when you threw in Harold Robbins.'

In a North Dublin pub Kate had fallen into chat with a bus driver who put Kate right about some aspects of *Finnegans Wake* and both of them joined heads interpreting *Waiting for Godot*.

'This Dara Holden, Kate, he's sure to be one of them. And listen, I know the Micks, secretly they laugh at us. The reason only half the universities are up all night figuring Joyce is the other half are punch drunk deciphering Beckett. And we make apes of ourselves coming over here with magnifying glasses tracing the footsteps of two conmen. Give me Brendan Behan any day.'

'Bush, you want we should talk acting.'

'Chrissakes no,' Bush Vine lied.

Dara Holden was twisted with fright that he might not make an immediate impression on the actor. But when Bush Vine did appear Dara did not look at him. Unlike Stanley Callaghan who preached that it was a sin to have intercourse before marriage, Dara was not a virgin and was smug about his five conquests so far within the amateur drama movement, all fine women he thought until now he was vouchsafed his first sight of Kate Flynn. He could not take his eyes off her. Bush Vine gripped his arm and said: 'Yes, son. You *are* looking at the most beautiful woman in the world, and thank you. But Kate's okay, she doesn't bite, let's all have a drink and get to know each other.'

'What – what'll you have – am – can I call you Bush?'

'You'd kill me if you called me anything else, Dara, son. And Kate's Kate. Right, Kate?'

'Right.'

'Now let me get the drinks while you and Kate get comfortable.'

'No, no. I'll get them. Who's ever in the bar first buys first. Local rule.'

'Well then. Mine's sherry. And Kate will have – Kate?'

'A glass of Guinness, Dara, please.'

Dara began to relax as he waited at the bar counter for the drinks. Hank Harold had written that Bush Vine would be accompanied by his ward. Dara vaguely remembered reading that Bush Vine had adopted an orphan he came across filming *Without a Past*. To be sitting in Hanrahan's Hotel, not just with Bush Vine, but with a woman who looked – there was a thud as Bazook deposited a muddy Aer Lingus bag at Dara's feet.

'Dara, found you. Stanley said you'd be here. I got your boots from your mother, we've a match against the Institute at half seven.'

The sherry, the Guinness and Dara's lager were placed before him. He tendered a ten shilling note and stared suspiciously at Bazook.

'Stanley sent you?'

'Yeah. He said to hurry.'

'That idiot knows I can't play any bloody match tonight. And when did it come up?'

'A phone call today someplace. I don't know. Stanley's waiting down in the Nook with the lads. Even with you we might be short. Jake's having to round up a couple of strangers.'

Dara glanced briefly at Bush Vine and Kate Flynn seated around the open hearth. He hissed: 'Now listen, Bazook. You go back to the Nook and tell Stanley I said to go and fuck himself. All right?'

'He'll kill me if you don't come.'

'Keep your voice down. Don't look now but I'm with the people over there. I said don't look. That's Bush Vine. *Bush Vine.* Will you explain that to Stanley, for fuck sake will you remind him who I'm with? Now buzz. Here . . . take the bloody bag with you.'

Shaken, Dara Holden brought the drinks over to his company.

'All right, Dara, boy?'

'Yeah. That was an emissary from a pal of mine,' Dara forced a chuckle. 'He wanted me to play a soccer match. They'll have to manage without the star of the team for once, I'm afraid.'

'Is it big league stuff?'

'A pub against a pub or something. Kid stuff.'

'Oh, well, here's a thousand million welcomes or whatever the saying is.'

'Cheers,' Dara replied.

'So. You want to make an actor, fella. What do you think, Kate? Dara *look* an actor?'

Kate studied him. 'Hmm. I'd say Dara would make a fine actor, Bush.'

'Except actors don't usually blush. It's okay, Dara. I blush myself when Kate tells me I'm not looking bad for eighty.'

'Eighty? You're not – eighty?' Dara knew Bush Vine's age to the day.

'Every minute of it, son. Mack Sennet gave me my first break. That's how eighty I am. Now then, back to you. There's acting and acting. Where do you see yourself, Dara? Straight? Comedy? Western?'

'I want to do O'Neill.'

Bush smiled. He patted his ward on the knee. 'Yeah, O'Neill. Met him a couple of times. Not bad for a Mi . . . I got an okay with Eugene.'

'You actually *met* him?'

'Yeah. I . . .' Dara Holden was seated facing them, his back to the door. Bush thought there was something odd about the guy standing with his arms folded behind Dara who was blatantly listening to the conversation. Slowly, Dara Holden turned round.

'Stanley!'

'Mr Vine, would you please forgive me interrupting, but I need this man desperately for an hour or so.'

'Bush, this is a friend of mine, Stanley Callaghan. I . . . '

'How are you, Stanley? This is my ward, Kate Flynn.'

'Mr Vine, this is an honour. I've seen all your movies. I'm your second biggest fan in Mellick. Dara's number one. Pleased to meet you, miss. You don't mind my borrowing him?'

'Cut that out, Stanley.'

'Dara, we're short.'

'Stop messing, Stanley. Go on. Just cut it out.'

Stanley shook his head and stared at the floor. 'Come on, Dara.'

'Stanley, sit down and have a drink or else blow.'

'Dara, it's twenty-five past. We're late as it is. Are you coming, yes or no?'

'No.'

'Dara, what am I going to tell Stevie Mack? That you're letting us down? You know I wouldn't be able to stop him. He'd come in and take it out on that mirror there. Look, why don't your friends come. Miss Flynn, wouldn't you like to see Dara play?'

'I'll kill you, Stanley.'

'Hey, that's not such a bad idea, Kate, huh?'

'I don't mind, Bush.'

'Let's go, kid. Bazook has your gear.' Stanley led the way out of Hanrahan's, pausing to hold the door open for Kate Flynn. Outside he announced: 'We have a couple of cars down outside the Nook. I think we'll all squeeze in.'

'You need a car, I got my Avis if you need a car.'

'Great. Look, Dara you nip down to the Nook and get the lads moving, I'll travel with Mr Vine and show the way.'

Bush Vine insisted that Stanley sit beside him in front. 'Left on to the main street,' Stanley directed, 'and straight for about half a mile until I tell you turn left again.'

In the rearview mirror Stanley caught Kate Flynn's eye for a moment but immediately dropped his.

'So you're a pal of Dara's, that right, Stanley?'

'We're best friends, Mr Vine. Grew up together. Went to school together.'

'Bush. Just plain Bush. You see he does what he's told?'

'Pardon?'

'He didn't seem to want to play this match.'

'Oh. He wanted to play all right. It was just that the match came up at the last minute. It's unfortunate that it clashed with his meeting yourself. You couldn't blame him for getting his priorities scrambled. He was so excited. It's lucky he told me or I wouldn't have known where to find him. You don't mind that much – for an hour? I mean we really need him badly.'

'This match is important then. It's sort of a big moment around here playing these matches?'

Stanley turned to see if the actor was ribbing him. 'Big moment? Good God, no. It's just that we have this pub team, and we got this challenge from the Institute . . . '

'The Institute?'

'Well, everyone calls it that. I don't even know its real name. But it's a club. High class. They play hockey and tennis and cricket, for the better off, all educated by the Jesuits whereas Dara and myself and the lads, we had to go to the Christian Brothers where education is free. Anyway the game, it's not that important, it's cutting into drinking time for one thing, but we don't like to lose to *anyone* and certainly not this shower . . . maybe you think we're mad . . . '

'No, no. I wouldn't say that. Would you say that, Kate?' Out of ordinary good manners – beaten into him by the Christian Brothers – Stanley turned to face the lady's reply.

'I'm going to cheer for Stanley's team.' This time she smiled directly at Stanley who cleared his throat and turned away not quite understanding the effect she was having on him but capable of an educated guess.

'Left here before the traffic lights.'

A few moments later they entered the drive of the Institute.

Stanley rushed away from them to tog up. Bush Vine swept a seasoned eye over the scene as he held the door open for Kate. Two games of mixed doubles were in progress on the courts; pairs straggled around the nine hole pitch and putt course – the stumps were in place on the cricket field though nobody was playing. On the hockey pitch where the soccer match was about to take place a few of the already togged out Institute limbered up. The club was situated only a few minutes from the city yet it had a rural setting. Bush Vine inhaled the trees and fields and remembered having spotted a stream a few hundred yards back. The gentle May evening, the still warm sun and the setting drew from Bush the actor: 'Kate, Isn't this wonderful? Young men on a May evening engaged in friendly combat for the honour of a bar and a club. Where did we lose this, Kate? We must have had this once. That Stanley guy, he has his priorities right. There we were boozing in Hanrahan's and in he comes to jolt us out to the clean air of the playing fields of Mellick.'

Smiling, Kate walked with him towards the hockey pitch where the Institute eleven could be seen splendidly attired in the red and black jerseys of the hockey side. Bush observed the Nook strip near a hedge bordering the pitch.

'I see that as Homeric, Kate. Stripping off in the open.'

The Nook did not have jerseys. Some wore vests, some T-shirts, others pullovers. Some of the shorts were a filthy white, some a filthy black, and one guy, Bush was thrilled to see, wore his long trousers. 'At least Kate, they seem to have boots. No, there's a guy in sneakers.' In officious contrast, the referee, impatiently blowing his whistle and looking at his watch, was dressed in the full black regalia of a League of Ireland soccer referee, which he once had been.

Bush was bored by the game itself. It was not baseball. The referee blew the whistle. Somebody kicked the ball and both teams ran up and down the pitch in pursuit.

'Still, Kate, young men content to play for the honour . . . '

Suddenly, though the plot may have seemed poor to the actor, the dialogue began to sparkle. The Nook goalkeeper, a small chap, apparently called Bazook, saved a shot and was charged by an Institute forward. The babble of the small crowd didn't muffle Bazook's: 'Come in on me again like that and you'll get a kick in the bollix.'

The bystanders began to crowd around Bush Vine as they recognised him. From one of them Bush enquired the rules of the game, a man with the curious name of Tom Splendid, who wore four watches on each arm and whose pockets were stuffed with the shillings and half-crowns and two bobs of the Nook team who did not mind what was robbed belonging to them as long as it was not their money. Tom Splendid explained that the goals were makeshift as it was a hockey pitch. They were using two flag poles and the amenities did not run to a crossbar. This explanation was necessary because play had ceased and there was an angry crowd around the referee in the Nook goal mouth and Bazook was plainly heard again: 'Who's a fucking midget?'

Time and again play stopped in the Nook goalmouth and always due to the same contentious issue. Any ball that went over Bazook's head the Institute claimed as a goal and they were forced to press the point when it became obvious that Bazook was unbeatable by a low shot. Though it was a foreign game to Bush Vine he was gradually able to decipher certain characteristics of some of the players on the Nook team. There was a strong, red-headed guy they called Stevie, who was so clumsy that every time he contested a ball in the air or on the ground he managed to injure someone. Bush was beginning to wonder how accident prone the red-head really was when someone gleefully commented to the gentleman with the watches: 'Did you see the knee in the back when he went up for the header?'

Two guys, known as the twins, Bush could see, were very bad players. Dara Holden and Stanley Callaghan didn't stand out one way or the other but there was a lanky guy called Jake who seemed to do more of what everybody else did and he seemed to do it better. Usually he stayed in the Nook half of the field – where the ball was most of the time and where all the arguments occurred – but once, this guy Jake pushed the ball a little in front of him into the other half of the field and kept going until he was thirty yards from the Institute goalkeeper. Then he kicked the ball past him and in between the two poles sticking out of the ground. This was a score, Bush deduced, when Tom Splendid leapt into his arms and hugged him and the bystanders patted him on the back knowing he was up for the Nook.

At half time Bush and Kate sat on the grass while the Institute team ate oranges and the Nook smoked cigarettes and drank from the bottles of cider thoughtfully provided by Tom Splendid.

The second half to Bush Vine's eyes was a boring procession of the Nook kicking for touch, particularly the Jake guy who drew cheers from the bystanders every time he sent the ball out over the trees. When it finally ended Bush joined in the exultation that rewarded the Nook victory. And it was having thus entered into the spirit of things that made him unprepared for the behaviour of Stanley Callaghan after the game.

Bush and Kate waited at a modest distance from where the Nook team dressed, Bush watching Dara and Stanley chat to each other as they slipped into their trousers.

'That's a sign of best pals indeed,' he said to Kate, 'to be alongside each other talking whether waiting to enter the gas ovens or sharing a sporting victory.' He was the son of fin de siècle immigrants from Belorussia. At eighty, dying, the clean innocent exchanges of young, healthy sportsmen after a game in leafy May surroundings, saddened him.

'Are you coming to the Nook?'

'I'm not going to the Nook. And fuck you, you bollix. I'm going straight back to Hanrahan's where I was rudely interrupted. And by Bazook of all people. He looking like a – like a – a *thing* – in a carpeted hotel. Now I've got to start from scratch again. And isn't she something? Even you noticed her. Stanley, I'd nearly abandon my career to fuck her.'

'You're crude, Dara. You've had the same advantages as me. Decent parents, a good school, respectable neighbours and you end up like this. Can't you think – *cleanly* of women *at all?* She's his granddaughter or ward or something?'

'That's their story but you know what? I'd bet my flute she's his mistress.'

'Don't be disgusting.'

'Who am I talking to. What do you know? All you know is you're about to become a teacher and have three months holidays in the year, you fucking pea brain, you small, parochial, unambitious drone. I have a feeling about the two of them. It's there all right.'

'What proof have you? I mean, Jesus, it's disgusting to even think it.'

'All right, sonny. I admit it. I never sat on a high stool watching the two of them in bed. Okay? And I can't prove there was a second world war either apart from a dim recollection of brown sugar.'

Almost hoarse with disgust – and longing – Stanley asked: 'What age is she?'

'I don't know. Twenty-six? Who cares. Stanley, why don't you drop into Hanrahan's after I make my pitch. Gimme an hour. They probably won't mind.'

'Are you sure? Fuck you, Dara, An eighty-year old rapist won't object to my company? Thanks. Anyway, I don't drink in hotels.'

'You're going to live in the Nook for the rest of your life.'

'Dara, listen to me. Listen to me for the last time before it's too late. In case this Bush bollix is dumb enough to take you on. Dara, only a madman would leave here to go to America. You want to become an actor. All right. Become an actor. Look at MacLiammor, he doesn't have to go to America. He doesn't even have to go to England. F.J. McCormack, what part of America did he make his name? Dara, stay here. Please? I begged you to go to training school with me. No. You're too dumb. Next September, just picture this, Dara. In in the morning at nine. Finish at half three. Christmas, two weeks paid holidays. Easter another two weeks. Two whole months in the summer. After a couple of years a few caravans. Money rolling in, nothing to do but swim and lie in the sun. You could still do it, Dara, you were better than me at school. You could do it in three years. Go for a BA in Uni full time. Look, I'll back you with half my wages, what more can I fucking well do?'

Dara Holden flicked the loose strands from his comb. He put a hand on Stanley's shoulder. 'Do you mean that?'

'Yes. I mean it.'

'I do believe you do. You've never gone this far before. Stanley I'm touched, and to tell you the truth, I wish I could. But you've never listened to me. I want to be an actor. I want to do O'Neill. Not with the College Players. On Broadway. Where it belongs. Come with me, Stanley. They need teachers in America. It would broaden your mind.'

Stanley changed the subject. 'Look at your man walking away. He was handy. Who is he?'

'I don't know. Jake got him. Gabriel something. Are you going to join us in Hanrahan's?'

'Dara, the famine's over. People don't bum passages to America any more.'

'What's the use. We've been through this so many times, we're like long playing records. Let's go.'

'You ride back with your friends, Dara. I'll go with the lads.'

'Aw, come on, Stanley. Say goodbye then. I don't want them to think you've no manners.'

'I don't care what rapists think.'

'Rapists? Jesus.'

'You don't have any decency left, Dara. No morals. You condone mistresses, you sleep with women yourself. You don't go to mass or confession. There's no strength in you, Dara. Good luck. I'll see you.'

Sadly, Dara watched him go and rejoin the Nook. He knew he could not save Stanley Callaghan. He had tried and tried and tried over coffee and cigarettes and whiskey and cigarettes and pint bottles and cigarettes into the fag end of drunken mornings over five years.

'Your friend not coming with us, Dara?'

'No. He's going to the Nook for the celebrations.' Dara regretted letting that slip when Kate enquired: 'Oh! What way do they celebrate?'

'Drink.' Dara scrambled into the back seat praying it would blow over but as Bush Vine pressed his elegant foot on the accelerator he muttered: 'And singing, I bet? That's funny, Kate, we haven't come across any singing.'

'We've been in too many hotels, Bush. Hotels aren't the places for singing, are they Dara?'

'No. But neither are pubs any more. Since the television started last year. The Nook doesn't have television. But there's no singing there, either. Singing isn't allowed. There's a sign up on the wall.'

'This is it, Dara, right here?'

They pulled up outside the hotel.

'Yes.'

'Well, I could do with a real drink after the excitement. I shouldn't, but whiskey it's gonna be. May as well celebrate ourselves. Who wants to live to be a hundred and fifty anyway. What about you, Dara? Join an old man in writing a night off?'

'Sure.'

All three began with large Jamesons. Bush and Kate were relaxed whereas Dara was noticeably uneasy. 'Good stuff,' Bush Vine complimented the whiskey. 'Now where were we? Ah yes. O'Neill. Dara, my advice to you is to forget O'Neill for a while. Now, I haven't heard of some of the stuff you mentioned in your letter to Hank, except O'Casey, of course, but why don't we get to the bottom line on this straightaway and then we can settle down to serious drinking. Dara . . . what exactly can I do for you?'

Bush Vine sat back, unsmiling, eyes frank with enquiry. Dara fidgeted with the ashtray.

'It isn't easy to ask face to face.'

'You speak your mind, Dara. I like straight talk.'

'It's just . . . to me the States is the only place to make it, but I can't get there. I don't have a single relative or friend out there to claim me over. And I thought even if I had I'd still be lost. What I wondered is, could you get Mr Harold to take me on?'

'Dara, I don't know that you know agents. Hank will take *anybody* on. Well, maybe not anybody. As for claiming you out as you call it, I'd stand by you there myself. You just give me your word you won't become a burden on the American economy.'

'Of course . . . '

' . . . the problem is Dara, there's more to it than that . . . '

'I know. I know. It's up to me. But I know I can make it. It's just the introductions, where, how to peddle my wares. You see, acting, I've never held a steady job. I've been in and out of factories, at the moment I'm with sps in Shannon, three shifts, the money isn't great but I calculate that chucking booze and fags I could save the fare in four or five months. After that I don't want to waste a second when I land. If Mr Harold showed me a door, I'd do the rest. I know I can.'

'I like confidence in an actor. Never met one that hadn't got it. I don't see any problem here. I'll fix it with Hank. If I'm still around. Eighty and not getting younger. Say, listen. Now that that's outa the way, why don't we join your buddies in the Nook? What do you think, Kate? Had enough of hotels?'

'Good idea, Bush. Would we be gatecrashing, Dara?'

'Pardon? No, no. Of course not.' Dara was dry-throated. He had missed his chance. He could almost see Stanley laughing at him. He had to draw on his limited acting experience to hide his feelings but Bush Vine was an actor too.

'Kate, why don't you just powder your nose and then we'll hit this Nook.' Bush winked at her. Obediently she left them alone.

Bush Vine drew his cheque book from his jacket inside pocket: 'No need to spend four months in a sweatshop, Dara.'

'Hold on. Please . . . '

Bush Vine put a finger to his lips. He began to write. He looked up and chuckled: 'Dara, an old man has a poor memory. I've forgotten your second name.'

'Holden. But I couldn't do this. Honestly . . . '

'I'm doing the doing. Hell, a goddamned plane ticket. I can run to a plane ticket. And when you get on your feet you can pay me back. Here, that oughta cover it. Now you gotta get a passport, visa in order, your arm jabbed, that business. I expect to see you in New York in a month. I'm not there, Hank will tell you where to get a cheap room in the Village. Okay, son?'

Slowly Dara put out his hand towards the proferred cheque but without taking it he slumped back in his chair and put his face in his hands.

'I haven't been straight with you. I thought I could go through with it but I can't. The truth is, I've already seen to passport, visa, and so on. I could go in the morning. I – anticipated your decency. Stanley – my pal – he said I was disgusting. He said I was a bum, a beggar. He was right. He told me to ask you straight out for the fare – out of respect for you – but I didn't, I couldn't, I was cowardly . . . '

'Some day, Dara boy, I'll tell you how I got to Los Angeles. My old lady had put by for a rainy day. Kept it under her mattress . . . ' Bush Vine gripped the bridge of his nose with thumb and forefinger. Anyone who did not know him, anyone other than Hank Harold would have taken the gesture as evidence that Bush was distraught at the memory. 'And she didn't even live to see me make it. So, Dara kid, old Bush understands. Better than you know. So let's you and me get drunk tonight. And your buddy, Stanley. I like that guy, something about him. Ah, isn't she beautiful?'

'She certainly is. And thanks.'

Kate Flynn linked them both down the road to the Nook.

Dara Holden detached himself from Bush and Kate and led the way into the snug. It comprised an L-shaped form, a table on which there would not have been room for three breakfasts but had often accommodated nine at poker, and one tubular chair immediately inside the door and tucked under the table. Kate Flynn sat facing the door, her back to the wall. Bush and Dara sat together on the form facing the hatch which Dara pushed open and which afforded a television view of the bar.

'Dara, you order three doubles. I'll pick up the tab.'

Mrs Trehy was in residence on her high stool. The team and supporters were gathered round Stanley. Thanks to the cheque in his pocket Dara was able to maintain a certain equanimity in spite of the 'cunts', 'bollixes' and 'shitheads' that wafted smokily towards the snug. That was what Stanley Callaghan wanted him to stay at home and remain part of. It was not that Dara did not like Stevie Mack or Jake or Tolly or Bazook or Cocoa – he had grown up on the same street with them, he was doomed for life to like them, but collectively they were a shambles. Dara could see it and he didn't understand why Stanley refused to see it. If he were in the bar with them now he would be part of the admiring throng around Stanley. Dara would be no better than themselves in their eyes. They did not understand ambition let alone respect the greatness of Dara's. All they knew was that Stanley was the boss. Stanley had always been the boss. As kids on the corner of the street checking their fourpences it was Stanley who decided what picture they should see. It was Stanley who had almost succeeded in killing Stevie Mack with his notion to expose the Great Blondini. With Bush Vine's cheque warm in his pocket Dara Holden began to soar away from them all. He saw a day when he would return home rich and famous and with a woman like Kate Flynn on his arm – if not in fact Kate Flynn . . .

Tom Splendid's wife, Peggy, took the order. The babble subsided briefly in honour of the purchase of three large whiskeys. Dara caught Stanley's eye but as readily lost it.

It was the woman with the actor that drained Stanley Callaghan of all joy and confidence. She was what he had always dreamed about, the never-to-be-realised ideal that contented one with hoping some day to settle for and be rewarded with less. Unable to look at Dara he buried his face in the pint; he was a nobody, a prospective teacher who could have no business in the snug except as Dara's pal. Dara was an actor, one of their own.

'Dara, would your friend Stanley join us for a drink?'

Dara poked his head through the hatch and shouted: Stanley! Stanley left the bar and opened the snug door.

'Stanley, Bush would like to buy you a drink.'

'Hell, I'd like to buy everyone a drink. You're a fine bunch of guys. Drinks on the house, Stanley.'

'I don't think so, Mr Vine – Bush. I'd be very glad to have a drink with you myself, but please, not for the house. They're a peculiar lot. They have their pride. Knowing you were here they would find the drink tasteless. I've seen it happen. But if you gave Tom Splendid the money for a drink for the house for tomorrow, they'd drink it then and love you and toast you in your absence.'

Stanley didn't smile or blush when Dara stared at him in disbelief. Bush Vine nodded with understanding.

'I see. I'll do that later then. But you must sit down here, Stanley, and tell us about yourself.'

It was then that Teresa Green made her entrance in time to see her husband give Mrs Trehy a victorious squeeze. Stanley looked over the partition at the commotion while Dara, Bush and Kate viewed through the hatch. A pint of Guinness flowed wastefully down Johnny Green's face as Teresa threw herself at him digging her nails into his face. All Johnny did was shield himself, making no effort to fight back. Teresa stood up, unsatisfied, grabbed a half-pint glass from the counter, broke it and attempted a jab at her husband's throat. Jake O'Dea, reluctantly, led the charge to disarm her. It was all over in less that two minutes. Johnny Green left or was dragged away by his wife, Stanley was not sure which. He sat down. He was thrilled to think that the incident would lower Dara in Bush Vine's eyes and astonished to realise he felt shame himself at what the woman would think of him. Ever alert, Bush Vine consoled: 'Never a dull moment here, I'd say.'

But Stanley only looked in sequence from Dara to Bush to Kate Flynn and then down at his fingers drumming sadly on the table.

'She's some cookie?' Bush smiled at Dara but Dara had no answer.

'That's not the problem,' Stanley revived. 'The problem is that Johnny Green is a gentleman and she takes advantage of it. She knows he would never hit her. A gentleman fallen on hard times. Johnny Green sang Holy Night from the high altar of the Redemptorists two Christmases in a row. Now look at him — at seventeen!'

Dara Holden glowed briefly with love for Stanley.

'Maybe someone should sing a song here, cheer everyone up? Huh, Dara? Stanley?'

Dara Holden indicated the sign: ONLY SAD SONGS ON SAD OCCASIONS ONLY. 'I'm afraid, Bush, that songs in the Nook aren't meant to cheer people up.'

'I don't get that,' Bush admitted.

'It means what it says. The only time singing is allowed is after a funeral or something like that. It's a perk we allow the proprietor. That notice was up before we started drinking. We inherited it.'

'I feel almost hungry for a song knowing it's forbidden.' Kate Flynn spoke wistfully. 'Would he not make an exception just for tonight, Dara?'

Dara Holden looked at Stanley and so Bush Vine and Kate Flynn looked at Stanley. Stanley smiled, made a hopeless gesture and stood up; he navigated the long hall and re-entered the bar. The occupants of the snug observed him approach Tom Splendid. The proprieter did a double take of disbelief. He shook his head and washed his hands symbolically of Stanley Callaghan's entreaties. The bar fell silent.

'Look, Tom, once wouldn't kill you.'

'No.'

'It's a sad occasion, Tom.'

'Sad? We just beat the Institute. Where's the sadness?'

'Tom, look at poor Johnny Green. Isn't that sad? Don't you think that's sad?'

'You're joking. The best entertainment in ten years. No, Stanley. I'm sorry. I won't have sadness devalued in my bar.'

'Just one. Just Bazook. One song.'

'No.'

'All right.' Stanley did not know where the inspiration was coming from. 'All right, Tom. You're forcing me to announce something I wanted to remain secret. I suppose I'd have to tell you some time. I am about to be married.'

Dara Holden was astounded at Stanley's acting talent. The announcement was greeted first with silence, then titters, then guffaws. But Stanley managed so well the look of one indeed about to suffer that fate that silence returned and Tom Splendid was obliged to enquire – sarcastically – though a little unsure of himself: 'And who is the lucky woman?'

Stanley gazed at the floor. Slowly he directed his eyes to the snug: 'The lady's name is Kate Flynn. And it is in her honour I want the song.'

All eyes turned to the snug. Kate Flynn withdrew from the hatch and sat out of general view, blushing. Dara Holden whispered: 'He'll do anything to get his way.'

'Splendid job. But. Is it a sad occasion? 'Twill do. One song. One sad song only.'

'Thank you, Tom. Bazook, your best.'

Bazook, braced by a benedictory swallow from his pint, climbed down off his stool and took short steps to the centre of the bar. He tugged with both hands at the lapels of his short coat. Then he rested his right fist lightly on the counter, retained his left-handed grip on his left lapel, coughed and began:

> Dearest, our day is over,
> Ended the dream divine;
> You must go back to your life,
> I must go back to mine.
> Back to the joyless duties,
> Back to the fruitless tears;
> Loving and yet divided,
> All through the empty years.

In the snug Kate Flynn leaned forward from her seat and peered once again through the hatch. Dara Holden closed his eyes. Bush Vine stood on the form and looked over the partition. The hush in the bar was almost visible, the only movement in fact being the drift of cigarette smoke. The general reverence was well deserved. Bazook, of the buck-toothed foul vocabulary and common Mellick flat accent on the field of play, was no more.

> How can I live without you?
> How can I let you go?
> I that you love so well, dear,
> You that I worship so.

Bazook drank from his glass, re-assumed his stance and continued.

> Dearest, the night is passing,
> Waneth the trembling moon;
> Hark! How the wind ariseth,
> Morn will be here so soon.
> Tell me again you love me,

Kiss me on lips and brow;
Love of my soul, I love you,
How can I leave you now?

Humbly, the bar joined in:

How can I live without you?
How can I let you go?
I that you live so well, dear,
You that I worship so.

The applause from the bar was much louder than usual. They all knew the snug was impressed. The snug was on its feet clapping, including Dara, a victim of Bazook's tenor wizardry despite the absurdity of the occasion. Stanley Callaghan sneaked a glance at Kate Flynn who remained with her elbows on the hatch and her attentive palms framing her face. Thanks to the merciful effect the drink was at last having on him Stanley forced himself back to the snug.

'I trust I may be forgiven the liberties taken to have a song sung here.'

'Stanley boy, it was sure worth it. Good thinking. Kate, it was worth it?'

'It was beautiful. Such beautiful words. I wonder who wrote them.'

Stanley beat Dara Holden to the hatch and roared: 'Bazook, Bazook, who wrote the words?'

'Tosti. F.Paolo Tosti.'

'Good man, Bazook.'

'He even knows who wrote it?' Bush Vine was flabbergasted.

'He's a music buff. Hey, Stanley, who was it, Joe Kennedy, he used to haunt the Nook one time trying to get Bazook to train his voice.'

'That's right. He claimed he could get Bazook sent to Rome or Milan or wherever. Just as well. We wouldn't have beaten the Institute without him.'

Bush Vine and Kate Flynn laughed. Dara Holden was not amused, knowing as he did that Stanley was serious.

'Sister Aquinas used to sing songs like that to me when I was a little child,' Kate Flynn offered dreamily. 'She hadn't a voice like Bazook's, of course. She would only sing to the small girls in the orphanage. She was shy about it.'

This woman a whore. This woman a mistress. Dara had so little control over his base self that he was capable of believing anything.

'You were in an orphanage?' Stanley groped.

Kate nodded. Bush Vine answered on her behalf. He was conscious of the glamour of the abandoned and he liked to project this aspect of Kate's desirability in much the same way that he might – given appropriate circumstances – have drawn attention to her beautiful legs.

'Yes. Kate is an orphan. But a good Catholic one. She was found in St Patrick's Cathedral and she was reared by Sister Aquinas better than I guess any parents could have done. Until old Bush here happened along and got Kate to look after me in my old age. I tell you fellas, my goddamn wives never minded me like this angel does.'

The lovely girl sitting opposite Stanley in the snug was adopted by a genial old fogy and how did Dara interpret that? A whore. Stanley should have known better. The freaks attached to the College Players could do everything but act. Dara was always claiming that every other so and so was a homosexual – he actually said it about Michael MacLiammor – and Stanley in his innocence had believed him.

'Yep,' Bush continued even though Kate tried to stop him. 'Some woman. Streets ahead of her class in school and college. Thought you wanted to be a teacher, my dear? Bush knew better. Kate's in real estate. And how! There isn't a negotiator in the village of New York in the same league as Kate.'

'Real estate?' Stanley asked. 'Isn't that what we call auctioneering?'

'Yes,' Kate answered. 'And don't listen to Bush. He oversells me. That wouldn't do in real estate.'

'See what I mean? She knows how not to oversell. Been wasted as a teacher.'

Stanley realised the old actor did not intend a slur on his vocation. But presented with the germ of a performance Stanley saw his opportunity to impress the lady. As naively as he could express himself he asked: 'But – you're not actually qualified to teach?'

'She most certainly is. I saw to that. Kate, I never mentioned real estate or any other career until you were qualified, did I?

But I knew you had enough of schooling being reared in one. I figured it would cramp your style. And I was right.'

'No you weren't.' The words were out of Stanley and in a tone he had not intended before he realised. Dara Holden's eyes widened: 'What exactly is that supposed to mean?'

'Nothing.' Stanley spoke mildly. 'I'm just saying it's wrong to put real estate before learning.'

'Not so fast, Stanley. I'm not knocking learning.'

'You're not knocking it but you're saying it doesn't square up to flogging houses?'

'Well, now, I wouldn't put it as crudely as that.'

'You just did.'

'Hold on now . . . '

'I'm not blaming you. You just don't know what you're talking about in this instance.' He had their attention. All he could think of was that he had their attention.

'Stanley . . . '

'Stay out of this, Dara. There are some things that just can't be let pass. I'm putting it to Mr Vine that it's a crime to dissuade anyone from teaching and two crimes to divert them into selling houses . . . '

'That's enough. Can it, Stanley. I'm sorry, Bush.'

'No. It's okay. Let Stanley finish. I wanna hear this. And no more Mr Vine please, Stanley.'

'It needs to be said. A moment ago you claimed you were not knocking learning. Do you expect a decoration for not knocking learning? Do you not realise where you are? This is the island of Saints and Scholars. Nobody, not Bush Vine or anyone else in this world can knock learning. Because in this world learning is what matters most. And no one can learn unless he's taught. Now I'm not *blaming* you. It's easier for me, us, an old country to see it. America's young . . . '

'You just hold it right there, Stanley. Don't hand me that "only two hundred years old" crap. I won't take it.'

'I'm not handing you crap. And I'm not *criticising* America for being born yesterday. I'm just trying to point out in a civil fashion that if you were as old as we are you wouldn't put anyone off teaching no matter how well meant you were. I'm not criticising *you*. You don't know any better . . . '

'Stanley . . . '

'Shut up, Dara. I'm about to become a teacher myself and I

won't let anyone devalue the *vocation*.'

It was not working out the way he intended. He had Bush Vine's unfazed attention. Even when Kate Flynn put her hand to her forehead and began to sniffle, Bush did not turn to look at her. He fingered his glass but otherwise regarded Stanley with neither hostility nor pleasure. Dara Holden gripped Stanley's arm fiercely and hissed: 'Get out.'

'All right, Dara. Take it easy. My apologies to you all. I've been trying to oversell teaching. I'd never make a hot shot negotiator.' Nobody laughed. 'I'll leave now. Do have a pleasant stay in Ireland.'

He walked back out the hall and into the bar.

Stanley Callaghan was drunk with jealousy now. He knew what he should do. Out of respect for himself and out of friendship for Dara he should go back to the snug and make a genuine apology to the old man and at the same time tell the truth and he should then leave them and go and lick his self-inflicted wounds. But he could not face it.

Knowing the truth, Dara Holden contributed: 'That was uncharacteristic of him. All I can say is that he must have too much taken.'

'You know, Dara, maybe the guy is right? You would have been a great teacher, Kate. And *he'll* make a great teacher. He has the ideals. You're lucky to have a pal like that, Dara. I never had.'

'Dara, excuse me but where's the ladies?'

'I'm afraid, Kate, the Nook doesn't run to one. But you can go upstairs. I'll get the key.'

Dara tapped on the hatch and discreetly drew Peggy Splendid's attention. He mimed, by twisting his wrist, and Peggy responded by smuggling the key out of a drawer and passing it guiltily to Dara. It was considered a shameful business to go to the lavatory and the publican took advantage of the national psyche by providing a shameful lack of accommodation. Dara directed Kate down the hall and stood by until she opened the door leading upstairs.

'Turn left on the landing. Ignore a small kitchen. Next door after it.'

Without Kate there was no embarrassment in the snug. Bush Vine was eighty and had left that class of emotion behind him.

He understood why she sniffed – on his behalf and he had not been in the least offended. Idealism had never given him offence. He admired it. And pitied it. It hadn't a chance.

Dara Holden was angry. Stanley was the one person he knew whom he would have been happy to bring anyplace with him. He was well reared, good in conversation, knowing when to listen. Stanley could have done a snow job on the Americans on Dara's behalf that would have had Bush reaching a second time for his cheque book and insisting that America needed Stanley too. But instead he had given that ludicrous exhibition.

'I just don't understand it, Bush,' Dara lied. 'I just don't.'

'Dara, son, leave it. In many ways Stanley is so right.'

Dara did not see any point in trying to enlighten him.

'Jake, mind my pint. I'll be back in a second.'

There was no danger to Stanley's pint. Drink was not robbed in the Nook. His remark was to cushion the oddity of his sudden departure. He had spotted the handing over of the key. He watched Dara's return to the snug. He waited in the hall not knowing what he was going to say or exactly why he wanted to say anything. He told himself that this was an opportunity to apologise privately. He listened for the footsteps on the stairs, tip-toed back out the hall and began to walk in again to coincide with her coming out.

'Oh!' He managed surprise. Kate Flynn nodded, smiled and turned to lock the door. Having achieved accidentally bumping into her he was now totally on his own. To put on an act now did not even occur to him.

'Listen, please, I'd like . . . '

'Pardon?' She turned clutching the key.

'What I want to say is, I can't tell you how sorry I am about back there . . . ' Stanley discovered he was not afraid of her.

'Oh. Not at all. There's nothing to be sorry about.'

'Yes there is. I was offside. I really was and I'm sorry. I could die.'

'But honestly.' He might have been a child she was comforting. It was a narrow hall. They stood close to each other. 'Honestly, no one took offence. And everything you said was quite true for you.'

'I made you cry.'

'No you did not. I shed a small tear but for a different reason.'

'Thank you for saying that anyway.'

'It's true.' It was true. She had thought Bush might have felt remorse at having directed her away from teaching but when she saw that he was not offended she recovered at once and left to make up her face. Stanley had his back to the door of the bar. Kate had her back to the wall. She was at her ease; there was no mistaking his discomfiture. His mouth opened and closed again without utterance. She would move out the hall, back into the snug and out of his life if he did not say something immediately.

'I . . . ' he tried. But there was no follow through.

'Yes?'

'Oh, nothing. I don't know what to say.'

'Come on in and have another drink.'

'Good God, no.'

'Why not? You're not afraid of dear old Bush?'

'No. It's Dara. I just couldn't face him now. D'you understand? I'll see him tomorrow. Both of us will have sick heads. I'll bump into him on the street. He'll glare at me. I'll glare at him. One of us will say: the hell with it.'

Something was working. She wasn't moving. She was standing there in front of him, chuckling, amused. Then she said: 'I'd better go back in.'

'Wait!' The word leapt from him.

'Yes?'

'Just one second. I wanted to say something.'

'Yes?'

'God. I'm a coward. I can't say what I want to say. I mean I'm afraid to say what I want to say. But I'm going to say it, Dara might never look at me again, you might think I should be locked up, if it would only come out of my mouth, what I want to say, it sounds ridiculous even before I say it . . . Miss Flynn, I'm in love with you. I've never seen anyone like you in my life, never imagined there could be anyone like you. There. That's it. You go back to Dara and Bush. I'll nip into the bar. I swear to you, if I could have stopped myself, I would. But I had to say it. Please forgive me.'

He had not looked at her while he spoke. He looked at her now. She dropped her eyes and mumbled: 'Thank you. Thank you very much.'

'Please. Don't thank *me*.' Kate studied him frankly for a

second. 'You know, I like you too.'

'There's no need for you to say that. But thanks anyway.'

'But I do.'

'Are you really serious?'

'Why shouldn't I like you? You don't hate yourself, I bet.'

Dara Holden opened the snug door and poked his head into the hall.

'Kate, are you all right there?'

'I'm grand. I'm fine, Dara. Be with you in a moment.'

Dara allowed his suspicious look to linger on Stanley and then reluctantly withdrew.

'Gas man, Dara. Would you mind if I asked you one question. What age are you?'

'Twenty-eight.'

'I'm only twenty-three. You'd consider me too young for you I suppose.'

She saw him growing in confidence and found herself replying coyly: 'Too young for what?'

'Could I do one thing and then I'll go away. Could I give you one kiss? Just once. A small kiss.'

'All right.'

There was only a foot between them. It might have been an ocean to a crazed mariner so long did it take Stanley to go into action. He was thumbs, knees and elbows and the kiss was not hot enough to be chaste. There had never been a moment like this in his life; what overwhelmed Kate was that she felt as excited as she had the day Bush Vine took her to the lodge in the Catskills when he first made love to her.

'Thanks.'

'And thank you too, sir.'

'I've shot my bolt now I'm afraid. Even I haven't the neck to say what I feel like saying now.'

In dark moments Kate had faced the fact that Bush Vine would die and she would be alone again without a friend – with the exception of Hank Harold and Hank thought of himself as ridiculous let alone it being a secret from anyone else. When she thought of the chilliness of New York without Bush Vine she was not being spiritually unfaithful; he had himself bluntly suggested a dozen men he thought worthy of her. Often he had half-heartedly tried to revert to the father and daughter relationship so that she would be unclouded in her sexual

attitude to those he deemed prospective husbands. He had
sometimes been so resolute in his abstinence that she had had
to outrightly seduce him.

'Say it, Stanley.'

'Say what?'

'Say it. Go on. Say it.'

'Will you ... '

'Will I? Would you be kind?'

'Kind? My name is known throughout the length and breadth
of the Nook for kindness. Ask anyone.'

'You're on then young Stanley.' Her shyness evaporated. She
smiled fixedly at him.

'But ... '

'But what?'

'You're joking.'

'Am I?'

'I mean – I've no money. I'm just – just nearly a poor teacher.'

'I have money. Or I have no money. Which do you prefer?'

'I prefer you with no money.'

'It's a deal then? Let's close it. I hate loose ends.' Kate put out
her hand. Stanley examined it. He wiped his sweaty plam on his
chest. So unambiguous was the look they exchanged for the
second that they shook hands it might have been after a month
of exhaustive negotiation.

'Now. Let's go and break the good news to Bush and Dara.'

'Ladies first – Kate.'

Dara Holden and Bush Vine swung their knees to the right to
allow Kate to resume her seat. Stanley stood immediately
inside the door with his elbow on the hatch.

'Ah, Stanley,' Bush Vine greeted.

'Behave yourself this time,' Dara instructed, 'show them
your good side. I've been telling Bush you have a good side.'

Stanley laughed, rubbed Dara's hair and mutely shook hands
with a delighted Bush Vine. 'Bush, don't mind me. Kate ... I
don't know how to tell them, Kate. You tell them.'

Dara Holden thought it was typical of him to use her
christian name as though she were his sister. He was one thing
or the other. He turned to Kate for the revelation. Bush Vine
looked straight ahead, his left ear doing the seeing. But it was
directly to Bush that Kate spoke after staring at him for what

seemed to Dara a hypnotic length of time.

'Stanley and I are going to be married.'

Very slowly Bush Vine turned to her. Her eyes beseeched him. Bush nodded, leaned towards her and kissed her forehead. Once again he extended his hand to Stanley.

'Good. Good, good, good. Congratulations young man. Now this does call for that drink for the house – for everyone – and to hell with their feelings. The drink's on Bush Vine.' He pushed open the hatch. 'Innkeeper!'

'Stanley? Stanley, what is this? What trick did you pull now? Come on – somebody – let me in on this.'

'It's all right, Dara. There was no dirty work at the crossroads. Come on. Give us a smile.'

What Stanley Callaghan had earlier posited – that Nookites might be embarrassed at having a drink bought for them – appeared briefly a tenable notion when Bush Vine announced the betrothal. He was greeted with collective stony stares sadly directed at Stanley Callaghan. It might have been his death that had been announced.

The union was discussed from every angle in Hanrahan's Hotel and Dara Holden's house. The four of them were drunk leaving the Nook and they played out a comedy outside the hotel; Dara and Bush standing aside while Stanley and Kate arranged to meet the following night.

And now, fully clothed, Bush and Kate sat on the bed puffing cigarettes. In the circumstances Bush was reluctant to as much as loosen his tie.

'It's extraordinary, Kate. That time when Stanley announced you were going to be married, just so that Bazook could sing, I thought about it then. Imagined it. As a good idea. You're happy, Kate?'

'Bush, tell me not to go through with it.'

'Certainly not. Unless you want me to. You want me to?'

Kate stubbed out her cigarette and sat with her hands under her thighs kicking her legs. The schoolgirlish pose seemed appropriate to Bush Vine.

'Bush – I felt, just looking at him, even that time when he came in first downstairs and stood behind Dara, I can't describe it, I . . . '

Bush Vine placed his hand on her knee: 'It's not meant to be describable.' He took away his hand. 'I like him. Don't ask me why either. But I do. And Kate, you've often heard me going on about the Micks, well, I'll say this much for them, they take marriages seriously in Ireland. No Reno. No Vegas. It's for keeps. And you gotta think of that, Kate. And frankly, my dear, I do give a damn. Heh heh. Here now, Kate? What is it, Kate? Not tears?'

Kate knelt on the floor and put her head on the actor's knees. She whispered: 'Bush . . . Bush, I love you so much. So much. I'm afraid for you.'

Bush ran his fingers through her hair. 'Afraid for old Bush? My dear, how silly . . . ' It was very hard for him to think now, as he was thinking, that it was not on to share a bed tonight. And yet he was relieved, almost ready to die of relief that she would be in good hands. And yet again the thought of her body, of her fragrance, of her total commitment to loving that he himself had taught her, trespassed on his eagerness to sacrifice. He pulled himself together and said jauntily: 'You know, it occurs to me that Hank and I haven't had a game of checkers in years. I think I'd like that, play a few games with Hank, chew the fat about the old days. So there. Old Bush is going to hit the hay now. Can't carry the liquor these days. Kate . . . stop that now, Kate. No tears. Come on. Tears! On such a face! But I do know why, Kate. And I thank you. But pull yourself together now and hop into bed. And start thinking of Stanley.'

He stood up and lifted Kate till she stood facing him. 'Bush, we must be together tonight.'

'No, Kate. I've had a good run. There's a time, Kate, even for the proprieties.'

Bush kissed her on the forehead but she clung to him, whimpering. He forced her hands from around him and made her sit on the bed. He left her there and quietly went to the adjoining bedroom. He was laying awake twenty minutes later when Kate came in.

'Now, Kate . . . ' He left it at that. And in her own way, on their last night together Kate Flynn repaid Bush Vine for everything he had done for her. A lesser man would have died from the pleasure.

Over the mugs of tea in Dara Holden's kitchen Stanley

Callaghan responded to the inquisition. 'Dara, everything I've told you – word for word – is exactly the way it happened. I'm as amazed as you are.'

'You couldn't be.'

'Is it that big a mystery? My native charm, would that not account for it?'

'The only thing native to you is your cunning. Okay, let's suppose the woman was ripe for romance. How the hell didn't she see me?'

'Dara, you got what you wanted. You're off to the States to do O'Neill. I'm happy. You're happy.'

'You're happy? You don't want me to stay at home and become a teacher any more so you can have someone to play you snooker at four o'clock? Where did you get that bullshit about the nobility of learning and teaching? Christ! I bet that's what did it. She believed you. Good God, she thinks that's you. She doesn't know that you're fucking well rotten through and through. And you're meeting her tomorrow. Jesus. What are you going to do tomorrow?'

'Assuming she doesn't change her mind, assuming nobody tries to make her change her mind – we'll go and see a priest and set the letters of freedom business in motion.'

'Letters of freedom?'

'Kate wasn't born around the corner from me. She'll have to get a letter of freedom from all the parishes she's lived in.'

'And you won't have to get any?'

'Of course not. You've forgotten your own religion, Dara. I'm not a travelled man.'

'Travelled?' Dara Holden sniggered. 'You can move fast though, can't you? I'll tell you something, Stanley. I've never had much time for the black army but I'll say this: a priest who would give you a letter of freedom, he should be defrocked, gouged, have his bollix kicked in and his poor box robbed. I'm going to bed. I suggest you fuck off home and examine your conscience – Jesus, what am I saying? You? Conscience? Jesus!'

After Stanley left Dara made another pot of tea and set about another packet of cigarettes. It had happened at last. He was going to America to do O'Neill. He had praised America so often to Stanley as an antidote to having to listen so often to Stanley knocking America – not America specifically but any place that was not Mellick, but not Mellick specifically – any place that was not the Nook. All through their schooldays when they would go home at four and have a few hours of homework to do and no money Stanley could not get it out of his head that teachers were home at four, had money and that that was considered to be work. Stanley cited God's curse on Cain. Work was a curse to be avoided. Stanley was amazed at how easy it was to become a teacher and how comparatively few people seemed to know this. Even doctors and solicitors worked all hours.

'Dara, let me paint the picture for you. Four o'clock, the two of us straight down town for a few games of snooker and then a few pints before the tea. No school, Saturday, Dara. Just think of the summer, we could be stretched out on the grass beside the headrace getting a colour. And then dive into forty feet of water in the canal to cool down. Jesus, Dara, it's heaven on earth, imagine, being *paid* for two months holidays in the summer. And no need for conscientious shit. I can see myself telling the class to read the Lives of the Saints during Christian Doctrine while I correct compositions.'

Dara saw no chance of saving him now. He might have been Bob Tracey the way he came out with the guff about learning. Except that Bob Tracey did believe in it. It was ironic that Dara himself believed in it but that Stanley didn't.

'I want to shake off the parish pump, Stanley, and make something of myself and that sticks in your craw, doesn't it, leaving you behind to preside over the Nook.'

'Wrong. I'm trying to show you your own backyard.'

'Thanks. I see it.'

It was already nine o'clock and dark when they came out of the presbytery. The parish priest knew Stanley to come from a good Catholic family. He declared he would proceed with expedition. But earlier in the day Bush Vine had telephoned Hank Harold and letters of freedom were on their way to the parish priest before the parish priest wrote for them. For the first time in his life Stanley Callaghan was on a date and almost totally innocent of procedure. He held Kate's hand as they walked down town.

'This is O'Connell Street, Kate, named after Daniel O'Connell, the Liberator. There's a place down here I want to show you, the Cat's Hole, it's a little cul-de-sac responsible for its own share of liberation among my generation. Or so I'm told. I've never been there.'

It was late in the day for Stanley Callaghan's generation to walk out into the country and too early for them to own motor cars. Lana Turner's sweater gave them bad thoughts and they learned of the frailty of man from the Redemptorist missioners who not alone had condemned Bush Vine from the pulpit but who also identified Elizabeth Taylor without equivocation by referring to her as 'a certain actress who shall be nameless'. The Cat's Hole was as much a landmark in the relationships of that Mellick generation as buying a watch or meeting the parents. By day the Cat's Hole cul-de-sac off O'Connell Street throbbed with a second-hand car repairs wizard, a basket weaver's, a bicycle shop, a coal merchant's, an upholsterer's and sundry fugitives from the rates. White-washed and cobble-stoned, at night, the entrepreneurs having bolted and shuttered, the Cat's Hole was a pitch dark lane where couples courted.

'Down there, Kate, that's where all the courting couples go.'

'It's dark.'

'Yeah. People are probably shy of kissing without the cloak of night. I know I wouldn't have been able to kiss you last night only I was jarred.'

'Stanley, is that an Irish compliment?'

'I didn't exactly put that beautifully did I? You know, I mean I'd be shy about it in daylight.'

'Stanley, after you.'

It was much darker than they realised, not the dark of the cinema that brightens with adjustment. It was dark and remained dark the way an impenetrable jungle remains impenetrable. They stumbled along. From the sporadic evidence of their ears there were about half a dozen couples grappling in the Cat's Hole that night. By the glimmer of a white-washed portion of the wall against which they leaned, Stanley put his arms around Kate and kissed her. He squeezed her body to him and maintained the kiss as long as he could knowing that stamina was a sign of experience. They kissed and kissed and kissed because Stanley was thrilled with kissing and would not have dreamed of anything else. He knew of those who put their hands underneath their girl friends' dresses before marriage not to mention how shamelessly far Dara went. But Dara had lost his religion. As they kissed they heard from less than ten yards away a hoarse and muffled avowal: Honest, I'll pull it out in time.

Between kisses Stanley told Kate that he loved her and she said: 'Me too.'

Three days later Bush Vine and Dara Holden flew to New York. Kate stayed in Hanrahan's. Stanley courted her for three weeks. He called for her every night. Sometimes they went for a long walk and kissed, sometimes they went to the pictures and kissed and after the pictures went to the Cat's Hole and kissed. Once Kate smuggled Stanley into her room in Hanrahan's and there they also kissed, leading to Kate lying on the bed and Stanley lying on top of her, both of them fully clothed. Panting, Stanley emerged from kissing to announce: 'I can't wait until we're married.'

But he was going to wait until they were married, Kate could see, and it struck her that that was probably what love was – patience. She also waited. Bush came back for the wedding to give her away. Jake O'Dea was best man. There were no other guests. Although Stanley did tell Jake to make sure a big collection was made for him in the Nook and to hand it over unpolluted by a change into Waterford glass.

12

A Lion

Cocoa Brown rang Stanley Callaghan at the school with the news that Ralph O'Shea had been selected for the British and Irish Lions squad to tour South Africa.

'I read it. So?'

'The Institute will be a man short!'

'Who told you to fix the day of the replay for May 5?'

'Come on Stanley, you didn't know he was going to be picked.'

'The day after Mike Gibson announced his retirement I told you get the match on May 5, remember?'

'You didn't know then that the two Welsh centres would have broken legs.'

'I didn't. But I knew that the first Test against the Springboks was scheduled for May 5 and there was a possibility he'd make third centre with Gibson gone. Anyway, don't think I'm wounded because you don't appreciate my foresight.'

'All right, Stanley. Well done. There's another snag. The Institute aren't allowed the use of their grounds.'

'Why not?'

'I don't know. They don't appreciate soccer or something. We've to meet Tony O'Neill to come up with a venue.'

'Sign nothing without my approval.'

'Tony,' Henry Corr shouted into the phone, 'get your ass over here pronto. We got problems.'

Sitting in Henry Corr's office Tony O'Neill decided on the tactic of humouring Henry Corr. The American vocabulary cut into him like a lash. He didn't want to hear any more of it. He was not yet recovered from the ground literally being swept from under him. And worse, he had to agree with their decision. It wasn't that they objected to soccer, which they did; it was not their distaste at the prospect of adult messenger boys from the Nook lowering the tone of the Institute, which indeed appalled them. What put up the back of the assembled elders of the Institute was a remark overheard by the assembled elders in reference to themselves: 'Tony, you soft soap the fossilized pricks and get the goddamn pitch. Be nice to the cocksuckers.'

But now Tony O'Neill discovered Henry Corr in an uncharacteristically amiable mood. Henry folded his newspaper and handed it over, tapping the relevant news item.

'I'll just ring for tea and biscuits for you, kid, while you throw your eye over that.'

'No thanks, Henry. I had a cup before I left.'

'Shit, have another cup. I click my fingers, tea comes. No point being able to click my finger and tea comes without I click my fingers and tea comes. What fucking button is it, Kathleen? Kathleen, tea for two and biscuits. Plain, not chocolate. And no sugar in the tea. Thassmygirl. Well, Tony, what do you think?'

'I read it this morning,' Tony O'Neill became emotional. 'I can hardly believe it. One of our own. Ralph will get a civic reception for this. Just think, Henry, a boy we grew up with – a Lion! We'll have to make a presentation to him from the Institute . . . '

'Tony . . . Tony, we gotta think hard on this. I'm not a rugby nut myself, the gauchos haven't even got the shape of the ball right, but even so you bet we'll have a whip round for Ralph. But Tony, let's you and me be selfish for a minute. May 5. That's the day we play the Nook. Right?'

Henry Corr watched Tony O'Neill piece it together.

'Ralph won't be able to play!'

'Right.'

'Dammit. I never thought of that. I see the problem now, Henry. We can change the date or get a sub. I think it would be better to change the date. We don't have anyone as good as Ralph.'

'Just when we were getting organised, Tony. We have a positive atmosphere going at the breakfasts. This would happen. Tony, this Callaghan, I don't want to send you cap in hand looking for a sub or change of date if you're going to get the bum's rush. But I been outa town. America's a tough country. The weak go down. Stay down. You gotta be tough to make it, but even so, if it was one of their bunch I'd be all for obliging them, but Tony, suppose – suppose the motherfuckers say no way?'

'They wouldn't do that, Henry. Stanley Callaghan, he's respected, he's a teacher, famous for his principles.'

'But suppose? I know it's hard for us to imagine – we've breeding – but suppose they just won't play ball.'

'They will.'

'Tony, please? *Suppose?*'

Tony O'Neill supposed. Grimly he decided: 'If that was the case, Henry, we'd play them with ten men. And we'd beat them. If I have to train all night to do it.'

'Yeah. Only this isn't Ireland, Tony. Until this match is over, this is America. And we play the percentages. None of that ten men emotional stuff. Eleven's better than ten any day and fuck the romance. But I'll let you give it a try. Get on to that prick, whatsisname, Cocoa. Get on to the Cocoa prick and kick it around. Call me. Okay?'

HOLDEN TURNS DOWN $6,000,000 TO PLAY SOCCER! The headlines screamed even as Dara Holden was over the Atlantic. The Jumbo touched down in Heathrow where Dara was collared in the VIP lounge by Roderick Mann, who had been traced and primed by Hank Harold. Charged into believing half the stuff he found himself telling the famous columnist, Dara decided to spend a few days in London fornicating before going on to the chaste stomping ground of Mellick. He booked into a hotel, sent a taxi to pick up Stevie Mack in Fulham and both of them went to a club, Stevie in his capacity of a boxer Dara had a share in whom good judges predicted would be the next white hope. Stevie – ring name Battling Murphy – monosyllabically slept that night with a coloured model.

Tolly Holliday was already waiting with his taxi when Dara Holden and Stevie Mack emerged from customs. Dara had phoned on from London. They shook hands without a word, Stevie Mack nor the actor, Dara, able to disguise their consternation at Tolly's appearance.

'I know, Dara. Christ, I know. What can I do?'

'I don't think driving a taxi helps, Tolly.'

'What else can I do?' Tolly opened the boot of the taxi and watched Dara and Stevie deposit their suitcases – Stevie's battered one, Dara's quality three. Tolly made no offer to lift any of them. Stevie Mack sat in the back; Dara sat in the passenger seat and yet had to half turn round to see Tolly's face even though Tolly's stomach was wedged into the steering wheel.

'If I couldn't adjust the seat I couldn't get into the car,' Tolly explained. 'I can't take three passengers because there isn't room for the invisible man to sit back of me. I'm fucked.'

'You should get out of the taxi business just like Dara said.'

'Stevie, I'm only in it because it's the only business will have me. Sometimes when the cab drivers get talking it's like being in a cell. You know? What are you in for type of thing.'

Dara Holden smiled: 'Jesus, Tolly, once was funny; twice, well sometimes people have to put their fingers in the wounds; but you should have kept your hands in your pockets the third time.'

'It was only five quid the first time. How did I know I was lightfingered, it's a disease, like alcoholism, except it doesn't get recognition. I didn't know I was that way till I saw petty cash. Dara, I never as much as dealt from the bottom in the Nook, you both know that.'

'Stevie would have broken both your hands.'

'You said it, mate.'

'All right. But money just lying there in a fucking Oxo box stuck in a drawer. 'Twas – unnatural. The prick of a manager called a meeting of the staff and told them the firm was not going to prosecute. But I had to be sacked. A warning to them all.'

'The decent thing to do would have been to prosecute,' Dara Holden encouraged him, familiar with the story.

'Of course. And then Floyds. Wearing a green coat and selling paint and wallpaper over a counter. We had to put the money into a fucking cable car and send it up to the office for change. How I got away with it for a year I'll never know. I put more work into the two sets of books. Having to go on holidays fucked it up. Come back bronzed and fit, defrocked of my green coat. They did the decent thing, Floyds. They prosecuted. The fuckers.'

'What I don't understand is how you got a third job. Mellick's a small town.' Dara Holden yawned. Tolly loved his own life story.

'I got away with a fine but the old man had to cough up. He beat me down to confession. Inside in the box, you know how it is, the healing power of confession and the shit frightened out of me by the old man, I told the priest everything. He wanted to know what I was going to do. I told him. England. That's what fucking England seems to be there for. Present company excepted, Stevie.

'The priest had been on the English mission. He wouldn't hear of me going to England. And there did happen to be a vacancy. The general dogsbody had dropped dead a week before. Polishing brass knockers, cleaning windows up ladders and looking after mass cards. He was as good as Christ himself that priest was putting me in charge of mass cards. None of us said a word but 'twas plain from his face that he trusted me. Putting me directly in the way of temptation. And do you know what, Dara? Stevie? I'd never have let him down only for Jake and his fucking tip. He got it from some bollix in the post office. Nine to two, all I put on was two quid. Second. There was a thing going in the next at evens. I put a fiver on figuring I'd be able to put back the two quid and have three for myself. Last. Last in an eight horse race. Down seven quid. There was one race left . . . '

'Peggy's Leg.'

'Peggy's fucking leg is right. Three to one on. Twenty-one quid was all I needed to get back the seven but I got greedy. 'Twas only a four horse race. There was fifty quid in the mass card box, 'twas that fierce winter, bitter. I put the fifty on. Peggy's fucking Leg. It came over the last a furlong – a furlong – in front of the field . . . '

'And slipped on the flat. It wasn't your day, Tolly.'

'I couldn't face the priest. I left him a note and borrowed the fare to Dublin from Cocoa. Funny, I don't think I ever paid Cocoa back . . . '

'You did one thing right that day, mate.'

'The priest didn't prosecute. He didn't go to my father. I often think he'd have let me stay on.'

'Dara, you want to stop off in Durty Nellies for a few?'

'No, Stevie. I have to see Stanley first. Anyway, I'd be mobbed in there. How is he, Tolly?'

'Stanley? Stanley's Stanley.'

'And yourself? Are you doing okay?'

'Dara, you bought the taxi. I'll never forget that. Against all Stanley's rules, you bought me a taxi. You saved my life.'

'Fuck Stanley. And you paid me back anyway.'

'Did you know a fella will never fiddle his own money? Hey, money. That reminds me. You got something against money all of a sudden, Dara. Today's *Express* says you threw up six million dollars to play for the Nook. Are we supposed to believe that?'

'The honour of the Nook, Tolly.'

'You could be Stanley.'

'How is he, Tolly? How's he taking this replay?'

'Stanley? You tell me Dara. You're closer to him. Is he – I know this is a lousy thing to say – but between the three of us, could he be gone off his game?'

'No. Unfortunately he's sane. How's everyone else? Jake? Cocoa? Johnny?'

'All draggin'. Listen, we must have a right night now that ye've arrived. We haven't all been together – with Stanley I mean – in fifteen years. Apart from Jake's wedding. Do you know he won't let us train for the match?'

'Who?'

'Stanley. Who do you think? Can you beat it? Personally I'm not complaining. I ran after a little shithead a month ago who jumped out without paying his fare. Sixty pence.'

'Did you catch him?'

'Of course I caught him. And beat the head off him. But I didn't get my breath back for four hours after. Jake's training on the quiet. He runs miles every night and swims across the river and back to cool down. Thank God for Jake.'

'Thank God for Jake is right. Listen, Tolly, I want you to drop me a few doors from Stanley's house. I want to surprise him. You take Stevie on home. I'll pay you now.'

'On the house, Dara.'

'No it isn't. How much?'

'Eighteen, if you insist.'

'What's it normally? If it wasn't me and Stevie?'

'Fifteen.'

'You're afraid I'll give you a tip.'

'Please, Dara. Just don't give me *too* much.'

Dara extracted his three suitcases from the boot and tossed twenty pounds through the window. He struggled with his cases the fifty yards to Katstanco. Inside Stanley was reading the Roderick Mann interview in the *Sunday Express*.

'It's Dara!' Kate squealed and ran with Conor to the gate. Stanley remained behind his newspaper. He had a full armoury of clippings in his notebook with which to needle Dara but the sight of the actor provided fresh ammunition. Dara stood leaning against the jamb of the sitting-room door while Kate and Conor dragged in his luggage. He was wearing svelte knee high boots of a mawkish pale blue into which were tucked scarlet cords. Stanley appraised him over the *Express*.

'Obligatory attire between jet set airports, Dara?'

Dara put his arm around Kate and a paternal hand on Conor's shoulder. 'As Hank Harold says, you're not spotted in an airport you're dead in the business. Stanley, don't let me get you excited. I'm just one of the neighbours dropped in for the loan of a cup of sugar.'

Stanley went back to his newspaper. He stretched his hand out over the top of the page. Dara went and shook it briefly.

'Kate, you look wonderful. And look at Conor. You're growing. What are we reading these days, Conor? Finish *Treasure Island*?'

'Yes. I'm on *Glenanaar* now.'

Dara stared significantly in the direction of the father plodding through the *Sunday Express*. Kate said: 'I'll make you a breakfast, Dara, you must be ravenous.'

'I am, Kate.'

'Come on, Conor. Let's leave the grown-ups.'

Dara brought a chair over beside Stanley and sat on it cowboy style. He articulated the one word: '*Glenanaar*?' Stanley did not reply.

'*Glenanaar*, Stanley. You'd feed that crap to your own son. Haven't you done enough to inherit the Bob Tracey mantle? How's the teaching these days? Playing snooker at four o'clock?'

Stanley folded the newspaper and let it rest on his lap. 'Dara, it's not your fault that God gave you a hairy chest and hairy arms. But surely you can afford clothes to cover them up? Where'd you get the medallion, Buddha? And tell me, tell me my eyes are deceiving me. Please tell me that is *not* a digital watch?'

'I knew there was something. Conor. *Conor*, come here a minute.'

The boy came running from the kitchen. 'Here, open the suitcase, I have something there for you.'

Conor inserted the key and after the second click, delighted and puzzled and brandishing a gun, said: 'For me?'

'God. No. Let me have that.' He replaced the gun and opened a second suitcase and rooted out two digital watches.

'One for you, Conor. And one for your mother.'

'Gee. Thanks, Dara.'

'Don't say "gee", Conor. Please.'

'Sorry, Dad.'

'Go on now, take that trinket in to your mother.'

'Jesus, Stanley. What's with the "gee"?'

'I don't want Conor to have the vocabulary of a mentally indigent crew-cutted co-ed from some boondock high school.'

'Good man, Stanley. You get better all the time.'

'The gun, Dara? You have news for us about that gun?'

'Don't ride me. New York's New York. It's not the sleepy hamlet of Mellick. And I'm known, Stanley. You'll admit that, I am known.'

'I do. I admit that. From Sweden to Japan they know all about the acupuncture to increase your sex drive.'

'Not increase it. Decrease it. Get Hank's handout right. I see you've been reading good old Roderick. Hank didn't let the grass grow there either.'

'Good old Roderick says you were drinking coffee in Heathrow, evidence of your determination to give your best for the Nook. I'm not having this, Dara. I won't have abstinence. We go clean on to the sward.'

'There's no mileage in drunkenness in our business any more. It's in to be on the wagon. Anyway, I made up for it with Stevie the past few days.'

'When's he coming?'

'He's here. I brought him with me.'

'But I want to see him. Why didn't you bring him round?'

'I didn't want to share you with anyone, darling . . . Stanley, should I take my breakfast before you tell me what you're up to or will I throw up now?'

'Go and eat. And thanks for coming.'

Kate and Conor left Dara to buckle down to his breakfast alone in the kitchen but impatiently Stanley joined him claiming to need a cup of tea. Dara chewed his bacon and spoke out of the side of his mouth.

'How come you're so calm? I thought you'd be excited making a comeback after fifteen years.'

'One doesn't disturb the noiseless tenor of one's ways.'

'Stanley, cut the Goldsmith shit on my first day. Not at breakfast.'

'Not Goldsmith, my dear fellow,' the teacher beamed.

'I know it's not Goldsmith, bollix. I was referring to how we're supposed to be amazed how your one small head can carry all you know. And don't tell me you're getting your quotations right these days. All six of them. Do you ever read?'

'What a question.'

'Yeah. What's the answer. What do you think of Updike? John Fowles?'

'I don't read Americans.'

'Fowles is English. You read C.P. Snow?'

'Who would he be?'

'Jesus! Okay you don't read. Who's surprised? How do you sleep knowing you're a fraud? Wordsworth, Shelley, Yeats, Goldsmith and now Gray apparently, a handful of poems you were forced to learn by rote at school and you're living off them. *Glenanaar* down your son's throat, straight pens, Latin litanies . . . '

Kate knocked on her own kitchen door and entered excitedly: 'Stanley, the phone. It's – he says he's Danny Blanchflower.'

In mid-chew Dara Holden swivelled his eyes from wife to husband to wife. On his feet but unable to move Stanley croaked: 'Danny Blanchflower? Are you sure, Kate?'

'Well he said he was. From the *Sunday Express*.'

Dara and Stanley gaped at each other. 'Stanley, go and answer your own phone.'

Stanley walked slowly toward the instrument in the hall. He wiped the palm of his hand down the side of his coat and eyed the receiver as though it were a snake. Dara Holden abandoned his breakfast and commanded: 'Pick it up.'

'Hello? . . . Yes. Speaking . . . Of course I heard of you. If it is you. . . . Sorry. Yes. All right. Ask away . . . That's true. As a matter of fact he's with me at the moment, just arrived from London this morning. No. I do not share your colleague's sense of wonderment . . . I mean Mr Mann *has* lived so long amidst the – the tinsel – I wouldn't blame him if he's forgotten the old values. $6,000,000 is exactly right . . . Pardon? . . . No. The way I see it Dara Holden didn't have any choice. . . . Hmm? No. I mean he didn't have a *moral* choice . . . A crusade? Well, that's a bit strong . . . Sorry? . . . I don't know, I'd have to think about it, publicity is exactly what I want to avoid . . . To be honest with you I wouldn't have come to the phone if you weren't who you are . . . Don't mention it . . . Impressed? Oh. The $6,000,000 . . . No. That doesn't impress Dara's team mates one farthing . . . Dara Holden understands loyalty, honour . . . High standards? No. Well, standards are standards, it's not that we don't appreciate Dara's sacrifice but he's more than a film star to us, he's – he's one of us, we expected him to rally round and he did . . . Pardon? Do you mean as distinct from the way we're talking now? I don't know, I honestly don't want to answer straight off without thinking about it. I don't quite follow the "personal" angle . . . Sean Senior? Really? You'd do the *game*? . . . Of course I'm – I'm flabbergasted . . . and flattered, thank you . . . The – *The Times*? You're kidding me . . . all of them? Ah! The $6,000,000. I see . . . . Yes, but can I believe it's not that with you. I read your column every Sunday . . . Well, can I have a few days to think about it? Yes, this is the number. After four . . . Fair enough . . . don't mention it. And thank you for your interest.'

Dara Holden stood, his mouth half open, his thumb stroking his lower lip. 'We're all ears.'

'He says it's the talk of Fleet Street. They're going to descend on Mellick. Sean Senior wants to do me from a personal angle. Blanchflower wants to cover the match.'

'All right, Stanley. I got your letter. I'm here. Now, what the hell are you up to?'

'Nothing. A local soccer match. Blown up out of all proportion because you're in a profession that has forsworn all truth. Okay. I believe you when you say you don't have acupuncture or whatever it is to recharge or run down your batteries, it's Hank Harold. But couldn't you have come and played the match without lying about it to the world? And without all this ridiculous publicity.'

'Listen to you. You were like a schoolgirl there on the phone to Blanchflower. And I didn't lie. When I got your letter I *thought* I was turning my back on six million bucks. The fact is The Dara Holden File is for the axe. Hank knew it. Cardone knew it.'

'Is that the truth?'

'Yes. Let's go for a pint.'

'I usually go for a Sunday morning stroll with Conor. I don't drink on Sunday mornings.'

'Is that true, Kate?'

'Yes, Dara.'

'Still President of CRAM, Stanley?'

'One plays one's part.'

'That, I can believe. Come on. Play your part over a pint for a change.'

They walked into town, easing the journey by discussing the File.

'Why is it coming off? I thought it was so successful.'

'It was. It is. But it seems that America's tired of anti-smoking or that's what Cardone anticipates and CBS can't afford to be wrong. Not with the cost of a point in the Neilsen ratings. The individual is back in a big way – part of the Nixon legacy. My problem is being so closely identified with the anti-smoking league in the File. Hank's already at work on a new image but I don't give a damn. Your letter came at the right time. I think I might buy a cottage here and do some fishing, get it together . . . why are we crossing the road?'

'We're going to Brigid's.'

'We're not. We're going to the Nook.'

'Dara. I'm breaking the habit of fifteen years by going to a pub with you on Sunday. So it's going to be Brigid's.'

They went into the snug in Brigid's where Stanley ordered a pint for Dara and a tomato juice for himself. Brigid, after shaking hands with the celebrity and serving the drinks, discreetly gave them privacy.

'Is that breaking out? Tomato juice?'

'Dara. I don't like what you've been telling me. What about O'Neill?'

'A dream. A daydream. Get off my back and tell me about this match.'

Stanley took out his cigarettes and sipped his tomato juice.

'I came in here with Kate, minding our own business . . . '

Dara took in the story without interrupting. When the tale was told he commented: 'You threw a pint glass at them through the partition?'

'Yes.'

'Stanley, you're still alive. But tell me, this Corr wants a replay, we give him a replay. The man wants a bet, we accept a bet. The whole business of course is beneath me but in your narrow little world the mechanics should be simple. What did you have to clothe a simple challenge with all that "those who can, do, those who can't, teach" resentment? It's not as though you're a teacher. Anyway, what's with the Wilde bullshit. It was Shaw, you dummy.'

'No. Corr had it right. Kate says so.'

'Kate is infected from living with you. It was Shaw.'

'No matter. I am what I say I am, Dara. I am now a teacher as Bob Tracey was a teacher. My pupils can all spell, add, multiply, subtract and do long division and they will have an excellent hand before the year is out . . . '

'They going to be monks?'

'Okay, sneer. My colleagues sneer.'

'Wonderful. I love you, Stanley. Now let's get back to the match.'

'Dara, there's something that puzzles me and you're the only one can sort it out. Henry Corr. He came in here like a stage American. His clothes. His speech. And I know he was setting me up. Now, someone comes to set me up, he'd have to be shrewd. If he was shrewd he wouldn't be stagey. You know?'

'You hate America, Stanley. You hate it because it's beyond you. It's the real world. You're terrified of it. That's why you make fun of it. From the way you describe Henry Corr he's typical. I think Henry Corr is American and nothing wrong with him. And you'd appear to any civilized American as big an asshole as Corr apparently seems to you. Forget it. Relax. I'll pick up the tab. You're looking for reds under the bed because of the money. I don't want you worrying over a miserable eleven grand.'

'No.'

'What no?'

'It's my bet.'

'Have you eleven grand?'

'I can get it from a bank with you as guarantor.'

'What's the difference? Why can't I just give it to you?'

'Because, but you wouldn't understand. It's out of the same stables as Peter Dempsey sponsoring us – on condition we wear the Mikimoto jerseys.'

'Look, what are we doing here? Why aren't we in the Nook with all the lads, falling around the place laughing at this Dempsey nut?'

'Dara . . . '

'Yeah.'

'Dara . . . I want you to be serious for one minute if you can. I want you to remember something. Did we hitch it to Dublin in 1957? When we were only fifteen years old? Was it to see representatives of Mikimoto cars? Was it?'

'No.'

'What was it then?'

'You know bloody well.'

'I want to hear you say it, Dara.'

'Duncan Edwards and Manchester United. Satisfied?'

'When we played around the streets you called yourself the tank after Duncan Edwards. Who cried his eyes out after Munich, Dara? Who went to mass every day for weeks while Duncan Edwards was hanging on? What hairy-chested, digital-watched, gun-toting, broad-belted star of the living-room screen had to be taken from the classroom in tears when I brought him the news that Duncan Edwards was dead?'

Without answering, Dara Holden paid Brigid for another beer.

'Dara, you don't go to mass any more. You screw around. You're thirty-eight and not married. I look at you on that television screen, plucking cigarettes out of people's mouths and telling them they're fulla shit and I remember you praying for Duncan Edwards . . . crying when he died . . . '

'Oh, for God's sake! You cried when Duncan Edwards died too. So don't act the hardboil. Every kid in Ireland cried – and England where they don't know how to cry.'

'I'm not ashamed of it though. I remember it. And that's why I'm not going to commit Mikimoto in his name.'

'We have to grow up some time.'

'Do we?'

It took Dara almost a minute to realise that Stanley had finished talking.

'I said "do we"?'

'Do we what?'

'You said we have to grow up some time. I said "do we"?'

'Look, Stanley, talk straight. I don't know you any more. I mean, I don't know who you're pretending to be any more. Tomato juice. Christ.'

Stanley called: 'Brigid, two large Jamesons, please.'

He smoked in silence until the drink arrived. He paid. He took one of the whiskeys and downed it in one swallow. He picked up the second whiskey and sipped it.

'Dara, I owe you something. For a long time. You're the only one who really knows me so it's you I must tell. Kate doesn't know me. I think – sometimes I think Jake does but he's not sure. There's too much evidence against what he thinks he thinks. First off, I'm no teacher like I say I am. All right. You've always known that. You don't know that I'm anti-work of any kind. Well I'm still that too. Dara, I tried to keep you and I failed. But you never knew that it was more than just you I wanted to keep. Ever since – ever since Duncan Edwards – Dara, I loved you the way you cried more than me. I cried but I never let on just what it meant to me because I didn't know until later. Dara, when Duncan Edwards died, I died. I died of a broken heart. I could look back and imagine that I died when Kennedy was killed but that wouldn't be true and anyway I would have come back from the dead once his banging all those women came out. No. It was Duncan Edwards with me. And with you and a lot more of us. Edwards, Tommy Taylor, Liam Whelan, they were more than just heroes, they were everything that *anyone* could aspire to be. Do I sound ridiculous?'

'No. Just different.'

'There's nobody in the world that anyone can look up to now. Okay, there's Mother Teresa, but there's no fun in that. Conor, my own son, he has photographs of Liverpool in his bedroom. Liverpool!'

'They're the best.'

'There's no best. There's no good. I stand at the door of the sitting room and watch him looking at the Boomtown Rats on Top of the Pops.'

'You liked Buddy Holly.'

'Dara, come a little of the way with me. Don't be difficult. I had a dream. You and me and Jake and Stevie and Tolly and young Johnny Green and Bazook and even Cocoa. I just wanted all of us to be together always, minding each other, one for all, that type of thing. That was my dream. And I never knew it couldn't happen. It never occurred to me that it couldn't last. You had a dream, I had a dream, the only difference was that yours was attainable, mine wasn't. Mine was good old-fashioned wishful thinking. I never intended staying away from the Nook, but Kate and I – you know there's a subject I can't be direct about – but the loving, sex, whatever you want to call it, for six months I couldn't see round it, it minded me like a bubble car, but when I could see clear again, even though I was as in love with Kate as I am now, as any man could be with any woman, I saw you were gone. Even then I wouldn't face it. But when Stevie Mack sent word he was having a goodbye night I didn't turn up. I knew it was over . . . '

Stanley downed his remaining whiskey. Dara Holden pointed hospitably at Stanley's empty glass but Stanley shook his head and went back to his tomato juice.

'I had spent fifteen years teaching. Fifteen years another man. And then Henry Corr comes in here. I'd gotten over my dream. Well, I thought I had. And then Corr starts bullshitting. Suddenly I missed the Nook, in one concentrated moment, with the intensity of all the fleeting pangs of those fifteen years. And it was only then that I fully accepted that it could never have been, that we have to grow up whether we like it or not. But I still wanted it. I wanted the old Nook back. And Jake and Tolly and Stevie and yourself and all the lads – and Kate Flynn with it. And Duncan Edwards and short back and sides. I wanted Cocoa Brown with his hair back on his bald head. I wanted, I wanted, I wanted. For the first time in fifteen years, I wanted . . . Dara, the tape's finished, let's pretend now it's erased. Let's talk business. I've been frightened that we'll lose . . . and I can't lose this game. This is instead of my dream. Now I've got you to talk to, I'm not so worried. Now let's hear your help.'

'How did we beat a team with Stockil and O'Shea in it?'

'That's not help, that sort of talk. Develop the ring of confidence. Thanks to who else but myself they won't have Ralph O'Shea. When Mike Gibson retired I figured O'Shea might make the Lions tour as third centre. So I fixed the match to coincide with the first Test. By an act of providence the two Welsh centres have broken legs so O'Shea's going as first centre.'

'It was good thinking, Stanley. You haven't lost your touch. And they can't have a sub as good as O'Shea. And even if they had we wouldn't agree. The sub should be an ordinary mortal like ourselves, within the proper spirit of the contest.'

Stanley drained his tomato juice. 'Dara, it *was* America you were in the past fifteen years? There isn't going to be any sub. They're going to have to play with ten men.'

'No holds barred stuff?'

'No holds barred.'

'Good old Stanley. Now let's drink. What do you want, short? Pints?'

'No more. I have to go home.'

'Come on. Kate'll understand. So the dinner's burned. Your pal's home.'

'It's not that.'

'What is it?'

'We make love every Sunday afternoon.' He was immediately sorry he had not been inventive. The truth made Dara Holden colour. 'Even a robot like me needs a bit of pleasure,' Stanley joked trying not to notice how much Dara desired his wife.

'By Jesus,' Tony O'Neill exclaimed and Henry Corr nodded. 'Henry, we'll beat them for this. They're not playing the game.'

Henry Corr hunched his shoulders: 'I told you, kid, I told you. That crowd would eat their mothers, Tony, we're not going to take this lying down ... '

'I'll train morning, noon and night. I'll ... '

' ... yeah. Listen, Tony. Tell me about Ralph. Away fifteen years you lose touch. Ralph wasn't the brightest – okay, he had it over me, my school was life – but Ralph wasn't in your league, Tony. What's this he's at again?'

'He's a sales rep. The crowd that sell the new German lager. Minegen. It's very strong. Two bottles of Minegen, I'd be under the table. He's bound to be promoted now, a Lion ... '

'I don't like it.'

'It doesn't taste too bad, it's the effect ... '

'Not the goddamn drink, Tony. Look. Ralph O'Shea. Rugby international. Lion. Trying to sell Minegen in Ireland. Tony, a Barry John or a Phil Bennet couldn't give that stuff away in Wales and Ralph's trying to sell it here. Here! Did you ever look into an Irish drinker's face? They're faithful to porter like they never clung to religion. You know?'

Tony O'Neill did not know but he nodded anyway.

'Tony, its a waste of Ralph O'Shea. I always liked Ralph. Ralph's a nice guy. Good manners. Tony, where's he from?'

'How d'you mean?'

'Where's Ralph O'Shea from? Where's he going to settle when he's finished with rugby? He's born in Mellick, he's gonna die in Mellick. He brought honour to Mellick. Mellick owes him, Tony. In a big way. It's funny the way things click in your mind. Only last week my kid, Dean – he's a baseball nut – we searched Mellick for a baseball bat. Big search. One miserable sports store in Mellick that was here before I was even born. Missus whatsername. A goddamn thousand year old woman owns the only sports shop in Mellick for Chrissake . . . '

'Mrs O'Mahoney. Her son runs it now.'

'That's it, that was the cocksucker. Her son. Sixty-nine if he's a day. Listen, Tony. They threw a suit on Ralph O'Shea and made him a rep. Pigeon-holed him. Okay, he goes to South Africa or New Zealand, big deal. He's a Lion. Big deal. Can he put his medals and his caps on the table, tell his kids, eat that? Can he? Bollox. Ralph O'Shea deserves better than that. Tony, I got a few bob. Mind you I earned it. Every cent. Don't talk to me about work. What this town needs is fresh air. One goddamn sports shop, what do they stock? Paddles for Noah's fucking ark. You know what that O'Mahoney motherfucker said to Dean? The cocksucker grinned and said: Sonny, what you really want is a hurley. Dean didn't say anything, all my kids are well behaved, I wouldn't have it any other way. But no cocksucker was gonna talk to a son of mine like that. Listen, I said, my kid knows what he wants so shut your hole and serve him. What does he say to that? There's no need to adopt that attitude! That's their out, their taking the Fifth. Course they don't have baseball bats. Shannon airport's crawling with Americans, same here in Mellick, we're on our fucking knees begging for industry and what do we give them when they get here? We tell them play hurling.'

Tony O'Neill was lost. He had answered the summons. He took refuge in yet another cup of cold and sugarless tea hoping Henry's question was rhetorical as most of them were. One minute it was the match and Ralph O'Shea, the next it was baseball bats and industrialists and everything coated with that awful word 'cocksuckers'. Mercifully, Henry began to stride up and down and Tony was able to relax for a moment. He could blink. He had always to keep his eyes open listening to Henry who had said on a previous occasion: Whatsamatter, am I boring you? because Tony was not looking straight at him. If it wasn't for Henry Corr, Tony O'Neill could have been in Hanrahan's Hotel having coffee with his fellow insurance brokers or with a contact who might tell him of who was about to go self-employed and would be ripe for a policy.

'You know what I see, Tony? I see an opening in this town for a sports shop. A *stocked* sports shop. I'd put those motherfucking O'Mahoneys out of business in a month. But I'm not dumb, Tony. I know my Mellick. Small. Small minded. You know? What Henry Corr would he be now? That kinda shit. Who's behind him? That bolloxology. But, Tony, you take Ralph O'Shea. That they'd understand. Jesus, it's wide open. With my business sense and Ralph's name I see a sports shop with kids fighting to go in and buy. Me, I don't give a damn. But I'm thinking of Ralph. He deserves better. What do you think, Tony? Am I missing something? You think it would go?'

For once Tony O'Neill was delighted that the question was not rhetorical.

'Henry, I think it's a brilliant idea. I'm amazed it hasn't been thought of before.'

'Thought of? Tony, you must be joking. Thought makes illegal entry into this country. But here's another thought for you. What do you think of this. Now take your time, Tony. A good idea needs to be thought about. I want you to see the headlines. Tony, just picture: O'SHEA TURNS DOWN LIONS TOUR TO HELP BOYHOOD PALS.

'Can you picture that, Tony? Isn't it beautiful? That wanker Holden and his six million bucks, that's in the ha'penny place. Ralph O'Shea. He's gonna live in Mellick. He's gonna have that sports shop. The people of Mellick will remember his loyalty to his pals. I tell you, Tony, turning down that Lions tour will be the best thing ever to happen to Ralph O'Shea.'

Turning down the Lions tour was what Tony O'Neill imagined Henry Corr said the first time. Now Henry repeated it. For the first time in Henry's company Tony O'Neill laughed. It was the embarrassed mirth reserved for simpletons or deranged ladies who talked aloud to nobody in the street.

'Okay, Tony. What's so funny? Me? I'm dumb, I can't see the joke. What's funny?'

'Henry, you can't expect a man to turn down a Lions tour to play a soccer match against a pub.'

'I can't? Why can't I? Who are these Lions motherfuckers anyway? They haven't even got the shape of the ball right.'

'It's the greatest honour . . . '

'Honour! Do you put salt or vinegar on that? Do you boil it, fry it? Listen, Tony, you sound him out. Talk to Ralph. We can try. I see a big opening for a sports shop. If Ralph isn't interested maybe Timmie Stockil will be. You sound him out. Okay kid?'

'Me sound him out.' Tony O'Neill shook his head, giggling. 'I can't, Henry.'

'Why not, for Chrissake?'

'He – he might hit me.'

'He won't hit you. Tell him – no. I may as well handle it myself. I gotta do everything. You want something done give it to a busy man. Tony, get Ralph to drop by and see me. If he doesn't see the right side of this then he's so dumb maybe we are better off with ten men. What you call it? Minegen? Jesus!'

Dutifully and in accordance with precedent and decorum, Ralph O'Shea first informed the Irish Rugby Football Union. An official of the IRFU contacted Ralph O'Shea by telephone to check the validity of the letter. The IRFU was then forced to the conclusion that Ralph O'Shea was insane or, worse, had sold his soul. The IRFU did not have the authority to adjudicate on his mental condition but they did ban him from playing rugby union at any level for life and he was forbidden entry to any ground or pavilion under IRFU jurisdiction, even as a spectator.

Overnight the replay became the hottest news in all the leading newspapers of the British Isles, New Zealand, South Africa, Australia, Argentina, France and Russia. The defection in particular sent Fleet Street gaga. It happened at a time when there was no news. Readers yawned daily over reports that an innocent man was shot through the forehead on answering a knock at his door in Belfast. Only fools answered indiscriminate knocks at their doors. And so it went on. Unerringly the press of three continents identified Stanley Callaghan as the key story. Dara Holden might have forfeited $6,000,000; Ralph O'Shea might have turned down a Lions tour; but Stanley Callaghan hogged the limelight by his decision to shun publicity. A few days before the replay there was not a single bed to be had in Mellick. Stanley Callaghan was nowhere to be found. But nineteen days before the replay Stanley Callaghan was available to Danny Blanchflower who arrived on a reconnaissance visit with Sean Senior. Blanchflower rang from Shannon airport. Stanley made a deal over the phone: He would not accept one penny but he was willing to give an exclusive interview to the former Spurs double captain on condition that Blanchflower quoted him verbatim.

13

Brother Gibson

Before Stanley granted the one exclusive interview to Danny Blanchflower and Sean Senior he was involved in two other interviews, the second of which he conducted himself. The first was with Brother Gibson. The second with the Nook team.

For the Brother Gibson interview he was summoned to the Superior's study at three in the afternoon. He left his class unattended with the stricture: You have the opportunity to justify my boast that you do not need invigilance. Do not let me down.

Brother Gibson uncapped the bottle of whiskey in his study. Stanley accepted a small one – Bob Tracey would have.

'Stanley, your good health.'

'And yours, Brother.' The Superior was seventy-nine.

'Stanley, you know what I think of you?' Modestly, Stanley did not reply. 'I think you are the finest lay teacher we have today. And I'm not saying that because you stood by me in the Locky incident. Not since Bob Tracey – he'd be ninety-nine if he was alive today. Twenty years my senior and yet every morning when I stood at the school gate cuffing the stragglers he used to doff his hat to me and say "Good morning, Brother". And on a day he was bareheaded, he saluted – brought his fingertips to his temple . . . '

'A true gentleman . . . '

'Yes. But I'm only teasing myself. I've had my fair share of reality this past ten years. Never thought I'd live to see it. But Bob Tracey. And all the lay teachers of those days. I wasn't even Superior. Just an ordinary Brother. But we had the power, Stanley, and we exacted respect. And why not? It was *our* school. It was our school for over a hundred and fifty years before there was ever a government in this country.'

Stanley sipped his whiskey in unison with Brother Gibson. He had listened often in the past to Brother Gibson on the subject of the erosion of religious dominance.

'Tell me about this match,' Brother Gibson continued, seeming to cut in on his own reminiscences.

'I dare say you've read about it, Brother.'

'Yes. It is getting its share of publicity. Do you know, Stanley, that I've never really yearned for the trappings of power. As such? No. Ours is a calling of humility – if it isn't vainglorious of me to say so. I don't think I'd mind in the least being treated with condescension if the new order was getting results.' Brother Gibson pawed at a bundle of papers on his desk. 'Letters of instruction from guess who? The federated union of employers, telling us the type of pupil *they* want turned out. The way things are going, Stanley, they'll get them. Have you any idea what it's like at the school management meetings? You haven't and I appreciate your non-attendance. They give me a stiff hearing. Parents and lay teachers, their views are in accord. To them I'm a left-over savage from the days when we beat education into pupils – as if there was any other way. The latest bit of sabotage is that they want to have us retired at eighty. How they'd love to see me fangless, selling pennyworths of foolscap in the school shop, a coat over my shoulders. Stanley, you stood by me in the Locky case.'

'Brother, I could see your point of view.'

'Yes. But I lost. We both lost. And it was a bad defeat. Any time I open my mouth it's cited as a precedent. They won't let me forget. I wouldn't mind but I thought I was reasonable with the man. But I hadn't realised how far the rot had spread. Mr Locky, I said, this is a proud school. Associated since 1884 with the national games of Hurling, Gaelic Football and Handball. I told Mr Locky – politely – how I had always turned a blind eye to his rugby playing. The whole business came back to me, Stanley, reading about this O'Shea person. I pointed out to Mr Locky that *his* selection for Ireland threatened the traditions of the school. But of course I was wasting my breath. I can see the stubborn look on his face now. In the interests of this academy, I pleaded with him – I must ask you to forego the notoriety of playing a foreign game for Ireland. Do – you – know what Mr Locky said to me?'

'He refused.'

'He said he was sorry but – I quote – whether he played marbles for Hong Kong or rugby for Ireland was none of my business. Those were his exact words.'

Brother Gibson went for his glass. Stanley joined him.

'His exact words. It was then I told him that he would have to seek alternative employment. And what did the bold Mr Locky reply to that? Brother Gibson, you're living in the past. Of course he was a young man. A few years older than yourself at the time. Certainly not over thirty. I deferred to his black hairs. As charitably as I could I said: Mr Locky, I will overlook the subordinate nature of your vocabulary. Patiently, I pointed out that the school was already in difficulties – we hadn't won the Harty Cup in four years. I showed him how his example might encourage the boys to play rugby outside school in misguided emulation of his achievements. I was wasting my time. He had been exposed to the very West Briton influences in his rugby club that our boys were protected from here at school.'

Brother Gibson took out his tobacco pouch from the recesses of his soutane. He gnawed on his pipe as he kneaded his tobacco. Stanley, thinking back now on the incident, was thrilled with his own scab role. They were out on strike for three days in support of Locky who had been dismissed and (Mr Locky claimed) assaulted by Brother Gibson who was then sixty-nine.

'It wasn't enough for them to take a stand on the dismissal,' Brother Gibson resumed, shrouded in pipe smoke. 'No. They had no faith in themselves, you see. I stood accused of assaulting the man. I denied it strenuously. But of course it was true. Big second row forward that he was I knocked three of his teeth out. I had taught the chap as a lad and he stood there defying me. Of course I hit him. I never thought he'd mention it though. No class. Well, they won, Stanley. They won. I was instructed to back down. Ours is also an order of obedience. Stanley, would you think of me as bitter?'

'Anything but, Brother. You seem to have accepted the shift in power with admirable grace.'

'Ah, you're good for me, Stanley. And good for yourself, I dare say. Stanley, let me share a secret with you. I was bitter. I am bitter. And while God spares me I will be bitter until I get my own back on them. Which brings me to the point. This soccer match of yours. Some might say it's futile to be concerned with the image of the school nowadays – it's *fourteen* years since we saw the Harty Cup. Stanley, you're involved in a *soccer* match, for a *gamble*, and this is no clandestine affray, shouting it from the roof tops you are. A nice example to the pupils, Stanley. Would you have held your post in, say, the pre-Locky days, Stanley?'

'Brother, in the pre-Locky days the thought of playing soccer wouldn't have occurred to me.'

'Exactly. Have another drop. But today anything goes. Or does it? Stanley, do you know that I'd sack you in five minutes if I could. But what would happen? They'd go on strike again. Even though they don't love you. To them you're a scab. And yet they'd go out again to keep me in my place. Be honest with me, Stanley, what ammunition have I? Is it enough that you're an admitted gambler to the tune of a thousand pounds? I think I could whip up feeling among, say, the parents who don't invest ten pence on Grand National day. What do you think, will I give you the sack?'

'First of all, Brother, it's more than a thousand. I'm sticking my neck out for the whole team. It's eleven thousand. But even so. My honest opinion is that you would lose – maybe narrowly – but you would lose and they certainly would strike, even for me. I could write their manifesto for you now and I could see them hauling in photographic evidence of Christian Brothers and clergymen at coursing and dog meetings. The debate would drag on. The very best you could hope for would be a pyrrhic victory.'

'Hm. The losses on my side wouldn't worry me I can tell you. Pull the house down around me if I thought I could beat them before I died. What's left anyway?' Brother Gibson again stabbed the letters on his desk. 'People writing to ask us to concentrate more on integrated circuits and less on Livy. No Harty Cup for fourteen years. You're standing over eleven thousand! Why Stanley? You don't even have that sort of money.'

Brother Gibson's emphatic prod of the letters on his desk isolated sufficient of a letter from the pile for Stanley to see that it bore the signature of Henry Corr.

'Brother, may I glance at that for a moment?'

'Help yourself. If you have the stomach for it.'

DATALOG in computer style lettering was printed in gold ink, the eight point italic 'Manufacturers of Integrated Circuits' was printed in grey, the letter itself was typed on an IBM Executive in mid-century typeface and was phrased in a language Stanley Callaghan recognised as vintage Henry Corr. The directors' names at the bottom of the A4 sheet were printed in black save for H. Corr, the Irish director, which was printed in silver. This was to distinguish him, Stanley mused, if distinction was necessary, from the likes of J. Martinez, E. Kumm, R. Eckert, E.Z. Jones . . .

'Are you all right Stanley . . . ?'

'Sorry, Brother. The mind was just boggling at what under heaven an integrated circuit might be. You were saying?'

'Eleven thousand pounds. You're not rich?'

'No, I'm far from rich Brother but I have decided to compete in a fashion that precludes the possibility of losing.'

'You have?' Brother Gibson eased himself up in his chair. 'Dirty work, Stanley? Dirty work?'

Stanley nodded. 'I can't elaborate.'

'Wonderful. And there I was thinking of sacking you now. I'll wait. Between that film star Holden – to think he passed through this academy – and the bizarre characters on your team I'll surely get enough rope to hang you. Will I?'

'I'd say that was a pretty safe bet, Brother Gibson.'

'I love you, Stanley. You're my only real teacher but I'd sack my mother to beat them. Anyway, you can always get a job at that non-denominational school outside the city. They *look* for perversion in a teacher. You say you can't lose?'

'Yes.'

Brother Gibson produced a set of keys from one of the manifold repositories about his person and unlocked a drawer. He opened a cash box and selected a five pound note.

'Stanley, can you place this for me? On the Nook of course. None of that draw-I-lose business. And no tax. I'll take as low as two to one.'

'All right.' Stanley took the note.

'I was a coursing man myself once, till the blood sport cranks got on to the bishops. Which reminds me, I might just turn the collar of my coat up and take a look at this epic. Where is it to be held?'

'I don't know yet. It was to be the Institute pitch but they refused permission. As it turned out we couldn't have played there anyway. With all the publicity there could be thirty, forty thousand at it. The only ground in Mellick to hold a crowd like that is the Gaelic Grounds. We've written to the County Board.'

'I don't believe this.'

'On my mother's grave, Brother.'

'Soccer? In the Gaelic Grounds? Don't you know as chairman of the youth board I'm ex-officio on the County Board? And I happen to be on the sub-committee that deals with the use of the Gaelic Grounds.'

'I didn't, Brother.'

'I opposed the nuclear festival. They over-ruled me. I opposed the folk festival. I was shot down. But as sure as *my* mother is in the grave, I'll fight this, Stanley. Not the Gaelic Grounds.'

'Of course.'

When Stanley returned to his classroom he instructed the pupils to continue whatever it was they had been doing in his absence. He gazed out the window musing on Brother Gibson's determination to preserve the purity of the Gaelic Grounds. At least that is what he remembered afterwards but his thoughts must have strayed because he did not even notice the scraping of chairs to remind him that it was four o'clock.

'*Virgo potens*' . . . '*Ora pro nobis*.' '*Virgo clemens*' . . . '*Ora pro nobis*.' 'Suttons Coals' . . . '*Ora pro nobis*.'

Stanley was oblivious to the giggled response. But when he continued: 'Metro Cleaners' there was no response. The laughter astonished him. He roared SILENCE and then stared the laughter to a standstill as Bob Tracey might have done, at the same time deftly checking to see if his fly was open. It was not. And it could not be the drink. He was able for the few whiskeys.

'Crowe, what is this? What is this outrage?'

'It's what you said, sir. We couldn't help it.'

Stanley had no idea where he was in the litany.

'And what, pray, did I say?'

'You said "Suttons Coals" first, sir.' The class laughed. Stanley glanced out the window and there in the yard was the Suttons' lorry delivering coal.

'So. Homer nods. And what else did I say?'

'Metro Cleaners, sir.'

'And?'

'That's all, sir.' It was enough, Stanley admitted to himself but there was nothing he could do about it now. He could not bring himself to ask them where in the litany he had deviated from the authorised version. He crossed himself and waved them home. Alone in the classroom he smoked two cigarettes and confronted the fact that he was rattled by the fear of losing.

The second of Stanley's pre-Blanchflower interviews was held in the Nook that same night, between seven and eight o'clock, with the front door bolted. Gabriel Storan was smuggled out of the asylum – in the boot of a car – to benefit from the camaraderie of the occasion. Johnny Green was absent on a gig. Everybody cheered Stanley when he made his entrance but he did nothing to acknowledge the party spirit of the gathering.

'Gentlemen, I'll be very brief and I want you all to listen carefully. I'm going away for a couple of weeks. Thanks to Dara and that lunatic Ralph O'Shea, reporters are knocking down my door. I've given one interview to Danny Blanchflower that you can read next Sunday and all I'm saying now is basically what I said to him. First of all, you all stand to make two thousand quid and you've nothing to lose. I have, which means I'm the boss and what I say goes. I let the Mikimoto business go even though I won't wear the jersey, and I'm letting you wear the Three Star boots . . . '

'No boots, no boots.'

'It's all right, Gabriel, you can wear tackies. I didn't charge Blanchflower a bob but you can all make what you can out of interviews – if the journalists are thick enough to pay . . . But there's one thing I insist on. There's to be no training. It's out. Smoke and drink as usual. Is that understood? No training. Drink and fags as usual. I'm going into hiding in Kilmogany, Co. Kilkenny and I don't want that to get out. All right? Any questions?'

There were none. Neither were there any cheers. There was no manoeuvring to be nearest Stanley and nobody bankrupted himself to buy him a pint. It was a suddenly very muted gathering, testimony to a prevailing lack of faith. Only Dara Holden joined him.

'All right asshole. What are you up to?'

'I need to have peace and quiet while I plot and Dara, if I'm discovered in Kilmogany, I'll blame you. I have to go now. See that they maintain their drinking standards.'

'What are you bullshitting about? You don't have to go any place now. Come on, you set the drinking standards.'

'My hour is not yet come in that regard, Dara.'

'Jesus. I do believe you do believe you're Him!'

With Kate and Conor Stanley went into retreat not in Kilmogany, as he had announced, knowing the location would be leaked, but to the chalet they usually rented in West Cork in summer. Brother Gibson had granted Stanley compassionate leave.

At ten o'clock on Sunday morning Jake O'Dea knocked up Tom Splendid. He had not been able to sleep on and such was his confidence in his credit that he ordered three pints of Guinness, instructing the proprietor to pour the first two down the sink.

'I can't afford to start off with a bad pint. Not with this' – Jake tapped the *Sunday Express* – 'to keep down after a breakfast.'

'Three pints, two for the knacker's yard. Splendid job.'

'Chewing gum is out.'

'I beg your pardon?'

'I'll read it out. Listen to this. It starts off with, you know, we're a team of Sunday footballers having this replay after fifteen years etcetera, then the business of the Mikimoto and the boots then, here it is. Danny Blanchflower: Mr Callaghan, you do not approve of sponsorship and yet are willing to be part of an eleven thousand pound bet? Stanley Callaghan: A gentleman wagers, he does not accept sponsorship. Jesus!'

'Splendid.'

'Hold on. Danny Blanchflower: Is it true that you will not allow your team to chew gum? Stanley: Yes. Not for any amount of money will any of my team be allowed to chew gum. Blanchflower says, why? Stanley says, pardon? Blanchflower says: Most of the top professionals in Britain chew gum. They find it relaxes them. Stanley says: I can believe that, none of them has broken out of a trot in years. Wait, I must take a slug out of that before I go on. Put the three of them down on the No 2. It won't be long now, Tom. All accounts will be wiped out. Where are we, yes. Danny Blanchflower: Do you hold English football in high regard? Stanley: It died in February 1958. There's a heap of writing then explaining what happened in February 1958, they must be very thick in England if they don't remember *that*. Blanchflower then says: You thought highly of the Manchester United team that was wiped out in the crash? Stanley says: Yes. Then he goes on to name the United team. Hey, he has it wrong, he has Roger Byrne down here at left full, Byrne was right full, I could catch Cocoa with this, bet him a fiver he couldn't tell me what's wrong with this article, he'd never spot it, even Blanchflower – his own brother was on the team – even Blanchflower didn't spot it, or else it's a printer's mistake. Wood, Byrne, Foulkes, Coleman, Jones or Blanchflower (Jackie), Edwards, God be with Duncan Edwards, Pegg, Violet, Taylor, Liam Whelan or Charlton, Berry . . . He seems to have the rest of it right. Stanley goes on anyway: Yes, you could say I thought highly of them. Football did struggle on a few more years, your own Spurs side of '61 was not entirely discreditable. Throw us out twenty fags there, Tom, this is priceless.'

There was a tap at the window. Tom Splendid squinted through the curtains at Mrs Trehy peering in. He opened the door sufficiently to get a view up and down and then allowed her to scrape in past him. Jake O'Dea had not seen Mrs Trehy before so early in the morning and without her make up and without whatever it was she did to her hair on duty she looked to Jake like Mrs Trehy's mother, if she had one. His mouth was full of porter that was undecided whether to retreat or advance. Stanley Callaghan, on the night when he was making laws, maintained that no drinker should ever throw up. It was true that Stanley himself had never done so and after the enactment of this new law Jake could not remember anyone – even Cocoa – ever throwing up again. So Jake swallowed his mouthful and looked away from Mrs Trehy who breakfasted on a pint bottle and a packet of crisps.

Jake read on but to himself lest he attract Mrs Trehy's attention.

> D.B. Thank you. I have been known to cast a jaundiced eye on modern football. It's no secret. But back to the replay. Dara Holden turns down $6,000,000 to play

this match; Ralph O'Shea turns his back on a Lions tour. Are these not extraordinary gestures?

S.C. Yes. But only in the sense that an expression of loyalty is considered extraordinary these days. It is unfortunate that these gestures have drawn the attention of the media. Incidentally, I hope you will point out that I am not accepting a farthing for this interview.

D.B. Certainly. I will put it on record though I forebore to point out to you that it is not *Express* policy to pay for interviews in the first place. And now may I ask you about your approach to the game? Your tactics? Training schedules? Will you play 4-3-3 or the more adventurous 4-2-4?' (Mr Callaghan looked at me witheringly as can be imagined from his replv.)

Dara Holden pounded on the front door. He was accompanied by Stevie Mack. They stood either side of Jake O'Dea looking over his shoulder as Jake traced with his finger the conclusion of the interview.

S.C. You used the expression "Sunday footballers" to describe us. Fair enough. We approach this game with the spirit of the Sunday footballer. We do not train. Our tactics are 1-5-5, a goalie, five backs, five forwards as it was in the days when the air was clean. If we win, we win. If we lose, we lose.

Jake's finger reached the end of the interview skipping the formalities of the parting. He looked up at Dara Holden and Stevie Mack. It was Stevie who, in the circumstances, made an appropriate remark: 'What's the pint like?'

'It could be worse.'

'Two pints, Tom,' Dara Holden ordered and continued to Stevie Mack in a whisper: 'Jesus, look at her. I mean don't look at her. The pint would want to be good.'

Johnny Green's whistle through the keyhole achieved his admittance. He had a broken arm and a black eye.

'Jesus, what happened to you?'

'Tripped over the bloody wires. They were lying slack. 'Twas Butch Madden's guitar solo and I was going for a drink. I forgot he jumps in the air.'

Though the arm was in a cast, Jake O'Dea begged, 'Is it – it's not broken, Johnny, is it?'

'Yeah. I'm lucky to have my eye. Banged it on the edge of the drum.'

'When will it be fixed?' Dara Holden asked, calmly.

'The plaster won't come off for a month at least. I'll have to drum with one hand.'

'Johnny,' Jake O'Dea became uncharacteristically emotional, 'fuck you and your drums. You won't have it off for the match!'

They drank in silence broken only by the arrival of Bazook, Tolly Holliday, Cocoa and the twins who, in turn, had related to them how Johnny Green had broken his arm and blackened his eye. It was Dara Holden who took command: 'Stanley should be here. He should be here – now!'

Caught by the anxiety in Dara's tone Jake O'Dea asked: 'What's he up to, Dara?'

'Fucked if even he knows. The bullshit's there in the paper. Who is this man – do any of us know him?'

As though to franc the question Stevie Mack answered: 'Hey, Dara, 'member the night we put the goat in missus whatsername's parlour? Bleedin' lark that was, eh?'

'Yeah, Stevie. I'd almost forgotten that.' Dara spoke without enthusiasm. What in God's name was the point in remembering such things?

Bazook did not usually speak unless he was spoken to. As an ex-docker he thought of himself as above dustmen and beneath everyone else. Because he was born in the same street in the Fairgreen he was now friendly with a film star and a teacher who had married a beautiful American. This was a light in his life that he had no desire to extinguish by opening his mouth and putting his foot in it. But he was emboldened now to recall: 'What about the day the Guard was after him for streakin'? He came in the front door, the guard after him, over the counter and out again. And he bollox naked. 'Twas a panic.'

Dara Holden stared at Bazook as though listening to the story for the first time.

'That was for a bet that was. My bleedin' quid he won too.'

Cocoa remembered a story about an orchard but Dara couldn't hide his impatience. 'Listen fellas,' Dara cut in, 'I have bad news.' He was greeted with immediate order. 'Stanley's gone over the top. *We've* got to do something. We can't leave this to him any more. He's burnt out. He can't make decisions.

He's avoiding the whole issue. And the bullshit is there in the *Express* to prove it. Jake?'

'What, Dara?'

'Come on, Jake. You know what I'm saying's true. If we're to win this match we gotta do something to help him. Even if we gotta do it behind his back.'

'I'm not doing anything behind his back.'

'Why, Jake? Why?'

'I don't know why. That's why.'

It was almost half twelve. The law abiding clientele began to tap on the front door. Dara Holden raised his hand to Tom Splendid: 'Tom, let the fuckers gasp or go next door. Till we finish.'

'Splendid job.'

'Stevie, you getting on okay over?'

'Me? Sure, mate. Why?'

'London's tougher than Mellick, Stevie?'

'I get by,' Stevie modestly admitted.

'Sure you do. You think New York's a village? And I get by. But how would Stanley – this today Stanley, how would he fare in London or New York? So Stanley streaked – fifteen years ago. So he robbed orchards and put goats in parlours – fifteen years ago. He's fifteen years a teacher. He's *changed*. He was the boss when we were kids but now it's different. Are we all going to sit back like Stanley was the schoolmaster? Do nothing? Wait for a miracle? We have to win this match without him – for his sake. He told me it means everything to him. But he's living in the past. It's there in the paper. He's worried about chewing gum. There's eleven thousand of his own money at stake, money he had to borrow and what's worrying him? The Mikimoto and chewing gum. So. Are you going to help me help him win this match? Stanley, I'm sorry to say, has – lost – his – touch.'

Dara paused to let them consider this pronouncement. Cocoa Brown was first to comment.

'We were training. He came in here and made us drink. Tom Lewis never smoked in his life, Stanley shoved a fag in his mouth.'

'Jake, come on Jake, for Christ's sake admit it. He can't win this match the way he's carrying on.'

'Dara, Stanley was always off his game and he always came

through. He never let us down.'

'All right, Jake, I'll ask you one question. Suppose there was no Stanley. Suppose this was your team. Your money. How would you approach the match? Would you tell everyone come in here every night smoking and drinking? Would you, Jake?'

Jake didn't answer. Dara allowed a silence reign that he finally broke himself in exasperation: 'Anybody, has *anybody anything* to offer?'

The body who had something to offer shocked Dara Holden with his offering.

'He told me to beat the wife,' said Johnny Green.

Dara had always maintained that nothing could surprise him about Stanley but now he was genuinely flabbergasted.

'What did you say, Johnny?'

'Stanley. He told me I should beat Teresa.'

'Jesus!'

'A few weeks ago, the night he told me about the replay. It's no secret me and Teresa have our rows. I was talking to Stanley about it and he said I should beat her. Teresa thinks I play around. Last night we were up the country and Butch had a crate of beer in the wagon. I got pissed on the way back. I was late. Teresa went bazook, claimed I was ridin'. And I wasn't. It must have been the beer. Stanley's advice came back to me—but Teresa hit me first—and then I clocked her. Women have fierce strength when they go mad, you know. She got me in the eye with her hair brush and then fucked me down the stairs. That's how I broke the arm. It's okay now, we made it up after I came back from the hospital.'

'Tom, give us another round, in the name of Jesus, Mary and Joseph.'

Dara walked to where Jake O'Dea was installed at the end of the counter. 'Well? He's telling people to beat their wives. So now Johnny has a broken arm.'

'Dara, what do you want to do?'

'We've less than three weeks. Train. That's what we're gonna do. Train and work out a system. Agreed? Jake? Stevie?'

'But Dara, he told us no training. And Stanley saved my life.'

'Saved your life? The day he set you on fire like Blondini? Okay, so he saved your life. How're you going to thank him? By losing the replay? Now come on. Are you with us?'

'It's up to Jake.'

'It's always up to Jake. Dara, I want everyone here to witness that I'm going along with you under protest. And as for training, I haven't stopped since I first heard about the match and Stanley knows it.'

'Good man, Jake. Okay. Everyone on the wagon. After today. We'll murder today. Fags out. Every night collective training and a team talk afterwards. We'll do the AA on it. Anyone tempted to cave in ring me at Stanley's. I have to stay there in case he rings with instructions. And tactics. First thing we have to do is work on tactics. Jake, what do you think? I'd say we should play 4-4-2. If they don't score we can't lose. We can throw the twins up front . . . '

14

The Twins

'Tom,' Mick Murphy, the owner of the American Express Shoe Repair Service shouted into the repair shop, 'have you Mr Mulrooney's ready yet?'

Tom Lewis, clutching an awl and wiping a sweaty hand on his apron came out to the counter. 'What were they, Mr Murphy?'

'Black brogue, leather sole, steel tips on the heels. I gave them to you first thing this morning.'

'You gave me no black brogues today, Mr Murphy.'

'I gave them to you before you hung up your coat. Before you finished your fag. I told you they were wanted this afternoon.'

'Mr Murphy, I'm Tom. I don't smoke. You gave 'em to Joe.'

'Well, one of you, it doesn't matter, they're wanted.'

The twins had joined the American Express Shoe Repair service when they were fifteen and though by then they had grown dissimilar Mick Murphy saw them as identical. Tom Lewis was insulted that they could be mistaken for each other now. He had perfect eyesight and black hair. His brother Joe was bald and wore thick-rimmed spectacles. When they had first joined the American Express Shoe Repair Service they were dressed in identical suits but as soon as Tom Lewis was in a position to pay for his own clothes he bought grey if Joe bought blue and spaced his haircuts so that his was short when Joe's was long or long when Joe's was short. Tom loved his brother but hated his appearance. He was happy when Joe grew a moustache.

'Have you black brogues leather sole steel tips ready?' Tom Lewis growled at his brother.

'I sent them out half an hour ago.'

'Well, go out and show the blind bollix where they are will you.'

When Joe returned Tom controlled his anger and continued:
'Joe, listen. I'm a minute older than you but you make me feel a
hundred years older when you act so dumb. Five hundred
pounds, do you realise how much that is? Can you count that
far? And it's two five hundreds we're talking about. We could
start out on our own, can you imagine? Instead of making that
blind bollix rich. You know how he started? In a shed down the
Cat's Hole. Are you listening?'
'I couldn't do it.'
'Do what?' Tom Lewis hissed. 'You don't have to do anything.
All you have to do is go out on the field and be yourself. You
know how bad you are. You're worse than me for fuck sake. If
you scored ten own goals no one would notice anything wrong
with your play.'
'It's not the point. It's the principle. Bad as we are we must try
and do our best for our side.'
'Jesus Christ.'
'I told you before not to swear.'
Tom Lewis' hand tightened on the awl. An urge that must
have been with him in the womb almost overcame him.
'All right. All right. We'll take the money and pretend we're
going to try and score an own goal between us and then we'll do
our best for the Nook. Okay? Satisfied?'
'I don't know. That wouldn't be right either.'
'Will you listen? Will you listen to your older brother for
once in your life?'
'I told you before not to be going on about being older.'
'All right.' Tom Lewis chewed his lip. 'You're up for the
Nook, right?' Joe Lewis nodded. 'You're against the Institute.
We've a chance to relieve the Institute of a thousand pounds
and we can still die for the Nook. Do you want Jesus to come
down from the cross to show you what's all right about that?'
'Will you stop swearing, will you?'
Tom Lewis tore off his apron and flung the awl across the
repair shop. 'I'm going to ask for my cards and this time I mean
it.'
'Don't start that again.'
'I won't work another minute with you. You want to see me
penniless all my life.'
'If you saved like I do you wouldn't always be short. I'm
telling you that for the past twenty-three years.'

'Before I go out and tell him he's a blind bollix I'll ask you for the last time. Is it a deal? It won't kill you. Is it?'

Tom Lewis had threatened to resign many times before. Something told him it would break Joe's heart. And he was right. Though younger by a minute, Joe was the sensible brother and had minded Tom all his life, the way sense minds spirit. Tom's face was redder and angrier now than Joe had ever seen it in the past.

'All right. But we play straight.'

Immediately after work Joe went to the Nook for a mineral before tea. He had left Tom to confirm the arrangement with Henry Corr. Cocoa Brown and Jake O'Dea were there before him. The news was too good for Joe to keep to himself. He rattled off developments but did not mention that Tom wanted to collaborate all the way.

Cocoa Brown eyed Jake O'Dea as they listened to the tale.

'With five hundred each and the bank to back us and the couple of thousand if we win the match we could nearly go out on our own,' Joe Lewis concluded. 'Let me get the two of you a drink.'

'A tomato juice – a large one.'

'That's handy money for nothing, isn't it Joe,' Jake O'Dea said.

'I can't believe our luck when I think of it.'

In training Jake O'Dea took charge of Cocoa and Tom and Joe Lewis. Dara Holden, Stevie Mack, Bazook and Johnny Green, when he was available, trained indoors in a municipal sports complex rented by the hour. It was the only way Dara could have any privacy. It was decided that it would be too dangerous to train Tolly Holliday. And Gabriel was fit – from what nobody knew. Neither Jake nor Cocoa said much to Tom Lewis when he turned up and admitted that he had received the first payment of a hundred each in cash. 'I can't believe how foolish some people are,' Jake said. 'I can't believe it myself,' agreed Tom Lewis, thinking Jake was meaning someone else.

Later that night, in Tom Splendid's kitchen, Tom Lewis was educated on the nature of folly by Stevie Mack. Stevie did not need to become physical. He outlined the fidelity those who grew up in the street expected of each other and though the twins were not from the street Stevie confided that the same high standards were expected of them. 'Else I'd have to break your fucking neck, wouldn't I, mate?' Cocoa Brown then took charge of the money on behalf of the Nook until Stanley Callaghan was available to adjudicate.

The intimacy of the West Cork chalet out of season drew Stanley and Kate closer together than they had ever been. Though Stanley could not know it their sex life had always been as vigorous as that of film stars but now because Kate was so reminded of the solitude of the lodge with Bush Vine she did things they had never done before. Of course Stanley still thought of any new refinement as a mutual discovery.

Conor had brought his books and every night Stanley took him a few pages further in all of them – except the new maths and the technical subjects. Conor had to get along on his own in those. Stanley also set Conor exercises and it was while Conor was so preoccupied that Stanley and Kate strolled on what was in effect their private beach. They held hands walking on the beach, stopped, kissed, gave each other a little feel and concluded the fondness later in bed. That was on the first night. On the second they stripped each other and made love on the beach. On the third they had intercourse with their clothes on, huddled from the wind in the shelter of the rocks and fortified by almost total darkness. It was there, suddenly, that Stanley said: 'Kate . . . Kate, I have a terrible confession to make to you.'

'Stanley, even in the dark, you *look* like someone with something terrible to confess. Come on. Make love to me, love.'

'I just did.'

'Once! Come on, come on.'

'Kate, stop. Let me keep a cool head. Later . . . although later you mightn't feel that way about me any more.'

'Stanley, what on earth are you talking about? You're not going to run off with Mrs Trehy?'

'Please, Kate. It's not that long since I've eaten. Kate, ever since I was a boy, I had one ambition . . . '

'To teach.'

'Not quite. I never wanted to be anything else but a school teacher. But not because I wanted to teach. I didn't want to work. I wanted the two months holiday in the summer.'

'Stanley, don't be ridiculous. Come on. Put your hand here.'

'Kate, will you listen to me. Just listen. Don't interrupt. Please. I have to get this out once and for all. It's true. I wanted a teacher's job because of the short hours and the long holidays. And when I got older, when I was only seventeen, I saw myself buying caravans and renting them. Kate, let me finish. And if you can't look at me, don't. I don't blame you. I was never a respectable person, Kate. Exactly one month before I met you I took off all my clothes for a pound bet and streaked. A civic guard chased me. And I did mad things before that . . . '

'The Great Blondini.'

'Kate, don't be flippant. Not now. The night Dara produced you and Bush Vine I was crazy with jealousy. I was jealous of Dara even knowing such exotic people. He was going away, leaving me behind, King of the Nook as he called it. In the snug I almost hated you for being in Dara's company and not mine. And when it came out you were qualified and had gone into real estate I thought I saw a chance to impress. I made my big speech . . . '

'You were marvellous, Stanley.'

'I couldn't tell you the truth. All these years I've lived a lie. I modelled myself on Bob Tracey, knowing the image of me you fell in love with . . . '

'Stanley . . . '

'Please. Let me finish, Kate.'

'You're finished. You big dope. I don't want to hear it. You don't know what I fell in love with. Will I tell you? Will I tell you exactly what I fell in love with?'

'All right.'

'I fell in love with *you*, Stanley.' Stanley waited for more but all Kate did was nod over and over as if agreeing with herself.

'I don't get you, Kate.'

'Yes you do. You get me. And you got me. But let me put it another way. Can I go to confession now? I have a sin to confess too, you know. And I was afraid to tell you. And I must have been mad to have been afraid. Stanley, I told you how Bush rescued me in the convent . . . ?'

'Yes. A wonderful man.'

'In the twelve years I knew Bush Vine I was his mistress for the last six.'

'But you weren't a whore.'

'A whore? What are you talking about, of course I wasn't a whore!'

'I mean – it wasn't like you were a gangster's moll,' Stanley blustered.

Kate shrieked. 'That's fabulous. Well, that's my confession, Stanley, what do you think of my confession?'

'I think it's good one of us knew something about the business. Did you love him, Kate?'

'Bush? I adored him. But not – not like you, Stanley. And not towards the end when he was getting old, I mean really old. Oh, I loved him with all my heart and he was never feeble but even though I didn't realise it my body wanted a body like yours but it had to have something to go with it. Bush spent all his time drilling that into me. A man had to be decent. I was lucky. I fell for you the moment I saw you and you turned out decent . . . '

'Kate, don't say I'm decent. Not after what I just told you.'

'But you are. No matter what you say or do. You're decent.'

'I'm as crooked as a corkscrew. Listen, do you know what I do at CRAM meetings? Just to get through them I dream of sabotaging the whole thing. I imagine a hardened Nook cadre combating the sweep-in. No sooner would the vigilantes have cleaned a street than I'd see a Jake O'Dea marshalled quorum of urchins arriving with sacks full of scatterabilia like chicken boxes, coke cans, ashes to float on the breeze, used condoms . . .'

'He-hee!'

'You find that funny, Kate?'

'Of course I do. Don't you?'

'I suppose so. But I haven't thought seriously like that in fifteen years. You know the straight pens the kids use at school? I must have robbed the post office of every village we ever drove through. Didn't you ever notice how I'm always stopping to post some letter?'

'You mean – that's what you were doing. Marvellous.'

'About ten months ago – since the pens dried up in the post offices – I wrote to a crowd in Warley, it's in the English West Midlands, they sent me a catalogue of stuff to the school admitting they introduced plastic handles to keep costs down but that there was no danger of them ceasing to produce the nibs. Kate, and this is what amazed me. I was thrilled! I wasn't just pretending. I had *become* a Bob Tracey. But then Henry Corr changed everything. I knew that night I'd have to revert but it's only now that I realise how completely. I have to go back to being Stanley Callaghan the nut. And, Kate, this isn't a delusion of grandeur or mad modesty but you have no idea what a real nut I am. I'm such a nut I don't want to make love now. I don't want to make love now until I can put a mad proposition to you. Let's go to the pub and I'll explain. But Kate, you might want to leave me after you hear it.'

'After I hear it – whatever it is – I'm going to teach you something you've never been taught before. It's the ace that was up Bush Vine's sleeve . . . '

They returned to the chalet which did not sport a television. They brought Conor out to the local and planked him with lemonade in front of the set. Though it was late at night a children's programme was showing – Dallas. Stanley ordered a large whiskey and a pint of Murphy for himself but Kate would have no more than a chaste sherry. They took themselves to a corner of the pub and Stanley told Kate of his interview with Brother Gibson.

'Kate, I'm not going to let him down.'

'How? How are you not going to let him down?'

'I have something in mind that will put a cloud over my head – if it doesn't land me in jail.'

'Lovely.'

'Kate, please be serious.'

'I am. Do you realise I have a brand new husband? And you have a brand new wife? It's like swapping partners without the nasty aftertaste.'

'The plan would have to have your blessing.'

Kate made a sign of the cross.

'Wait until you hear it, Kate.'

Stanley was appalled and delighted when Kate immediately agreed to it. Then she encouraged him to have another large whiskey and pint of Murphy though she would not have any more herself. 'It's best for the man to be a little tipsy and the woman sober,' she explained. Once Conor was asleep they left the chalet and went to the beach. It was no night to be naked yet Kate insisted that they strip.

'Now, Bush,' she said, 'maintained that a couple could whip

up a frenzy just by saying certain words.'

Stanley had heard of this. And he was suddenly ashamed of Kate. How could she think this sort of thing would please him? It had nothing to do with him thinking he was Bob Tracey. The old Stanley Callaghan or any Stanley Callaghan thought shouting obscenities belonged to the type of people he imagined Dara knew.

'Just say: Kate, I love you.' Stanley did not know whether to be surprised or not. It was probably leading up to it.

'Kate, I love you.'

'You could say it as though you meant it. I love you, Stanley.'

'I love you, Kate.'

'Isn't it good? Wasn't Bush original to come up with that?'

They stood five feet apart on the beach. 'Stanley, I love you. You're the most wonderful person in the world.'

'No, Kate. You are.'

'I thank God every day that he made you. I love you Stanley.'

He understood his wife again.

'Kate, Kate . . . my God, Kate . . . ' It was proved that Bush Vine could do no wrong.

They worked out the details over the next three days. Kate provided the obstacles and Stanley plotted a way round them.

15

The Venue

In 1952 an ad hoc committee of one, Sonny Hagen, the celebrated consigleore, was sent on a fact-finding tour of the smaller European countries. His search was for the power behind the thrones. He began in Ireland and in less than a week found his quarry. Since the foundation of the state the government – whether in government or in opposition – was the Fianna Fail party and the consistent strain among the members of the Fianna Fail party was not so much Catholicism or Republicanism – both of which all the deputies did of course have in common – but the predominance, among those same deputies, of those who had excelled at the national games of hurling and Gaelic football.

Sonny Hagen prepared himself for a detailed analysis of the structure and infra-structures of the Gaelic Athletic Association – the GAA. There was a GAA club in every parish and townland in the country. By way of steeling himself for all the reading between the lines his background led him to expect he applied for and found readily accessible a copy of the previous year's Statement of Accounts and Balance Sheet. There he discovered, not between the lines, but boldly admitted under Expenditure:

> To Blotting Paper £274,009 14s 8½d

The accounts were certified by a firm of auditors established thirty years before the end of British Rule. Sonny Hagen flew on to Denmark.

The Grounds Letting Committee of the Mellick County Board Gaelic Athletic Association held its meeting in the chill Gaelic League hall. The committee consisted of two trustees, Sean

Bawn Walsh and Cathal Og Shannon, both in their early nineties; Davy McMahon, the Board PRO who was twenty-two; and Brother Gibson.

'I think,' Brother Gibson began, 'it's enough to make the cat laugh. Soccer!'

The nonagenarians nodded. Davy McMahon extracted a bank statement from his briefcase and placed it on the table before the trio.

'I hope you find that pleasant reading.'

The Mellick Gaelic Grounds had been modernised. Now it seated – *seated* – seventy thousand under covered stands which were reached by twenty-seven different entrances to a vomatorium underneath which were five modern dressing-rooms and a bar and above which was a ceili hall and function room. Because of television, affluence and laziness the sporting five-eight was no longer content to stand on an uncovered embankment and urinate into his neighbour's pocket. The resultant white elephant was the new *super* stadium in Mellick.

Almost coincident with the completion of the new stadium the Cork and Tipperary hurlers went into, what was for them, a decline and the Mellick hurling team reached every final – finals that had to be played at a neutral venue in conformity with a by-law of the Association. The Mellick County Board was now skint and in massive debt to the banks (which were largely staffed by ex-rugby players). The Mellick shopkeepers and restaurateurs suffered the loss of revenue attendant on seventy thousand people turning up everywhere but Mellick for the big games.

Sean Bawn Walsh passed the bank statement to Cathal Og Shannon who took out his reading glasses the lens of which had not been changed in twenty-five years.

'It's still soccer,' Sean Bawn Walsh said.

'But gentlemen, we're using the ceili hall and function room for discos,' Davy McMahon patiently reminded them.

'That's different,' Brother Gibson cut in and was grateful that Davy McMahon did not pursue the supposed difference. Davy McMahon never made a point a second time though he proceeded now to make a second point.

'We sanctioned a folk festival. And the anti-nuclear rally.'

'There wasn't much difference between the two of them,' Cathal Og Shannon observed as indeed he would be entitled to at his age. 'Long hairs fornicating in tents. Saving your presence, Brother.'

Brother Gibson nodded to show he was not taking any offence. Impatiently now, Davy McMahon snapped: 'I had the Chamber of Commerce on to me. They cited the instance of the Association in Dublin giving Croke Park for the Champ versus Young Mulcahy fight – a *foreign* game. After all expenses were taken into account the proceeds were donated to the handicapped children. The Chamber wants to know what have we got against the handicapped children. I have letters from the Lions, Rotary, the hoteliers . . . '

Everything was now ready for the replay. The fact that it now possessed the benediction of the GAA released all hurling and Gaelic football afficionados from the unwritten pledge never to watch a foreign game. There was speculation that the crowd might exceed fifty thousand. Davy McMahon, the County Board PRO, told the press that they expected crowds from as far away as West Kerry. The venue was agreed; the referee agreed; there were representatives of press, radio and television of half a dozen foreign countries already in Mellick; and both teams claimed to be fit and well. And at the time the claims were made they were.

16

Bazook

Stanley, back now from Cork, was in rare form having stopped at six pubs along the way and throwing back a pint and a Jameson in every one of them. He kicked open the inner swing doors of the Nook and caught them empty-handed.

'TRAITORS!' he roared. He stood with his back to the doors and eyed them one by one. Bazook was on the corner stool minding a rock shandy. The twins leaned against the counter watching the Muppet Show. Dara Holden, Jake O'Dea, Cocoa Brown and Stevie Mack were playing solo. There were four pints of cidona on the table. Gabriel Storan was in St Joseph's; Tolly Holliday was out driving his taxi, and Johnny Green was on a gig playing the drums with one hand and resurrecting his ventriloquist act to smooth over his sub-standard performance.

'Traitors!'

'Now take it easy, Stanley.' Stanley ignored Dara's injunction. He walked to the counter and ordered: 'A pint and a small one and hand me out the brush please, Tom.'

'A pint, a small one and a brush. Splendid job.'

'Excuse me,' Stanley hissed at the twins who immediately stood back from the counter. Stanley swept their glasses of orange and Bazook's rock shandy to the ground. At the solo table play ceased and nobody tried to preserve his drink. Stanley cleared the table.

'Tom, drink for your customers, please. It's on – no, it's not on me. It's on Dara. Come on, Dara, buy us a drink.'

The actor rose and joined him. 'Stanley, you can get pissed – you are pissed – but we're on the dry. We're on the dry and off the fags and we're training. Now just let me finish and then you can bullshit all you want. We're doing this for you.'

'Dara, I love you kid. I love you all. That's why I had to get away to think. I have a brain none of you have and that's meant as a compliment. It's a twisted brain that's needed now. We're not going to lose our hard-earned money to a bunch of snobs. So. Who's going to have a drink with Stanley the lush? Dara? Cocoa? Jesus, he looks away. Can't even look at me. Stevie? Bazook? Come on Bazook, what are you having? . . . *Bazook!* Am I talking to the fucking wall?'

'They won't let me, Stanley. Honest . . . '

'Won't let you. Won't let you . . . Jake . . . ?'

'I'll have a pint.'

'Good man, Jake. Tom a pint and a small one for Jake.'

'Splendid.'

'Stevie? Stevie . . . I saved your life once . . . will you drink with me?'

'I'll 'ave one then.'

'Keep filling, Tom. Cocoa?'

'Lunatic.'

'*Cocoa!*'

'*All right*. It's your money. Why should I care?'

'Good. Bazook, you can drink now too. Dara, drinks for everyone and cigarettes for everyone,' Stanley turned to the twins, 'whether everyone smokes or drinks or not. And then follow me upstairs. By Christ, I'll show ye planning.'

Stanley Callaghan was in no condition to drink as he had used to. Fifteen years of moderation had its effect. Upstairs in Tom Splendid's kitchen he sat on the floor and gazed foggily at Cocoa, Jake and Stevie sitting on the table and Dara, the twins and Bazook standing. Everyone was now smoking and drinking.

'Right. We're going to play a goalie and ten backs. The minimum we'll achieve is a scoreless draw. Timmie Stockil and Ralph O'Shea, I've worked out a plan to stop them. Dara, you'll be our secret weapon. They'll be expecting rough stuff from Stevie but no. Stevie you're to play like a gentleman. But you can teach Dara how to get them with the elbow. And we can form a mêlée. Or a ruck. Then Dara can put the boot in. I want no fancy football. We're going to play dirty. Are you all with me?'

Jake O'Dea eyed Dara Holden. The actor said: 'We're with you. Of course we're with you.' But his smile said: 'Humour him.'

Stanley continued to garble through two further rounds of

drink. His advice was contradictory: 'Keep the ball moving/Slow it down to our pace ... '

After the fifth round the team began to re-discover their normal appetites and concentrated less on Stanley's dribble than on the quickening gallop into drunkenness. Bazook, who missed drink most, ate the stuff now. Stanley's pep talk petered out with his own barely coherent instruction that they go back downstairs. He had matched them drink for drink and so legless was he now that he fell the last flight. He struggled to his feet and stared at the steps, questioning their alignment. In the bar he sat on the floor, his head drooped towards his chest and just as he was about to drop off rallied with the slurred cry: Up the Nook.

There had been great drunkenness in the Nook before and with Stanley Callaghan in the driving seat but the sight of him drunk now and groping to stay awake brought the gloomy recollection home to them all that they were fifteen years older than they should have been and though they all drank themselves as drunk as time and Dara's generosity allowed, the collective heart was not in it. There was no conversation, only a vigil over *the* collective heart now dribbling asleep on the floor.

The night ended limply without anyone calling an official halt.

'Stevie, give me a hand to get him in the car. I'll see you fellas tomorrow night. We'll get back on the rails.'

Jake O'Dea, with no desire now ever to be back on the rails, nodded: 'See you, Dara. Mind him.'

It was the following morning, though it seemed to Dara that only ten minutes sleep had elapsed, that Jake O'Dea rang Katstanco to tell him that Bazook was dead.

With the circumlocution of close friends Jake announced: Dara? Bazook's dead. Dara held the phone a suspicious foot from his mouth and stared at it.

'Jake? Is this a joke?'

'No.'

'Well for Christ's sake, give it to me. Tell me what happened.'

Dara made tea and toast and sat over his breakfast before going back upstairs to wake Stanley. He had to resort to pouring cold water from a kettle over the teacher's head.

'Did you really have to do that?'

'No. But why deprive myself of the pleasure. I woke you to tell you something. Stanley, Bazook is dead.'

Stanley lay on his back and continued to rub his eyes with the back of his hand. He stared up at Dara who continued to stare down at him. Every second that neither of them blinked was an answer to an unspoken question and when the time elapsed constituted Bazook not alone dead but in his grave Stanley rose slowly and tottered past Dara to the bathroom muttering: 'Make some tea.'

'It's made.'

Downstairs Stanley poured tea and nibbled at the toast.

'Dara?'

'Yeah?'

'No joke?'

'No joke.'

'All right. Talk.'

'Jake rang over half an hour ago. Bazook was cycling home – pissed – he must have swerved to avoid a car and went up onto the footpath. Out over the handlebars. Head meets wall.'

'Jesus.'

'Stanley . . .' Dara's tone was uncharacteristically sympathetic.

'Hm?'

'Stanley, you're not to blame yourself. It was an accident. It could have happened to anyone.'

'What the fuck are you talking about? What would I blame myself for?'

'Take it easy, kid. I know what you're feeling. If you hadn't bust in and got us all drinking – but that's not the way to look at it. Drunk or sober cyclists are killed every other day.'

Stanley lit a cigarette and nodded.

'What in Christ's name was he doing on a bicycle? At thirty-eight years of age?'

'It was part of his training.'

'Training! And now we're going to be a man short. I told you not to train.'

'Ah, Jesus, Stanley . . .'

'Don't act that, Dara. So God took him. I'll miss him as much you or anyone else. But it won't bring him back letting the replay out of sight. With only ten men, we're in real trouble. If it had only been one of the twins. Or both. Guys like Timmie Stockil, nowadays it's part of their trade to learn how to exploit ten men. I can just imagine Henry Corr.'

Dara stood up. 'It's true for Cocoa. You are sick. A lunatic. I'm going to the Nook for a cure. And rest easy. Training's finished. I don't give a fuck now whether we win or lose. It's the piss for me for the next seven days . . . '

When Stanley reached the Nook at twelve o'clock he was cheered with the result of a post mortem that had been held earlier: although Bazook had indeed gone over the handlebars the cause of death was no more romantic than a hardening of the arteries. Fortified with this news Stanley returned to Katstanco without having a drink.

Bazook had no relatives in England or America – a rarity for an Irish corpse – so his body was brought to church that evening. His death was announced on the lunchtime radio news and the evening radio and television bulletins. 'The death has occurred following an accident of Paschal Halvey of Mellick, otherwise known as Bazook . . . '. It was also printed in the two national evening papers. Bazook might have been a celebrity, Stanley thought, as he prepared for the funeral and then realised that they were all celebrities now. In the church Stanley was spruce and fresh in contrast to Dara and the rest who had tippled out of sympathy from the moment Tom Splendid had opened that morning. After the prayers were said over the coffin Stanley joined the throng up the middle aisle to sympathise with Bazook's mother. Mrs Trehy immediately preceded him. She placed her mass card on the coffin and then shook hands with Mrs Halvey and said: 'The Light of Heaven to his soul, Mam.'

The Nook was closed except for regulars. The funeral had been massive. The people did not turn out to pay their respects. They were there to gawk. Dara Holden was an obvious focus. He was pestered for autographs. The press could not believe their luck. Stanley roughly pushed them out of his way outside the church, affecting not to hear their questions. He noticed Blanchflower standing respectfully aloof. Stanley held up eight fingers and two thumbs, and shrugged his shoulders. Blanch-flower nodded. Stanley walked over to him.

'Where are you staying?'

'Hanrahan's.'

'I'll be in touch. I expect a scoop that will put everything that's happened so far in the shade. It will be all yours.'

'Thank you.' Nothing shocked an old pro.

Every nationality has its version of the stiff upper lip. The Irish take refuge in the inconsequential. It was no surprise to anyone when Dara observed over his first pint: 'We're a filthy race. Backward. Apathetic. How often do we wash? We still have the Saturday night bath. Went out with the Dark Ages. A fella shovelling shit for a living six days a week talks of his Saturday night bath. I was ashamed of Bazook lying there in the coffin . . . '

'I wouldn't call Bazook dirty. And there isn't a bathroom in his house.'

'Jake, I'm not talking about dirt.' Dara downed a quarter of his pint.

'You could have fooled me,' prompted Stanley.

'I know Bazook was clean. We're all clean. I'm not talking about us and I'm not talking about baths.'

'Dara,' Stanley was neutral enough now to help anyone along. 'Dara, what exactly *are* you talking about?'

'Teeth. I'm talking about teeth, what else do you think I'm talking about. Bazook's teeth. We had to look at him there in the coffin. His yellow teeth sticking out like Bugs fucking Bunny. You're born with buck teeth in Ireland, it's accepted as though it was a hump. They correct things like buck teeth in America . . . ' Dara concluded with a futile wave. He was drunk but hanging on after a rough day. His contribution was hardly vintage stuff, Stanley noted, but he appreciated the decorum of the effort. And what Dara was really telling him, Stanley realised, was that he, Stanley, as representative of the bygone Nook, should have been taking the lead in establishing the mood of the wake. There was a tap at the window. Mrs Trehy was admitted. Stanley put a pound on the counter: 'A drink for Mrs Trehy.' She nodded her thanks.

'He didn't look well in the coffin. I agree with you there, Dara. But we should be grateful. If his mother had money think of how well he would have looked. Give me Grade D funerals any time. I was at a funeral a few month's back, Mr Locky's father, you'd feel like jumping into the coffin beside him. Like a film star.'

The effort was lamer than Dara's and Stanley knew it. It did not strike a chord in Jake, Cocoa or Stevie Mack. But Stanley pressed on: 'Do they dicky them up in London, Stevie?'

'Dunno. Aunt of my landlady kicked the bucket couple a year ago. Me landlady dropped round to see if there was any few bob bein' left. 'Er aunt didn't 'ave fuckall. Eed – that's me landlady, she come home fuckin' an' blindin'. Couple a days later I asked 'er when 'er aunt was bein' buried. She said, "Ow should I know? Bleedin' undertaker looks after all that, don't 'e." They have no God in England.'

Still nothing.

'It's dead in here tonight.'

'Jesus, Stanley, you sick bollix.'

'Dara, all I mean is someone should sing.'

'I'd prefer to hear about our prospects of winning with ten men, and I don't want to hear that either.'

But that was what they all did want to hear. It was all over their faces. They had had almost three months of nothing but the replay and not even Bazook's death could put it out of their minds.

'Bazook would understand that we have to face the replay some time.'

'Jesus! He's not buried yet.' The exclamation was rhetorical. Dara was frothing to discuss the game.

'Cocoa, let's start with you. What do you think?'

'Have we grounds for a sub?'

Stanley shook his head: 'I wouldn't even let you ask.'

'All that money down the drain.'

'Cocoa, the Nook will win.'

'Even Jake wouldn't agree with you now. Jake? Will the Nook win?'

'If you'd died instead of Bazook our chances would have improved. But Bazook is a loss and we can't play Johnny in goal with a broken hand . . . '

Johnny Green abjectly nodded agreement. He hated the mention of his broken hand. It was an embarrassment to Stanley, Johnny thought, having been the cause of it, telling him to clock Teresa. But Stanley wasn't even listening. He was thinking that Plan A unadulterated – going out to win the match like gentlemen – was never really on. That was why he had worked out Plan B with Kate. And now a Plan C began to take root. To concentrate on Plan C he urged Jake O'Dea: 'Dara's right. We shouldn't talk about the match now. Not tonight. Jake, sing the song Bazook used to sing.'

'I don't know it all.'

'Start it. We'll all join in.'

> Dearest our day is over,
> Ended the dream divine . . .

Jake did not have Bazook's voice. He sang softly and they joined in with him softly. When they came to: 'How can I live without you?' everyone, including Mrs Trehy and Tom Splendid joined in, softly. It was by any standards a fitting and tasteful remembrance. There was a minute's silence, all the more poignant for not being solicited, to follow the elegiac tribute. They were all rather proud of themselves in genuinely experiencing grief. So much so that of all people Cocoa broke the silence with: 'Stanley's right. We will beat them. Even with ten men. For Bazook's sake.'

'Cocoa, no more about the match. Tom? It's a sad occasion?'

'Yes. Splendid.' Tom led the community singing of sad and appropriate songs until closing time. During this singing Stevie Mack had to go to the toilet where he was joined by Dara Holden. Dara found him urinating almost as high as the ceiling and he noticed this was not because Stevie aimed high, Stevie had his hands in his pockets.

'Horny?'

'Yeah. Miss the ol' bag. How you manage for it, Dara? Here, I mean?'

'I don't. Like yourself. I do without it.'

'Jesus, I'd love a fuck. I'd fuck Mrs Trehy an' all.'

'So would I.'

'Would you though? Straight up, mate, would you?'

'Would you?'

'Yeah. You on then?'

After the burial the next day Stanley called Stevie Mack aside and gave him confidential instructions. To the rest, who were horrified at his not joining them for a post burial drink to consummate the death, Stanley announced that he was withdrawing to his retreat in County Kilkenny and then set off for West Cork to rejoin Kate and Conor. He would reappear on the night before the replay. This messianic promise convinced all but Stevie Mack that Stanley was mad but there was so little time to the match there was no other choice but to have faith in him. Stevie Mack, correctly deciphering his confidential instructions, was sick with fright.

17

The Sub

The night before the replay Dara Holden, Jake O'Dea, Cocoa Brown, Johnny Green, Stevie Mack and Tolly Holliday were gathered round a card table in Katstanco. They had brought pint bottles with them from the Nook having drunk in the pub until ten o'clock.

'Come on, Stevie,' Dara Holden pleaded for the sixth time, 'tell me.'

'Can't tell you. All's I was supposed to tell you is meet here and wait for the call. 'E said everyone was to have at least six pints and be here between ten and eleven. It's only half ten now. Your nerves are at you, Dara. It's off for a quid.'

'Why did he tell *you*? Why didn't he tell me?'

'Dunno. He just told me to do certain things an' I done 'em.'

'What things?'

'Can't tell you.'

'Why did he leave out the twins? Why didn't he want Gabriel here?'

'Look, it's off for a quid, who's playin'? If we're playin' cards let's play cards . . . '

The phone rang. Dara Holden leaped upon it.

'Katstanco.'

'Put Stevie on.'

'What the hell are you up to?'

'Put Stevie on for Christ's sake. It's important.'

Proudly, Stevie Mack accepted the phone.

'Yeah, mate?'

'Did you get the van?'

'Yeah.'

'The gear?'

'Yeah. Said I would, didn't I?'

'Where?'

'Down the dock – near the old weighbridge.'

'Right. You go straight there with the lads. I'm just going to Patsy Naughton's for a sausage and chip, I haven't had a bite all day. See you in ten minutes and for God's sake don't open the van till I get there.'

Ranged around a black van Dara Holden beseeched Stevie Mack: 'Stevie, just tell me what you *think* he's up to.'

'Dara, I don't want to think about what I think he's up to. 'Ere 'e is anyway.'

Stanley Callaghan took the last sausage from the bag and ate it like a sword swallower. He wiped his vinegary fingers on his handkerchief and though his mouth was full he managed to bark: 'Nobody talk. All into the van. Stevie, you and Johnny in front, the rest in the back.'

Stanley squatted on the floor of the van, Tolly Holliday and Jake O'Dea on his left, Cocoa Brown and Dara on his right and Stevie Mack and Johnny Green leaning back over the front seats. By the light of their cigarettes Stanley briefed them.

'All right, gentlemen, it's Plan B time. It's an emergency measure in case we're in danger of losing the match. Now, I want to clear one thing up first. In case any of you have scruples. I want you all to know I've given this a great deal of thought and I honestly believe we're morally justified . . . '

'Hey . . . '

'Shut up, Cocoa. All I'm saying is that it isn't very clever of us to play the match with ten men.'

It was the way Stanley looked at each of them that made them dwell on his exact words. Dara Holden half rose and uncovered the tarpaulin on which he had been uncomfortably perched. It revealed shovels and ropes.

'Yes, Dara. We're going to play Bazook.'

Nobody spoke. For a few moments they could hear each other breathing. And then suddenly all that remained of Cocoa Brown in their midst was his ankle and the shoe so quickly grabbed by Stanley. Cocoa had his hand on the back door of the van. He managed to wriggle out of the shoe and clambered on to the road. He shouted 'lunatic' and took off, his shod foot clopping a morse tattoo in his wake. Stanley Callaghan and Jake O'Dea did not catch up with him for a quarter of a mile. Stanley put his arm around Cocoa and a hand on his mouth and held him until Stevie Mack arrived to help them carry him back to the van.

'Now. Take your time, Cocoa. Get your breath back and calm down. And tell us your problem.'

'I have no problem. You have a problem. Gabriel should be teaching in the Christian Brothers and you should be locked up.'

'Cocoa, let's talk about it. I'm not a dictator. All I said was that we're going to play Bazook. He was on the team. It's not a crime, is it? In all justice, Cocoa, decide yourself, are we not entitled to play him?'

Uncharacteristic tears formed in Cocoa's eyes. 'Stanley, Bazook is dead. Somebody – Dara, you tell him. Tell him Bazook is dead.'

'Bazook is dead, Stanley.'

'Of course he's dead. We wouldn't be going to this trouble if he was alive. Dammit, he was ours in the first place. You've nothing to worry about, Cocoa. I have it all planned out. You won't have to do any heavy work. The rest of us will take turns with the digging and then you can help guide the coffin into the van . . . And try not to be sick. Come on, pull yourself together. I said you won't have anything to do, I just didn't want you to feel left out. Think of the Nook. Never beaten. No one ever let the side down.'

'Who ever had any choice? You won't even let the dead rest in peace.'

'That's it, a bit of humour, Cocoa. You're going to be all right. Stevie, let's go. Now listen, from the second we get out of the van until we're back in it with Bazook, nobody speaks. Nobody coughs. Nobody spits. Tonight you behave like men. Like soldiers. Right? Move it, Stevie.'

It took ten minutes to reach the cemetery. Stanley lit a cigarette and every time he drew on it the light showed a contented smile about his lips. The rest of them looked at each other after every flash of the smile and they also smiled.

Three hours hard labour went into exhuming Bazook. All of them, including Cocoa, were needed to haul the coffin up and they were meticulous in refilling and re-sodding the grave. They hoisted the coffin into the van.

'Stevie, where are the levers?'

Seeing the consternation on Cocoa's face, Stanley explained: 'He's only down three days. The grave isn't marked. It's dark. The last thing we want to be caught at is playing the wrong man.'

A horrifying smell filled the van when they prised open the coffin. The corpse was legal. Cocoa could not take his eyes off Bazook. He began to swallow hard.

'Cocoa, keep it in. Please. Stevie, take her away.'

Stevie did not start the van immediately. He too stared at Bazook.

'Poor bugger. I don't know what it is, but he's givin' me a horn. Funny, isn't it? That's some name for that. I could fuck Mrs Trehy again, hah, Dara? I wonder where she hangs out. We give her another dart, Dara?'

'I'm gasping for a fag. Stanley, have a fag? Jake, smoke?'

'Stevie, what was that about Mrs Trehy?'

'Fucked 'er didn' we? Any old port in a storm. Me and Dara did.'

'Start the van.'

'Okay mate.'

Stanley looked at Dara Holden but Dara wouldn't raise his eyes from the still open coffin. With the first motion of the engine Stanley threw Patsy Naughton's sausage and chips up on top of Bazook.

18

First Half

Although the original Nook versus Institute game had been played in the evening both sides agreed to have the kick-off in the replay brought forward to three in the afternoon. The cast of Dara Holden, Timmie Stockil and Ralph O'Shea and Bazook's death led to wild speculation in the press regarding the possible size of the crowd. The actual attendance can be estimated from the admitted GAA receipts of £39,002 50p. The admission charges were one pound for adults and fifty pence for children. Given that it was contrary to the national character to pay for children (who were lifted over the stiles) and that the gatemen were of the voluntary breed accustomed to the rewards attendant on self-sacrifice a conservative estimate of the attendance hovered around the 60,000 mark. They travelled from all over Munster as though it were indeed a GAA fixture to supplement the huge crowd from Mellick itself. Itinerants hastily harnessed ponies. Hawkers manned the stalls. The disfigured gathered to beg and publicans diluted their stocks.

At one o'clock the Nook team assembled in the pub for a drink and tactical talk. Everyone except Gabriel and the twins looked sick. Gabriel and the twins were not yet privy to Plan B. When Stanley Callaghan arrived, with his gear wrapped in newspaper, he found them nursing half pints. He went from player to player examining their Manchester United, Leeds United, Liverpool, Chelsea gear holdalls.

'It seems I must go into this match clean alone. And half pints. Tom, pints, please.'

'Splendid.'

The Institute again wore their club colours of black and red squares and black knicks – the hockey outfit. The jerseys supplied to the Nook were green with white hoops with a square twelve inches by twelve across the chest flashing MIKIMOTO. In the dressing-room Stanley Callaghan ceremoniously cut out the square with a pair of scissors and donned the jersey over his vest. He had a small foot and through Conor borrowed a pair of boots size seven from a final year student. The rest of the team wore Three Star, supplied by Leary's. Gabriel wore tackies.

There was little talk in the dressing-room and no banter. Those privy to Plan B were burdened by the knowledge. The twins were ineffectual as ever and Gabriel so ashen of visage he might have been about to appear again before the metropolitan schoolboy international selectors. The Nook lined out:

GOAL	Joe Lewis
BACKS	Dara Holden
	Stevie Mack
	Stanley Callaghan
	Jake O'Dea
	Johnny Green
FORWARDS	Gabriel Storan
	Tom Lewis
	Tolly Holliday
	Cocoa Brown

The corpse was to be kept in reserve in case the Nook were behind at half time.

Because Bazook was dead, Johnny Green had a broken arm, Tolly Holliday weighed eighteen stone, the twins were the twins and the rest of the team had not wintered well over fifteen years, the first half, to the eye of the serious student of sport threatened to be a black comedy. 'You mean,' Sean Senior replied to his colleague Danny Blanchflower, 'a sick joke.'

The Nook lost the toss for choice of ends and were consoled with the doubtful honour of centering off and establishing the character of their approach. Tolly Holliday laboriously tapped the ball to Cocoa Brown who immediately passed the buck to Jake O'Dea. Jake eyed his four stationary forwards.

'Move. Move up. Who am I supposed to pass the fucking thing to. Run down the wing, Gabriel.'

The four forwards did not get into position fast enough and so Jake O'Dea, against all the principles that the Nook, through Stanley Callaghan, supposedly represented, was forced to pass the ball backwards to Johnny Green who mistakenly interpreted his reception of such a ball as a free pardon to pursue a continuum. He deftly returned the ball to Tom Lewis in goal. Tom Lewis gathered, threw the ball in the air to kick it clear and succeeded in sending it straight upwards. The stadium roared its delight at just how bad a soccer team could be and echoed the shout of a wit: COME ON THE TEN MEN!

Out of the disorder of Tom Lewis' absurd Garryowen Jake O'Dea won the ball and booted it down the right wing ahead of Gabriel who failed to reach it before Stafford Foy cleared to Ralph O'Shea who passed to Timmie Stockil who put a through ball for O'Shea to run on to – which he did – and only a desperate lunge from Jake O'Dea unbalanced the rugby player as he shot and the ball rebounded off the crossbar with Joe Lewis as a stiff onlooker. Dara Holden was nearest the rebound but his reflexes were so slow that it was Stanley Callaghan himself who cleared. For the next two minutes the Institute attacked non stop against a defence that was seemingly non-existent.

'Jake, what's wrong with you?'

'Leave me alone, Stanley. It's hitting me that there's people looking at us. They've paid to see us. I don't know whether to laugh or cry.'

The crowd stopped cheering for the Nook. They didn't cheer for the Institute either. There was support for both sides from friends and relatives of both sides but the crowd – as a crowd – was represented by an ominous mutter of disappointment. The Institute were the footballers and as such boring to the largely hurling and Gaelic supporters who were used to prolific scoring. And the Institute were in control. It was a twin, Tom Lewis who revived the crowd. Timmie Stockil and Ralph O'Shea did their by now usual one two until they were well into the Nook half and suddenly instead of going further Timmie Stockil passed to Tony O'Neill on the left wing. O'Neill loped goalwards and was challenged so ineffectively by Dara Holden that he found himself ten yards from the whites of the twin's frightened eyes. He shot. Tony O'Neill was not in Timmie Stockil's class as a footballer and he did not have the strength of Ralph O'Shea but he was fit from tennis and hockey and was only ten yards out. There is no reason to suppose that the best goalkeeper in the world would have saved his effort. But Tom

Lewis closed his eyes and, flinging himself in the air like a body jumping from a burning building, saved the ball with his nose. There was a full two minutes' delay while he recovered. The crowd clapped as though it had been a fine stroke in hurling. Stanley Callaghan pulled Stevie Mack away from the circle around the twin.

'Do O'Shea. And do it fast.'

'You mean it?'

'Yeah.'

'Am I to do him hard?'

'If you know how to do it, kill him. The fucker. Do him.'

During the next two minutes play Jake O'Dea continued to play better than anyone else on his own team but not anything as brilliantly as he was capable of. Two shots that might just as easily have been goals skimmed the post. Jake made a gallant effort to control himself. It had been so easy in the pub or training on his own to imagine a romantic victory. Now he saw twenty nil staring at them, if it stopped at twenty. And what Stanley proposed to accomplish bringing on a dead body at half time nobody knew. Jake collected the ball from a feeble Tom Lewis kick out and dribbled it slowly for a few yards looking for inspiration; the Institute, now that Jake had the ball, played the modern retreating defence. Jake roared at Cocoa Brown: 'Run, Cocoa. Down the wing. Go.'

Cocoa ran down the left wing. Jake kicked the ball after him. It was or would have been a perfectly judged lob only that Cocoa ran so fast in his enthusiasm that the ball, instead of dropping in front of him, landed on his head. Cocoa was stunned for a moment and then staggered forward. He lost his action so completely that he did not fall for another six yards. When he did the collapse was so ungainly that the crowd erupted. Jake O'Dea himself fell to his knees and clutched his stomach at the sight. That was the position he was in when the ball sailed over his head into the path of Ralph O'Shea who brushed past Stanley Callaghan to score, giving Tom Lewis no chance at all. Stanley Callaghan brought the ball from the net to the centre circle. As he passed Jake O'Dea, Jake grabbed his arm: 'Stanley, hold on. I couldn't help it. Listen it's over now. Relax. They won't pass again.'

From the centre off Jake O'Dea inevitably received the ball and this time booted it down the middle to see if Tolly Holliday had anything in him. Tolly was well beaten by a young O'Neill whose high clearance was contested by Ralph O'Shea, Dara Holden and Stevie Mack in the air. The back of Stevie's head rammed into Dara's forehead even as Stevie's knee dug into Ralph O'Shea's back. All three lay stretched on the ground. Referee Ronnie West stopped play. Ralph O'Shea struggled to his feet rubbing his back. Stevie examined his head to his own satisfaction. Dara Holden did not rise. The referee called the Knights of Malta on to the pitch and after three minutes Dara was able to stand. Referee Ronnie West asked: 'Are you all right?'

'Yes. Yes, I'm fine.'

'What's your name?'

Dara did not know. It was apparent to Ronnie West and the members of the Knights of Malta that Dara was concussed.

'Your name please,' the referee tried again.

'Hank Harold?' Dara guessed.

'Where are you?'

'I'm here.'

Ronnie West waved his hand in front of Dara's face but Dara didn't blink and then, as suddenly as he didn't blink, he collapsed. He was taken off on a stretcher to the applause of the sixty thousand spectators who now began to chant: COME ON THE NINE MEN!

And now Jake O'Dea was as good as his word. He began to play. His confidence spread to Stanley Callaghan and Stevie Mack. Though the Institute continued to attack non stop the uncanny anticipation and never-say-die spirit of Jake O'Dea kept them out. After fifteen minutes it began to dawn on the crowd that the Nook might not be massacred after all and their every odd attack was cheered. And the attacks were odd. Confronted by Timmie Stockil, Gabriel did a war dance, slipped the ball between his old team mate's legs, ran around him, beat Stafford Foy, Tony O'Neill, Henry Corr and then stopped. He stopped because there was no Institute defender to challenge him. He waited until he was again faced by Timmie Stockil whom he beat a second time by again putting the ball between his legs. By now all eighteen stone of Tolly Holliday and Johnny Green with his broken hand were in the penalty area gasping from the journey and waiting for the cross.

'Gabriel, cross it,' Jake O'Dea roared. But it was too late. A young O'Neill meekly dispossessed him. It was one of a handful of attacks mounted by the Nook in the first half.

19

Second Half

It was one thing to rob a grave in the dead of night, fortified with drink and the company of accomplices. Now Stanley Callaghan was confronted with actually parading the corpse. He sat in the dressing-room sucking a cigarette and staring at the concrete floor beneath his knees. There wasn't a sound. He was conscious of them all staring at him, including Dara whose disorientation was signposted by the idiotic grin on his face. Although Stanley was sitting down his legs were weak from nervous tension. He spat, took a final messy draw from his untidy cigarette and said: 'All right. Plan B. Gabriel, come over here.'

Gabriel sat beside him on the stool. Stanley put his arm around Gabriel's shoulders. 'How are you feeling? You're having a fine game, you made an ape out of Stockil.'

The inmate blushed. 'I'm okay.' Stanley thought it odd that a mental patient should redden. 'I hope you can take this in, Gabriel. And the twins. Come over here both of you. You three are the only ones unfamiliar with Plan B. This is it: Bazook, as you know is dead. Last night we dug him up. We're going to bring him out on to the field with us and take it from there. Now is the time for conscientious objectors. Have any of you any objection to playing with a dead man? Gabriel?'

'I don't mind.'

'I didn't think somehow you would. Lads?'

Though their outlooks could not have been more dissimilar Tom and Joe Lewis suddenly discovered that blood was thicker than water. Neither of them said anything.

'Right. Cocoa, you lead them out on to the field. Stevie, Jake, Tolly and myself, we'll get the stretcher.'

Dara Holden stood up though not knowing where he was or

what he was supposed to do. 'No, no, Dara. You're sound where you are. Sit down and have a fag.' Dara sat down.

The van was parked outside the grounds surrounded by the hawkers' stalls, the chip and ice cream merchants. Bazook was already laid out on the stretcher covered with a blanket. Stanley lifted the blanket and gazed at him. Earlier that morning on their return from the graveyard, when it was assumed that Stanley had played his final card, when they were consoling themselves with the certainty that nothing would ever surprise any of them again, Stanley had managed to astonish them.

Bazook had been laid out in his good suit. The suit was in fact such a good suit, though ill-fitting, that Jake O'Dea remarked: 'Funny, the first time I ever saw Bazook in a suit.'

It was then that Stanley opened the jacket and ran his fingers along the lining and the tailor's mark. 'It's brand new. He can't have had it long before he died.'

'I never heard him talking about buying a suit,' Jake O'Dea confided. 'Did he ever say anything to you, Cocoa?'

'No.'

It was a sad moment even for Stanley Callaghan. Given the society in which Bazook moved – from one end of the Nook counter to the other – the purchase of a new suit was a prolonged affair. Bazook would have said: How much are suits these days? And he would not have addressed the question to anyone in particular. He would have been answered: Suits? My brother-in-law bought a suit there a while back, and this was during the sale, 'twas a good suit all right, wool, but the lapels weren't hand-stitched or anything. I think he paid, I'm nearly positive it cost him sixty quid. Did he get it through the Provident? No, he's a mean bollix, saves like mad, gets a cut off for cash. What are the Provident charging now, a pound a week? Jesus, Bazook, how long is it since you bought a suit? You'd pay at least four quid a week to the Provident over twenty weeks, that would include interest. Fuck that for a yarn, it's something to cover me I want. A week later Bazook would have asked: Where do the Provident have their office now?

'New suit, new shirt, new tie, new socks, new shoes,' Stanley opened the zip of the trousers, 'and new underwear. His mother must have gone up to her neck to bury him. Get it off him. People don't play soccer in their Sunday suits.'

Bazook was duly togged out in the Nook colours. Stanley

considered cutting the Mikimoto out of the chest but decided to leave it. They covered Bazook with a blanket and carried him on to the pitch. They lifted him from the stretcher and placed him just beyond the half-way line in the outside left position. At first a buzz went round the stadium that the figure on the grass was Dara Holden. The Nook players, after depositing Bazook, walked back to their own half for the centre off. Tony O'Neill was first to approach the horizontal figure. He could not believe his eyes. He touched the body with the toe of his boot and backed away as his colleagues joined him.

'Jesus,' Henry Corr declared, 'I knew that bunch were sick but I didn't think that sick. Ref! Hey, ref!'

The referee, Ronnie West, examined the body.

'Who is this?' he asked, beckoning with his finger in the direction of the Nook team. Stanley Callaghan responded: 'He's one of our team. He wasn't fit for the first half.'

'He doesn't look fit for the second. The man's dead.'

'Yes. The Lord have mercy on him.'

Ronnie West looked steadily at Stanley Callaghan and though the teacher did not blink the referee didn't trust him. And this man he knew was considered the flower of the Nook. He did not trust himself to contemplate the weeds lest he forgot his mission in life to persecute the Institute and behave as nearly as possible like an English gentleman.

'You're sick, buddy,' Henry Corr broke in. 'You robbed a grave, that's how fucking sick you are. Now Ronnie, get him off and let's get on with the massacre.'

'Ref, is there any reason why Bazook can't play the second half?'

'For Jesus Christ Almighty sake . . . '

'Your name please.' The referee got out his notebook.

'Come on, Ronnie, for fuck . . . '

'Your name please. Or do you want your walking papers now?'

'What the hell. Henry. Henry Corr.'

Ronnie West wrote in his notebook. 'You, sir, with your abominable tongue, are a disgrace to the Institute and you are fortunate that I am not listening to you in my capacity as representative of the club today. But as referee whom you will please address as Mister West if at all. I must warn you that one more uncouth syllable and you go to the line. And you, sir, is that genuinely the Bazook person who died?'

'Yes, Mr West.'

Without a word Ronnie West went to the centre circle, checked his watch and blew his whistle to start the second half. Henry Corr was genuinely baffled. They had robbed a grave, dressed the corpse in football gear and brought him on to the pitch at half time. Even for people who drank in the Nook it must have been a dangerous waste of time. What could they possibly hope to gain? Five minutes into the second half he began to understand.

The Institute, who had attacked so freely in the first half, became tentative and panicky. And in contrast the Nook were controlled and fiery. Every ball cleared by Jake O'Dea was booted in the direction of Bazook and the mere presence of the corpse on the left wing discouraged the Institute. Henry Corr realised that he himself was conscious of the presence and made an effort to lead by example. The crowd, by now aware of the identity of the corpse, shrieked over and over again: COME ON THE DEAD MEN.

The next ball that was fought for near Bazook inspired Henry Corr to plough in and hack for possession, at the same time managing accidentally on purpose to kick Bazook on the thigh. Stevie Mack immediately grabbed him by the throat. 'You fucking bollix, do that again and I'll kill you.'

Ronnie West had blown for the free against Bazook. He called Stevie Mack aside and took his name. 'You retaliated and you used an expletive. You have one leg on the sideline, my friend.'

The foul on Bazook provoked the nasty element in the crowd. Though the attendance was almost a hundred per cent GAA there were small pockets of choirs scattered about the ground who feebly rendered You'll Never Walk Alone, When the Saints Go Marching In and the Institute are a shower of Shits. But now these *summa cum laude* graduates of the Jimmy Hill Academy for the sons of welfare recipients were joined in their chorus of boos by the GAA fraternity who hated all referees on principle. Fifteen minutes of cat-calling, booing, obscene chants elapsed during which period the Institute did not go near mounting an attack but at the same time neither did the Nook. The up-the-left-wing ploy was contested by the Institute as though the corpse was no more than a puddle of water. And then Tony O'Neill whispered something to Henry Corr who immediately called his defence together. When Jake O'Dea next cleared the ball the entire Institute team immediately ran inside the Nook half and Tony O'Neill shouted, 'Offside, ref!' Tony O'Neill was pointing at Bazook. Ronnie West blew his whistle. He was instantly ashamed at not having spotted it at the centre off – the only other occasion that Bazook was actually offside. This free for the Institute against the corpse was described by O'Grady Says as 'the key that lifted the Bazook bogey'. Sporting journalists are catholic in their theft of the cliché. Now the Nook had to lift Bazook back into their own half and this retreat inspired the Institute to, according to O'Grady Says, 'parade all their talents'. The next five minutes saw the Nook camped in front of their goal buckrooting for touch. The crowd, with little of a positive nature to cheer, sang to the air of Colonel Bogey:

> The Institute – are a shower of shits,
> A shower of shits,
> A shower of shits.
> The Institute – are . . . etc.

Stanley Callaghan, inspired by a line of poetry – 'the centre cannot hold' – from, he was positive, Robert Bridges – drew Jake O'Dea to one side, then instructed Johnny Green to go to centre forward and called Gabriel over: 'Gabriel, the next ball you get, hare down the right wing and play for a corner. Go as far as the flag and wait until you're tackled. Then work a corner. Can you do it?'

'I can.'

'Then do it.'

Jake O'Dea was in possession. He ambled as usual down the left side where, up to now, he had played Bazook's wing. The Institute, as usual, were waiting in a cluster by the corpse. Jake stopped, changed direction and sent a long ball out to Gabriel on the right. Gabriel tore as far as the corner flag and waited for Timmie Stockil's challenge. The ex-Caledonian schoolboy team mates played patience until finally Timmie Stockil lunged and Gabriel kicked the ball off him over the line for a corner.

'Good man, Gabriel,' Stanley Callaghan shouted. 'Right, Jake, you take the corner. Stevie, you and Tolly give me a hand.'

They lifted Bazook and carried him up to the penalty area

where they stood him between Stevie Mack and Tolly Holliday. Jake O'Dea's cross was perfectly judged; the ball hung in the air above Bazook. Johnny Green summoned all that had ever stood to him as a ventriloquist and roared: 'My ball!'

The shout coincided with Tolly Holliday and Stevie Mack lifting Bazook up in the air. The Institute defence, thinking the cry came from the corpse, was, according to O'Grady Says, 'paralysed'. The ball bounced off Bazook's head and bounced once more before trickling past goalkeeper Eric O'Neill who was 'rooted to the ground'. Following Stanley Callaghan's bad example the entire Nook team hugged and kissed Bazook. The roar of the crowd was heard two miles away in the centre of the city. When the shaken Institute lined up for the centre off, Stanley Callaghan could not resist roaring at Johnny Green: 'Bazook wants some chewing gum? Have you any to spare?'

The Institute were shattered for a few minutes, their every touch of the ball jeered by what had now become a mob, yet they recovered once again through the agency of Tony O'Neill, and with Bazook's help. The corpse had now to remain in his own half of the field lest he be blown for offside. There was a shemozzle for possession near Bazook and Tony O'Neill roared out of the mêlée: 'Hand ball, ref! It hit his hand.'

'It was accidental,' Stanley Callaghan claimed. But Ronnie West, dispelling any notion that he might not have noticed earlier hand balls and astounding those who knew him by entering into the spirit of things added: 'I've let him off three times already for hand ball. It can't be accidental all the time. Institute free.'

Though the Institute did not score as a result of the free against Bazook their morale was so restored that for the remaining ten minutes they attacked as they had done at the start of the game. It was now Jake O'Dea versus the Institute. And this pairing was somewhat one sided: Jake O'Dea, swimmer of rivers and lover of prizes of thousands of pounds held firm. In the very last minute of the game Jake broke out of defence and sent Gabriel away down the right wing again. Gabriel negotiated three tackles and crossed the ball into the square. It was the first time in his career that he had managed to be so direct. He was sick and tired of Stanley Callaghan and Jake O'Dea all the time shouting at him to play for a corner. None of the Nook team was in the square for the unexpected cross. It was a bad cross anyway – too direct. In fact it was more of a shot than a cross and the surprised Eric O'Neill in goal had to turn it over for a corner. As before Jake O'Dea went up to take the corner kick. And as before Bazook was borne into the square by Stevie Mack and Tolly Holliday. But the Institute were not to be caught napping twice.

'Watch that fucking corpse,' Henry Corr roared. Ronnie West acted swiftly. He raised his arm with Hitlerian firmness and pointed to the sideline as the crowd correctly interpreting the signal chanted: Off, off, off. Henry Corr left the pitch accompanied on the long walk by the non-stop booing of the crowd.

Almost the entire remaining Institute team surrounded Bazook and his handlers. Jake O'Dea paused, took stock. He kicked the ball much harder than anyone expected. It went over the heads of backs and forwards and landed at the foot of Gabriel Storan who side-footed with his tackie into the net.

20

The Third Man

The two head gatemen, Liam Leahy and Tom Collins, were visibly shaken as they recounted the tale for the seventh time. Tom Splendid, representing the Nook and Mr O'Neill, father of the O'Neills, representing the Institute, corroborated the gatemen's version of what had occurred. But Stanley Callaghan was not appeased. He roared red-faced, at the gatemen: 'Are you seriously expecting me to swallow that?' He glanced at Jake O'Dea for support. Jake was white in the face. His throat was dry. All along he had known, deep in his heart that it was too good to be true. The No 2 account would not be cleared in his lifetime let alone the No 1.

'Liam, you tell him,' Tom Collins appealed to his brother gateman, 'as sure as my mother is in the grave I'm not telling one word of a lie.'

Liam Leahy nodded. 'It's exactly as he said, Mr Callaghan.'

All the Nook team were squeezed into the counting room under the stand in the company of various GAA officials, two gardai and a few spectators who managed to gain admittance before the door was closed on the throng outside.

'Tom?' Stanley Callaghan turned to Tom Splendid, 'am I expected to believe this? They didn't take a penny of the gate money?'

'They demanded thirty two thousand five hundred pounds exactly. They spelled it out: the eleven thousand bet by each team, the ten thousand for wearing the jerseys and the five hundred for wearing the boots. They said they were the IRA and something about it being sacrilege to play soccer on a GAA pitch.'

'And you did nothing to stop them?'

'Stanley, all I saw was a gun and a voice telling me to face the wall. The gentlemen here gave out the money.'

Liam Leahy explained: 'Mr Callaghan, even though they had a gun, if they asked for the gate money they'd have had to shoot me first. But if I refused to hand over the soccer money I *would* have been shot. Right, Tom?'

'Yes. And it proves they were IRA. The IRA wouldn't steal Gaelic money.'

Dara Holden, still not able to take much in, stared quizzically at his jersey. He picked at the mud on the sleeve. He looked at the dirty jerseys of the rest of the Nook team and abruptly shouted: 'Hey, who won?'

Stanley Callaghan could see that Dara was out of his concussion.

'We did but the money has been robbed. Now shut up till I sort this out. What did they look like? How many of them were there?'

'They had stockings over their faces. And hats. There was three of them. The first guy, a thin chap, he told the small guy who was with him to go tell Louis to keep the car running. Something like that. That's how we figure there was three of them.'

'Louis? Louis?' Stanley Callaghan accused the gatemen, 'are you trying to get up on my back? Fucking *Louis?*'

'That was the name, Stanley. I heard it myself. Mr O'Neill heard it.' Mr O'Neill nodded to Tom Splendid.

'When did it happen?'

'Half way through the second half.'

Stanley Callaghan sat down and rubbed his palms down his face. 'My God,' he said, 'my God. What did I always say about that Institute crowd? They knew we had them. I knew Corr wouldn't let go. Fifteen years in America. You walk into a shop in America and buy a gun the same as if 'twas an apple. And then blaming the IRA. What were they wearing again? What kind of accents had they?'

Liam Leahy thought they were dressed in faded blue denim jackets and black wellington boots with Trilby hats pulled down over their stocking masks; Tom Collins thought the boots were green and the jackets and jeans grey corduroy and the hats Fedora. Neither Mr O'Neill nor Tom Splendid had a proper look at them. The thin guy, according to Liam Leahy, definitely had a North of Ireland accent. The small one didn't speak at all except to shout at Louis to keep the car running and

Liam Leahy thought he sounded like an American. Tom Collins, Mr O'Neill and Tom Splendid all agreed on the small one's accent but, respectively, they identified the thin chap by his voice as hailing from Dublin, Cork and Galway.

The Nook did not know whether to feel at a wedding or a wake. Only Dara Holden was in excellent form demanding to be told over again how the match was won. But Dara was a millionaire and did not miss the loss of a thousand pounds. The rest of them were of course proud of having won the match. Jake O'Dea did not know what to believe. He was drinking in company with Dara and Stevie Mack. 'Dara, tell me I imagined it. Tell me there was no robbery.'

'I wish I could, Jake. I'm proud of you. Everyone says you had a blinder. You deserve the money if anyone did. Look Jake, and you Stevie, I'm going to give you both a couple of grand of my own. Okay? And I won't take no for an answer.'

Jake O'Dea shook his head. Stevie Mack stiffened as though he had been offered a disease. Jake summed up: 'It never changes. The people you can't take money from offer it to you. Try and tap someone and you get no for an answer. I don't know whether to laugh or cry. Where is he, Dara? He'd know which.'

'He's in Henry Street. Swearing black and blue that he didn't rob a grave. Although that he'll have to admit. But he won't admit he robbed the Gaelic Grounds.'

'What? What do you mean?' Jake O'Dea begged hopefully.

'I went straight to Katstanco after the match. My gun's missing. Kate and Conor robbed the money. They left the bullets in my suitcase.'

'Dara? On the level? You mean the money is safe?'

'I'm on the level. But it doesn't mean the money's safe, Jake.'

'What d'you mean? If Kate and Conor have it, he put them up to it. Isn't that what you're saying?'

'Yes. He has the money.'

'Well then.'

'Well then what, Jake?'

Dara Holden handed Jake a note in Stanley's handwriting.

'He wouldn't do that to us.'

'Jake . . . he did.'

21

Success Story

A dusty spotlight of sun picked out Stanley Callaghan and Brother Gibson seated around the Superior's drop-leaf table – the leaves extended to accommodate the spread of thirty-two thousand five hundred pounds. Gently swirling his malt Stanley accepted the Brother's encomiums. 'You're a wizard and a thorough gentleman among graverobbers, Stanley. By God they can go on strike till their irons are hot now. You have your money, Stanley. And I have you.'

Stanley's fingers dipped idly among the notes. 'Brother, I wish I could share your confidence that the non-denominational will have me. Even they hardly run to graverobbers.'

'Good Lord, you'll be the jewel in their crown. Anyway, I've been in touch. Like everyplace else, they can do with a good man. Not that you need to worry with that lot.' He feasted his eyes on the bank notes.

When Stanley first revealed to Brother Gibson that he intended raising the corpse the Superior almost fell to his knees in thanksgiving. But when Stanley proposed robbing the gate receipts the good brother counselled wisely. 'Nook or Institute money by all means, Stanley. But not our money. Sean Bawn Walsh and Cathal Og Shannon are no longer young men. We don't want them to die of shock. Without them to back me up, that Davy McMahon would lease the grounds to fan dancers. I'll help you. I'll pick the gatemen. Their lack of, er, vigilance . . . fifty quid should cover that. If you want to leave it to me, I'll write the script for you.'

Stanley forced his eyes away from the money and chuckled: 'Brother, where, if you don't mind, did you get the "Louis" from?'

Brother Gibson blushed. 'I spent my youth in the gods of the picture houses. We used to sell jam jars for the price of admission. Was it not all right?'

'Oh, perfect. Wonderful, Brother.'

Stanley finished his drink. He stood up and walked around the table inspecting the money. Seated, Brother Gibson craned his neck to monitor the effect of the display on Stanley's face. He was puzzled to observe the teacher bite his lower lip. Stanley turned his back on the money, rested his hands on the window ledge and stared out into the school yard. The only movement in the study was the disturbance of a pound note by Brother Gibson's heavy breath. Stanley was two minutes looking out the window and Brother Gibson was at a loss to understand his sudden melancholy. Everything had gone like clockwork, he thought. He himself had driven Kate and Conor home from the Gaelic Grounds. He had taken charge of the suitcase full of money and given it sanctuary in the school. It was all there now on the table, the man should have been doing a jig. Stanley turned away from the window and further confused the Superior with: 'It's time to share out the gotten gains.' From the very large envelope that Stanley had brought with him he now extracted eleven almost as large envelopes and placed them on the table. On the first two Brother Gibson was able to read 'Bazook' and 'Gabriel'. So that accounted for the vigil by the window. A conscience at work.

'Stanley? What's come over you?'

Stanley smiled as he might have at a child: 'We were kids together. We grew up on the same street.'

It took them half an hour to fill the envelopes. When they had finished Stanley put them in the suitcase and then stretched his hand towards Brother Gibson. 'I'll say goodbye. And thanks for everything. I take it there won't be any problem about Conor staying on?'

'Of course not.'

'Well, then. I'll probably drop in and see you occasionally.'

'Please do.'

'And make sure you give your best, writing the letter of dismissal. I intend to treasure it. I'd better head for the Nook now. Goodbye, Brother.'

'Goodbye, Stanley.'

Brother Gibson watched his slow progress across the yard. He saw him pause and look up at the school clock then stare up at his own classroom for what was at least three minutes. At the school gate Stanley put down the suitcase for a last look. Brother Gibson ran from his study just as Stanley picked it up again.

'Stanley! Stanley! Come back here this instant.'

Brother Gibson continued running even though Stanley had already started to walk slowly back. When they met Brother Gibson grabbed his arm.

'What a fool I nearly was.'

'I beg your pardon, Brother?'

'Follow me.' Brother Gibson marched back to his study. He poured two glasses from the bottle and encouraged him to follow his lead in drinking as though to a narrow escape. 'Stanley, I can't go through with it either. I can't sack a Bob Tracey. There must be some other way to best them.'

'Brother, you have to sack me. A graverobber. A gambler. Think how long you've waited for this.'

'No, no. You never had the remotest intention of keeping that money, had you? Come on. The truth now.' Stanley's grimace of a grin confirmed the Superior's suspicion. 'Why did you want to steal it in the first place?'

'To mind it. In case Corr did. You are looking across the table, Brother, at a fraud. I'm not a Bob Tracey. I never was a Bob Tracey. In fact I'm not fit to lick a Bob Tracey's boots.' Brother Gibson shifted a little in his chair and widened his eyes. 'The only vocation I ever had in my life was for holidays. *That's* why I became a teacher. To holiday, not to teach. And it was always my intention to run caravans during vacation. I missed out on that, why, even I don't fully understand. So there you have it. I'm worse than the entire parents' council put together. So sack away and have no regrets.'

'Stanley, why don't you walk in the fresh air to the Nook? It might clear your head.'

'Brother, when I was fifteen . . . .'

'I'm not listening, Stanley.'

' . . . I spotted teachers worked the same hours as schoolboys except the teachers got paid . . . '

'I didn't hear a word.'

After the hysteria attendant on the distribution of the money

Stanley Callaghan announced his intention of withdrawing to the snug to gather his thoughts. Only Dara Holden questioned the grandeur of such a declaration. 'Are you going to put them in a thimble?' But this attempt at wit was not shared by the rest of the team for whom Stanley now had the status of a god. 'Don't upset him, Dara,' Jake O'Dea said. 'He might make the money disappear.' After giving his all in the match Jake was left with no more than the strength to hug his envelope and lift his glass. One after another the members of the team shouted for a drink for the house which in effect meant that each round contained eleven – it was accepted that Mrs Trehy was standing in for Bazook, though she did not of course buy. Gabriel had a beer mat from which he read the question: Who scored the winning goal?

From the snug Stanley surveyed his children. Eliminating the twins and Gabriel who did not hail from the street, he juggled with Cocoa, Stevie, Tolly, Jake, Johnny Green and Dara. All of them were replaying the replay, slapping each other on the back, every now and then shouting: Up the Nook. Dara stood out among them; it was true. But not in the way that Dara thought he stood out, Stanley concluded. Stanley tapped at the hatch and asked Tom Splendid to ask Dara to join him in the snug.

'This is an honour, your holiness.'

'Sit down. I've been taking stock.'

'You're always taking something. Bodies, money, the mickey. Well, I'm all ears.'

'I discovered tonight that I'm a success. I'm a good teacher and I never realised it.'

'Are you drunk already? What does all that mean?'

'You can't see it, can you? I've got to show you what it means. Look out there. Look at Stevie Mack. Now there's a success for you. I'm proud of that man.'

'I didn't think you exactly approved of Stevie.'

'Approved?' Dara was startled by the sudden anger. 'It was none of my business. He came from the same street but he never let the street down. So he cavorts with his landlady. Good for him. He's happy. She's happy. Where's the damage? No damage to the street, no damage to Stevie. Can't you see that?'

'No. And what about your famous religious scruples? Were they sham too?'

'They're *mine*. They're not for Stevie. And then there's Jake. He's a monumental success. Maybe the happiest man of us all. And he didn't need a Kate Flynn.' Stanley clamped his jaw shut having forced that out. 'That Molly is some woman,' he continued, not looking at Dara, his eyes on his children in the bar. 'Tolly – he stole a few shillings in his day. So what? People work round the clock printing pound notes and minting coins. Tolly didn't cause a shortage. And Johnny Green. Marvellous. He likes what he does and he's happy with that bitch. Cocoa. Was there ever fear of him? As for Bazook. Ex-docker. Unemployed and unemployable. Hideous, apart from the voice. He must have been the last singer of that song left in the world. God knew it. Canonised him . . . '

'Are you sure you're not drunk? You called me in here to listen to this – this bilge?'

Stanley turned away from his children in the bar to his child in the snug. 'You, what can I say about you, Dara?'

'You'll think of something.'

'You're a disaster. You fell for your flukey success, didn't you? O'Neill? No O'Neill. Wife? No wife. Where's your O'Neill, Dara? Where in the name of Christ is your wife?'

'Shut up, Stanley.'

'I'm trying to talk to you.'

'Talking and being vicious are two different things.'

'Tell me then, why *did* you never get married?'

'I've told you fifty times. All actresses are whores. Anyone else who was half-way decent I couldn't know whether they were interested in my money or me.'

'Fuck you and your fame and your money. You seriously expect some woman to isolate what you imagine are your attractive spots and then fall in love with the rest?'

'I dunno.'

'All right then. We've made a start.'

'We? Listen, stay out of my life, please. You think I'm one of the kids on *your* street. Like Stevie. He still thinks you saved his life.'

'You fucked Mrs Trehy.'

'What's that to you?'

'It's as though a funeral horse left fresh green shit on my street and no one cleaned it up. I'm trying to help you. Fucking Mrs Trehy. Look at her!'

Astride her stool, her hands limp by her sides, Mrs Trehy's face was mashed into the counter as though about to be beheaded. Her flop hat and handbag on either side of her mop of white hair, she was like a boozed altar. Dara stared at her trying to recapture what he had seen in her the other night. He had been aroused all over the world since he first set forth to do O'Neill and in his early days by frugal stenographers and drug store assistants. As his fame grew and his experiences multiplied he joined the cosmopolitans for whom sex was a rattling match between afficionados. And he had gone on to poke Mrs Trehy. Slowly he took his eyes off the creature.

'I must have been pissed.'

'Dara,' Stanley looked at his watch, 'you have seven minutes. I've done as much as I can. The rest is up to you. And remember, your date is a woman who couldn't be after you for your money or fame, because for one thing she's in the same boat, she needs a man interested in her for herself and not her material possessions. And it wasn't easy, I had to work on her, I had to persuade her you're a catch . . . '

'What on earth are you talking about?' Dara asked dreading the reply.

'I've found a woman for you. It's as simple as that. And there'll be no handling charges. You've a date in – six minutes now.'

'Stanley, you don't look like your joking. Tell me you're joking.'

'I'm not joking, Dara. I took the liberty – and don't get mad, I knew it was a liberty I was taking – I mentioned to a certain person, I did it, well, Kate will tell you, actually both of us did it . . . '

'Stanley, stop talking for one second. Just one second.' They drank in silence for nearer a minute while Dara Holden constructed his appeal. 'I want to ask you a favour. If our friendship means anything to you answer me this question straight. Are you honestly telling me that you have set up a date for me?'

'Yes. With Brigid. You often said she was a fine woman, it was a scandal she'd never married. Ring Kate if you like. It's in four minutes time.'

'Jesus!'

'Brigid *is* a fine woman.'

'I know, I know. Or rather I don't know. I've never really looked at her. Jesus. What a thing to do. Jesus, you're sick.'

'If she doesn't see you there she won't turn up. You'd better go now.'

'Where? Tell me where, you fucker.'

'Hanrahan's lounge.'

'What am I going to do? Christ, what can I do?'

'It's up to you now, Dara. Take her out the country to some converted barn that charges a score for rechristened fish if that's your style. You're on your own.'

Dara Holden considered his situation glancing intermittently at Stanley as he gnawed his knuckles. He rose and went to the bar where he borrowed Jake O'Dea's pint and sent it crashing into the snug and then left. It was all he could think of to hide his excitement.

Stanley remained alone in the snug without bothering to disentangle himself from the splinters of glass and baptism of porter while in the bar Jake O'Dea tried to convince Tom Splendid that he was due a pint on the house in reparation.

His eyes closed the better to see into the future Stanley Callaghan smiled in anticipation of what he foresaw as the wedding of the year. He would have none of the quiet wedding business from them. That was for the pregnant brigade – a six o'clock in the morning caper and rashers for breakfast. No. Brigid would be sent off as befitted a woman without a stain to her name. Jake O'Dea's had been the only real Nook wedding and it had not been what it should have been. Too low key. This time everyone would be there. A guard of honour outside the church symbolic of – he would have to work on that . . . Gabriel would have to be brought out. And he would get Kate to get on to Hank Harold to handle the international aspects. It occurred to him suddenly that the wedding was already getting out of hand. He began to see it clearly, breakfast in a giant marquee in the Gaelic Grounds – the social event of the decade . . .

His smile dimmed; Bazook would not be in church to sing the Ave Maria. Still, if everything went okay and Dara didn't cock it up the wedding could go on in a month's time. What condition would a body be in then? The Church authorities might not smile on dead bodies at weddings yet, without Bazook, it wouldn't be the same. He could have a carnation in his new suit. It would be a wonderful surprise for Dara to be greeted at the end of the aisle by Bazook. It could be a surprise wedding present. Of course, everything would depend on Bazook's condition. He would have to pass a fitness test.